I0622488

Knot of the Slain

Blood Angels
Book One

T. C. Archer

ISBN: 978-069236157x
ISBN 13: 978-0692361573

Author's Website: www.tcarcher.com
Facebook: Facebook.com/tcarcherauthor
Twitter:@TCArcher

Cover/Interior Art: Dreams2Media

First Trade Paperback Printing by Broken Arm Publishing: January 2015

10 9 8 7 6 5 4 3 2

Table of Contents

Acknowledgements

Much thanks to Kimberly Comeau, editor extraordinaire. Also, a very big thank you to Rebecca Poole, who created this gorgeous cover.

Trademarks Acknowledgement

PART ONE

Ice cold veins on a river of fire.

TWISTED

I have kissed thee ere I killed thee, no way but this, killing myself to die upon a kiss.

William Shakespeare

Prologue

Stakkholtsgja, Iceland, 1705

ALARR GAZED DOWN the precipice. He, an assassin's assassin, hunted among the sharp shadows cast by a three-quarter moon. Wind whipped at the long, woolen cloak and hood that concealed his blond hair as he surveyed the valley. He stood, a shadow within a shadow, the midnight world around him alive—crickets, rich loam, even the living rock of the cliff beneath his feet. A fine salt, along with faint whale songs, floated on the breeze from the North Atlantic more than a league away. Life forces sliced through him, resonating with every nerve.

A lone rider, dressed in leather britches and jerkin, appeared around a bend in the canyon below. Freyja: his quarry. She rode relaxed in the saddle, hands loose on the reins, allowing her stallion to choose his way across the rocky terrain that bordered the river. Alarr snorted softly. How quaint. Only Valkyrie assassins preferred equine transport above the superior swiftness of their own limbs. As they had their entire history, these females preserved their energy so they didn't have to feed on human blood.

He focused on her face, on the long golden hair that blew about high cheekbones and a strong mouth. He could almost feel her smooth skin, her firm breasts. His tongue throbbed in anticipation. Her blood would still have the tang of youth, despite the century that had passed since the gothi high priest made her a Valkyrie assassin through the bite of her high priestess.

How he wished he had seen her in battle, testing the strength of her sword against those of mortal Norse warriors. He longed to watch her deliver the kiss of death. Desire pulsed through his veins. Their union would be slow, sweet, and controlled.

Alarr leaped from the cliff, sailing for an instant on the fierce Icelandic wind before landing with a crunch of boots on the rocky soil in front of Freyja's horse. She pulled the stallion up short. Her pupils dilated. Did she understand he intended to kill her as the other *Aptrgangr* sent by the gothi less than a month ago? When that other *Aptrgangr* faced her, she did what no Valkyrie assassin had done. She killed him. Now, he must send her to the gods she served. But how could he, *sómaherji*—honorable warrior—vanquish such beauty? Disgust roiled through him. The gothi had created Freyja. Why couldn't the priest deal with her like the god he claimed to be?

Her upper lip lifted in a sneer. Pride and sadness wound around his heart. Yes. She understood all too well.

"Shh, sweet," he whispered.

Freyja dropped the reins and drew her sword in one fluid motion, bringing the blade to a diagonal Nastak defensive posture in front of her chest. Alarr couldn't take his eyes off her. How was it possible such beauty should be extinguished from the world?

Curse the gothi and their hold over his clan. His kind, the legendary Aptrgangr, walkers of death, *the clan cast from heaven*, had borne the blame of mortal sin across the centuries. Why had they accepted the role as *God's* assassin? Alarr had taken five Valkyrie assassins since the rogue gothi rose to power. Surely this beauty was the last. Anger twisted through Alarr. Mortal and immortal alike were fools; mortals for holding the Aptrgangr accountable for man's wrongdoings, and the Aptrgangr for accepting the role. Christianity had replaced the Norse gods centuries ago. Yet, this gothi…this god had continued in secret for six hundred years—with the help of Freyja's kind. Perhaps it was time to break the bond between the gothi and the Aptrgangr, and purge the world of the gothi pestilence.

Alarr stepped forward. Freyja swung a leg over the horse and dropped to the ground noiselessly, her sword vertical, in a two handed Vefyat attack stance. He drew two daggers from his belt and crossed them in front of his chest. She toyed with him. A seasoned warrior such as she knew there were no less than three effective parries to defend against a Vefyat strike. He gave a low, mocking laugh. Surely she wouldn't try the Vefyat—and against duel daggers! She could shift to only one of two possible stances before he had her neck between his fangs. Let her choose, and quickly, or he would do so for her.

She leveled her sword at his chest and lunged. Alarr turned aside, deflected the blade with one dagger, the other pointed at her exposed flank. He held his strike. Her lunge must be a gambit. Little fool to think he wouldn't know. She had purposely exposed her side. She would use his switch from defense to offense—parry to strike—as an opening for a blow or strike to his head.

As expected, Freyja aborted her thrust to his midsection. She stepped aside and spun, swinging her sword in a tight circle toward his throat. He leaned backward and the blade whistled through the air a hair's breadth from his face. She pivoted and, gripping the hilt hand over hand, sliced downward.

Alarr spun, fanning his cloak around him to diffuse and distract. Her blade cut air where his head had been an instant before. She stepped back and stood, sword now in a left-handed Nastak.

He faced her, daggers again crossed in front of him. "Beautiful," he murmured.

She snarled and struck again, swinging, slicing, lunging in a flurry of movement. Alarr deflected and twisted, steel striking steel ringing across a night gone silent. He chose only to defend, to study her form, how her body moved, her muscles toned and feminine under supple leather britches and jerkin. What pleasure she must have given her master.

She drove him backward into the water. Another instant, and he was ankle deep. The deeper water behind him made further retreat foolhardy. She pressed her attack, but he held his ground, forcing her aside by feigning an opening on his left. She swept her sword at his flank, and he sidestepped ashore. She was good. Faster than he had ever seen. Her gothi master was a fool to have allowed her beauty to captivate him. He had delayed her death, and she had grown in power beyond any Valkyrie before her.

Her sword flashed in a downward strike. Alarr dropped his daggers and caught the blade between his palms an eyelash's breadth from his face. Before she could move, he snapped the blade in half, ducked left, grabbed her arm, and spun her into his grasp, her face inches from his.

She snarled, baring extended fangs. Her broken sword clattered to the ground as she tried to force her hands between her chest and his. He tightened his hold in an embrace that would have crushed a mortal woman. Her breasts pressed against him. He felt her muscles tense, her energy build. Freyja snarled deep within her throat and kicked his shin. Pain shot through him, desire hot on its heels.

He lowered his head and whispered "Shh," as he touched his lips to her cool skin. "I must take you."

She kicked his shin again as he pierced her flesh, the warrior in her unable to accept defeat. She hooked her leg around his and yanked in an effort to drag him to the ground, but he was stronger. Alarr pulled back from her neck, thrilled and anguished to let her blood trickle unconsumed even for an instant. He slipped a hand beneath her knees and drew her close. Her glare blazed up at him. She understood he had robbed her of the necessary leverage to topple him. He returned to feed on her neck, shivers of lust rippling through him.

"Hush, my love," he whispered with his mind as he braced for the title wave of her memories.

The taste of blood flooded his senses as if he were starved. A few more drops—a few more, more—he sucked now, hard, feeding on her. Freyja's struggles weakened as their minds merged. He saw her as a human child in a walled community of women, warm, sweet, and alive. Sula, she had been called: the sun.

She grew into a young woman, then—Alarr faltered and dropped to his knees, still joined with her—came the memory of the nights she spent with the gothi so that she might be filled with his child. The gothi took her without care for her sensitivities, her innocence. Six nights she was forced to lay with him. Her fear faded only with the birth of a son nine months later. A son meant an end to her nights as the gothi concubine.

Eighteen months passed in bliss, then she stood in a great stone chamber, tapestries hung on the walls, the stone floor, bare and cold. Alarr struggled through numbing emotions while she held her whimpering, yellow-haired son. Tears streamed down his chubby face from eyes as blue as his mother's. She bid farewell in her mind, but promised her son she would return. Alarr felt her tears, the soft warmth of her son's body in her arms as she now lay in his. He slowed his drinking and the events in her mind slowed in tandem.

The high priestess led Sula away. She glanced over her shoulder. Through her eyes, Alarr gazed at her son. His chest tightened at sight of his small arms outstretched toward the mother he would never again see. Sula smiled softly and faced forward in the dark corridor of the temple.

The child's single cry preceded her into the gloom.

Cool air gave way to a deeper chill as the rough-hewn temple stairway Sula and the priestess descended opened into a chamber she hadn't known existed. The high priestess stopped before an age-stained, oak door and bid her enter. In her innocence, she obeyed. Alarr jarred at the bleak clank as the door locked behind her.

In the dimly lit room, seven priests waited in gray communion robes. Their cold fingers sent a shiver down her spine as they removed her simple woolen robe. She recognized the man in front of her as the grown son of her maid-in-waiting. He reached out and her gaze caught on his middle finger, on the gold band decorated with a red gem and a crooked cross—*the ring of the Gothi High Priest, Mótsognir.*

Sula leaped back in alarm. His eyes darkened and she instinctively recognized the centuries old soul of her god now living inside the young man's body. She gasped as he seized her arm. A chill enveloped her naked body. She cried out and tried to yank free.

Mótsognir's grip tightened even as his eyes beckoned. "Come, my prized priestess."

Alarr sensed the presence of the Aptrgangr high priestess lurking in the dark even before Sula revealed her in their shared memory. The priestess left the shadows and drew close. Fear overshadowed Sula's earlier anguish when the female Aptrgangr grasped her shoulders and drew her breast to breast. Sula screamed, then voiced one high-pitched shriek as the high priestess tore open her neck and fed.

A shiver of pleasure rippled through Alarr in the instant before he withdrew his fangs. Breath coming in labored gasps, he caressed the puncture wounds with his tongue, mending the lesions with his saliva. Then he hugged Freyja's limp body and collapsed, a crumpled heap on the pebbled shore.

Chapter One

T WELVE-YEAR-OLD GERRY FORSTNER huddled on the couch beneath Grandma's afghan and peered at the black and white television screen.

A commercial jingle faded and a TV announcer said, "Welcome back. We rejoin our midnight presentation, *The Undead of the Black Forest* as Hargrave, our intrepid vampire hunter, enters the cemetery of the damned."

Chilly Billy, the host of KDKT's late, late Chiller Theater was dressed in a tuxedo, complete with cape and fangs. Even in black and white, the black liquid trickling down his chin looked like real blood.

"It reminds me of the time I was on the prowl for fresh blood." Chilly Billy rolled the word 'blood' off his tongue as if he were savoring that meal all over again.

Shivers crawled up Gerry's spine. He knew he shouldn't be watching TV at this hour, but heck, he'd be a teenager next year. Things would change then, by golly.

Chilly Billy licked his lips. "But that story will have to wait until the next break. Join me in a cup of life as we return to our movie, *The Undead of the Black Forest.*" The last words echoed in the studio and the cameraman zoomed in on Chilly as he picked up a silver chalice and took a long drink.

Gerry popped out from under the afghan, suddenly not at all frightened by the hokey special effects from the local Omaha studio. Everybody in school knew Chilly Billy Cardilly was Bill Cardill, the same guy who did the five o'clock news and hosted *Bowling for Dollars.* Mom said he was part owner of KDKT.

The picture faded to black and was replaced by a scene in front of the wrought iron gates of Whitcomb Graveyard. Gerry pulled the afghan up around his chin, ready to dive under its protection again.

A footstep sounded on Gerry's front porch. He froze, heart pounding, and listened, then glanced at the closet under the stairs—his safe haven. The key turned in the lock. Gerry nearly jumped out of his skin. Mom! He threw back the afghan, leaped from the sofa, ran to the TV, and twisted the knob to the off position. He started to turn away, but stopped when the picture wavered, then shrank to a tiny white dot at the center. Dang it. Mom was sure to notice that.

He raced to the front door landing. The lock clicked, echoing in the stark entryway. Gerry gripped the newel post, whipped around the banister, and took the stairs two at a time. The door handle jiggled between thuds of his footfalls.

Just below the top of the stairs, he heard the door creak open. He skidded to a halt, dropped to squat, and peered through the banister to make sure it was Mom and not some night creature.

"Gerry, I heard you." She closed the door, turned, and stared up into the shadows. "You better be in bed by the time I get upstairs."

Gerry leaped up the final stair, slipping and sliding in his stocking feet as he raced to his bedroom and did a face-plant onto his pillow.

Chapter Two

Stakkholtsgja, Iceland
Fifteen years later… present day

PAIN SHOT THROUGH Freyja's ice-cold veins on a river of fire. She convulsed as though struck by lightning and choked on damp earth. Buried. She had been buried *alive*! She struggled to move her arms, legs, to break through the packed earth. Muscles burned with the futile effort and, at last, breath coming in heaves, she stilled.

Life-blood filtered into every pore with the same slow precision it had when drained from her. Memory rose of a dark face. She stiffened, then softly gasped at the recollection of her son's final cry that day so long ago when she had been changed.

A heavy rumble shook the ground. Sula cringed. The sound, like a landslide, pierced her blood-warmed core. Another rumble sounded—closer—louder. The earth above her unexpectedly rolled away. Waves of burning sunlight rippled across her body, penetrating her closed lids.

She screamed.

A JOLT OF awareness raced up homicide detective Gerry Forstner's back. He jerked his gaze from the long line of people waiting to enter Miami's premier club, *The Hot Spot*, past the full parking lot to the darkness beyond. The only other time he had experienced that same *someone just walked over my grave* feeling had been during the *Keepers of the Secret* investigation.

Memory of the case returned with a vividness that belied the five years that had passed since the clues dead ended in the Florida Everglades. It had been his first assignment as head of Miami's Serial Killer Task Force and the mental connection he had made with the killer that night had faded into a more rational sense of disbelief—until now. A spider-like sense of legs crawling inside his brain tickled the fringes of consciousness, then vanished.

Oppressive pressure crushed his chest. Gerry drew a slow breath to ease the constriction. A February gust sent a wave of goose bumps up his arms. He froze as a mental throb receded into the blackness of his mind. Where had that come from? What the hell was it?

Like a window shade that snapped up, music blared through the open door of the club, jarring him back to the sight of two women pressed close in a dirty dancing gyration. The taller of the women rubbed silicone double-Ds strapped into a sequined halter top against the other woman's c-cup breasts. Several men had stepped out of line to watch. Gerry grimaced at the garish makeup the women wore and inhaled a shaky breath as he shifted his gaze to the line of glitterati backed up halfway down the block.

In the sea of heavenly female bodies, his gaze latched onto a busty dyed blonde waiting in line. She smiled, but he turned away. Whether it was the brassiness of the bottled color or the fact the woman was easily a foot shorter than his six feet, the knot in his gut told him he couldn't stomach another blonde. An unexpected desire to unravel that knot with a scotch surfaced. He'd been down that road before and nearly destroyed his life. No way was he going back. He headed for the front of the line and stopped beside the bouncer.

The big Cuban with no neck gave him a quick glance. "Back of the line," he said, and motioned the two brunettes at the front of the line into the club with a nod.

Gerry watched the women sashay under the yellow neon light that flashed *The Hot Spot,* then step through the club's open door.

"Busy tonight," Gerry said.

The man glared. Gerry pulled the badge from his back pocket and flipped it open.

The bouncer glanced at it. "Yeah?" he grunted as he motioned two more women into the club.

Digitized bass boomed in an abrupt crescendo and Gerry winced. "Is it always like this?" He motioned to the crowd.

"Thursday night's always busy."

"Got a lot of regulars?"

"Dunno." He waved in the two young women who'd been dancing together.

Gerry watched them enter the club. The sequined beauty cast a dark-eyed glance over her shoulder before disappearing inside. Damn, she'd known he was watching.

He looked back at the bouncer. "You're new here."

The bouncer gave him an appraising look, then gave in. "Richie," he replied.

Gerry reached inside his pullover sweater, located his shirt pocket, and retrieved the photo of Frank Vitelli. He held it out. "Recognize this guy?"

Richie looked at the photo. "Yeah. I seen him."

"Was he here last night?"

The bouncer shrugged, bunching up what little neck he had until shoulders and jaw met. "Don't remember. I seen lots of folks come and go."

"You sure? This guy used his credit card here last night."

He shrugged again and asked for the IDs of the young couple who stepped up next. Gerry pocketed the picture and brushed past him into the club. The fetid combination of sweet liquor, perfume, and sweat assaulted his nostrils. Dance music hammered his eardrums and multicolored lights flashed. He hadn't been in *The Hot Spot* in a while, but its black walls and suspended tile ceiling still needed remodeling.

He scanned the tables, the dance floor, and the bar along the left wall. The place was jam-packed. He glanced at the occupancy sign. Two hundred and twelve, by order of the fire marshal. Twice that many were shoehorned inside. Gerry squeezed through the throng to the bar. He flashed his badge to get the nearest bartender's attention. The barkeep nodded and grabbed a bottle of gin as a softer Latin tune played through the sound system.

"What's your name?" Gerry asked.

"Collin."

"Collin, did you see this guy last night?" He slid Vitelli's mug-shot across the bar as the bartender set the gin on the counter and reached for two glasses from the overhead rack.

Collin dug each one through the ice machine beneath the bar as he studied the picture. "Yeah." He metered a shot of gin into each glass. "Frankie. Big tipper."

"Was he with anyone?"

Collin grabbed one of the dispenser lines in front of him and filled the glass to the rim with tonic. "Not at first. He cruised the floor until this woman he knows showed up."

Gerry paused while reaching inside his sweater for a notepad and pen. "A woman he knows?"

After placing the two drinks at the waiter's station to his right, Collin turned back to Gerry. "A blonde, tall, mid-shoulder-length hair. They hung out at the bar over there." He jerked a thumb at the far end of the bar.

Gerry glanced in the mirror behind the bar at the hundred other blondes who fit that description. "Can you narrow it down? How about a name?"

Collin shook his head. "Naw."

Gerry flipped open his pad. "What time did she arrive?"

Collin turned, dug into the beer cooler and came up with a Heineken. "Maybe twelve-thirty."

"Can you describe her?"

The bartender set the beer on the waiter's station, grabbed the towel hanging over his shoulder, and wiped his hands. He leaned against the counter. "Good looking, but Frankie only goes for the lookers."

Gerry began jotting notes. "How old?"

"Between twenty and twenty-five."

"Height, weight?"

"Five-eight, five-nine. One fifteen, maybe."

"What was she wearing?"

He thought for a moment. "Short knit top—black—with her belly button showing. White skirt. Great legs. Despite the trendy outfit, she had a real goddess thing going on."

Gerry looked up from his notes. "Goddess thing?"

"Yeah. You know, tall, angled features, the classical look. Remember that sculpture, the Wings of Nike?"

"The goddess Nike?"

"Yeah." Collin gazed upward, his expression deliberate as he recited, "'When an August dawn wakes over you, your atmosphere is potent with their life, and sometimes a young ethereal figure indistinct, in rapid flight, wings across your hills.'" He refocused on Gerry. "Constantine Cavafy."

Gerry raised a brow.

Collin grinned. "I dated an art major in college." His grin widened. "She was something of a goddess herself."

Gerry grinned back. He'd dated a goddess or two in his lifetime. "Our blonde goddess, what was she drinking?"

"Same as him, vodka martinis."

"Did you notice anything out of the ordinary with Frankie?"

"No—" Collin snapped his fingers. "Wait, Frankie's a pretty laid back guy, but I thought he was going to punch this chick."

"The blonde?"

"Yeah."

"What were they arguing about?"

Collin shook his head. "Frankie raised his voice. I turned and saw them almost nose-to-nose. I started for them, but Frankie saw me and laughed. The chick's got balls. She grabbed his hand with that god-awful ring he was wearing, shoved it into his face, and laughed." Collin whistled. "He's big, she's small. He could kill her with one punch."

A glint in Gerry's peripheral vision startled him. "Sounds like the violent type," he answered mildly as he turned his head toward the flicker. A moonlit river of grass stretched out in an endless silvery-tinted mass. The quiet drone of an air boat racing atop Everglades jumpstarted his heart. He inhaled sharply and got a nostril full of swampy air. His choke was cut off as the boat veered left and he clutched at empty space. How the hell—

"Look," Collin's voice yanked him from that night in the Glades, and the club tune playing over the PA boomed in his ear, "in this business, you learn fast how to size up a guy. Frankie liked a good time, but was more flash than hard knocks. He made the dough, or acted like he did, and made sure the chicks knew it."

A short, redheaded waitress appeared at Gerry's side. "I need a pina colada and a Bud draft."

"Get Roy to do it, will you, baby?" Collin said. "I'm kinda busy."

She gave Gerry a curious glance. He stared, his heart still thudding so loudly he felt sure she could hear it. She shrugged and headed to the other side of the bar.

"You okay?" Collin asked.

Gerry looked back at him. "Yeah. This blonde, you know her?"

"She started hanging around with Frankie about a month ago."

Gerry studied him. "You sound pretty sure about that."

"You don't forget a woman like that."

"Were they good friends?"

"They had a thing going."

"Thing?" Gerry repeated.

A loud whoop went up from the dance floor. The bartender flicked a glance over Gerry's shoulder before answering, "Thing, chemistry. Maybe a love-hate thing."

"The other night was the first time Frankie was…aggressive?"

"I wouldn't call it aggressive. More like…short tempered."

"Did this short temper start when he began hanging around with the blonde?"

Collin looked startled. "I guess it did."

"You know anything about his business?"

Collin held up both hands, palms out. "Whoa, man. Frankie considers himself some sort of player. Fantasy or not, I don't want any piece of that action."

Gerry gave a small nod. "But he was a good tipper."

"Yeah. He was one of those guys who wanted to be somebody. Can't blame a guy for wanting respect."

"Nope," Gerry agreed. "Can't blame a guy for that. You don't know anything else about this blonde? Did she have a jealous ex-boyfriend?"

"I see a lot of people in here. I don't know anything about them outside of what goes on here."

Gerry reached into his shirt pocket, pulled out a business card, and placed it on the bar. "If you remember anything else, call me." He reached for the picture.

Collin grabbed his wrist. "Is Frankie in trouble?"

Gerry paused. Damn. The guy didn't read the papers. An hour after Gerry had been assigned the case, the story broke about Frank Vitelli, the third victim in what the newspapers dubbed *The Valknut Murders*. Chief Herrero had already gotten a phone call from the local Asatru community. They were concerned about the fact some nut was using the three interlocked triangle of their Valknut holy symbol as a signature for murder. Who knew what that concern would turn into if they discovered that the Valknut had been drawn on each of the three dead bodies with the blood of the following victim?

Gerry pulled loose of Collin's grip. "Frankie was murdered last night."

"Jesus," he breathed. "What happened?"

The crime scene photo of Vitelli's body flashed before Gerry. He hadn't been able to shrug off the unnerving feeling he'd experienced upon seeing the calculated sterility of the small, neat cut to the jugular. Why the jugular—as if Vitelli were a sacrificial bull? All three victims had been sliced in the same way and left to bleed to death.

Gerry tapped the card as he retrieved Frankie's photo. "If you see that woman again, call me."

He squeezed through the crowd and out onto the sidewalk. He strolled along the line of people waiting to enter the club, scanning for a blonde goddess, his mind half on where that flashback in the bar had come from when his cell phone chortled the tune *Send in the Clowns*. He unclipped the phone from his front pants pocket and flipped it open.

"Forstner."

"Gerry, you haven't called." His ex-wife, Brenda's voice rattled his concentration.

That's what he got for not checking the caller ID. He really needed to program a special ring for her number. "I've been tied up." He slowed, his attention on the crowd.

"You're going to pick up Joey tomorrow, right? It's your weekend. Joey wants you to take him to his soccer match, and you promised to take him to Daytona for the NASCAR race. He's really looking forward to it."

The tickets lay on his kitchen counter. Four hundred bucks apiece. It had taken two months to save the money. "I wouldn't miss it for the world," he said.

"Just making sure. I know you're working that Valknut case—"

Gerry halted. "Who told you that?"

A second of silence passed. "My connection said it was assigned to you this afternoon. Three dead."

Her connections were too damned good. His name hadn't been mentioned in the newspaper report. Brent Douglas was murdered three days after Darryl Michaels. Douglas' blood was the blood used to draw the Valknut on Michael's chest.

The department had classified the case as a multiple, not serial murder, and assigned the case to Miami Detective Mark Blakely. This morning, Vitelli turned up murdered. Four hours ago, his blood was identified as the blood used to draw the Valknut on Darryl Michaels' chest. Three murders. The first and second victims had the Valknut written on their chests with the blood of the next victim. The blood on Vitelli's chest hadn't yet been identified. Find out who that blood belonged to and Gerry might prevent the next murder.

The case was reclassified as a serial murder and reassigned to him. Between the one hour meeting with Herrero and the ride to *The Hot Spot* Gerry had realized there was a possibility that the killer stood alongside his next victim while he committed the murder. Gerry had a long way to go to wrap his head around that one. What the hell was the killer trying to say by marking his victim with his next victim's blood? Was he thumbing his nose at the cops?

"The papers say those guys were slime buckets anyway, Gerry."

His attention snapped back to Brenda, his gut tightening in that all-too-familiar way. She was spouting her version of justice again. *Put all the criminals in a bag and drop them into the Atlantic.*

He'd once asked *Why not toss the court system in there with them?*

She'd shot him a scowl that said he needed to get the board out of his by-the-book-ass. He knew she was calculating the money he would have made defending those crooks if he had finished his law degree.

Brenda wasn't in the habit of stopping to consider circumstances that didn't directly affect her. She didn't give a damn that Derryl Michaels had worked two jobs and had been two semesters away from a business degree on the day he died. All she would have seen was the prison record he had worked hard to put behind him.

"You promised Joey," she went on. "What's one more dead criminal anyway? And," she added—Gerry tensed, *there was that tone*—"if you blow me off like before, I'm calling my lawyer."

"That happened once."

"Twice," she snapped.

"Fine."

"I have plans for the weekend," she said.

Gerry halted. Did the plans include the new boyfriend she'd neglected to mention? Joey had innocently dropped that bomb. Gerry knew she'd date again. He'd even fantasized she'd marry a rich guy who would whisk her away to some exotic place while they left Joey with him. The fantasy hadn't included the new boyfriend being a top Miami lawyer who took

Joey to the Superbowl, something Gerry couldn't afford. His anxiety at being a weekend father surfaced with a vengeance.

He stepped off the curb. "Brenda, do—"

"And I don't want to hear you dropped him at your mother's," she added.

He gave a low laugh. "Haven't sucked enough of my blood?"

"Another thing, I haven't got my check yet," she snapped.

He winced. Guess he'd gone too far with the bloodsucking crack. He paused for a passing car. "Yeah, I'll bring it with me."

He flipped the phone closed. Amazing, he could handle every freak in Miami except his ex-wife. He wondered if the commendation he'd received for catching the Ted Bundy copycat included recognition for *not* giving that freak the names and addresses of every ex-wife in Miami.

He crossed the jammed parking lot, headed for his gray Impala, and spotted Hargrave in the front seat. The day Chief Ramirez of the K9 Corps paired him with Hargrave was the second happiest day of his life— until he brought the Shepherd home. Brenda had left without saying a word and returned an hour later with Fluffy, as well as enough kitty litter to last a year. She informed Gerry that Hargrave and Fluffy couldn't live in the same house. But he knew she meant, *you and I can't live in the same house.*

Damn her. When they met, they couldn't get enough of each other. They'd talked for hours, made love all night long, and planned the life they'd have. He would win every high profile case and she'd raise the two kids they planned to have. But he fell in love with law enforcement, and Brenda fell out of love with him. Maybe he wasn't the man she married. Maybe. But she didn't have to buy that damn cat.

As Gerry approached the car, Hargrave stuck his snout through the crack in the window and sniffed. A wave of affection rippled through Gerry. The dog was his ex-partner and best friend, and the mutt knew it. Hargrave hopped into the back while Gerry opened the car door and slid behind the wheel. The dog sniffed at his ear, then curled up on the back seat, ears pinned down, staring.

Gerry stared past the cars and the street at the point where the streetlights gave way to nothingness. He didn't spook easily. So how come the Valknut case had him jumping at his own shadow? Because some psycho had people killing each other. Wind whipped through the crack in the window and Hargrave whined. Something was coming.

Gerry didn't know what it was, but it was bad. The last thing he needed was Brenda tying him in knots. Or maybe the last thing he needed was another walk on the dark side.

Chapter Three

A T FIVE-THIRTY THE following morning, after four hours sleep, Gerry placed a second cup of coffee on his desk at home and dropped into the swivel chair as Hargrave stretched out beside him and fell asleep. In preparation for the report Herrero wanted for the Mayor's press conference that afternoon, Gerry had planned on reading the Valknut murder files. Instead, the *Keepers of the Secret* file filled his monitor screen. He had woken with the inexplicable certainty of a connection between the two cases.

Five years ago, when Sarah Matthew's body turned up short six pints of blood, the Bahia Honda Key chief of police got on the phone to the Miami Task Force. Some maniac was draining people of blood, and forensics had no clue how. *Beam me up, Scotty,* Chief Decker had said. The blood was simply gone.

With two days under his belt as head of the task force, Gerry headed for the Keys. Decker had been right, no cuts, puncture marks, or wounds. The blood seemed to have disappeared. A thorough search of past murders turned up another body with the same MO two years prior, farther south in Big Pine Key. The kicker had been when Gerry discovered each of the victims were terminally ill.

Rumors of a cult called the *Keepers of the Secret* eventually led him to the Everglades. He recalled the strange flashback he'd experienced a few hours ago at *The Hot Spot* and gooseflesh raced across his arms. He'd never experienced a memory so vividly. Vivid? Hell, for those two seconds he'd been back in the Keys. Gerry grabbed the mouse and logged out of the file on his monitor. Nothing he'd found in the file justified rehashing that failure. He had too much to do to worry about a case long dead. Aside from Herrero's report due today, he had an early morning meeting with Reyna Jacobs of the local Asatru community. Gerry's studies in ancient history and religions only touched on the Norse.

He opened Google, started to type in Asatru, then changed his mind and typed the word Valknut. The first ten of twenty thousand eight hundred results loaded. He hit the first link and a page loaded showing the three interlinked unilateral triangles found at each of the murder scenes.

Beneath, he read: *This symbol found on Old Norse stone carvings is called "Hrungnir's heart" after the legendary giant of the* Eddas. *Best known as the Valknut or knot of the slain, it is common on funerary motifs, signifying the afterlife. The Valknut can be drawn in one stroke, making it a popular talisman of protection against spirits.*

…drawn in one stroke…

Gerry shifted his gaze to the three-triangled symbol and stared as he had upon first seeing the Valknut on the victim's chest in crime scene photos, painted in blood with a forefinger. The intricate interlocking shape had been drawn with painstaking precision. No smudges or misalignments…as if *drawn in a single stroke.*

If the blood in the Valknut drawn on Vitelli's chest followed the pattern, it would be the next victim's blood. Yet none of the victims fit a cult member profile. What was the connection? Was the owner of the blood present during the murder? If not, how did the murderer get the blood? How many people could draw that Valknut so meticulously? The same person had to have drawn the symbol on each victim's chest. That meant at least two men took part in each murder. One, knowing his next victim stood beside him, the other unaware he stood alongside his killer.

Gerry refocused on the Valknut. With news of the three murders all over the media, had the psychopathic mother fucker already killed the guy who helped him murder Vitelli, or would he somehow convince the guy to slice his own throat and lay down and bleed to death?

✦

FIVE HOURS LATER, Gerry shook hands with Reyna Jacobs, then took the chair she indicated across from her glass top desk. Upon entering the office, Gerry's attention had fixed upon the painting that hung on the wall behind her desk. Yggdrasil, the Norse *World Tree.* Deer stood beneath the thick branches and stared up at the tree, while the tree's roots descended into the earth through the mythological *nine worlds.*

"Kevin Crossley-Holland," Gerry said.

"You know him?" Reyna asked as she seated herself in the leather chair behind her immaculate desk.

Gerry shifted his gaze to her. "*The Norse Myths* was required reading for my world histories course."

Gerry liked Reyna Jacobs. Maybe it was her lack of pretense or that she wasn't defensive, as he expected. The fact she wasn't old and dumpy didn't hurt. She was a buxom fifty-eight year old brunette, dressed in a conservative pantsuit, and her tone was low and cultured. The fact she owned a small but successful public relations company that represented international companies doing business in the U.S didn't hide the underlying spark that suggested her sixties flower-power fling had extended well into the seventies, maybe even the eighties.

"Yggdrasil," she said.

"The world tree," Gerry murmured. "A sacred ash spanning heaven and hell, tended by the Norns, goddesses of past, present, and future."

Reyna beamed. "I'm impressed."

Gerry retuned her smile. "Don't be. It was all part of my ancient history classes."

"And probably a large part of the reason you're Director of the Miami Serial Killer Task Force," she said.

"Now I'm impressed," he replied.

She gave a hearty laugh. "It's all over the newspapers, Detective."

"Then you know why I'm here."

"I'm not foolish enough to think it's only because I've called the Mayor and expressed our concerns."

Mayor Blakely had thoroughly investigated all known Asatru members in the greater Miami area and come up empty. "You think you're a suspect?" Gerry asked.

Her gaze sharpened. "Our members are being harassed. We've already had two death threats."

Gerry straightened. "The news hit the papers less than twenty-four hours ago. I hope—"

"Your Chief Herrero has someone on the case."

"Was one of the threats against you?"

She gave a throaty laugh. "I see why you head the task force."

"Were you targeted because of your position as *Symbeldis* for the Coral Gables Asatru community?"

"As *Symbeldis*, the responsibility to represent the Asatru community falls to me. It's only natural I would be singled out. Add that to the fact that the office of *Symbel* can only be held by a woman…" She grinned again. "Some feel no religion has the right to elevate women to a status that excludes men."

Gerry couldn't prevent a laugh. "I don't know a thing about what it means to be *Symbel*. What's got them in knots?"

"The ritual of *Symbel* is the most holy of Asatru group religious rites." She snorted. "They probably think we're conducting orgies."

"Group rites?" Gerry asked.

"Yes. The *Symbeldis* bestows the right to hold a *Symbel* to the leader of the rite. She also fills the horn or cup, then carries it from person to person during the sacred rounds of the ritual. She is a crucial spiritual representative of the Kindred, as she represents the Fates who offer a sip from the Well of Wyrd to each person. In essence, she presides over the creation and resolution of the group-destiny. Do you know anything about the Asatru?"

"A few historical tidbits. Asatru belongs to the Neo-pagan family of religions. Modern Asatru, unlike, say, Wicca, which evolved into different traditions, closely follows surviving Norse records. The word Asatru is Icelandic for the Danish Asetro and means belief in the Asir, the Gods. Throughout Scandinavia the religion is called Forn Siðr, meaning the ancient way or tradition."

She grinned. "Isn't Google wonderful?"

He grinned back. "What can you tell me about the Valknut?"

"The Valknut is a very ancient and holy symbol. It's most widely known as the Valknut, but also goes by knot of the slain, Hrungnir's heart or, in Scandinavia, Knot of the Vala."

"Vala?"

"A female spirit ruling the fates of men, a Valkyrie," she said.

"The airborne horsewomen of death."

Reyna nodded. "They were warrior maidens known as choosers of the slain and, Freyja, goddess of love, fertility and beauty, also known as the Goddess of battle and death, is said to have ruled them."

"Avenging angel?" Gerry asked.

"Avenging angel, angel of death, something like that."

"I thought Hel was the goddess of death."

"You *have* done your homework," Reyna said. "Hel dwells in the land of shades. Odin gave her power over the nine worlds, so that she could determine where everyone should dwell *after* death. Freya, on the other hand, chooses who is to die."

"How many choosers of death do you know, Ms. Jacobs?"

She laughed without rancor. "None, I'm relieved to say."

"Who might?"

"Detective Forstner, the Asatru community is small. There are about five thousand worldwide."

"*Five thousand.* You weren't kidding."

"I don't know them all," she said, "but a member who decided to conduct the blot with a human sacrifice would be big news."

"Human sacrifice?" Gerry repeated. "What is this blot and what's it got to do with human sacrifice?"

She regarded him. "Is what the papers say true about the victims having bled to death due to a cut on the neck?"

Gerry blanched inwardly. When he found out who leaked that fact, he'd have his ass. "Yes," he replied.

"The killer is performing some sort of blood ritual," Reyna said. "In Asatru, the blood ritual is called the blot, which was originally animal sacrifice. There is a very large difference, however, between the Asatru's outlook on sacrifice and most other ancient religions. In Asatru, we are more than worshipers of the gods, we're physically related to them. Humankind is gifted with Ond, or *the gift of ecstasy*. This ecstasy—Ond— is a force of the gods, and is what separates us from other creatures. Ond connects us to the gods, makes us part of their tribe...their kin, if you will. Through the blot we share in this ecstasy. Therefore, we aren't simply buying off the gods by offering something they want, but are sharing something we all take joy in. By sharing a blot with the gods we reaffirm our connection to them and, therefore, reawaken their powers within us and their watchfulness over our world."

"Are you saying the killer is trying to attain the gods' powers?"

"The victim's blood is drained—spilled. That, combined with the use of the Valknut strongly implies sacrifice. The Valknut—" Reyna broke off, her mouth gone thin. She looked Gerry in the eye. "The Valknut is something of a lucky charm. It's believed to have properties that aid in protection against spirits. Its three interlocking shapes and nine points relate to rebirth and reincarnation and are also associated with the interrelatedness of earth, Hell, the heavens, and the nine domains. Protection against evil spirits, reincarnation, rebirth, heaven, Hell," she paused, adding with emphasis, "reawakening of power through the blot. Think of the Phoenix arising from the funeral pyre."

A funeral pyre of his victims, Gerry thought, and cursed.

Chapter Four

THAT AFTERNOON GERRY leaned back in the chair in his office and watched the slow screen fill on his monitor for the *Morgunbladid*, the Daily Newspaper in Reykjavik, Iceland. His Google search for the combined words *murdered*, *blood*, and *valknut* had turned up nothing of interest—except the Icelandic newspaper. Maybe. The killer was using a Scandinavian holy symbol. What could a Scandinavian newspaper have to report that included those three keywords? The painfully slow load had revealed the article's date—a year ago—the heading, and two pictures beneath the Icelandic letters; a freighter, and a man's head shot.

Gerry leaned back in his chair. Human sacrifice and avenging angels. The Valknut killer sounded like David Koresh and Charles Manson rolled into one smart killer. If Reyna was right, and the killer saw himself drawing on the gods' powers, maybe he saw himself as God, and had taken it upon himself to dispense his brand of justice. Frank Vitelli was a small time hood, Brent Douglas spent three years in prison for possession of cocaine, and Derryl Michaels did a long stint for robbing a small grocery store.

Justice, any way you cut it, sometimes sucked. Derryl Michaels' girl-friend, Shannon, had come by the office an hour ago. The young black woman spoke softly when she mentioned reading about Vitelli's murder in the papers and had asked if any progress had been made in Derryl's murder. His life insurance policy would be null and void if he had died during the commission of a crime. Gerry didn't believe the young man had committed any crime. The insurance company was slow rolling Shannon.

Gerry hadn't been able to get the picture of Shannon struggling with their baby out of his mind, and hoped she took his suggestion and kept quiet about Derryl being aloof the last few days of his life. The kid sounded as if he was getting his life back on track, but if he'd decided to take a short cut...

Gerry leaned back in his chair and brought his thoughts back to Vitelli. *On edge* had been Collin's description of Vitelli. Brent Douglas had recently divorced and had no family. His ex got the house and, apparently, their friends. Douglas might have dated the blonde and angered an ex-boyfriend, but not Michaels. Gerry made a note to check if Douglas had been dating a blonde, then turned back to his computer. While the newspaper loaded, he navigated back to Google and typed *valknut, murder,* and *ritual.* Google returned one hundred and seven hits, all about a cyberpunk band named *The Norwegians* whose lyrics included those key words. He rechecked the newspaper page and stared at a jumble of words in Icelandic with no sign of the expected link to an English translation.

"Damn," he muttered. "So much for the modern age."

He switched windows to the Norwegian-English dictionary and started his Black Widow program to copy the dictionary onto his computer. The progress bar reported a ten-minute wait. He glanced at the dictionary and blew out a breath. There had to be a better way.

"Of course," he murmured, and reached for the phone. He punched up the research jockey, Jake Quinlen, at headquarters. Voicemail answered. "Quin, this is Forstner. As soon as you get in, I need you to find me the number of a Professor Janice Hastings, former head of the Foreign Languages Department at Brown University. I think she lives in Cambridge now. Thanks."

Gerry hung up as Richard Lummus stepped into his office and tossed a file onto his desk. At six-two, long and lean, Lummus looked good on TV in his thousand-dollar suits and spit-shined shoes, but he'd never broken out of his back-country, South Carolina mentality. He liked to be called Richey, but behind his back, everyone called him Dick. *You can put lipstick on a pig, but you still have a pig* was the standard joke.

Gerry tilted his head and read on the folder tab, *Coroner's Report Frank Vitelli.* "Anything good?"

Lummus mouth twisted upward in condescension. "You're the hot shot. You tell me."

Gerry picked up the file and opened it. "Talk to Brent Douglas' friends, anyone you can find. See if he'd been dating anyone who fit the description of Vitelli's blonde."

"No jealous boyfriend is going to do all this," Lummus said.

"Check it out," Gerry said without looking up.

Lummus whirled and Gerry shifted his gaze to his retreating back. Lummus weaved through the desks in the outer office with an arrogance that told Gerry he knew his boss was watching. Lummus was a competent cop and next in line to inherit Gerry's job, but his shitty attitude was bad for business. Gerry shook his head. The real loser would be Lummus' partner, Martin. When Martin's broken leg healed and this case was over, he was going to be stuck with Lummus a lot longer than Gerry. Unless— he grimaced—this case didn't get solved anytime soon. He barked a laugh. That was incentive, if ever he'd needed it.

He returned his attention to the file, skipped the standard weights and measures of body, brain, and organs, and read the line describing cause of death, *Jugular sliced open in a half millimeter wide and five points long cut*, before catching sight of a yellow post it stuck at the bottom of the page.

Gerry:

Give me a call.

Pam

He grunted. No wonder Lummus had copped an attitude. He'd had a thing for Pam, but had gotten nowhere. Gerry picked up the phone and dialed the coroner's office. The phone rang four times before someone picked up.

"Coroner's office," Pam Harris said.

A whir of small machinery sounded in the background and he tried not to think about what Pam and her intern might be cutting up. Pam was a gorgeous redhead divorcee, but Gerry couldn't think beyond the fact she worked with cadavers for a living.

"Pam, it's Gerry Forstner."

"Gerry, hold on a sec."

A second later, the noise stopped as if a faucet had been shut off, and Pam said,

"Sorry. It gets a little noisy in the examination room. I bet you got the file on Vitelli."

"Yeah. What's up?"

"Did you notice the old wound on his neck?"

Gerry looked at the open page. "Old wound?"

"Yeah. I stuck a note next to the info."

He found the line and read: *Two puncture wounds two point three centimeters apart, estimated to be ten years old located on victim's neck in the parotid gland region.*

"Okay," he said. "Weird, but what about it?"

"I'm sending you a link. Take a look."

His computer inbox chimed an arrival. He double clicked the link. A picture loaded, and Gerry recognized the man in the eight by ten murder scene photo. Johnny Enriques, a small time drug peddler who frequented junior high schools. For six years, every PD in Dade County had been trying to nail him, but he always had the best lawyers money could buy. Johnny lay on the beach, his body tangled in enough seaweed to choke the Loch Ness monster.

Gerry whistled. "Looks like Johnny finally pissed off the wrong guy."

"Yeah," Pam replied. "And that guy must have gone to the same school for assholes your Valknut killer attended."

"What are you talking about?"

"Three days ago, Enriques washed up in Miami short six pints of blood."

"I don't like where this is going," Gerry said under his breath.

"It gets better. Scroll down to item fifteen, part A."

Gerry hit the page down button and found the line: *Two puncture wounds, two point six centimeters apart, estimated to be ten years old located on neck where subclavian vein joins with the internal jugular.*

"Shit," he murmured. "What kind of puncture marks?"

"Pinpoint."

"Needles?"

"Needle punctures wouldn't be discernible after ten years."

"Any signs of a cut on Enriques like those on the Valknut victims?" Gerry asked.

"Nope."

"Could the puncture marks be a catheter?"

"Catheter would leave a bigger scar."

"Shit," he said again. Twin ten-year-old vampire-like bite scars. "If Enriques bled to death from those wounds on the neck, how can the puncture wounds be ten years old?"

"He didn't bleed to death from those ten year old puncture wounds."

Gerry grimaced. "I was afraid you'd say that."

"I knew you'd appreciate my efforts."

"There's nothing in the reports on Michaels or Douglas about old wounds."

"Right," Pam replied.

"The puncture marks on Enriques' neck are four millimeters wider than the cut on Vitelli's neck," Gerry said. "But are located in the same place Vitelli got cut."

"Looks like your killer has been around for a while," she said.

"Fucking coincidences," Gerry muttered, then added a "Sorry" before saying, "I better talk to the investigation officer. Who's working the case?"

"I've attached the file."

"You're the best," he said. "Any progress on the blood used to draw the Valknut?"

"Yep. Don't know whose it is, but it's not the victim's."

"Shit," he muttered, and Pam said, "Yeah."

A BLAST OF *Send in the Clowns* brought Gerry wide awake. Hargrave woofed. Gerry groped the nightstand for the phone. Clock and phone fell to the floor. The jingle of Hargrave's tags accompanied the next stanza. 12:18 glowed up from the digital clock. Dammit, he'd been asleep for a whole two hours. Gerry clapped his hands and the bedside lamp blazed to life. He squinted. Hargrave sniffed the cell on the rug beside the bed.

Gerry scooped it up and flipped open the phone. "This better be good."

"Detective Forstner?" a male voice said.

"Yeah."

"This is Collin, the bartender at *The Hot Spot.*"

Gerry's head cleared in a flash.

"That blonde is here," Collin said.

Gerry sat up. "When did she arrive?"

"About five minutes ago."

"Is she with anyone?"

"Nope."

Gerry threw back the bed covers. "I'm on my way. If she tries to leave, give her a free drink or something, anything to keep her there without tipping her off."

"Got it," Collin replied.

Gerry closed the phone and tossed it on the bed when he jumped to his feet. Hargrave backed up a step as he hurried around the bed and grabbed the jeans he'd thrown over the chair beside the window. He had the waistband over his hips before remembering Joey. Gerry scooped the phone off the bed and hit 1 on speed dial. Two rings and he had his jeans zipped up.

His mother picked up after the third ring, and he spoke before she had a chance to say hello. "Ma."

"Gerry?" came her sleepy voice.

"Ma, I've got Joey this weekend and I have to go out. Can you come over and stay with him?" Gerry crossed to the chest of drawers and located a cotton pullover.

"Right now?" she said. "It's after midnight."

"Sorry, but I got a call." He held the phone away from his ear and pulled the shirt down over his head.

"—bring him over here," his mother was saying when he returned the phone to his ear.

"Ma," he paused. Damn, he'd never lied to her, and she was no fool when it came to Brenda. "Ma," he began, "Brenda said—"

"That grandson of mine will need a hearty breakfast," she interrupted. "I expect you have all the fixin's for a good country breakfast?"

God, he loved his mother. "Yeah, just like on the farm in Nebraska." She had grown up on a farm, and had perpetuated her family's tradition of a big country breakfast every Saturday morning.

"I'll be over in half an hour," she said.

"Use your key," he said.

"You're not going to leave him alone?"

"He won't be alone. Hargrave will be here."

"Gerry—"

"You know how it was with Pop on the force."

"Yes," she said in a low voice, and Gerry cursed his forgetfulness. To him, his father would always be the cop who wouldn't take a bribe. To his mother, he'd be the husband who hadn't made it home one night. Putting Pop in the ground was hard on both of them.

"I'll make sure Joey isn't alone, Ma," he said. "Just hurry."

"I'll be right over." She hung up. Gerry tossed the phone onto the bed, and stuffed his arms into the sleeves of his shirt. He pulled on a sweatshirt, grabbed the phone again, and dialed Lummus.

The phone rang twice, then, "Yeah."

"Lummus, Forstner. We got a lead on that blonde at *The Hot Spot*. She's there now. I'm headed over. Meet me there."

"Sure, *boss*," he replied, and hung up.

Gerry snorted in derision as he dialed the precinct. The asshole still hadn't gotten over the fact the governor had practically begged Gerry to head the task force when Jones was promoted to Section Chief.

Gerry dialed the Duty Officer, the principal contact at headquarters for Investigative Offices, off duty detectives, and management. The phone rang once and Dee Kelly's voice came over the line. "Duty Desk."

The best part of Gerry twitched to life. He'd been fighting that twitch the entire eight months Dee had been assigned to the precinct. He could ignore the urge if she didn't have that husky voice—that and she was a helluva cop. Four months ago, she'd tackled a suspect in the bullpen as the guy reached for Detective Rigs' gun when the detective turned to pull a form from his desk drawer.

Gerry had gotten two steps out of his office when Dee had the suspect on the floor, her knee in the small of his back. A shaken Riggs grabbed the guy's arm and barely allowed Dee time to move before yanking the asshole to his feet and shoving him back into his chair. Gerry heard her mutter, "Jerk pistol whipped an old woman," as she filed through the quiet room, and he realized the suspect was the guy wanted for a string of convenience store robberies, during which he'd badly beaten a store owner. That was the first time he'd wondered why he hadn't met someone like her twelve years ago.

"Dee," he said into the phone, "It's Gerry. I need backup."

"Where?" she asked.

He hurried to the closet, slid open the door, and pulled his shoulder holster from a hook on the wall. "I just got a call from *The Hot Spot*. The blonde last seen with Vitelli is there."

Gerry lodged the phone between ear and shoulder as he slipped into the holster and snapped it closed. "I'm heading over. Lummus is meeting me there." He reached between the blankets stacked on the closet's top shelf, grabbed his 9mm, then slammed it into the holster. "Who's near my place? My son's here and I need someone to keep an eye on the house until my mother arrives."

There was a pause. "You want me to dispatch a patrol to baby sit?"

Two years as a part-time father was catching up with him. Maybe his mother was right. How many times could he go charging off after the bad guy when he should be home with his son? He glanced at the clock. 12:28. She would be another seventeen minutes. This wouldn't be the first time he'd been the last on a scene because he had to wait for someone to sit with his son. Maybe Brenda had been right after all: toss 'em all in the Atlantic.

"Life in the twenty-first century," he said. "I want someone here, and fast."

"I'll call dispatch," Dee said, and disconnected.

He scooped up the hand held radio from his nightstand. "Come on, boy," he called Hargrave, and headed for Joey's room.

Joey lay on his stomach, arms tucked under his pillow. Gerry pulled the blanket up over his shoulders and kissed the top of his head. "Down, Hargrave."

The Shepherd dropped to his stomach, paws stretched out before him.

Gerry squatted and stroked his head. "Okay, big guy. Keep an eye open. No bad guys allowed."

Chapter Five

F IFTEEN MINUTES LATER, Gerry pulled into the club's parking lot. He flipped his cell phone closed. He had waited three minutes until the black and white had arrived at his house before leaving, and his mother had just called to say she'd arrived five minutes ahead of schedule. The tension in his gut relaxed a fraction. He scanned the crowd for Lummus. No sign of him. Gerry parked at the far end of the lot, grabbed his handheld from the passenger seat, clipped it to belt, and hurried to the club. He brushed past the line of people and flashed his badge at Richie, the bouncer.

"Hey!" a man in line yelled. Fingers closed over Gerry's shoulder.

He whirled. "Police." He shoved his badge in the guy's face.

The guy backed up, hands raised, palms out. Gerry headed for the bar. The music boomed with a Latin beat. Collin stood at the far end of the counter where a group of women watched raptly as he flipped a shaker in the air then caught it. They broke into applause. Collin grinned, removed the lid, and began pouring their drinks. He didn't appear to have noticed Gerry, but nodded to the left.

Gerry pushed through the crowd and stopped at sight of the blonde at the end of the bar. Her back faced him. Her blonde hair hung in a ponytail that exposed a slim neck. And that hair…nothing fake about that color. He gave a slow, silent whistle at the clothes: sheik, not the trendy stuff Collin had described. She stiffened as if he had called her by name. An abrasive static crackled like a blown speaker. Slowly, she brought her gaze to eye level in the bar's mirror and fastened her deep blue eyes onto him.

Gerry's breath hitched. Christ, Collin had been right; a blonde of goddess proportions. The cacophony of music receded into the background and his surroundings blurred into a mass of black, white, and blood red. A sucking force emptied his lungs, asphyxia brought on a wave of dizziness. The static sound became a metal-on-metal shriek. The blur of colored lights and shifting forms twisted around her eyes. The whirl picked up speed. Gerry clutched at the moving whirlpool, his fingers closing on the hard back of a chair.

Music suddenly blared and the flash of the strobe lights blinded him. *What the hell?* He shook his head, refocused. The blonde was gone. He spun. She was ten feet away, headed for the exit. She glanced over her shoulder and her blue eyes swallowed him. Then she turned away.

Gerry yanked free the badge clipped to his belt and thrust it above his head. "Police!" he shouted over the noise of the club.

Everyone within twenty feet froze. He pushed past the bystanders and grabbed the blonde's wrist. She looked down at his hand. Curiosity splashed across her face, then melted into a frown. She brought her gaze up to his. Her eyes were the bluest he'd ever seen, an ocean of blue where he could lose himself.

He swayed for a heartbeat, then stammered, "I need to talk to you."

With a twist of her arm, she broke his hold and bolted through the door. Gerry lunged after her. He collided with three women entering the club. They shrieked and one buxom Cuban girl clutched at Gerry, taking him to the floor with her.

He mumbled "Sorry," shot to his feet, and flew out the door.

Gerry hit the street in time to see the blonde fifty feet away, turning the corner onto Water Street. How the hell had she gotten that far ahead of him? He spotted Lummus sauntering up to the club. Gerry stuffed his badge into his back pocket and dashed after her.

"Hey!" Lummus called.

"Call for backup! The blonde bolted." Gerry hollered over his shoulder.

He reached the corner within four seconds, but she was nowhere in sight. He raced down the busy block, checking storefront alcoves and alleyways. He finally slowed to a jog. Where the hell was she?

His handheld crackled to life. "All units in the vicinity of Fifth and Main, 459a reported at Cray's Jewelers. Repeat; all units in the vicinity of Fifth and Main, 459a at Cray's Jewelers."

459—burglary—a block east.

"This is unit thirty-five," came a voice over the radio. "We're ten minutes away. Anyone closer?"

"Negative, unit thirty-five. Unit one-oh-three is fifteen minutes away."

"Damn," Gerry said. It had been years since he'd answered a call for anything other than homicide, and by the time he arrived the murderer was always gone. He grabbed the handheld from his belt and keyed the radio. "Dispatch, this is Forstner. I'm at Fourth and Water. ETA sixty seconds."

So much for the blonde. He spun and sprinted across Water Street. A blue minivan screeched to a halt. He skidded into the fender and pushed off. The woman driver stared wide-eyed as he swerved out of the way. He reclipped the radio to his belt, flipped it off, and veered left into an alley that dumped out onto Fifth. Traffic noise receded and the burglar alarm sounded loud and clear in the darkness ahead.

Gerry yanked out his weapon and dodged dumpsters and piles of trash as he ran. Halting at the intersection of another alley halfway to Fifth, he concentrated on the alarm. It blared from the left, down a gloomy alley that passed behind several stores, including Cray's, then opened onto Main.

Heart pounding, he crept into the gloom. Dumpsters, crates and unrecognizable junk littered the alley. A critter shot across his path and scurried into a dark hole. Five feet farther down, a pair of disembodied eyes glinted from the darkest shadows. Halfway down, a steel door swung open and crashed against the brick wall. Gerry skidded to a halt as two men, one short, one tall, dashed out the door. The short guy stopped and stared in Gerry's direction.

Gerry aimed. "Halt! Police!"

"Move!" The tall man shoved the short guy and they started running.

Gerry cursed. Both men clutched cloth bags, but he hadn't seen a weapon. Damn. No weapon, no shooting. The pad of their shoes on asphalt grew distant. Gerry chased them, running a slalom course through refuse and filth.

The tall man shot out of the shadows at the far end of the alley, turned onto Main, and disappeared to the right. The smaller man dashed from the rear of a trash bin like he was on fire. Gerry accelerated, burst onto Main Street on the short guy's heels, and tore right. The tall guy ducked into a gap between storefronts half a block from Cray's.

"Where the hell is backup?" Gerry growled as the smaller guy ducked into the same gap.

Gerry rounded the building and plunged through a gap barely as wide as his arm-span. He scanned the fire escapes, then slowed. Lights on Main illuminated the empty alley—and the dead end, a hundred feet away. *Trapped.*

"Shit," he swore, and started to swing around.

The short guy lunged from an alcove. Steel flashed. A slicing pain penetrated Gerry's gut as the thief thrust. Gerry staggered back, tried to raise his 9mm, but his grip loosened and the weapon clattered to the asphalt. He clutched his stomach. Wetness seeped through his fingers. He looked down at the stain spreading across his shirt.

"Shit," he wheezed, and sank to his knees. He squinted up at his attacker.

"Die, motherfucker!" the man hissed.

Gerry blinked. How would he hold his guts in long enough to get back to his car? His sight dimmed and his balance wavered as he tried to remain upright. He pitched backwards, tensed for contact, and hit asphalt. A black sheet abruptly dropped between him and his attacker. A scream sounded as if deep within a tunnel and Gerry felt the silkiness of the sheet envelope him. A tall, lithe figure loomed over him, then knelt at his side.

The blonde from the club.

So this is hell's door.

Somehow, Gerry wasn't surprised that his mind had chosen a beautiful woman to represent the Angel of Death. What better justice than to spend eternity in Hell with the reminder of such earthly beauty?

She yanked his shirttail free and leaned over him. Gerry stiffened as a hot poker rammed into his gut and a current raced through his veins like a runaway locomotive. He arched with the electric energy, body flailing in a burst of adrenaline. His wrists were grabbed, forced back against a rough surface, and held with merciless strength. Fiery liquid surged from his belly and up into his throat. His mouth filled with liquid—the coppery heaviness of blood. He choked and felt his eyes roll back into his head.

This is it. I'm drowning in my own blood.

Coolness like that of vaporous hot ice crawled across his skin. An ethereal sensation of life flowing through then out the wound startled him. Falling through nothingness, then a slow turn like that of a 747 angling around on approach. He catapulted from his body and…he wasn't alone. An unearthly presence accompanied him, unseen, unheard. The Angel of Death.

His lips felt wet and the metallic taste had taken on a cool, sweet flavor. He felt the thickness of blood as it retreated back *down* his throat. A memory of himself at eight rose with more clarity than real life. He saw himself—was himself—as he mounted his neighbor's pony, Dusty, and felt horseflesh move between his thighs. Gerry clutched the pony's mane as the beast started forward in a slow amble.

Time flowed past in the form of a thick ribbon of quicksilver, and the pony vaporized as Gerry now sat at the head of the stairs listening to his parents argue. He crammed his hands against his ears to block out the insults, the profanity—more sorrow than he remembered overwhelmed him.

He shuddered and found himself at his senior prom, slow dancing with Jenny Myers, her hip pressing his hard-on. His body convulsed again with the energy jamming through his veins. His memory jumped to his wedding day. Admiration enveloped him at the devotion and love he felt for his young bride.

His first commendation replaced the vision, then Joey's birth...and intense pride. The university, K-9 school. Flash after flash—draw after draw—he sank deeper and deeper into darkness. His body grew heavier, heavier. He shot forward into shared nothingness. Another surge raced through him. A jolt hit like lightning. His sight unexpectedly filled with sunlight shining off a horizon of white that went on forever.

Christ. Someone made a mistake and sent me upstairs.

He couldn't prevent a laugh.

Another jolt and he stood on a country road beneath a cloudless blue sky. His surroundings had taken on a pristine, 3-D, Technicolor appearance. The sky was bluer than any he'd ever seen. The trees, the stream—another jolt, this one harder than the last, and quicker—darkness closed in around him. A towheaded boy was ripped from his arms. Then a woman led him through a labyrinth of tunnels, down, down, down.

They'd discovered their mistake and were sending him into hellfire, after all.

Gerry broke from darkness into a candlelit chamber. Men dressed in monk-like robes approached. The icy touch of their hands sent a shiver down his spine as they slipped the robe from his shoulders. One man reached out. Gerry caught the flash of a thick gold band decorated with a red gem on the man's middle finger, a crooked cross glowed within the circle deep in the jewel. The man caressed his chest with cool fingers. Gerry shivered. The man's gaze deepened and Gerry stepped back in terror. The man seized his wrist. Gerry cried out at sight of the willowy arm attached to his own body. He looked down at his feminine forearm and hand with long, sensitive fingers.

The man tugged him forward. Hair brushed Gerry's shoulders and his hips moved with an unfamiliar sway as he allowed himself to be led from the room and through a stone passageway. Damp cold enveloped him. He shivered again. He looked down at his chest to discover bare breasts—full, female breasts on his chest. He cried out and tried to yank free of the man's hold.

The man looked back and said something, but Gerry only saw his lips move. No sound. No sound at all in this place, he realized. He looked down again at his body—at the feminine body he inhabited—and jammed his eyes shut. *This is Hell. I'll spend eternity being raped by monsters.*

Abruptly, he sat atop his pony—no—a horse. He rode. The three-quarter moon waned in the western sky. Cliffs rose high on both sides. The river his horse followed soothed him. A male figure suddenly landed on the path a few feet ahead. Gerry stiffened. This creature, too, was beautiful, as beautiful as the blonde, but this male had been conjured from somewhere deeper in Gerry's psyche.

The creature's dark gaze latched onto his. Fear lanced through Gerry. The thing meant to kill him! Gerry leaped from the horse, drawing his sword before his feet touched ground. The creature drew two daggers and crossed them in front of his chest. Gerry leveled his sword. The engraved tree of Yggdrasil glittered on the sword's shaft.

A cold roughness on the back of his head imposed itself into the silent surroundings. Gerry gasped as darkness returned and the blare of a car horn roared past. He snapped open his eyes and straightened to a sitting position, his breath coming in heavy gasps. He looked wildly about for his attacker, but the alley was deserted. He felt…alone, more alone than he ever remembered feeling. A crushing emptiness settled deep in his gut. He doubled over and vomited onto the pavement.

LOW VOICES IN argument filtered down the hallway as Gerry clicked shut his front door. Mom had fallen asleep in front of the TV. He paused in the hallway and slipped a shaky hand beneath the blue scrubs the doctor had given him at the hospital. No injury. One look at the bloody shirt and front waistband of his jeans and the ER nurse put him at the head of the waiting line—then reached for the phone to call headquarters. Gerry prevented the call with a flash of his badge. After the doctor found no serious wound, Gerry didn't contradict his conclusion that the blood must have belonged to the thief.

He let his hand drop to his side and padded down the hallway to the living room. He paused in the doorway. Mom lay on the recliner, Grandma's worn afghan askew across her midsection, her feet propped up on the footrest. Warmth washed over him. Back in the alley, the hallucinations seemed real. He had felt the knife slice deep in his gut, had touched Collin's blonde goddess, even glimpsed heaven and hell. Yet he now stood in his house, uninjured, surrounded by the people who loved him.

This is real.

Gerry crossed to his mother. He picked up the remote from the floor beside her and hit the off button.

She jarred awake. "Oh."

Gerry smiled down at her. "Go back to sleep, Ma."

She started to push the recliner upright. He grabbed the back of the chair, stopping it from righting, and bent and kissed her forehead. "Go back to sleep." He arranged the afghan more squarely around her.

She frowned. "What are you wearing? Are those—" Her eyes widened. "What's wrong?"

"Nothing's wrong," he soothed. "I spilled coffee on my clothes."

"But—"

"No buts." He dropped another kiss on her forehead.

"You sure you don't need—" she began.

"I don't need a thing. Go back to sleep."

She glanced at his clothes, then gave a small nod and closed her eyes.

A moment later, Gerry eased open Joey's room. Hargrave looked up from beside the bed. "Hey, boy," Gerry whispered as he entered.

The dog jumped to his feet, met him halfway across the room, and followed him back to the bed. Gerry rubbed him behind the ears as he paused beside the bed. Joey hadn't moved an inch. Gerry tilted his head to get a better look at his son's face. The kid slept in blissful peace. A love heavily tinged with the depth like that he had felt in the alley's dream flooded him. Gerry breathed deep, kissed Joey's cheek, then tiptoed to his room and flopped onto the bed.

Hargrave padded in and laid his head across Gerry's leg. Gerry closed his eyes and felt himself slip over the edge into sleep. Clear blue eyes stared in the darkness. Steel flashed. He jerked awake. His vision focused and registered the white ceiling. What the hell had happened? Psychedelic lights, visions, and a scratch that couldn't have bled enough to soak a Band-Aid much less his shirt and jeans. Then there was the blonde, the strange priest with the ring, the disgust of his touch, and the creature standing in the shadow. The memory of its burning eyes…like the blond man with the daggers he knew, but didn't know. Dispatch said he was AWOL for twenty-seven minutes. That half an hour had passed in seconds and seemed like a lifetime. Two lifetimes.

Wide awake, Gerry pushed to his feet. Hargrave backed up. Each step felt like quicksand. He ignored exhaustion and crossed to the dresser, exchanged the scrubs for a sweatshirt and jeans, then let Hargrave out into the backyard. After the Shepherd relieved himself, Gerry led him back to Joey's room.

"Stay."

Hargrave's butt dropped to the floor.

Gerry rubbed the dog's neck. "Lay," he said. "You're going to stay here tonight."

The dog stretched out as he had before, settling his nose between his paws. Gerry crossed to the door and closed it behind him just short of clicking shut.

Chapter Six

GERRY JOLTED AWAKE. Blackness filled his vision, and he blinked for several seconds before realizing he stared at the blank computer screen in his office.

"You look like hell," a husky feminine voice said.

He jerked his head toward the voice. Dee stood over him like an angel in a blazer. Despite the ghost of a smile in her brown eyes, a deep frown creased her brow. Parted in the middle, her long, straight rust-brown hair framed high cheekbones, dark eyebrows, a straight nose, and full, sensuous lips. Lips now compressed into a thin line that echoed the concern in her eyes.

A soft female scent conjured visions of satin sheets, soft murmurs, and her hundred and fifteen pound body beneath his. A phone rang in the bull pen outside his office, breaking the spell, and Gerry glanced past her through the door. The precinct's Saturday morning grind was in full swing. He winced inwardly. He'd passed out at his desk. No wonder Dee thought he was a nut. He lifted his hand. The notes he'd been working on last night stuck to his sweaty palm. He shook the paper loose and looked up at her.

"It's been a long night."

Dee leaned forward. Gerry jerked back. She paused, her hand hovering pec level, six inches from his chest. She gave him a dry look and pointed at his gut.

"What happened?"

Gerry glanced down. A dime-sized dark spot had appeared on his gray sweatshirt over his belly. The wound that wasn't had oozed. "An old sweat shirt," he said.

Dee continued to stare. "I'm going for breakfast."

Gerry stared stupidly at her.

She snorted a soft laugh and shook her head. The smile hinted at in her eyes, became a full-fledged laugh. "Come on." She motioned toward the door.

He glanced at the cork board filled with Valknut crime scene photos and notes and she laughed again. "I'm buying. Tell me you can refuse that."

He couldn't.

✦

GERRY WAS HALFWAY through his eggs and hash browns when his cell phone played *Send in the Clowns*. Dee raised a brow, and he felt his face go warm. A corner of her mouth twitched in obvious amusement and he couldn't help a grin. He shrugged, removed the phone from a jacket pocket, and flipped it open.

"Yeah." He grimaced inwardly, belatedly realizing he hadn't checked the caller ID. If this was Brenda—

"Forstner," a male voice said, "this is Johnson. We've got another murder with the Valknut MO."

"Who?" Gerry demanded.

"John Kinnison."

"The Kinnison who walked on that child molestation charge six months ago?"

"That's him," Johnson replied.

"Christ, talk about justice. Where'd it happen?"

"His apartment. 4A, 6341 3rd Avenue. Corner of 63rd and third."

Gerry knew the neighborhood: Middle class town houses and snow-bird condos. He was betting they now had their match for the blood used to draw the Valknut on Vitelli's chest. "Who's on the scene?" he asked.

"Forensics and Lummus."

Gerry glanced at his watch. Seven-ten. Leave it to Lummus to deal him out. "Be right there." He flipped the phone shut and slipped it into his pocket.

"Another murder?" Dee asked.

"Yeah." He reached for his wallet.

"Nope," she said.

He looked up.

"I said I was buying." Dee looked at him over a spoonful of cantaloupe. She slid the fruit between her full lips and began to chew.

He felt a distinct thickening in his groin. Strike two. He'd better get out while he still could. A mental image of the blonde from *The Hot Spot* rose to mind and he was startled to see the picture metamorphose into him stroking the curls between her legs. He quickly slid the wallet back into his pocket, hoping like hell Dee hadn't noticed the tremble in his hand.

He rose. "Thanks. I needed this."

"Sure."

"Dinner, tomorrow night?" he asked.

She looked thoughtful and for a split second he thought he'd miscalculated. Strike three.

"Sure," she said.

"Okay. I'll call after I drop off my son."

Dee nodded, the tips of her hair moving almost infinitesimally against her cheeks. The olive skin of her Italian heritage softened the darker brown of her Seminole ancestry. He had been right: He should have gotten out while he could.

HELLUVA WAY TO start Saturday morning, Gerry thought as he pushed through half a dozen reporters gathered outside Kinnison's apartment building, a beat-up six-story gray adobe that probably used to be white with inset lanai's for each unit. Rust-stains ran down the stucco under each balcony's railing. He was supposed to wake up this morning with Joey jumping on his chest. Instead, his son was at home with Grandma, while his father chased another freak—another freak who inhabited a dump. Justice left a lot to be desired.

"Why has the Valknut murderer killed again so soon?" a young brunette reporter Gerry didn't know shouted above the other questioners as he showed his badge to the uniformed officer who barred their way down the open walkway leading to Kinnison's unit.

"Come on, Forstner," Linda Beaumont of KPAC called. "If you don't give us the truth, we'll be forced to make up something."

Gerry averted his face so Linda wouldn't see the grin he hadn't been quick enough to prevent. He liked Linda. She wasn't above haranguing him for a story, but she was a straight shooter, despite the tough act.

"Give it up, Forstner," she shouted over the other reporters.

"Talk to Public Relations," he threw back as he started toward Kinnison's apartment. "I don't give interviews."

A moment later, he closed the apartment door behind him and released a breath when the quiet bustle of forensics replaced the reporters' din. Across the room, Lacey MacKenzie snapped pictures of blood splatters on the entertainment center. Gerry took two steps forward, then caught sight of Kinnison's naked body lying in a puddle of its own blood on the other side of the couch. Sightless eyes stared up at the dirty popcorn acoustic ceiling. The Valknut drawn in blood spanned his chest.

Gerry's attention jarred onto a pile of flesh lying three feet to Kinnison's right like a gruesome dishrag. Gerry's stomach turned. That wasn't just some *pile of flesh.* Those were Kinnison's genitals. Christ, the bastard had suffered. Had the sick pleasure he'd derived from those parts been worth the pain he'd suffered the last minutes of his life?

Fuck. Why hadn't he stayed in K-9? Had it been the two years of theology? The theology had been Mom's idea. Maybe it had been scoring in the top nineteenth percentile in criminal psychology? No. Neither one was the real reason he'd gravitated toward cult hunting. He had a knack for getting into the mind of these sick fucks. He'd spent many sleepless nights wondering what that said about him.

He released a breath and strode around the couch, stopping short of the blood surrounding Kinnison. No signs of violence had been present at the other three murder scenes, and nothing about them indicated they were sexually motivated. Why this violence? Was the killer making an example of Kinnison? Or maybe this was just special treatment for the child molester. Had Kinnison broken some cult law by molesting children?

Gerry shifted his attention to the body. While Kinnison's heart pumped blood from his veins onto the carpet, the killer had knelt beside him and drawn the Valknut on the dying body.

"Cool and calculated," Gerry murmured. Too cool. No hurry. No fear. Smarter than the average serial killer.

"Lacey," he called, "you got pictures of the body?"

The photographer snapped a picture of the sliding glass door leading to the balcony, stepped around Francis, who was dusting the table beside her for prints, and replied, "Yep," as she snapped a second shot.

Gerry squatted and examined Kinnison's neck. Sure enough, his juggler had been opened with the same cut found on the other victims. Pam had said the cut was meant to trickle blood at a rate more like soy sauce than catsup, yet didn't coagulate. Toxicology of prior victims showed no sign of blood thinners. The puddle of blood wasn't smeared, stepped in, or tracked around the carpet. It was as if Kinnison had painted a Valknut on his chest, ripped off his own genitals, slit his throat, then laid down to bleed to death.

Gerry cursed, remembering his thoughts yesterday morning about the killer talking his next victim into slicing his own throat.

"Any signs of forced entry?" Gerry asked Lacey without taking his eyes off the body.

"No, and no sign of a struggle either," she replied.

Gerry hadn't thought so. Kinnison had let the murderer in...then let him slice open his neck. Whose blood had the killer used this time to draw this Valknut? How possible was it anyone would be willing to help him murder another victim when they had to know they were next? About as possible as Kinnison letting someone that was all over the news as a serial killer's MO perform a sacrificial ritual on him.

Gerry's gut tightened with the vision of Kinnison opening the door for the blonde from *The Hot Spot*, then kneeling, head upturned as he offered the beautiful cult goddess the ultimate gift of his life. What power could she possibly have that could induce a man to let her make him a sacrificial lamb? Gerry recalled the attraction that had transfixed him when their eyes first met, then the intimacy of the dream in the alley, and shuddered. He never wanted to find out.

"What's the matter, Forstner?" Lummus spoke behind him. "Feeling queasy?"

Gerry twisted and locked his gaze onto Lummus' dark eyes. "Who discovered the body?"

"I did. A match on the blood used to draw that monstrosity on Vitelli's chest came back this morning as Kinnison's. I came over to haul him in and found the door ajar."

Gerry rose and faced Lummus. "Did you talk to the other residents?"

"No one saw or heard anything unusual."

"Are there surveillance cameras?"

"No cameras. There's a service entrance, but anyone entering has to get an okay from the Super." Gerry opened his mouth to ask about the superintendent, but Lummus held up a hand. "I've already talked to him." Lummus produced a sheet of paper from a jacket pocket. "A copy of yesterday's deliveries. Nothing suspicious, but we'll check it out."

"Get some help. Pull in Sheridan."

A corner of Lummus' lip turned up in a condescending glower, but Gerry only looked back at Kinnison. His attention flicked to the genitals, but he forced his eyes onto the Valknut drawn on the chest and said, "Kinnison was a pedophile and Vitelli a small time wise guy. Check their rap sheets. Vitelli never did hard time, but they might have met in some local joint. Talk to your street contacts. Maybe they shared a prostitute or had a local hang out."

"You gotta wonder how come no one heard him cry out," Lummus said.

Gerry jerked his gaze onto Lummus. That was the smartest thing he'd heard from the guy—except Lummus hadn't felt what Gerry had upon seeing the blonde at *The Hot Spot*. If she showed up at Kinnison's door that would why he let a killer in, and maybe why he went without a whimper. Gerry paused at seeing a smart phone lying on the coffee table.

He crossed in front of Lummus. "Find out why no one heard anything." He bent over the smart phone and studied the screen. "Did you get this, Francis?"

"Yeah," he replied.

Gerry pulled latex gloves from his back pocket and slipped them on before picking up the phone. He opened the address book and scrolled through the contact list. The name Skip Jackson came into view. Skip Jackson, where did he know that name—Judge Jackson—the judge who presided over Kinnison's trial.

"Holy shit," Gerry whispered.

GERRY TYPED THE code into his home computer that allowed him access to Kinnison's file on the precinct's mainframe. To Gerry's surprise, the file loaded in three seconds. About time. The department had been trying to get new software online the last two months. He scrolled down the screen and stopped short at the picture of seven-year-old Ben Phillips. The boy was a dead ringer for Joey two years ago. Gerry scanned the case report. His stomach turned. Kinnison had coached Ben's soccer team. Ben's father was habitually late picking up his son after soccer practice. This particular Saturday afternoon when he was late, Kinnison took the kid home—Kinnison's home.

Gerry leaned aside and peered down the hall into the living room. Joey lounged in the easy chair, soccer ball in hand. Gerry watched his son toss the ball up a foot and catch it. An hour ago, Joey had begged him to go out back and help him warm up before his game. He still waited.

Gerry glanced at the phone numbers written on the yellow pad sitting on his desk. One of the two numbers that assistant DA, Pete Nelson, gave him for Jackson's residence matched the number in Kinnison's PDA. A muted thud sounded from the living room. Joey's ball striking the carpet. When Joey talked about playing soccer, his eyes shined twice as brightly as they had when he'd told Gerry about the Superbowl game with David Myles, Brenda's new boyfriend. Gerry closed out Kinnison's file and headed down the hallway to his son.

✦

AFTER ANOTHER SOCCER match where Gerry almost arrested two abusive fathers, Gerry took a left off Coral Way onto SW 19th Avenue, headed toward the ocean and the swanky part of town. Joey glanced at him with a quizzical expression.

"I've got to check out this guy's house before it gets dark," Gerry said. "Then we'll go to the Pup and Taco like I promised."

"Sure, Dad."

Gerry frowned. Joey was too accustomed to these detours. "It'll only take a minute," he promised, and leaned forward to read the street signs. Judge Jackson's street should be next. He didn't know what he'd find, but curiosity had gotten the better of him. Jackson could be on the take, or maybe child molesters ran in packs, in which case…what would he see? If Jackson was a cult member, maybe he would be good enough to have a Valknut on his mailbox or front door. Gerry had seen crazier things.

The sign for Espanola Drive came up. Hedges and brick walls lined the sidewalk, broken at intervals by gated driveways that led to mansions set back behind palms. Gerry read the house numbers painted on the curb and slowed as he approached Jackson's house on the right.

An eight-foot wall of white stucco draped with passionflower vines fronted the property. An iron-gated driveway plunged into various tropical bushes and dwarf palms. Gerry peered through his passenger window and caught flashes of terracotta roof tiles and white stucco beyond palm trees. Well to do, but not opulent, and no Valknut.

The street curved to the right and a pedestrian came into view up ahead on the sidewalk. His gaze riveted to her ass, the feminine sway of hips, and Levi-clad legs. Wavy blonde hair fell midway down her back, caressing a pink, rayon Gucci top. She strutted like a debutante out on a stroll.

"No dog and no cars parked along the street," Gerry murmured. "Where you going, baby?"

As Gerry pulled abreast, he let off the accelerator. Something about the classical jaw line and cheekbones…she turned with unhurried ease and made eye contact. He stared into the ocean blue eyes of the blonde from *The Hot Spot*—those same eyes from that dream in the alley. He felt slippage and fought the feeling he was falling.

Her eyes narrowed—then softened with recognition. A jolt of adrenaline gripped his chest. What the hell was she doing in Jackson's neighborhood? The corner of her mouth turned up with a curious twist. That mouth, a man could—

"Dad!"

The front tire clipped the curb with a jolt. Gerry corrected and reflexively grabbed Joey's arm to steady him. Joey clutched the door grip with one hand, the other braced against the dashboard. He stared out the window at the blonde. The boy's reflection in the window mirrored the same blank stare Gerry had experienced when he'd seen her at *The Hot Spot*. Gerry jerked his gaze back onto her. She had locked eyes with Joey.

Fear shot down Gerry's spine. Never before had he put his family in the crosshairs. He stomped on the accelerator. The engine bogged, then the car lurched. He grabbed Joey's shoulder and spun him to face forward while watching the blonde in his rearview mirror. Her eyes swung to meet his. He ripped his gaze free and whipped the car around the corner.

Chapter Seven

THE FOLLOWING MORNING, Gerry surveyed Sunday's country breakfast carnage scattered across the kitchen table: remnants of scrambled eggs, pancakes, grits, bacon, sausage, toast, biscuits and gravy. The breakfast had been more for him than Joey. Having slept little, he rose early, poured coffee down his gullet, and started cooking to stay busy.

"Okay, Buddy, you better get dressed or we'll miss the warm-up laps at Daytona."

Hargrave woofed as Joey jumped up from his seat, barely dodging his paws. "Sorry," Joey called in his race toward his room.

Gerry paused in carrying the dirty dishes to the sink and watched through the open kitchen door as his son bolted down the hallway to his room. He smiled, set the dishes in the sink, and turned on the water.

The phone rang. He grabbed the wall phone's receiver. "Hello."

"Forstner, this is Andrews. You got a call from," there was a pause, "a Collin Norman, the bartender down at *The Hot Spot*. He said the blonde showed up again last night and swiped your business card from the register top."

"What—?" Steam rolled up in waves across Gerry's face from the hot water. He turned his head aside and twisted the faucet off. She'd seen Joey, had time to memorize his face. Now she had Gerry's name and mobile number. "We need a description of her on the wire. Who's on duty for sketches?"

"Max Hayes."

"Let him know I'll be down in half an hour. Get Lummus on the bartender."

"Will do." Andrews hung up.

Gerry replaced the phone on its hook. Why had the blonde gone back to *The Hot Spot*? Given the fact Gerry had seen her at the club and outside Jackson's place, her return didn't make sense. Was it some weird coincidence that she'd noticed his card on the register? Seeing her outside Jackson's had convinced Gerry the judge was a cult member. But if that were the case, Jackson could have given her Gerry's work and home numbers. Maybe Jackson's above-board reputation was on the money and he hadn't allowed even cult law to countermand his personal sense of duty. That might explain the blonde's actions. If Jackson wouldn't hand over the information, she might have gone looking for it, despite knowing Gerry was looking for her.

A chill cut into his gut. *She's hunting me—and wants me to know.*

Joey. Gerry's home number was unlisted—Brenda's wasn't. She hadn't switched back to her maiden name. She was too angry to realize that someone with a score to settle against him would start by looking in the phone book under Forstner. Goddammit, he'd begged her to get an unlisted number. That had been his mistake—begging.

Gerry surveyed the remnants of breakfast. He and Joey wouldn't make the practice laps. They would make the driver introductions and race if he skipped the cleanup. He grabbed a marrowbone for Hargrave from the fridge. The Shepherd's alert brown eyes sent a pang of guilt through Gerry. Hargrave knew a fresh bone meant he'd be left home alone. Gerry squatted and scratched the dog behind the ears as he set the bone between his paws.

"You know the drill, big guy," he murmured. "No vampires allowed. Now that they can get SPF-60 sunscreen, I hear they can come out during the day."

Hargrave was already gnawing the bone as if it were his last meal. The sound of Joey's sneakers echoed in the hallway and Gerry gave Hargrave a final scratch before rising. Joey stood in the kitchen doorway, Intimidator hat on his head, hearing protection headset in hand, and a questioning expression. The kid had heard the phone ring too often when the two of them had plans to mistake what it meant.

Gerry ignored the deepening sense of guilt as he headed for the door. "Come on. We have to bolt. I have to swing by the station."

GERRY DROPPED JOEY off at Brenda's long after dark, his ears still ringing from the roar of the race engines. He circled through her quiet residential neighborhood twice before assuring himself all the cars parked in the driveways belonged there. No blonde. The tension didn't ease.

Joey hadn't said a word about her cool, compelling stare, but Gerry had caught him staring at a slim blonde two rows down from their bleacher seats. She had been the only woman that had held Joey's attention, but Gerry had been distracted by every blonde at the track. Images like those he'd imagined of Kinnison kneeling before her warred with the softer look of recognition she'd given him outside Jackson's. Goddammit, he was confusing beauty with goodness.

As he turned down Brick Hill Road, the muffled jingle of his cell phone emanated from the glove box where he had stuffed it before the race. He retrieved the phone and checked the caller ID. Headquarters. Dee was on duty. An erotic image of her sprawled naked across the armrest between the car's front seats, her breasts arched toward him, rose in his mind, and his insides finally relaxed a notch.

He connected. "Forstner."

"Gerry, Lummus has been trying to get in touch with you for the past hour," Dee said.

"What's up?"

There was a heartbeat of silence, before she said, "Hold on," and placed him on hold. He took a right onto Grand Avenue, went through a green light, then merged onto the highway. A candy apple red Toyota Celica, lowered, with wide tires and a brushed aluminum airfoil in back, whizzed past. Gerry settled in behind a panel van in lane two.

"Gerry," Dee's voice came back on the line, "Lummus answered a 317 in Coral Gables."

"A break-in at Jackson's place," Gerry demanded.

"Yeah."

"I'll be there right away."

"Lummus wanted you to call him," Dee said.

I bet he does, Gerry thought. "Okay. Listen," he paused, suddenly tongue tied.

"What do you need? This place is a madhouse tonight."

She was all business. Gerry hesitated. "We still on for dinner?"

"Sure." No sexy note of anticipation in her voice. "Pick me up at ten."

She signed off as his phone chirped another incoming call.

Modern women. Gerry grimaced and glanced at the screen. Lummus. He accepted the call. "Forstner."

"Forstner, this is Lummus. I'm at Judge Jackson's place. There's been a break-in."

"What's that have to do with homicide?"

"Jackson came out of his shower and caught a woman in his bedroom. He recognized her from your sketch."

"Her?" Gerry demanded.

"The woman from *The Hot Spot.* Apparently, the judge surprised her as much as she surprised him."

A tingle spread through Gerry's midsection. Why would Jackson report seeing the blonde as a burglar if he and they were fellow cult members? "What happened?" An opening appeared in the right hand lane. He accelerated.

"Jackson doesn't remember much. He doesn't know how she got in or out."

"What do you mean?" The headlights of the car he'd passed receded and Gerry merged into the right lane. "She didn't run when he caught her?"

"That's the odd thing. He remembers stepping from the master bathroom into the bedroom and seeing her rifling his desk, and demanded to know who she was. His wife called to him from an adjoining room. She had been out for the night—some charity thing—but came home early. Jackson yelled for her to get out and call the cops. He heard her ask what was wrong, heard her footsteps approach the connecting door, then his memory went blank until the cops showed up. Mrs. Jackson found her husband on the floor. She figured it for a heart attack and dialed 911. By the time the paramedics arrived, Jackson had revived and called the Chief. The paramedics didn't find a thing wrong."

Gerry took the 47th Street off ramp. Damn. Finding a blonde goddess in his bedroom would give any guy a stroke. "Does Jackson know what she was after?"

"Nope," Lummus said. Gerry's phone crackled and he heard, "—baffled. Jackson's wife—didn't see—Their Scotty dog barked like—"

The light at the end of the off-ramp was green and Gerry turned right onto Denny. "I'm on my way."

"Don't bother, Chief," Lummus said. Lummus-the-asshole was back. "Jackson refuses to answer any more questions. He's already gone to bed.

He's promised to come to the precinct tomorrow for further questioning. I've stationed a couple uniforms outside for the night."

"Good of you to call and give me a heads up," Gerry said.

"Did it out of the goodness of my heart."

"Have your report on my desk tomorrow morning."

A second of silence passed, then Lummus' "Yeah, right" was followed by a click.

"Right," Gerry repeated, and disconnected.

He rested the phone on his leg. The blonde had returned to *The Hot Spot* and Jackson's place. Her appearance at *The Hot Spot* made no sense, but if Gerry was right about the judge being involved in a cult that could account for her going back to his place. That could also mean the judge had good reason to lie.

An affair? Cult member and a judge? Jackson was seventy-two, still sitting on the bench, and healthy as a horse. Maybe he let her into the house and she was in his bedroom when his wife arrived home. The blonde split and Jackson claimed she was an intruder. Gerry let out a slow breath, not liking the final possibility. If the blonde was an intruder and hit Jackson with the same look she gave him at *The Hot Spot*, that would explain why he blacked out.

✦

A COOL FEBRUARY breeze kicked up from the beach, blowing strands of Dee's hair across her face. The hot wing poised at her lips trembled slightly and Gerry noticed goose bumps running the length of her slim arm. Despite the exhaust generated by the cars on the busy street beside the *Sandbox Café*, a winter chill permeated the ocean air.

"Here." Gerry slipped off his navy blue jacket.

"Really," she began, but he was already up and around the table.

He placed the jacket over her shoulders. She twisted and slid an arm into the sleeve. He was sorry to see the arm disappear beneath dark fabric. She slipped the other arm in and smiled at him. A wave of embarrassment rolled over him. He was staring like a school boy. He stepped back to his chair as she picked up the chicken wing she'd been about to eat.

"Why are you being called in on that break-in at Jackson's?" Dee bit into the chicken and, before he could reply, added, "Did the call have anything to do with the trespassing complaint last January?"

"What?" Gerry demanded.

Dee stopped chewing and regarded him.

"Sorry." He grimaced a smile. "You caught me off guard."

She gave him an assessing look. "Remind me never to do that again."

"It's not you." He shoved his plate aside and leaned back against the chair.

"No?"

"No." It was all him and the way he was letting this case get to him.

She nodded. "A call came in from a neighbor about a trespasser cutting across their adjacent properties."

Gerry frowned. "Those estates occupy several acres, most with walled grounds. Who would cut across that much private property? Who answered the call?"

Dee finished the chicken wing and set the bone on her plate. "Hernandez and Manning."

"Do you remember when in January?"

She paused. "The twenty-fourth."

"Good memory," Gerry commented.

She tore off a piece of quesadilla and popped it into her mouth. "Kinda like a photographic memory.

Gerry's attention caught on a brunette sitting alone three tables to their right. A glass of water sat in front of her, and he had the distinct feeling she had been stood up. She rose and weaved between tables toward the street. Gerry stared, transfixed by something in her ethereal glide. The long cashmere coat she wore accentuated the shapely motion in her hips. She reminded him of someone…

"That woman needs an upper body workout," Dee said.

Gerry looked at Dee. "Huh?"

Dee motioned with her chin toward the woman. She stood at the curb, watching oncoming traffic. "See the legs?"

He dropped his attention to her slender calves and ankles.

"She's got too much bulk on her upper body," Dee said. "A lot of women make that mistake."

Gerry looked back at Dee. "What mistake?"

"Working the legs while ignoring the abs and upper body. Women think great legs will get a man to ignore a belly that sticks out past their breasts. I work it all."

A mental picture of her *working it all* jumped to mind and he dropped his gaze to the remnants of their appetizers, praying the erotic picture hadn't reflected in his eyes. An unexpected chill rolled across his shoulders, sending a wave of goose bumps up his arms. Memory rose of five years ago, Sarah Matthew's leukemia wracked body lying on a cold slab in Bahia Honda Key morgue. Sarah hadn't needed an upper body workout. She'd needed a whole new body. Gerry jerked his attention onto the empty sidewalk where the brunette had been standing.

"What's wrong?" Dee demanded. A Porsche sped past.

"Gerry?"

He shifted his attention onto her. "Sorry. I thought I saw…someone I knew."

Wind whipped strands of hair across her mouth. She smiled. It had been far too long since a woman smiled at him like that. He glanced at his watch. One a.m. Even if she'd let him make a move, it was too late for anything but a quick romp. Not a good idea for a first date—or the first time. No, for the first time, he planned it slow and easy.

"I hate to be a deadhead," he said, "but it's getting late. Monday morning department meeting at eight sharp."

She looked uncertain, and his gut clenched. If his expression had given away his thoughts…

"You must be beat," she said. "I don't usually get up until one or two. By then, you've put in a day's work."

The tension relaxed. He signaled the waitress, then said, "If you think of anything else concerning Jackson, let me know. I don't trust Lummus to keep me informed."

She snorted. "You haven't made a friend there. Of course, Lummus' only friend his partner." She laughed. "And that's probably because Martin hasn't had a chance to see Lummus' charming side yet. Just wait'll Martin recovers from that broken leg."

Gerry grinned. Damn, he liked the woman.

Chapter Eight

GERRY LOOKED AT Dee as they turned the corner and strolled along Fair Street. She stared back, brows lifted with a question he instinctively knew he wasn't ready to answer.

"Why switch from law to law enforcement?" she asked before he could think of some way to stop her. "And why go from the K-9 Corps to detective?"

He looked straight ahead. At the precinct only eight months and she already knew half his life history. He sighed mentally. Why go from law to law enforcement? He hadn't wanted that law degree. Brenda had. *Mom had.* A part of Mom had died the day a drug dealer killed his father. He decided he couldn't do that to woman, so he tried the next best thing: law. The next best thing left him empty. Mom accepted his decision to move into law enforcement with a nod. Brenda's reaction was another story. Her shock lasted five minutes. Then the shit hit the fan and the stink lasted seven years.

"Being a cop is bad for business," he said more to himself than Dee.

"What's that?" she asked.

"Something my father used to say," he replied, remembering one of the days his father had been in the doghouse. His father hadn't come home the night before and his mother had cried herself to sleep thinking he'd been shot or killed. That wasn't the first time Gerry heard his father say that being a cop was bad for business. It just happened to be the last. Turned out, he'd been right. Gerry had been seventeen years old.

"I loved the law," Gerry said, "just hated the way lawyers twisted it." He flashed a lopsided grin. "My pop was on the force. I guess it's in the blood."

Dee grinned back. "There's nothing like piecing together the puzzle."

"You're the first cop in your family?" he asked.

"I've got a cousin in Sacramento who's a deputy sheriff, but that didn't mean much to my folks. My friends went to college and I spent four years in the Navy as a Radioman. When I got out, I entered the police academy. Mom broke down when I dropped the bomb. Dad made me promise to start with something more sedate than a beat. I worked patrol, made Sergeant, then passed the detective exam. I figured if I was going to move into real investigative work, I had to move to the big city."

"Working a desk."

"For now." She lowered her lashes. "You've gotten pretty far doing field work. Maybe you could coach me?"

Gerry had visions of coaching, all right, but kept his voice level as he said, "Yeah, I can give you a few tips."

She gave a husky laugh and he knew she'd read every blessed thought he'd had. They turned down 32nd Street. The Impala came into view, parked a few feet away. Hargrave stuck his snout out the crack in the window as Gerry reached for the keys.

"Where'd you get the name Hargrave?" Dee rubbed the dog's nose.

Gerry hit the remote unlock button. "Hargrave was the vampire hunter in this old movie I loved as a kid." He opened the passenger door.

"Vampire hunter, are you?"

The Shepherd whirled and scrambled between the seats and leaped from the car.

Dee fell back a pace. "Whoa!" she laughed.

He darted to the rear bumper and stopped, his gaze fixed on the corner they had just turned. Gerry followed Hargrave's point. The hair on his neck rose. *Someone is watching.* A chill rolled across his shoulders. He took a step forward. Time slowed. Color faded to black and white. He jammed his eyes shut. Streetlamps flared and filled his vision, despite the closed eyelids. Hargrave woofed and Gerry snapped open his eyes to the sight of the dog's ear-pricked stare. Hargrave was never wrong. Why hadn't he taken the Shepherd with him to the Keys?

"You okay?" The sound of Dee's voice jerked Gerry's attention onto her.

"Yeah. Fine." He opened the back door and ordered Hargrave inside. The Shepherd jumped inside, and Gerry looked at Dee. "Ready?"

She studied him. "Want me to drive?"

He gave a small laugh. "I'm okay."

She got in. He closed the door, and circled the car.

"You coming down with something?" Dee asked as he slid behind the wheel and fit the key into the ignition. "When's the last time you had a good night's sleep?"

He fired up the Impala. *That's the sixty-four thousand dollar question.* He glanced into the rearview mirror then maneuvered the car onto the deserted street. He eased down on the brake for the red light ahead.

"Sorry. I…" He brought the car to a stop. "It's this case. Damn thing's got me spooked."

"It must be rough investigating serial killers. Add the occasional holy war…"

He shrugged. "Gang wars, holy wars, it's all the same." The light turned green and he accelerated.

"I think you need a good night's sleep," she said. "And maybe a good meal."

Gerry thought he heard a touch of humor and glanced at her. She was grinning.

"I'm a pretty good cook," she said. "Half my family—" she leaned toward him, "—the formidable half—is Italian. I make a mean linguini with pesto."

Despite years out of circulation, he recognized the invitation. "Yeah?" he said, then cursed the idiotic response.

She straightened and looked ahead. "Maybe one of these days you'll get lucky enough to get a taste."

His belly did a flip.

HE WATCHED THE Impala lights fade down Ocean, yanked the lit cigarette from between his lips, and flicked it to the sidewalk before casting a glare at the red tail lights that trailed up the Miami coastline. So many concerned with a destination, any destination, that took them anywhere but where they were.

The night, brimming with life. The city, devoid of emotion. Man had lost their humanity. The burning jewel of humanity, their instinct, buried so deep they might as well be so many automatons. The world was a colder place. He had God to thank for that.

T. C. ARCHER

Thankfully he could still move among humankind without a single one sensing his true nature. Except for *the man.* The man had sensed him even before the animal had. And, like the warrior princess, the man hadn't flinched.

She was here, and had shared her essence with him, that puny man, husk of blood and bone. The bond she'd created would draw them together.

He would watch and wait.

PART TWO

Justice served is justice denied.

NOOSE

Chapter One

TEN MINUTES LATER, Gerry pulled into the precinct parking lot.
"Which car is yours?" he asked Dee.

"Second row from the back."

He silently cursed. The parking lot lay in deep shadow. City administrators liked to pretend cops could see in the dark, and criminals wouldn't lurk near police stations. Gerry wished for the thousand time they could force every budget cutting politicians to stroll down that dead man's walk to the darkest corners on a cold, moonless night when the wind howled— and a criminal waited. Gerry sighed mentally. Just the sort of crimes he was supposed to protect people from.

He turned down the second to last row.

"There." Dee pointed out a red Alfa Romero.

He stopped behind the sports car. The license plate read: BONDGRL. "*That's* your car?"

"Yep."

He could see her in the car, unassuming girl next door disguised as sexy undercover secret agent. Or was it the other way around? He looked at her. "Into Bond?"

"Ian Fleming."

"Kinda pricy."

"Brutal." Dee smiled. She ran a hand along his velour seat back. "This Impala isn't too bad, either. Great color."

"All around gray," Gerry said.

Her brow furrowed. "Chevy calls it Pewter."

"Only to impress buyers."

Her head jerked up and her gaze locked with his. His heart rate kicked up. Christ, he had used his *fuck off, Brenda* voice. Dee gave a low laugh. Gerry's chest and groin tightened. She leaned forward. He remembered the faint scent of her perfume and imagined inhaling deeper of the perfume as their lips met. How would it feel to—her fond pat on his thigh shocked and embarrassed him.

"You still look a little shaken," she said. "You sure you're all right?"

Shaken was right, and stirred. Only it wasn't the eerie feeling he'd experienced earlier that had him in knots.

"I'm okay," he replied. "Maybe we can do this again sometime."

"Sure, any time."

Gerry fixed his gaze on her slender fingers as they grabbed the metal lever and pulled. She swung her legs out, shot a final glance over her shoulder, then stepped from the car and shut the door. He watched her walk away, ass swaying in the tight jeans, and blew a silent whistle as she opened the Alpha Romero's door and disappeared inside the little roadster. Gerry released a breath.

He waited until she'd started the car before moving. She backed out and followed him to the exit. He headed left, she turned right. He wondered how he'd keep the shit eating grin off his face tomorrow at the precinct.

✦

IN THE CAR'S rear view mirror, Gerry watched a Hummer inch closer as he nosed the Impala off the avenue into the parking lot of the all-night convenience store a quarter mile from home. The Hummer swerved and the horn blared as the driver sped past. A black and white leaped from a side street two blocks up, lights flashing, siren screaming.

Gerry set the hand held on the seat, his eye still on the Hummer. "Should have taken the hint and gotten off my ass when I tapped the brake six blocks back," he mused as the Hummer pulled to the side of the road, the black and white behind him.

Gerry glanced at the dashboard clock. One-fifty. Despite the late hour, warm thoughts of Dee mingling with remnants of his earlier chill had him wide awake. He brought the car to a halt in the first of five parking spaces and cut the engine.

"Keep an eye out while I pick up some orange juice," he told Hargrave, and shoved open the car door.

His feet hit the pavement and a shiver ran down his back. A flash of pale blond hair registered in his peripheral vision. Gerry spun, taking two steps toward the car's rear. Two brunettes walked toward him. Beyond them, a figure ducked down the side street just south of where he stood. Light colored hair—blond. In a city as big as Miami, that couldn't be her—unless she had been tailing him. He'd been focused on Dee, then the Hummer. Damn.

"Not this time," Gerry murmured, and sped toward the street.

At the corner where the figure had disappeared, he halted. An elderly man hobbled on a cane in his direction. The blonde had vanished again. But how—beyond the old man, the street opened onto Bolen Ave. A heaviness hung over the intersection. *Not again.* Gerry pushed past the feeling and dashed forward. As he approached the avenue, the city lights abruptly dimmed to a pinpoint against a wall of darkness.

He stumbled. "What the—"

Adrenaline burst through him and he shot onto Bolen like he was being pulled into a killing zone. His surroundings lurched and spun like a carnival ride jerking to life. He stumbled, dragged in a ragged breath as his vision snapped into focus, and caught sight of the blonde ducking down another street two blocks up and across the street.

"Mother fucker," he snarled, and dashed across the avenue.

A tiny bell rang and a young couple exited a coffee shop as he raced past on the sidewalk. Gerry rounded the corner the blonde had taken, and slowed. The sidewalks were deserted and businesses were closed. A car's taillights receded behind him, then turned right and winked out behind a building. There were no sounds of traffic, muffled TV from an apartment or two, or even the hum of neon or street lamp. Even the background city noise sounded far away.

Something was wrong. Life had been sucked from this block. The iron sky had a featureless overcast. If he called out, would anyone hear? Why had he left Hargrave in the car? He slowed to a walk, scanning the closed shops as he started to cross another side street. Awareness yanked his attention right. He halted. A male, six-four or five, long straight blond hair, late-twenties, stood in the middle of the deserted street, staring at him with blue eyes.

Gerry backed up. The man didn't move. Gerry ducked around the corner and slumped against the building. Christ, the blond he'd been chasing was male. He glanced left in the direction of the street. Still deserted. Gerry paused. He had been forty feet from the guy. How had he seen the color of those crystal blue eyes so clearly? Dread snaked through his gut. That guy had stood in the middle of the road staring at Gerry like he knew him—as if they had met. *They had.*

He straightened from the wall. The guy was the blond man from the hallucination in the alley. Gerry's stomach lurched. How could he have seen the man, drawn swords on him in some *vision,* before having set eyes on him? God, he needed Hargrave. Gerry reached inside his jacket and unsnapped the holster-strap on his 9mm. Hand on the weapon, he rounded the building's corner and looked into the street.

Empty.

He cut his gaze down the street. *A fucking dead end.* He faltered and forced himself to inventory the shops. A hairdresser, pizza joint, drycleaner, and pawnshop, all closed and barred. No alcoves or basement walkouts to duck into. The second story windows were dark. No balconies or fire escapes. Above that, nothing but depthless clouds. His hand tightened on the gun as he took a step forward, then stopped. This well-lit dead end street was no alley. No hiding places. *Oh yeah?* Then how had that guy disappeared?

The hand grasping the 9mm began to shake. Before he could stop the memory, Gerry saw the flash of the blade that had cut him two days ago outside Cray's, and jerked back to avoid the slash. He slammed back into the present, into a body shaking like a man coming down off a bad drug trip. He backed away from the dead end, heart pounding against his rib cage like it was going to drill a hole through his chest and make a run for it. Not until he had taken fifteen paces backwards did he stop, secure his weapon, and let his hand drop away.

He needed to talk to somebody. Not a police shrink. Someone private. If he didn't figure out what had happened outside Cray's, he didn't stand a chance of staying on the force. And if he didn't figure out how that guy just disappeared, he might as well walk away right now. Gerry stared into the dead end for a long moment, then headed forward to investigate.

Chapter Two

H USHED VOICES ISSUED from the briefing room as Gerry stepped inside for the eight a.m. meeting. A dozen department heads and assistants were assembled among the rows of folding chairs on a shiny tile floor. Valdez from vice, along with Famosa and Rigs from the Gang Task Force, stood in a tight knot in the back corner, deep in discussion, Rigs' leg thrown over the back of a chair. Master Sergeant Calvo occupied his usual spot in the front row, arms crossed. Lummus' seat in the far corner was empty.

Sheridan sat in the second row. He wore his signatory crumpled suit coat and mismatched pants. His comb-over looked sparser than usual, barely covering his bald pate. Dark circles under his eyes suggested he'd been up all night.

"Look alive, Forstner," Assistant Chief Herrero commanded behind him.

Gerry shot a grin over his shoulder. "Sure thing, Chief." Gerry scooted into the empty seat beside Sheridan.

Chief Herrero crossed to the podium and cleared his throat. Shuffling feet and sliding chairs replaced talk.

Gerry leaned toward Sheridan. "Anything from forensics on Kinnison?"

Sheridan shook his head.

"Damn." Gerry straightened.

"Okay, people," Herrero said. "We have a full docket." He looked at Gerry. "First, the Valknut case."

Gerry stood. "We had another murder Saturday night, John Kinnison, same MO. We're looking for a blonde female, five-foot nine, one hundred fifteen pounds, age, between twenty and thirty, wanted for questioning in connection with Vitelli's murder. Judge Jackson reported a break in at his house last night. The description of the intruder fits the blonde we're looking for. The sketch is being distributed."

Somebody behind Gerry muttered, "Looking for another blonde to replace his ex."

Gerry mentally winced. The upside was no one had gotten wind of him and Dee—yet. "The cut to the neck implies ritual," he went on. "No sign of forced entry and the only violence is Kinnison's genitals ripped from his body."

A murmur passed through the room.

"Kinnison was a real son-of-a-bitch," one detective said. "Some sorta avenging angel?"

"Maybe," Gerry said. "Valknut has strong religious connotations, which could mean cult. The symbolism could go as far as to include the power to choose who lives or dies and is a talisman used to ward off evil spirits.

"What about a copycat?" Calvo asked.

"No way. Kinnison's blood was used to draw the Valknut on Vitelli's chest," Gerry said. "Keep a lid on the blood trail. We're keeping it from the press."

"A fucking good luck charm," a cop interjected.

"Naw," Rigs said. "More like a St. Christopher metal." He withdrew a silver chain tucked inside his shirt and showed the small medallion hanging from the chain.

"Rigs got himself a rabbit's foot," someone said, and the room broke into laughter.

"*Jodete y aprieta el culo,*" Rigs said through tight lips.

"I don't think he can do that," someone laughed. "His dick isn't big enough to fuck himself."

The room broke out in raucous laughter.

"You're all going to hell," Rigs said. "I'm not taking any chances." He dropped the necklace back inside his shirt.

Gerry waited for the laughter to die down. "This guy isn't the typical cult leader."

"Sounds like that case down in Bahia Honda Key five years ago," Rigs said.

Gerry looked Rigs in the eye. "Killers in both cases are quiet and smart. Fortunately, in the Valknut case, we know how the victims are losing their blood."

"Johnny Enriques turned up short six pints of blood."

Gerry swung his gaze onto Mat Donaldson. "He took a bullet to the head. Pro job. Right?"

"Yeah. We figure it was his boss in Chicago, but got nothing to go on."

"The world's better off without that asshole," someone muttered.

"Think there's any connection with that group from the Keys, the Valknut case, and Johnny?" Donaldson asked.

"The only similarity is the loss of blood," Gerry replied evenly.

"Fuck," Calvo said, "that's a fucking big similarity."

"Yeah," Gerry agreed, "but, as Mat said, there's nothing else to go on." Gerry had read Enrique's file four times, looking for anything that might indicate the *Keepers of the Secret* had moved north into Miami, and hadn't found a goddamn thing.

"There wasn't much more than that to go on for the Bahia Honda Key case," Donaldson commented.

"If you guys turn up anything else on Enriques, let me know," Gerry said. "Everyone else, keep your eyes open. Any rumblings about a new cult or cult murders, anything, let me know ASAP. This guy's smart. He hasn't left a single clue at any of the scenes. Don't forget, we're keeping Kinnison's mutilation out of the press."

He sat down and Herrero continued, "I can't stress enough, this one is hot. The press is all over this case and the mayor is in daily contact. Apparently, Jackson chewed the mayor's ass raw this morning. Then I got the ass chewing. If any of you want any ass left, you better find this freak. He's a real nightmare."

Gerry reached for the back of the empty chair in front of him. The memory of the attack in the alley outside of Cray's flashed in his mind's eye. At sight of his trembling hand, he stopped mid-reach and let his arm drop back to his side. These memories were too vivid, too…real. Waking dreams, wasn't that what they were called?

"Item two," Herrero said. "Gang activity is on the rise in Little Havana. Reports show…" the Chef's voice droned on in the back of Gerry's hearing as he tried to remember where he'd read about the phenomena of waking dreams. Weren't they something like visions and who-do-voodoo bullshit? How did a waking dream explain the bloody jeans and shirt he had stuffed in a trash bag? The delirium that followed the attack was typical of shock, but what had caused the shock and more importantly, why did it continue?

Gerry's gaze caught on Manning walking past the briefing room's open door. Gerry glanced at his hand. Solid as a rock. He shook off the questions and slipped out. Manning was halfway to the elevators when Gerry called, "Manning," and jogged to catch up.

Manning turned. Big for a Miami cop, he stood six-six, weighed two-sixty, and wore a marine haircut. His partner, Hernandez, was five-two and chunky, with double-D boobs that entered a room before she did.

"Got a minute?" Gerry stopped beside him. "I want to ask you about the trespasser at the Jackson place in December."

Manning shrugged. "Jackson's got a bitch of a neighbor, Dorothea Hamilton, some trophy wife who got hers. She complained that someone from his place cut through her back yard."

"Cut through her back yard? Aren't those eight foot walls surrounding their estates?"

"Yep. But when you figure the trespasser was something out of her fantasies…" Manning gave a derisive snort.

"What do you mean?"

"Male, about my height, trench coat, long blonde hair, 'built like Adonis,' as she put it."

"Adonis?" Gerry blurted.

Manning added, "If you ask me, she needs to get laid."

Yesterday morning, Gerry would have agreed. But the description of the trespasser sounded too much like the man he had chased last night. Despite not having found any trace of the guy when he'd reentered the alley, Gerry had convinced himself that encountering a tall blonde male had been some cosmic joke. Goddamned blondes and alleys. He'd had enough of both. He refocused on Manning and found him staring. No sense trying to talk his way out of this one.

"Fucking case has me buggy," Gerry said. "Thanks." He turned and headed back to the briefing room.

"Gerry," he heard Dee call a second later, and turned.

The elevator doors were closing on Manning as she strode toward him. Gerry resisted the urge to glance back at the briefing room to see if anyone was watching. A measure of relief filtered through him when she gave him a noncommittal smile.

"You doing okay this morning?" she asked as she neared.

He grinned. "Just peachy." And he was.

She kept walking and Gerry fell in beside her. They would pass the briefing room in a moment. Aw, fuck it. "I thought your shift ended over an hour ago," he said.

"It did. I got in some target practice."

"Target practice? Nine-thirty, and you've already had target practice? How good are you?"

"I average a 47 out of 50." She blushed, and he was surprised to find himself wondering if she would blush like that while he was inside her. "Darn revolver jammed on me. I turned it in for repairs. I've got a piece I like better anyway," she said.

"Let me guess. A Beretta 90-2?"

"A Walther P99. I'll let you try it out someday."

"Like James Bond?"

"Nope. Bond had a PPK."

Gerry waited until they passed the briefing room before saying, "You work tonight?"

"I've got the duty desk, but I'm off tomorrow," she replied in such a nonchalant voice that he almost laughed.

"Want to get together? I'll take you to dinner."

Dee reached inside her purse and pulled out a card. "Call me." She handed it to him.

They reached the end of the hall and turned right. As they neared the locker room, the internal elevator at the far end of the hall opened and Lummus stepped off. His gaze met Gerry's and a faint smile creased Lummus' mouth when he flicked a glance at Dee.

Dee muttered something as Lummus passed and Gerry stopped with her outside the locker room door. "What did you say?"

She cast a glance past him at Lummus entering Herrero's briefing room. "He's jealous."

Gerry threw his head back and laughed.

BY NINE THAT night, Jackson hadn't shown up at the precinct, and by nine-thirty, Gerry pulled his Impala onto the judge's street. Tonight he'd chase down Jackson. Tomorrow, he'd hunt down Collin Norman. The bartender had dropped out of sight, but was scheduled to work tomorrow's evening shift.

The road veered gently left, the same curve that had brought the blonde into view last Saturday, and a Hummer parked four houses down from Jackson's place came into view. Gerry slowed, grabbed his hand held, and thumbed the secure channel to the duty officer. "DO, Forstner here. I need a 1028 on Echo, Able, Delta, nine, nine, three."

"Ten-four," Dee answered.

A fantasy of her sprawled across the armrest spread across Gerry's mind. He gave a low, breathy whistle while patting Hargrave, whose snout rested on the armrest. "Business tonight, buddy."

"Forstner," Dee came back over the radio, "2006 Hummer H2, Echo, Able, Delta, nine, nine, three, registered to a David Bradshaw of 1295 Gull Street, Miami. No arrests or warrants."

"Ten-four," Gerry said.

He couldn't suppress a chuckle. A midnight lover visiting a local socialite. Maybe Manning was wrong. Maybe the trophy wife who had made the trespassing complaint was getting some after all. His phone emitted a ding indicating an incoming email. He pulled to the curb behind the Hummer and cut the engine. He tuned out the police radio and tuned into Hargrave's even breathing as he picked up the phone. Gerry smiled. The low radio chatter was like tonic for the old boy. Dee's voice came over the secure channel reporting a list of aliases and warrants requested by another detective on a resident of lower Coral Gables. *Now that's a tonic for this old boy.*

He looked at the phone. In the screen's upper right hand corner, an envelope icon indicated a waiting email. He retrieved the message and smiled when he saw the sender was Joey. *Hi, Dad. I got my science test back today. B Plus.* Gerry hit reply and typed in *wtg, bud. we'll celebrate,* then hit send and exited from the email.

Drowsiness settled over him. He glanced at the clock. 9:50. Early yet. Four hours sleep wasn't cutting it anymore. Still, his eyes shouldn't feel so heavy. Maybe a day at his desk compiling reports was too much. His eyes closed. The phone grew heavy. Too heavy to hold. His arm drooped toward his thigh.

He tried to rouse, but lethargy settled heavier. He had come here to talk to Jackson. Gerry considered telling his body to straighten, wondered if he'd done so even as images of the previous night flowed through his mind. Drinking margaritas with Dee. Standing with her beside his car. Hargrave darting to the rear bumper. Him charging down the street after that man. Hargrave's growl—Hargrave's growl!

Gerry jerked awake and whipped his head around. Lip curled back, teeth bared, the Shepherd stared out the windshield. Tiny hairs on Gerry's neck stood at attention. A sense of someone unseen watching, *glaring*, like that he'd experienced when chasing the blond guy washed over him.

Gerry shook his head. *"No way."* Like a curtain yanked aside, the lethargy evaporated.

Hargr1ave turned and slathered Gerry's neck with his wet tongue.

He scratched the Shepherd's neck. "You felt it too, didn't you, boy?"

Hargrave panted hot air into his ear and licked his jaw.

"It's all right, buddy. I'm awake. It's all right." He glanced at the clock, 10:00. "Come on, let's take a walk."

Gerry grabbed the portable radio and Hargrave's leash from the passenger seat, then opened the door and got out. Hargrave jumped between the bucket seats, out the door, and halted next to him. Gerry flipped the radio off, clipped it to his belt, then attached the leash to Hargrave's collar. Gerry took two steps and spotted a black BMW 740i with tinted windows hidden in front of the Hummer facing the wrong way. He stopped and glanced at the five feet of space between the two front bumpers. Hargrave let out a growl.

"Stay." Gerry dropped the leash and Hargrave's rear hit the sidewalk. Gerry edged forward and halted at the Hummer's passenger door. He should have seen the Beamer when he'd parked. "Come on, boy." He patted his leg.

Hargrave trotted over. Gerry unhooked the leash and tossed it aside. "Hargrave, heel." Gerry grabbed the radio from his belt and turned it on as he stepped from the curb. "DO, Forstner here. I need another 1028 on a black BMW 740i, license, Delta-Robert-one nine-Echo-four."

"Ten-four," Dee came back.

Hargrave tensed. The car's precision headlights abruptly cut a beam across Gerry's legs. Behind the BMW's tinted glass, a slender figure shifted in the glow of the dashboard lights. A woman—*the blonde.*

Gerry thrust his badge forward. "Police!" he shouted, and started toward her door, Hargrave at his side.

The woman's head shifted as if her gaze followed him.

Gerry's heart pounded. *That's right, baby, keep your eyes on me.* He and Hargrave reached the driver side door and the Shepherd let out a low growl.

Gerry thrust his badge forward. "Open the car door, ma'am."

He recognized the sudden shifting of the car into gear. "Police!" He grabbed for the car door.

The BMW shot back a few feet, then hooked around the Hummer and sped down the street. He thumbed the radio's switch over to the general channel. "Dispatch, Forstner. Black BMW, license Delta-Robert-one nine-Echo-four, headed—" He began into the radio as the BMW turned right at 19th Street, "—west on SW 19th off of Espanola. The driver may be the blonde female wanted for questioning in connection with Valknut murders."

"Ten-four," Dispatch replied. "All units in the vicinity of—"

He switched over to the secure channel Dee monitored. "Dee, Forstner. I need a number for Judge Harold Jackson,"

"Negative," Dee replied. "Database is down."

"Dammit. All right. I'll be out of radio communication for a while. Call my cell if anyone catches that BMW." In a city full of black BMWs, he had a hunch they wouldn't. "Forstner out." He turned off the radio and headed to his car.

Chapter Three

A MINUTE LATER, Gerry pulled up to an intercom box affixed to a curved pole fifteen feet from Jackson's wrought iron gate and pressed the buzzer. A cultured Hispanic woman answered, "Jackson residence."

"This is Detective Forstner with the Coral Gables PD. I need to speak with the judge. It's urgent."

"One moment, please."

Headlights flickered on 19th, and a car turned onto Espanola. Gerry tensed. High-tech headlights. She couldn't be back? She knew his face, had his business card—knew he was on her trail. Did the *Valkyrie* chooser of the slain think he would be as easily taken as the first four victims? Gerry reached inside his jacket and unclipped the safety strap on his weapon. Judging from what happened at *The Hot Spot* he wondered if he could pull the weapon if needed. But, unlike the other victims, he'd be damned if he would going down without a fight.

Hargrave stared out the window, silent, attentive. The glare from the double-sun headlights hurt Gerry's eyes. He squinted, heart pounding. The car slowed. A hood ornament gleamed between the glare, round like a peace sign. The white Mercedes pulled into the drive across the street, two houses down. Gerry blew out the breath he held and let his hand fall from the gun. He'd really lost it.

"Detective Forstner?"

Gerry jumped at the sound of Jackson's voice over the intercom. He forced calm into his voice.

"Sorry to bother you so late, Judge, but I've just spotted your burglar near your house."

"My God, what was she doing? You didn't apprehend her?"

"Judge, please buzz me in. We need to talk."

The gate began a slow swing inward. Gerry reset the safety on his weapon while he waited for the gate to open wide enough to admit the Impala, then drove through. Four hundred feet into the manicured grounds, the driveway took a slow left in front of a three-story, Spanish-style, red brick adobe mansion. Two mature oaks stood sentinel, one near the entrance's columned portico, the other on the opposite side of the driveway where lush ferns grew. Nothing remotely like a Valknut adorned the façade. But then, nothing indicating the cult had been found at any of the victims' homes. How he longed for the days when the good guys wore white hats and the bad guys spoke like New York gangsters. Black and white.

"No such break, huh, buddy?" Gerry said to Hargrave. "But I bet Jackson's got an in ground pool back there. What do you think?"

Hargrave thumped his tail against the velour seat. Gerry brought the car to a halt in front of the mansion. As if on cue, the door opened and the woman he assumed had greeted him on the intercom appeared in the doorway.

"Stay," Gerry commanded Hargrave as he pushed open the car door.

Gerry hurried to the front porch and passed beneath a wrought iron porch light that hung from a medieval-style chain. He grimaced mentally. The chain, along with the arched, ten-foot tall, wood-paneled front door set in limestone casement, conjured up memories of dungeons and torture chambers derived from old movies.

The housekeeper ushered him into a library with book-lined walls and masculine reds and greens throughout. A stone fireplace dominated one wall and a grandfather clock in the far corner ticked. Jackson sat behind a highly polished Teakwood desk.

He rose to his full height of five foot five. "Detective. Please, have a seat." He motioned toward the chair that faced his desk.

As he sat, Gerry nodded at the Sir Lawrence Alma-Tadema's *A Sculpture Gallery* hanging on the wall behind the desk. "Beautiful."

Jackson glanced over his shoulder. "Yes," he replied. "A masterful piece of art, isn't it?"

"Yes," Gerry agreed. *Quite masterful.* Yet, the burglar hadn't touched it. "Judge, this break-in is no random burglary. I need a sketch from you immediately."

"Of course," Jackson replied.

Gerry met his gaze squarely. "Why is this woman dogging you?"

"I have enemies…"

"Anyone in particular?"

Jackson gave a low laugh. "After forty years on the bench, I've ended many a criminal's career."

"Why was your phone number in John Kinnison's phone?"

Jackson looked surprised. "I have no idea."

"Did Kinnison threaten you during that child molestation case? Despite the evidence against him, you let him walk."

The judge stiffened. "I never let anyone walk. That evidence you mentioned were accusations of an eight-year-old boy. He didn't testify, so the jury deadlocked."

The hard glint in the judge's eyes gave Gerry pause. He had a hard time seeing the older man agreeing to become an accomplice to murder. "No threats?" he pressed.

"No."

"Did Kinnison ever contact you?"

"No."

"Did you know any of the other Valknut victims?"

Jackson frowned. "I don't recall who they were."

"Darryl Michaels, Brent Douglas and Frank Vitelli."

"What does this line of questioning have to do with this burglary?" he demanded.

"You have no idea what the blonde was looking for?" Gerry shot back.

Jackson looked nonplussed. "What burglars look for: valuables."

"Did she steal any valuables?"

"No."

"This burglar returned, Judge. Why?"

"I don't know."

"What about surveillance cameras on your property?"

"I gave a full report on this to your investigator last night," he replied in an irritated tone. "Why rehash the details?"

"Because I saw this woman outside your house yesterday morning, Judge."

"Yesterday morning? That's impossible—"

"That's right," Gerry finished. "She hadn't broken into your house yet." He leaned forward. "She's wanted for questioning in connection with the Valknut murders. John Kinnison having walked six months earlier from your courtroom got me curious."

Jackson's mouth thinned. "What are you implying?"

"All I want is the truth."

The judge shoved his chair back and rose. "I've told you all I know. It's your job to catch this woman. I suggest you do it."

Gerry looked up at him. "I don't want you to be the next victim, Judge. These are nasty characters. You've got a wife…"

Jackson didn't break his gaze from Gerry's.

Gerry rose. "All right. I'll assign a squad car to extra rounds in the neighborhood."

"Your attention to this case will not go unnoticed, Detective." He pressed a button on the intercom sitting on his desk and the woman who had escorted him inside promptly opened the door.

"Maria will see you out. Keep me apprised of any developments."

"Sure," Gerry replied, and followed Maria down the corridor.

Outside, he strode to his car and slammed the door behind him. "Our attention to this case won't go unnoticed, Hargrave." Gerry looked at the dog. "What do you think?"

Hargrave thumbed his tail on the car seat.

"Yeah," Gerry said as he started the car. "The old man's in over his head."

He nosed the impala down the driveway. The gate opened and, as he pulled onto Espanola, a ding sounded through the fabric of his pocket. He glanced at the clock. 10:30. Another email from Joey? He parked twenty feet past the Hummer, retrieved his phone and pressed the message button. An email from Professor Janice Hastings filled the tiny screen.

Dear Gerry,

Attached is the translation you requested. The language is Icelandic. Despite the fact I speak German and Latin—Icelandic is related to both languages—I wasn't able to translate the article. Luckily, I have a friend who is the assistant to the head of the research library at the National and University Library of Iceland, Iris Hjortur, and she gladly helped. As it happens, Iris remembers the murder reported in the article. Very interesting.

Janice

Gerry opened the attachment and read.

Baby Killer Laurence Sander Found Dead on the Icelandic Cargo Ship Eimskip

*Laurence Sander, a crewmember of the cargo vessel Eimskip, was found dead in his quarters midway through the ship's fall voyage. He lay peacefully in his bed, and it was initially believed he died in his sleep. An investigation turned up a Valknut carved into the palm of his right hand—*Gerry cursed softly, but kept reading—*Captain Sjofn Sigurdsson froze the body in order to preserve it for forensics.*

"Around-the-clock guards were set up the moment we discovered Sander's body," Captain Sjofn Sigurdsson said. "This is my fifth year with most crew members, and my first mate has sailed with me for ten years. I found it hard to believe any of them were capable of murder. However, tension rose to the boiling point with reports of a leather-clad woman moving like a ghost throughout the ship. Pure superstition," the captain adds, "but you put a bunch of men on a ship with a dead body that has been marked with ancient holy symbol, and the more primitive reactions surface."

Sigurdsson reports this was Sanders' third voyage. "He was quiet, and always did his job. I never heard a cross word from him. If the authorities hadn't found the evidence in his personal affects, I would never have believed he was the Baby Killer."

The authorities were waiting when the ship reached Port Jersey. Examination by the New Jersey police medical examiner revealed the body had been drained of blood.

Gerry's gut tightened.

Because the murder took place outside U. S. jurisdiction, the New Jersey district attorney coordinated with the FBI and Icelandic authorities. However, to date, the investigation has turned up no clues as to the murderer's identity. No charges have been brought against any crewmember, and both U.S. and Icelandic investigations have reached a standstill.

He just bet they had.

P.S. Interestingly enough, Janice added, *the mention of the leather-clad woman jogged Iris' memory in regards to a burial site unearthed earlier last year in which a sword, leather scabbard, and two knives were found. The sword and scabbard were inscribed with the Valknut. Even more curious was the construction crew's claim to have seen a woman dressed in leather leap from the hole the bulldozer was digging. Pretty weird.*

Both groups of men reported seeing a woman dressed in leather? Gerry had to agree. Pretty damn weird. He made a mental note to have Janice send him a copy of the article about the sword and scabbard. The Valknut symbol had been left at a crime scene on the Eimskip, and blood drained from the body. Hargrave's bark jerked Gerry's attention up in time to see headlights splash from the judge's gated driveway, followed by his Mercedes. The car made a slow left, away from Gerry.

"Well, well." He punched the phone's end button and tossed it into the cup-holder. "Out for a little midnight drive, Judge?"

Gerry pulled from his parking space without headlights. Jackson turned right at the first intersection and headed toward the freeway. Gerry let the Mercedes get two blocks ahead, then flipped on his headlights. He tailed the Judge for five miles along the interstate, then Jackson turned off onto Biltmore Way. Three minutes later, he pulled into the VFW parking lot on Almeria Avenue.

Gerry slowed and watched him park beside a black Lexus with tinted windows. Jackson got out and hurried to the building's side door. He knocked. The door opened and he disappeared inside. Gerry parked between a Jeep Cherokee and a Corvette at the curb, cut the engine, and studied the building. Four other cars besides Jackson's sat in the lot.

He grabbed notepad and pen from the glove box and jotted down the Lexus license plate. Two spaces down sat an older model Buick LeSabre. He squinted to make out the plates, then scribbled down the info. A Caddy and Mazda Miata were parked at an angle closer to the door. He couldn't read the plates.

"Stay," he commanded Hargrave, and left the car.

Gerry jogged across North Street and hurried forward until he could see both plates. He wrote them down, then started back to his car. A prickly sensation zipped up his spine. He dropped to a crouch on the sidewalk and undid the lace on his sneaker. Carefully retying the lace, he glanced out the corner of his eye. A car passed on the street, but he detected no other movement. A tiny, creeping sensation in his brain made him think of Superman peering through him with x-ray vision.

The door to the VFW opened. Gerry cursed, gave the lace a final tug, then rose. No one called after him. He glanced over his shoulder and saw a person in the doorway—not Jackson—faced inside, talking with someone.

Gerry dodged between parked cars and cut onto the sidewalk, headed away from his Impala. A block down, he crossed the street, then started back for his car. As he neared the VFW the Lexus exited the parking lot. The car drove past. Tinted windows hid the driver from view. The Lexus turned the corner and the eerie feeling evaporated like a wet sidewalk in the summer sun.

Chapter Four

*G*ERRY WAS VAGUELY *aware that he rode a horse, and stared at his grimy fingers gripping leather reins. Shouts yanked his attention to an army of helmed men with raised shields and battleaxes, galloping down a grassy hill toward him in the moonlit night. He looked left and saw himself part of the front line of an army racing toward the enemy. Their thigh length, T-shaped chainmail gleamed in the moonlight. The lead horseman carried a tall standard, flying a red pendent decorated with a crooked cross within a circle in black. He had seen that cross and circle before.*

A piercing cry rang above the pounding of hooves. Gerry's horse faltered and he steadied the animal as if he'd handled him all his life. The cry sounded again and both armies halted. Silence fell, and he turned in the direction everyone stared. A lone figure sat on a dark stallion on a distant hill. His breath caught. The long, golden hair that whipped around the figure belonged to the blonde from The Hot Spot.

Throwing her head back, she thrust her sword high. Another cry—her cry— filled the air again. Gerry shivered. She had made the ungodly noise. She turned, her gaze on him. Air whirled around him and the ground rushed past as if he was being carried on the wind. He seized the pommel to keep from falling when the horse, the army, everything, faded into the background as he drew close to her. Her body became clear, her face sharpened in his vision, her ice blue eyes locked onto his.

Gerry halted so close, he jerked his head back. She reached forward and, with an icy finger, traced his jaw. She bent close and a frosty breeze preceded the touch of her lips on his as she—

A ringing sounded far away.

Gerry shook himself. A chill penetrated his body beneath the blankets. He shivered, the blonde's icy touch still on his cheek. The phone rang. He didn't move. Maybe the caller would give up. Another ring, then a third. He glanced at the glowing red numerals of the clock that read 7:30, then reached for the phone.

"Yeah?" he croaked.

"Not awake yet, old man?"

A jolt of excitement jerked Gerry from the remnants of the dream. Jake Quinlen wouldn't call so early if he didn't have something good. "Whatchya got, Wizard Quin?"

"I just emailed the info on those plates. You got something interesting going on."

"Give it to me."

"You've got a Jack McMillian, Glen Pentz, Martin Verdi and William Johnson Jr.. Various addresses in Miami, with Johnson from Fort Lauderdale. I got curious and checked them out. At first, I got all the usual stuff: birth dates and places, marriage dates, kids, shit like that. The first three served in the Army right after WWII, Johnson's father did too. I was about to call it quits when I noticed a glitch. All but Verdi served with the War Department's Legal Affairs Office, but the information specifying command or battalion was missing."

"Missing? Is that unusual?"

"Most times not, but in this case the information has obviously been blanked out. Erased. There were actually white spaces in sentences where the location or assignment had been covered in white-out. I love those mysteries. Sorta like tracing the Majestic 12."

"Majestic 12?"

"UFO conspiracy. Anyway, when I dug deeper with dates, commanders' names, travel records, I hit a dead end."

"What do you mean 'a dead end'?"

"Just that, a dead end, like those cartoons where it's raining on one side of the line and sunny on the other. When I tried to call up the info, it didn't exist, which is impossible, because out of four men, someone would leave a trail."

"So, this could all be a computer glitch," Gerry said.

"No way. Information doesn't systematically vanish."

"And you couldn't access anything more, at all?"

"I could breech national security, but I'm not willing to have those assholes hunting me."

"No need," Gerry said. "I can get the info from the catacombs."

"You'd better have some serious clearance. Captain Baker won't let me near that database."

Gerry laughed. "Can you blame him? You wouldn't be able to resist hacking into every system you came across. I owe you."

"Damn right you do," Quinlen replied. "I never get up before twelve."

"I'll send a vestal virgin as payment."

Quinlen snorted. "You don't know any virgins, much less vestal ones."

"I may *never* have known a virgin," Gerry said.

"You ain't missing much."

"Trouble in the love life?"

"No way," Quin shot back. "Not the E-Man."

Gerry laughed. Quin had once likened himself to the Energizer Bunny. Gerry had raised a brow and asked him if his ladies liked him warm, fuzzy, and pink? The E-Man responded with, "They don't care, so long as I can give a licking and keep on ticking." Gerry didn't bother telling him he'd mixed Timex's catchphrase with Energizer's.

"Okay, E-Man, keep those batteries charged."

"My battery has a life-time warranty."

The ignorance of youth, Gerry thought. What he wouldn't give to get it back. "Thanks. Let me know when you need a favor. Oh, what'd you get on the BMW?"

"Registered to a Linnette Howsten at 4049 Ponce De Leon Boulevard, Suite 580, Coral Gables."

"Ponce De Leon Boulevard," Gerry repeated. "That's a business district."

"Yep."

"I've got something else for you. This one may not be so easy. Think you can follow a trail outside the country?"

Gerry expected the kid to grab the bait like a hungry shark, but Quin surprised him by saying, "Where we talking?"

"Iceland."

There was a pause, then, "Valknut. Yeah, makes sense. What have you got?"

"I'll send it over as soon as I get up," Gerry said.

"Cool. Be seeing you." Quinlen hung up.

"Yeah," Gerry said into the dead receiver, and jumped from bed.

✦

INSIDE THE OFFICE building at 4049 Ponce De Leon Blvd, Gerry approached the security guard sitting behind a high desk, a man of about thirty who looked like he'd been born and raised in a gym.

The guard gave him an inquiring look.

"Who's in suite five-eighty?" Gerry asked.

"Intelligent Corporate Services."

Gerry couldn't help a laugh. "Isn't that an oxymoron?"

The guy cracked a smile. He had the grill to match his Mac truck frame.

"What do they do?" Gerry asked.

The guy's smile melted into a frown. No more play time. Gerry pulled his badge from his back pocket and opened it. He glanced at the nameplate on the desk as the guy looked at the badge. Raul looked back at Gerry, clearly unimpressed.

"That thing real?" he asked.

"You willing to chance that it isn't?"

Raul grinned. "Not for ten bucks an hour. They supply virtual offices."

"What the hell is that?"

"Phones, answering service, fax, internet, the whole shebang, including an office address. You can even hold conferences and meetings there."

Gerry whistled. Virtual offices for virtual criminals. He slipped his badge back into his pocket. "Fifth floor?"

Raul nodded.

"I gotta go up."

"It's your party," Raul said, and leaned back in his chair.

A minute later, the elevator doors opened to a large waiting room with a young brunette seated behind a half-circle receptionist's desk against the far wall. Gerry had almost expected to find a single geek sitting behind an array of computer screens. It would come down to that, eventually. Someday the Jake Quinlens would rule the world.

He headed for the receptionist.

A nameplate that read Lily sat on the desk in front of the brunette. Lily looked up and smiled. "Can I help you?"

"I need information on one of your customers, Linnette Howsten."

The routine followed the same pattern whenever he encountered some sweet thing at the front desk. She couldn't help, but knew who could. Lily phoned her superior, Kevin Matheson, and showed Gerry to an office where, yes, a tall, lanky, twenty-something geek sat behind a sterile desk with three twenty-inch flat-screen monitors to his right. How did these people spawn when they never left cyberspace?

Gerry stepped up to the desk. "I'm trying to track down one of your customers, Linnette Howsten. No," Gerry said, before Kevin could ask. The stubborn set of Kevin's jaw had telegraphed his question and Gerry wasn't in the mood to play footsies. "I don't have a warrant. Yes, I can get one and, no, you don't want me to. I head Miami's Serial Killer Task Force. Unless you want me down here with my crew going through every megabyte you have, you'll cough up her address and the list of services you provide for her."

Kevin's lips thinned. "Always glad to oblige the authorities."

I bet, Gerry thought with a surge of caveman satisfaction. Solids still had one up on cyberheads.

Kevin faced the monitors and typed in a few commands. The printer behind him hummed and began ejecting printed sheets. Kevin handed him a printout before the second hand on the clock behind him made a complete rotation. It looked like an invoice without the cost figures. He blew a mental breath. Kevin had moved up a notch on the food chain.

Gerry scanned through the printout, starting with Linnette's address: twenty-five eighteen Witherspoon, Miami, Florida. He looked at Kevin. "This is a business section of Miami."

"Yeah?"

Gerry stared at him for a long moment and felt sure the kid knew he was wondering how many mobsters had virtual offices with Intelligent Corporate Services. Gerry gave a single shake of his head and returned his attention to the report. Linnette Howsten and Harold Balder were listed at owners of T. Y. R Industries. The list of services included: mail forwarding, auto call routing, phone answering, fax, and email.

He looked at Kevin. "No server space, web services?"

Kevin shook his head. "They opted for our Easy Office Plan."

"Easy Office Plan?"

"Bottom of the line virtual office services. Gold members can have everything all the way up to hosting live meetings and conferences in state-of-the-art offices."

"All in this building?"

"Anything we can't handle, we lease or rent."

Gerry wondered what a room full of cult fanatics in a rented virtual conference room looked like. "What do Harold Balder and Linnette Howsten do?"

"Trade stocks."

That explained the BMW. "Of course, everything's on the up and up," Gerry said.

"We don't make the trades for them," Kevin replied. "Like I said—"

"Right," Gerry cut in. "You just take messages. What happens to the faxes and phone messages?"

"Faxes are received via the computer and go directly into their account. Phone calls are picked up by our automated service. We never see them."

No muss, no fuss, Gerry thought, and said, "You must have access—"

"I've got the admin passwords into their account, if that's what you're asking, but you'll need a warrant and your own computer expert to get any more than what I gave you."

Gerry was betting the software was Kevin's, and hacking in wouldn't be much of a problem for Quin. "How often do you see them in person?" he asked.

"We don't. That's the point of a virtual office."

"I'm betting they pay by credit card."

"It's a requirement."

Gerry just bet it was. "You don't worry some of your clients might be involved in criminal activity?"

Kevin didn't bat an eye. "That's your job."

Gerry pulled a card from his front pocket, and tossed it onto the desk. The card slid across the polished wood and slowed to a stop an inch from the edge. Kevin didn't bother looking at it.

"If you see or hear from Ms. Howsten, call me. I'm investigating a string of murders, and she's wanted for questioning."

Gerry held Kevin's gaze. He'd be back, and Kevin knew it. How soon depended on Kevin. Gerry turned and left.

Chapter Five

G ERRY PATIENTLY STOOD before Wayne Comerford's desk as the wiry IT kid studied the request form that allowed Gerry to access the federal database. First Quin, then Kevin, now Wayne. Gerry blew out a breath. He was getting old. All the precinct computer wizards were pimply-faced kids, and Wayne fit the bill right down the line. The only things on his desk were three twenty-inch flat-panel screens positioned in a semi-circle and a phone shaped like some sort of ray gun.

Wayne shifted uncomfortably in his seat, and Gerry said, "I'm doing some background investigation. If I need to use any of this, I'll come back with the proper signatures."

Wayne's finger moved along the lines of the document with a speed that would have made him wonder if the kid was showing off if he didn't know better. Though Gerry would never have said so to Quin, Wayne Comerford had a brilliance with computers that ran circles around Quin. Unfortunately, Wayne had refused all attempts at making friends. Gerry was pushing it by approaching the catacombs without signatures from the Chief and a Federal District Judge. If Brenda could see him breaking the rules now, she'd probably regret divorcing him.

"I really shouldn't give you access without the proper signatures," Wayne said.

Gerry started to reply, but the ray gun phone rang. The research department's number flashed across the top of the receiver. The phone rang a second, then third time before he looked at Wayne. The boy was staring at the phone as if it had morphed into an alien creature.

"Aren't you going to answer it?" Gerry asked.

"Huh?" Wayne looked at him with a dazed expression.

"You all right, kid?"

The phone rang and Wayne flinched again.

Gerry reached for the phone. He thought he heard a gasp from Wayne as he said into the receiver, "Catacombs."

There was a tiny pause on the other end of the line, then, "Detective Forstner?"

"Cindy? Yeah, it's me."

"What are you doing down there—I mean—oh God, I—"

"It's all right. I'm doing some research. Wayne was tied up, so I picked up the phone." Gerry winked at Wayne, who stared, eyes wide with sheer terror. Gerry frowned, then realized Cindy was talking. "What?"

"If Wayne is too busy, I can call back later."

"No. I'm sure he has time for you." But Wayne went another shade paler and frantically waved his hands in a crisscross formation. "Uh, wait, I may be—" Gerry held the phone out with a *you sure you don't want to talk to a beautiful woman* look, which elicited more frantic hand motions. Gerry pressed the receiver back to his ear. "I thought he was coming back, but must have ducked into the men's room." He cringed inwardly. Any woman who couldn't see through the lie—

"That's okay," she replied. The tone of her voice said she saw straight through the lie. When she added, "He's usually busy when I call," Gerry felt two inches tall.

"Pure coincidence," he said, then held his breath, praying the *I'm a man of the world and understand such things* tone would fool her. That tone had fooled Brenda the first six months of their marriage, maybe even the first year.

"Really?" Cindy asked.

"Really."

She hesitated. "Let him know I called. I have a question about a request form."

"Will do," Gerry said. The phone clicked in his ear, and he replaced the ray gun receiver on the hook. He looked at Wayne. "Nice girl, that Cindy."

Wayne nodded. Some of the color had seeped back into his thin cheeks, but he still looked as if he had one foot in the grave.

"She had a question about a request form."

"A request form?" Wayne repeated.

Gerry nodded, and Wayne started nodding as if playing Simon Says.

"Don't all departments have manuals on how to fill out forms?" Gerry asked.

"Yeah," the kid croaked.

"Odd that she would need your help." Gerry studied him. "It's been my experience a woman who needs something usually gets it. You realize today is Valentine's Day?"

Wayne swallowed and Gerry forced back a laugh. The kid had it bad. Lucky for him, it seemed Cindy did, too. Gerry looked at the request form. He controlled the twitch at the corner of his mouth. Wayne had balled the form in his fist.

Gerry pointed at the form. "Think you could see your way to get me into those records?"

Wayne glanced at the crushed form with confusion.

"You know," Gerry began, "if you want, I could do a little recon for you."

Wayne's head snapped up.

"Talk to Cindy. See what she's thinking." Gerry had a vision of himself in seventh grade, Ellen Gallagher doing recon on him for Sara Haines. He'd liked Ellen, and did a little recon of his own. Gerry stuck out his hand. "Deal?"

"You would do that?" Wayne asked in a voice almost as quiet as Cindy's.

"You bet."

"I wouldn't want her to know—"

"She won't have a clue." He hoped.

Wayne extended a tentative hand. Gerry gave it a vigorous shake. "I'll keep you posted. Now…" He looked meaningfully at the balled up request form.

A minute later, Gerry was following Wayne past the archives, long-term storage, and HVAC equipment rooms. Wayne stopped before a door with a pushbutton security lock. He keyed in a sequence and the lock clicked open. He pushed through the door and into a room that probably had been a broom closet in another life. Wayne flipped on the single light-bulb enclosed in a wire cage on the ceiling as Gerry took the two steps into the middle of the room.

A single table, two chairs and a computer terminal sat against the far wall. Despite discolored paint and holes where hooks and shelving had been, the ordinary terminal looked perfectly at home in the odd surroundings. He'd expected a bright red computer or something as strikingly ominous. He suppressed a grin. Dee wasn't the only one watching too many Bond movies.

The Unified Federal Database was new, born out of an experimental program to share information between agencies, a shotgun marriage between the Department of Homeland Security and community of first responders. Over the years, he had seen the Feds try sharing information. Give them time. This experiment, like preceding attempts, would be diagnosed as stillborn within a year.

Gerry seated himself at the terminal as Wayne walked to the door. Gerry felt the kid's anxious stare as he paused at the door. The shock over Cindy was wearing off.

Gerry twisted and met his gaze, now deadly serious. "You saw the names of the four victims on that form?"

Wayne nodded.

"I haven't been able to make any connection between those men. If you can come up with anything…"

"I'll poke around." Wayne pulled the door closed behind him.

As the door clicked shut, Gerry reached inside his jacket pocket and pulled out his notepad. He set the pad on the table, opened it to Jackson's info, and accessed the Army personnel database. The screen loaded in seconds and Gerry typed in Harold P. Jackson. He added the judge's service record: December 1944 through March 1950, then hit enter.

Three Harold Jackson's popped up and two Harold P. Jackson's. The second Harold P. Jackson turned out to be the judge. One by one, Gerry read the personnel records. Jackson's DD214, DD217, immunization records, the dates and places where he'd reported for duty at West Point in 1941 and was discharged eight years later. His duty roster listed twenty-eight duty assignments in four and a half years of Army active duty. All the information that had been blanked in the database Quin had accessed. Gerry began a bulleted list.

An hour into studying the assignment list, he stopped dead in his virtual tracks. There it was in black and white: U.S. Naval Air Station, *Keflavik, Iceland.*

Gerry looked at his bulleted list. Jackson had served as legal attaché and investigations detachment. He'd graduated from West Point five months before the war ended and never saw action. His post-war years were spent in various parts of Northern Europe investigating alleged Nazi war crimes.

Gerry gave a satisfied grunt. "And here I'd been wondering how a West Point officer could have such a lackluster service record."

He added the Iceland dates to his list, then searched other documents unsuccessfully for a list of the other men in Jackson's unit. There were hundreds of names, everyone from his commanding officers to his medic. Gerry flipped through his pad and found the four names Quin pulled from the plates of the cars outside the VFW. William Johnson, Jack McMillian, Glen Pentz, and Martin Verdi.

Gerry hit the home button and typed in William Johnson's name, and the dates Jackson served. A second later, the record appeared on the screen. Gerry scrolled down to the duty assignments.

"Well, well," he murmured. "U.S. Naval Air Station, Keflavik, Iceland."

He compared Jackson's info with the date Johnson was assigned in Iceland. Nineteen forty-six. The same. Gerry scrolled down the page to Johnson's post-war assignment: 1948 through 1950, investigating Nazi war crimes in northern Europe.

Twenty minutes later, Gerry stared at the words on the computer screen: *U.S. Naval Air Station, Keflavik, Iceland.* William Johnson, Glen Pentz, and John McMillian, had all served there with Jackson, but no Martin Verdi. Three of four were at the VFW with Jackson the night before.

Paydirt.

✛

JACKSON'S COMMANDING OFFICERS and the JAG attorneys he'd worked with were the only names written on the paper Gerry laid on Wayne's desk half an hour later. Yeah. Brenda would be proud. Gerry glanced at his watch. Twelve-thirty. Wayne was probably out to lunch. The idea struck him as funny. Wayne seemed more the type to sit in these dark catacombs and come out only when forced. He had the pallor of a person who hadn't seen the sun in months.

Gerry strode to the door, pushed through, and started down the gray corridor. "Hey!" he heard a moment later and turned to see Wayne trotting down the corridor toward him.

Wayne came to a stop in front of him and extended several sheets of computer printout.

Gerry glanced at the papers. "What's this?"

"The connection between your murder victims."

Gerry stared. "You found one?"

Wayne shrugged. "You told me to."

Gerry took the papers. Brent Douglas, Darryl Michaels, Frank Vitelli and John Kinnison were all listed beneath the header *Joseph M. Warner Laboratories for PSI Research*. He looked at Wayne.

"P-S-I?"

"Anomalous processes of information or energy transfer."

"English, kid."

"Psychic processes, say, like telepathy or ESP. You know, mind control."

"Mind control?" Gerry repeated. "What did the victims have to do with mind control?"

Wayne pointed to the printouts. "Look at page two."

Gerry flipped to the second page.

"See here?" Wayne pointed at the text. "John Kinnison was being tested for a high count of PSI."

"They can count that?"

"Yeah. This person might be able to guess what card the investigator is holding up five times out of ten. Whereas another—"

"Investigator?" Gerry studied him. Were all high tech geeks alike? Only this morning, Quin had mentioned UFO's. "Sounds like you know a lot about this stuff."

"A little. Look at this." Wayne ran a finger down the page and read, "Case three-three-three nine. Subject involved in systematic program to create and manipulate personalities as the foundation for programmed couriers resistant to torture. To date, experiments show the primary personality is not aware of the secret information being carried. Experiment number five is successful, as have been the past four experiments. Information has been summoned forth via post-hypnotic command or response to a pre-programmed cue."

"This sounds like science fiction," Gerry said.

Wayne nodded. "Yeah, so did Buck Rogers and Star Trek. But we went to the moon and string theory shows how the space-time metric can be bent into a warp field. The government's been doing paranormal research for years."

"I always thought that was bunk."

"Most people do. Look at this." Wayne flipped to the page with Darryl's name at the top.

"Consider telepathy as a problem in the transfer of information in a noisy environment. Experiments in the transmission of five distinct symbols via telepathy suggest a way of transmitting information using two symbols, namely Morse Code, Current ELF or VLF radio transmission methods for communicating with fleet ballistic missile submarines to issue launch orders involve very low data transfer rates, on the order of 3 to 30 bits per minute. Messages are short, consisting of pre-formulated action or targeting codes. I propose telepathic 'Zener Morse' as an operational technique for information transfer under severe signal to noise conditions."

"What the—"

"See," Wayne interrupted—Gerry saw the light of enthusiasm flood the kid's eyes—"this 'Zener Morse' is a type of Morse code."

"And they're using telepathy to transmit it," Gerry murmured.

Telepathy, PSI, psychic mumbo jumbo. But it wasn't mumbo jumbo. The idea hit him as somehow true and he had a sudden need to look behind him. He resisted the urge with effort. They were alone. No one could have entered that narrow hallway without him being aware of it—and no creepy crawly sensation itched inside his brain. So why couldn't he shake the sense that someone waited—for him? Just like the *Keepers of the Secret*. He hadn't been wrong back then.

Gerry forced his attention onto Wayne. "This is straight out of the movies."

The kid grinned. "Cool, ain't it?"

"What did you say the name of this place was?"

"Joseph M. Warner Laboratories for PSI Research."

Gerry narrowed his eyes on him. "How did you access these test cases?"

Wayne blushed.

"Christ. You cracked their system."

"Well, once the first couple of names came up, I had to. How else was I gonna get the info?"

"Thing is, kid, these test cases don't read like some nut-burger poking around in people's heads." Gerry winced inwardly at the terminology.

"This is government jargon." He scanned the paper. "Phrases like 'noisy environment,' 'transmission of information.' How about 'fleet ballistic missile submarines?' Does that sound like the average psychic bullshit to you? And this, according to what you're telling me, is PSI," Gerry looked at the documents and whistled under his breath. "Fucking PSI."

✦

A DRIZZLY DUSK rolled over Miami with the patter of soft rain against the car roof. Gerry sat parked in the Witherspoon strip mall. Hargrave moaned and shifted on the back seat.

Gerry reached back and scratched behind the dog's ears. "I know, buddy. Another stakeout."

He returned his attention to the laptop situated on the passenger seat, the screen facing him. He'd called in the warrant after visiting Witherspoon Stationary and Office Supply, where Linnette Howsten kept a private mailbox, and the surveillance videos had been waiting by the time he left the catacombs. He took possession of the videotapes an hour later and spent the remainder of the afternoon staking out the office supply store while studying the three black and white, jerky video clips of Linnette Howsten.

If the supply store clerk was correct about her mail collection routine, Gerry had a good chance of catching her tonight or tomorrow night. He focused on the video that looped over and over on his laptop screen. The black and white grainy quality hadn't improved in the waning light. Gerry had memorized her gait and mannerisms, the curve of her breasts and hips. Nothing about the video called forth even a sliver of the emotion he'd experienced in that morning's dream.

He hadn't been able to deny the disappointment. The feeling was nuts, but his attraction for her was—*had been*—almost primal. He grunted, and tried for the hundredth time to imagine her deep blue eyes in the black and white video, but couldn't. She kept her face averted from the camera. Maybe that's what put a damper on the deal.

Hargrave let out a low growl. Gerry looked at the street and spotted a set of high-tech headlights cutting through the twilight. This time he was ready. Droplets on the windshield distorted his view, but he discerned the outline of a luxury car. The BMW's distinctive double kidney bean grill came into focus through the glare between the headlights and Gerry snapped closed the laptop's lid, flipped on the ignition, and rolled down the window. Hargrave stood, muzzle at his ear, staring at the BMW as it turned into the strip mall lot.

"Stay." Gerry opened his door.

Hargrave let out a mournful whine over the chime that warned keys had been left in the ignition. The Shepherd jumped into the front seat as Gerry shut the door. Hargrave stared out the open window, intent on the BMW. Gerry hesitated, still torn about bringing him. Hargrave retired three years ago. He had acted professional outside Jackson's place, but dogs lived in the moment. Without recent training, the unexpected in a tense situation could trigger his prey-drive.

"Stay," he commanded, and turned.

He followed the car's progress to a parking spot two rows back. The driver's door opened as he slid between a Toyota and a Taurus in the adjacent row. A slim leg angled out the car door, and an ankle strapped in a black, spiked heel hit the wet asphalt. The leg pivoted as Linnette rose from the car. Gerry caught sight of a flared, red mini-skirt and low-cut silk tank top before her blue eyes met his.

His breath hitched. *She's not the blonde from The Hot Spot.*

Surprise flashed in her eyes.

Gerry realized he was staring and reached for his badge. "Coral Gables Police, ma'am. I need to talk—"

The waning twilight swam around him. Lights streamed off wet pavement and glittered from drops on cars, flickering, flowing, merging. His head pounded and ringing filled his ears. Gerry tried focusing on the blonde. He blinked and discerned the outline of her body even as he swayed. He was going down.

A loud bark pierced a relentless thudding. Gerry lurched forward on unsteady legs as if propelled into a body he didn't know. A silver blur streaked past him. Another bark. Air filled his lungs and he drank in great gulps as though he'd been underwater too long. He crashed to his knees. Pain radiated up his left leg. Soft fur brushed his jaw. Hargrave slathered his face with wet kisses. Gerry threw an arm over the dog's back and dropped his forehead onto it. Hargrave stood, unmoving, until Gerry finally lifted his head.

"What do you think, boy?" he asked in a rusty voice. "A throw back from the party days? Mom said I'd pay for the fun." Hargrave looked at him, head tilted left then right. "Yeah," Gerry said. "I'm not buying that story, either."

He abruptly remembered Linnette and pushed to his feet. His knee nearly buckled, then strengthened. He spun, but she and the car were gone. Gerry blew out a breath. So the Hummer outside Jackson's place had, in fact, belonged to someone visiting a lonely socialite. It hadn't occurred to him the blonde in the BMW had simply been in the wrong place at the wrong time. Why had she bolted just now? He groaned. Intelligent Corporate Services. Virtual offices for virtual criminals. It wasn't illegal to register a vehicle at a private mailbox, but it was suspicious. As suspicious as renting a virtual office. Driving away when ordered by a police officer to stop was obstruction.

"Fuck," he whispered. He'd spent a day chasing the wrong criminal.

Chapter Six

GERRY TURNED EAST into the morning sun and Granada Springs Estates. From his seat in the back, Hargrave gave his ear a wet kiss. Gerry laughed and swatted at him. The street sign for Sparrow Lane came up suddenly. He hit the brakes and made a hard right onto the lane. Hargrave yipped.

"Quit your bitching," Gerry warned. "That was your fault. Sit down. I can't afford an accident outside a suspect's house."

Hargrave whined, managed another quick lick on Gerry's jaw, then did two 360s and settled down on the seat. Gerry took the next right onto Sparrow Lane. He slowed until he found 2457 painted on a mailbox, then stopped in front of the house.

"Stay here," he ordered, and cut the engine.

Gerry glanced at the other houses along the street as he left the car and headed up the sidewalk toward 2457. They all mirrored McMillian's: one and two story adobes with terracotta tiled roofs. Three car garages. Three, like McMillian's, had covered porticos. Not one went for under a million bucks. Accounting had done well for John McMillian. Gerry stopped in front of the door and knocked. A moment later, the door was opened by a tall, fit man who didn't look old enough to have been in the war.

"Can I help you?" he asked.

"Yes," Gerry replied. "I need to speak with John McMillian."

"I'm John McMillian."

Gerry pulled his badge from the front pocket of his pullover. "Detective Forstner, Coral Gables PD. If I could come inside…"

McMillian glanced over his shoulder, then back at Gerry. "I'm busy,

Detective. What do you want?"

Of all the opening questions Gerry had in mind, McMillian's attitude left few choices. "What were you and Jackson involved with in Keflavik, Iceland?"

The man didn't blink. "War crimes. I'm not at liberty to discuss the specifics."

"Why not?" Gerry asked.

"The work was classified."

"All World War Two government operations were declassified years ago."

McMillian shook his head. "Due to the sensitive nature of the mission, these records will never be declassified."

That *could* explain the glitch Quinlen found. The military would be careful to purge public records. So much for declassification.

"What was the nature of your missions?" Gerry asked.

"I told you, Detective, all I can say is that we investigated Nazi war crimes."

"In Iceland?"

"German U-Boats landed on the Icelandic coast."

"Is that what you and Judge Jackson discussed during your Monday meeting?"

McMillian started. "What meeting?"

"The one at the VFW at one-twenty in the morning."

McMillian's gray-blue irises dilated. "Harold dropped in while I was there. What of it? Last I heard, running into an old friend wasn't against the law. Or is that one of the rights our government is methodically stealing from us?"

"Do you two meet there often?" Gerry asked.

"We run into one another occasionally."

"And William Johnson?"

McMillian's lips thinned. "Yes."

"What about Pentz?"

McMillian gave him a condescending look. "What did you do, Detective, have one of your computer whizzes dig into our private affairs?"

Damn TV crime shows, Gerry silently cursed. "What did you men discuss Monday night?"

"Ask Harold."

"Did you discuss the break-in at his place?"

Surprise flashed in McMillian's eyes.

"You men have one helluva bond after all these years," Gerry said nonchalantly.

"Lots of servicemen do."

Yeah, but usually only those who served in combat, Gerry thought, but said, "What happened in Iceland?"

"I can't—"

"I have four murders connected to you men."

"What—"

"I'm talking about the Valknut killer," Gerry cut in. "The Valknut is an Icelandic symbol. The most recent Valknut victim was John Kinnison. Judge Jackson presided over Kinnison's child molestation trial."

"Coincidence," McMillian snapped. "I don't know a thing about those murders."

"It's got something to do with what happened in Iceland."

"Nothing happened."

"Would the State Department agree?" Gerry asked. "Now, I'll ask again, what did you soldiers do?"

McMillian hesitated. "We investigated alleged Nazi sightings."

"Not war crimes?

"Iceland was an ally during the war. Any German activity on their soil would be considered spying. That is a war crime."

"Would the Icelandic authorities be interested in your activities?" Gerry demanded.

McMillian snorted. "The U.S. government coordinated with Iceland on all military projects. I've told you all I can. Good day." He stepped back and swung the door shut.

Gerry stared at the closed door. Bastard.

GERRY FIDDLED WITH his badge as he waited for an answer at the lower-middle class home of Glenn Pentz on Bonnie Street. Unlike McMillian's home, this house probably went for a hundred and seventy-five thousand. Apparently backhoe driving didn't pay as well as accounting. A moment later, a slight, gray haired woman opened the door.

"Yes?" she said.

"Good morning, ma'am, I'm Detective Gerry Forstner, Coral Gables

PD." Gerry showed his badge. "Is Glen Pentz home?"

Her eyes saddened. "I'm sorry, Glen is at Golden Acres. He hasn't lived here for six months."

"Are you Mrs. Pentz?"

She nodded. "He has Alzheimer's, you know."

"No. I didn't know. I'm sorry to bother you, but your husband's car was seen at the Almeria Avenue VFW. Why would that be?"

"Oh, our son, Sam, totaled his car a couple weeks ago. I gave him Glen's car. I suppose he hasn't gotten around to transferring the title yet." She frowned. "Is Sam in trouble?"

"No, ma'am. I'm mainly interested in talking to Glen."

"I'm afraid he's not with us much. Most days, he doesn't even know my name."

"Did he talk much about what he did in Iceland after the war?"

"Oh my," she chuckled. "You are going back a long way." She eyed him. "I don't suppose you like oatmeal cookies?"

Gerry grinned. "As a matter of fact, I do."

Five minutes later, Gerry settled in the breakfast nook of Mrs. Pentz's kitchen took another cookie from a plate piled to overflowing. "These cookies are the best I've ever had."

"You're too kind, Detective." She set another cup of coffee across from him and seated herself. "Now, where were we? Oh yes, Glen's assignment in Iceland. I wasn't there, you understand. Wives weren't allowed. You men want to keep all the adventure to yourselves." Her eyes twinkled, and Gerry caught a glimpse of the young woman Glen Pentz had married. "Well," she went on, "Glen understood my love of drama, and was good about indulging me." She sighed. "I miss him."

Gerry swallowed the last bit of cookie. "He's a lucky man, ma'am."

She beamed. "You're a charmer, just like Glen." She gave another sigh, this one mixed with satisfaction. "Glen interviewed sailors and officers about U-boat sightings. His job was to match Allied reports of attacks or sunken U-Boats in the North Atlantic with records confiscated from the German high command detailing where they thought U-Boats had been lost and where they had been headed. In the official record, Glen credited the captain and crew of USS whoever with the sinking of U-777, or some such thing."

"They didn't know for sure the U-Boats were sunk?"

"A submarine is supposed to submerge and sneak away, especially when damaged. All the reports had to be vetted. Apparently, there were many cases where a war ship thought they hit a U-Boat—oil slick and flotsam were visible—but that turned out to be a ploy to make the attacker think the sub had sunk. You know, they didn't paint the numbers on U-Boats during the war."

"I didn't know that," Gerry replied.

"It's true. The ships and crew didn't know which U-Boat they had hit."

"Are you sure you weren't the one investigating the subs?" he said with admiration. "You're quite the expert."

She laughed. "As I said, Glen was good about feeding my need for excitement."

"Wasn't this information classified?"

"Oh yes. At the time it was all top secret. But that ended. Now, anyone can access the records in the Naval Archives in Washington."

"All declassified," Gerry murmured.

"That's right. About ten years ago, some divers from New Jersey saw Glen's name on the reports and contacted him. They wanted to discuss a U-Boat they thought they'd located."

"Is that all? No war crimes?"

"He did investigate secret German camps on Iceland."

"Is that how he met Judge Jackson?"

"Yes. He and Harold spent a few months on some special team."

"How often did he meet Jackson and the others after they returned to the States?"

"Once or twice a month."

"Do you know why?"

Mrs. Pentz giggled like a schoolgirl. "It was all hush-hush. I wasn't supposed to know. They brought back German souvenirs from Iceland. Glen locked them in his desk. They acted like boys with a Playboy magazine. Closeting themselves up in his office and whispering so I wouldn't hear." She gave a little snort.

"You weren't curious?"

"I was very curious. But men like their secrets." She gave him a knowing look.

He countered with a hopeful raise of his brows. "Any idea what those souvenirs were?"

She grinned. "Books. Very old books. Pretty silly, huh?"

"Maybe not. What happened to those books?"

She paused. "I don't know. I haven't thought of them in years. The boys were quite fascinated with them when they first returned. I even remember him talking about immortality, as if that was possible. I guess I assumed that, like most other things connected to the war, they took a back seat to the lives they resumed."

"Did you, in…er, the course of feeding your love of adventure, see these books?"

She smiled, and Gerry knew she had.

A moment later, they stood in Glen Pentz's ten-by-ten office. She opened a drawer in the small roll top desk that occupied a corner. A picture of a good looking, dark haired man about Gerry's age sat on the upper right hand corner of the desk. Sam Pentz, Gerry bet. Mrs. Pentz located a folded paper and held it up.

"I never snooped, you understand. I found this while cleaning behind the desk. It must have fallen back there and Glen didn't realize it." She smiled innocently.

"Of course," Gerry said, and took the paper. He unfolded, then rotated the page right-side up. Three-quarters of the page was covered in carefully hand-written Icelandic. "Any idea what this is?"

Mrs. Pentz shook her head. "No. I can't read the language."

He grinned. "May I keep this?"

"Help yourself."

Gerry folded the page and tucked it into his shirt pocket, then pulled out a card. "I still need to speak with Glen. Maybe you can accompany me. It's better to have a loved one along to help trigger a recollection."

"Certainly."

"If you find he's having a good day, call." Gerry handed her the card. "Remember, anytime." He smiled. "Thanks for the world's best oatmeal cookies."

"I'll call you the first chance he comes around."

"I'd appreciate it. While I'm at it, can I get Sam's address and phone number?"

She grabbed paper and pen from the desk and jotted down the info, then saw him to the door. He said a final good-by and headed down the walkway.

Hargrave's snout rested on the open window. He woofed, tail wagging, as Gerry approached. "You smell those cookies, don't you, Pal?"

Hargrave woofed again as Gerry got into the car.

"Want to see what I have?" He pulled the page from his pocket and unfolded it. "Should have paid more attention in ancient history." He would FAX this over to Janice—along with the books Jackson was hiding.

Ancient manuscripts from Iceland and cult murders. A beautiful blonde and a judge. Gerry sighed. Things weren't looking good for the Judge. He looked at the yellow pad sitting on the car seat beside him. Verdi was the last name on the list of car owners at the VFW, but he hadn't served with Jackson so probably wasn't involved. William Johnson, Jr. had been there and Sam Pentz had been driving his father's car. Maybe whatever was going on was a family affair.

Gerry stuck the page Mrs. Pentz had given him inside the pad, then grabbed the pen clipped to the paper and noted the name Sam Pentz. He glanced at the dash clock. Two forty-five. He had enough time to swing by the VFW before his appointment at Joseph M. Warner Laboratories for fucking PSI Research.

Chapter Seven

A<small>T FOUR-THIRTY IN</small> the afternoon, Gerry followed Marjorie Wellington down the corridors of Joseph M. Warner Laboratories. Machinegun gray merged walls with doors in one long hallway, leaving Gerry even more uneasy than he had been when he arrived. Marjorie's long bottle-blonde hair was the only contrast to anything he'd seen in the building so far, which included her gray pen striped pantsuit that flattered a fine, tight ass. She stopped in front of a door with the name Alyssa Hamilton painted in thick, black lettering at eye level. None of the other doors bore markings. He thought of prison cells and wondered what sort of warden Alyssa Hamilton would prove to be.

Marjorie gave the door a perfunctory knock before pushing it open. "Detective Forstner," she announced, and stepped aside so that Gerry looked across a sparse room at the woman sitting behind a highly polished, dark cherrywood desk.

The contrast of the desk to the brightly lit gray walls paled in comparison to the piercing green eyes that met his. More uneasiness crept in. Dr. Alyssa Hamilton was fifty-two years old, five eight, one hundred and twenty-five pounds and had spectacular green eyes. Her shoulder length, wavy auburn hair had wisps of gray that looked perfectly natural on her.

Nothing in her file had prepared him for the woman. Not even the 1989 Vail, Colorado report on how she led a group of searchers to a lost girl. Miss Hamilton pinpointed the girl thirty miles north of the search radius. That was the first of thirteen cases where she assisted authorities in locating lost children. The final case occurred five years ago. The little boy was found dead. A month later, Miss Hamilton dropped off the radar.

She rose from her high back, leather office chair. "Please come in,

Detective."

Her voice was clear and strong, all business. Not surprising. One look at her, and a man wouldn't expect feminine wiles. She was beautiful, but unlike most women her age—hell, most women any age—looks weren't what made Alyssa Hamilton tick. This woman was a force to be reckoned with.

Gerry strode forward, sidestepped the brown leather Taylor Club chair in front of the desk, and clasped the hand she extended. Awareness snaked up his arm an instant before she released his hand. What the hell? The next thing you knew, his head would start spinning and he'd spit up pea soup.

She regarded him. "Something wrong, Detective?"

"Last night's pizza," he replied.

Alyssa gave him a quizzical look, then one corner of her mouth lifted. "Don't you hate it when that happens?"

A tiny jolt of agitation zipped through his body. If he didn't know better, he'd swear he'd been wired. Jesus, he was twelve years old again and fighting off the willies he got when watching those hokey vampire films. Must be the place. Tone down the contrast on the black and white TV, and you had the gray Joseph M. Warner walls.

"Yeah," he said.

"Please, sit down." Alyssa motioned to the chair.

Gerry glanced back and noticed the closed door before sitting. He leaned against the curved back of the Taylor Club chair as he sat, but couldn't relax. "Nice," he said, stroking the curved leather arm. "My wife—ex-wife," he amended with a rueful laugh, "had a thing for these chairs. It was one of the few things we agreed on."

"Thank God for small favors," Alyssa commented.

"Yeah." Gerry met her gaze. "How familiar are you with members of Joseph M. Warner Laboratories?"

"We have over ten thousand members. I couldn't possibly know most of them."

"All Florida residents?"

"No, and before you go on, Detective, let me add, many of our members are shunned by their families or cast out of their homes after their abilities surface. We offer an environment where they can explore who they are without fear. If I gave away information concerning them, it could shatter that security."

"I thought this was the New Age," Gerry said. "Police departments all over the world use psychics to help solve crimes. Psychics are making a bundle on nine hundred numbers."

Alyssa smiled indulgently. "Nine hundred numbers? Come now, Detective, there are as many charlatans in the psychic world as there are in…politics. The people who take those nine hundred number psychics seriously are being abducted by aliens on a weekly basis."

"Maybe, but this isn't the dark ages. Witches aren't burnt at the stake." He tried to sound casual when he asked, "What does Joseph M. Warner Laboratories do?"

She smiled politely. "Is the Coral Gables Police Department investigating us?"

"Depends on the link between Warner Laboratories and the Valknut murders. I know all four men were members."

Alyssa reached into a desk drawer and pulled out four files. She set them on the desk in front of him. The file names bore the names of the murder victims: Brent Douglas, Darryl Michaels, Frank Vitelli and John Kinnison. They'd even been stacked in order of death.

Gerry looked at her. "I thought you didn't know every one of your members."

"I don't. I had Marjorie check into it after you called. The connection was made by others who knew these men."

"And you didn't you report this? Jesus fucking Christ, what kind of show are you running here?"

"The kind run by a state licensed medical research facility."

Gerry bit back a curse. What idiots in the state legislature made mystic research a legitimate medical study? He leaned forward. "These *others* who made the connection, do they have any other information I should know—like who the next murder victim is?" Something flickered in her eyes. This time, chills ran the length of his body. "I'd advise you not to fuck with me, ma'am. I don't like it."

"I don't make the rules, Detective." Before Gerry could say that he knew good and well she was in charge, she added, "The idea that true evil might coexist on this plane or, even worse, on this earth, is beyond the ability of most people to accept." She paused, and her green eyes darkened. "Never underestimate the boogieman, Detective, and don't doubt your ability to know him."

He blinked. Was this how Columbia University Ph.D. psychology graduates applied their education? "The boogieman?" He hardened his voice though his stomach roiled. "I'll catch the boogieman next week. Right now, I'm interested in finding out who the next victim is and catching his would-be murderer."

"How do you know they aren't one and the same?"

Gerry stared into her green eyes. "Are you speaking of the murderer or the next victim?"

"Why not the murderer *and* the boogieman?"

"I have news for you, Miss Hamilton, there's a boogieman in every murderer." Gerry tapped the files with his forefinger. "I want to know who these four men associated with, when they were last seen together, and who, here, knew them."

Alyssa glanced at her watch. "It's only 3:30. You can probably have your warrant before Marjorie leaves for the day."

Gerry blinked, and something flickered in Alyssa's eyes. Amusement?

She picked up her phone. "Marjorie, could you make copies of these files I have on my desk, please?" She replaced the phone on the hook and looked at Gerry.

Christ, what could he say but "Thanks."

✦

AT TEN TO seven, Gerry walked up the stone steps of Jackson's mansion. The sun sat poised on the horizon as if refusing to rest until Gerry did. Before he could ring the doorbell, a metallic clank echoed and the door opened, revealing Judge Jackson in the doorway.

"Detective Forstner," he said.

"Evening, Judge."

Jackson stepped aside. "Come in."

A moment later, they entered Jackson's private study. Gerry repressed a shiver. He wished like hell he'd saved the interview with Alyssa Hamilton until after seeing the judge. He couldn't figure out what the hell she'd done to spook him, but she had.

Jackson sat behind his desk and Gerry lowered himself into the chair he'd occupied before and decided to forgo the preamble. Time to see how fortuitous coincidences could be.

"I know what your burglar was after," he said.

Surprise flashed on Jackson's face. "How—what—"

"She's after the books you and your men took from Iceland."

Fear flickered across the judge's face and was immediately replaced by a hardboiled expression. Not bad, Gerry thought as he reached into his back pocket and pulled out a copy of the document Mrs. Pentz had given him. He'd practiced the same look for years, but Jackson was better. Gerry unfolded the single sheet, set it on the desk, then sat back and looked Jackson in the eye.

"Where's your book?"

Jackson hesitated.

Satisfaction surged through Gerry. "If I contact the State Department, what will they say?" He leaned forward, "I know your record. You're straight. No scandals. Can't be bought. You don't want to go out this way." Gerry paused. "Did you know that Derryl Michaels was working two jobs and going to school? He had a wife and young child."

A moment of silence passed, then Jackson began. "I was assigned to a classified team of specialists who were sent to investigate Nazi medical experiments."

Gerry started. "Medical experiments? You mean like Mengele's experiments?"

"Yes. We came across a project of his delving into longevity."

Gerry frowned. Marilyn had mentioned longevity. "Like the fountain of youth?"

"Exactly. The Nazis believed they deserved to live forever. Death was the final enemy to be conquered. We compiled evidence on these experiments we had uncovered in an underground lair in Iceland."

"After all these years, this information must be declassified. How come I've never heard about it?"

He shrugged. "Neither have UFO investigations been declassified. If the government has a good reason, I'm not privy to it. The search for U-boats, war crimes against humanity, Mengele's experiments, which were too numerous and well documented to keep from the public, are the sorts of things people needed to hear in order to see that their government was doing its job. The experiments we investigated took place in a single underground cavern in Iceland during the war. They were gruesome. Perhaps our government feels the American people had seen enough Nazi brutality to convict every Nazi from here to kingdom come."

"Where do these books come in?" Gerry asked.

"The Nazi's discovered remnants of an extinct religion. They believed them to contain the secret to eternal life, and conducted experiments…" An expression of pain drifted across his face. "Horrific experiments. Nightmare quality. Near the end of the war, they abandoned the catacomb. Two years later, we discovered its remains. The lair they had occupied turned out to be much older than the Nazis."

"What kind of experiments?"

A shadow darkened the old man's features. "Have you seen war, Detective?"

"Not military," Gerry replied. "But my line of work comes with its own brand of war."

The judge nodded. "Yes. I can see that. However, when it gets to be too much, you can go home, turn on the TV, drink a beer, put on headphones and listen to music. We had no such luxuries. Day in, day out, you're there until discharged or you go home in a body bag, or worse, return less of a man than you were when you left. Death is a constant companion. Even if you make it, you know someone who didn't."

"You weren't in the war, Judge."

He gave a low, mocking laugh. "But I saw the effects. You would think that would make a man want to die, but it doesn't. You want to live, and you want to live a long time." He slumped back in his chair. "When we stumbled upon these books, we figured we deserved our piece of the pie." Jackson shook his head. "The stupidity of youth."

"What happened?"

"Nothing. We got home, resumed normal lives, and eventually grew old."

"You didn't pursue the idea?"

"When we first got back, we agreed to keep a low profile. But that was just a way of saying that we knew we'd been foolish. There is no fountain of youth."

"So these books are about the experiments?"

"No, about something much older. One of the demolition charges opened a hidden chamber the Nazis hadn't found."

"And?"

"And we found the books hidden inside." Jackson shrugged. "They looked old. We figured they'd make good souvenirs."

A long silence drew out before Gerry said, "I'll need the book, Judge."

Jackson gave a tired sigh and reached beneath his desk. A faint click sounded and the center drawer opened. He stabbed a gnarled index finger inside the drawer and pulled up a false bottom. From underneath, he withdrew an inch thick, leather-bound volume about the size of a three-ring binder.

He set the book on the desk. Two straps with metal latches bound the finely tooled leather cover. It looked like a witch's spell book straight from an old cheesy movie. Gerry leaned forward. The three triangles of the Valknut stood out amongst runes tooled into the cover. His pulse accelerated. It hadn't occurred to him that the Valknut would be on them—or that they would be so old. They had to be—his heart nearly stopped when Jackson pulled out a second volume.

Gerry pinned him with a hard stare. "You have two books with the Valknut and never connected them with the murders—not even after someone broke into your house?"

"I believed it was a coincidence. After all, I've had these books for decades." He pointed to the top volume. "I took this as a souvenir. The other belonged to Charles Thomas...John Kinnison's father."

Gerry stared at Jackson. "Charles Thomas was Kinnison's father? Christ, and you didn't recuse yourself from the case—or come forward when Kinnison was murdered?"

"Consider, his murder was only a few days ago and—"

"Don't give me that bologna, Judge. The Valknut has been plastered all over the media. We've been looking for a connection, and the biggest one was right under your nose. *And you knew it.* Any of the other Valknut victims related to your men?"

"No."

Gerry nodded toward the books. "What are those?"

Jackson unfastened the clasps on the top volume and opened it. Despite the faded ink, Gerry recognized the Icelandic script that filled the ledger rows. The second to last column contained dates. A lopsided cross, circumscribed with a circle in the final column grabbed his attention. His mind jarred as if the vaguely familiar symbol should shake something loose.

Jackson ran a finger down a column, breaking Gerry's concentration. "This is a simple registry that records births, deaths, baptisms, and unions for the Asatru order."

Jackson spun the volume around and Gerry studied the pages.

"A secret society," Gerry said. Son-of-a-bitch, it was worse than he'd thought.

"Impressive," Jackson said.

Gerry flicked him a *no it's not* look, then refocused on the book. This was all he needed, some kook who thought they were picking up where the ancient religion left off.

He looked up from the book. "I'll need the translations as well, Judge."

"Glen has the few translated pages. Old Norse manuscripts are rare, and—"

"These date back that far?" Gerry demanded.

"These are not contemporary. Perhaps now you can understand our concern. To take such ancient artifacts is high crime."

And the monetary value alone is enough to warrant murder, Gerry added silently. "Did the blonde search this room?"

"Forensics found no fingerprints. As far as I could tell, nothing had been disturbed."

Gerry pulled the journal toward him. The weight of past centuries washed over him as he scanned the exotic symbols with a sense of familiarity he couldn't place. He turned one of the thick pages and felt its texture between thumb and forefinger. Despite the passage of time, the paper was soft and supple. He closed the journal and ran a finger over the leather cover. Runes, along with other symbols he didn't recognized had been tooled around the Valknut sign, which sat in the center surrounded by a circle. A tingle resonated through him. He purposely broke the sensation by turning his attention back to Jackson.

"Do you have any other...souvenirs?"

"No.

"I have to confiscate these."

"I know."

Gerry picked up the books and stood. "Someone is onto the fact you have these books. I'll post an unmarked car outside. Stay home for a while, Judge."

Jackson gave a tired nod, but Gerry remembered the fact no one had seen Kinnison's murder come or go and couldn't repress a sense of dread.

Chapter Eight

A S GERRY SLOWED at the end of Jackson's driveway, Hargrave let out a deep growl. Gerry braked and twisted to look at the Shepherd. He stared out the passenger window behind him, lip curled back. Gerry scanned the street. Lamplight illuminated the street, but trees behind the walls barring entrance to the estates stretched upward into a moonless midnight blue void. No cars sat parked along the curb and the sidewalk was empty. Whatever had Hargrave on edge lurked behind one of those walls.

"What's there, boy?" Gerry murmured.

Hargrave's ears flattened.

Gerry pulled the car from the driveway and parked at the curb. He leashed Hargrave and stepped out. Hargrave bounded to the pavement and stood at attention, staring at a driveway across the street, two doors up. An eight foot wall hid the house and a wrought-iron gate anchored to sturdy buttresses blocked the driveway. Gerry's gaze caught on the nearest corner of gate and wall. The gate was set into the stone about three feet past the corner. From this vantage point, that corner lay concealed. A person could easily hide there. Gerry glanced at the books and Warner files on the passenger seat of the Impala. Where was the patrol car he'd called for before leaving Jackson's driveway?

Eyes on the hiding space, Gerry locked the car and choked up on the leash in readiness to cut the dog loose if needed. Hargrave remembered the posture and stepped close as Gerry started forward along Jackson's wall. The hiding place inched into view. He braced to release Hargrave. Headlights shined from around the curve. Dammit. He couldn't let Hargrave bolt across the street with a car just around that corner. Gerry quickened his pace. The headlights brightened. The hiding place angled into view. Nothing. Nobody hid there. A black-and-white rounded the curve.

About time.

Gerry let some slack on the leash as the car neared. He recognized Manning and, nodded as the car rolled by, then headed back to the Impala. Hargrave gave another low growl, then faced forward. Gerry realized his heart was pounding.

CROUCHED ON THE roof, he watched the patrol car pass, then swung his gaze back to the detective returning to his car. What did the detective want with the old man? He dared not look into the man's mind again. If the detective sensed him this time, the old man would end up under twenty-four hour guard.

The detective opened the car door and the dog leaped inside. Animals such as these had been bred to hunt night creatures. But that had been centuries ago. How had the animal sensed him so easily?

The Impala's headlights flared to life. He leaped to the ground and made the top of the wall in two steps. He watched until the car disappeared around the bend, then dropped to the ground. He could wait for his answers—and the warrior princess. She was somewhere in the city.

GERRY BREATHED EASIER now that the judge's books were in evidence lockup, being photographed and cataloged. The bullpen outside his office was quiet for a Wednesday night and his wire in-basket overflowed again. He thumbed through the folders and found only the run of the mill death reports for review, and signed off.

The chair squeaked as he reached for the Warner files. What did the institute for PSI research have on the four victims and what was their connection? None of the files were thick, but he'd noticed the lightweight feel of Kinnison's file when he tossed them on the Impala's passenger seat after serving the warrant at Warner Laboratories. He stared at the stack just as he had before starting the car and heading for Jackson's house.

He hadn't worked Kinnison's case, but what little Gerry knew said Kinnison was a son-of-a-bitch who deserved to die, maybe even deserved the death he'd gotten. Gerry paused. He'd gotten inside the minds of some nasty assholes, but he couldn't shake the feeling Kinnison's Warner Laboratories file might be getting too close. He grabbed the file and opened it to find a single sheet of paper.

Investigator's Note: Subject describes ESP experience as involving a state of detachment, abstraction, or relaxation. He closes his eyes and immediately drops into a light trance. The fact he perceives the images by hallucination, suggests he has achieved good abstraction from sensory disturbances.

"What the hell does that mean?" Gerry burst out. Hallucinations seem to be the order of the day on this case.

Gerry read on: *When I see something in Technicolor it is always correct. I close my eyes and gaze into a deep darkness. Images eventually emerge from the darkness—they sometimes metamorphous into something else.*

Investigator's Note: Until we know more about what inner states are associated with ESP, it is impossible to specify a frame of reference from which scientific reporting can be universalized.

They had investigators? Why didn't he think of that before wasting time in college? He could have gotten a cushy job making up the same kind of bullshit.

Gerry opened Brent Douglas' Warner file and read, *Sometimes, it takes half an hour before something like a white shimmer forms and condenses piece by piece into a recognizable image.* The next line headed, *Investigator's Notes* read: *I observed the subject for half an hour as the image appeared to him and gained an intensity approaching visual hallucination.*

Gerry paused. Two seconds had been all he'd needed for his hallucination to begin after he'd been stabbed. No, not stabbed. There hadn't been a wound.

He slowly reread, *In describing the process with which he receives impressions, the subject says…* Gerry ran his gaze down the paragraph and continued from…*something like a white shimmer forms, and condenses piece by piece into a recognizable image.*

He scanned the top of the page for the investigator's name. Jennifer

Moorhouse, then noted it on the pad sitting on the desk before continuing with the file.

The vision or impression may come through any sense-channel. Impressions seem to find a way, a chain of reasoning or association that doesn't seem to coincide with anything familiar to those present, but seems invented out of necessity.

Gerry paused. These so-called psychic impressions didn't associate with anything familiar to those present. Did that include the person experiencing the psychic phenomena? In the alley, he had seen the very thing that weighed most heavily on his mind—well, second most on his mind after the asshole with a knife: the blonde. If the subject couldn't associate anything with the impression, and he had been able to make an association, that would mean the hallucination in the alley was just that, a hallucination. At least he didn't have to worry about being psychic. That was a big relief. Gerry chuckled, then picked up Darryl Michaels' file.

Five minutes later, he wasn't laughing anymore.

Subject was instructed to describe how 'visions' or 'impressions' appear.
    "Sometimes a curved or straight line appears and some sort of outline takes shape. Other times the whole picture pops into my brain so close, it feels like someone is sharing my skin with me.

Gerry remembered with almost as much force as he had this morning when he'd dreamt about the blonde, her face so close to his, it felt like they shared the same skin. Dungeons, priests, and a creature that meant to kill him.

"Damn," he breathed. It was a dream, just a dream—A dream where someone invaded his psychic space. He grimaced. Until now, that term had simply meant *gotten too close.* Now—"Now it means I've lost my fucking mind." He eyed the file, wondering who he could get to read the rest of it, but his gaze inexorably, found, the next line:

Sometimes, everything rolls like a moving picture film. The pictures come and go fast. If something strikes me hard enough, sometimes I can force it to the front of my mind. I never know when I'm having the visions. I always have to 'remember' them right after they happen. I have a vision, then jerk from the trance and realize and remember at once what just happened.

I don't usually see just one picture. Sometimes it's a few, other times, one right after the other. Other times, I'll see something, then my mind will go blank for a little while, or it seems like I can think about what I just saw, then I'll suddenly realize I've just seen something else and didn't know it.

Investigator's Notes: Subject describes pictures as never in heavy lines, but sketched lightly, in a slightly deeper shade of gray than that of the mental canvas. He related how, once he realized these pictures were being impressed upon him, he remembered many such instances in the past when he saw other pictures. As is common with most subjects, these pictures can be so vague that one only gets a notion of how they look before they vanish.

Subject likes to stare with a "faraway look." He especially loves to stare out the window. He prefers this to closing his eyes, saying that the images were uncontrolled with the eyes closed.

Gerry closed Michaels' file and set it on top of Douglas' file. He reached for Frank Vitelli's file, but halted at sight of his trembling hand hovering over the file.

"Get a grip," he snarled, and snatched up the file.

Subject had no success in achieving true altered state on his own.

Gerry paused in reading the investigators' opening sentence. Nowhere on any of these files had he come across a date.

Production of hypnosis by means of simple oral medication, however, yielded precognitive results.

Drugs? Vitelli's toxicology scan didn't find drugs in his system. Gerry made a note to ask Pam what compounds the lab checked for, then went back to reading.

Subject predicted with accuracy mayoral loss due to sex-scandal, extensive damage caused by a hurricane that hit southern Florida with devastating results in mid September of this year, and that the local police would find the murder of a little girl gone missing six years ago.

With no further medication, hypnosis was reinforced daily during the following four days. On the fifth day, subject entered a meditative trance where he described the following past life regression:

"Flames everywhere! I can't see them, but I can feel them, sense them. I am afraid, not of the fire, but because I can't move. Why? I'm bound—no, I'm paralyzed, drugged maybe. Yeah, it feels like my mind is muddled, my body lethargic. I must be drugged.

"Darkness—no, wait, a lit room. The room is old somehow, not in this time, and is small. A candle on the wall near the door is the only light. I'm lying on a small bed and there's a man. He saved me from the fire. He wants to know what I was doing there—was I a sacrifice? I was lying on some sort of altar. I wasn't alone. Several other women were with me. Everyone thought we were dead and left us there to die when they burned the temple. A temple—we were in a temple.

"Dylan saved me. He's a soldier, tall, not so young, fifty-five maybe, but very strong. He is one of the men assigned to deal with us—no, not us, no one knew about us. There is someone else, I feel like I should know who. I want to ask Dylan, but his hate for the priests is palpable. Priests? Yes, the men who came to destroy us. I don't understand why they would want to destroy us. If we are part of the church, why—

Investigator's Notes: The regression abruptly ended and subject awoke. I quizzed him as we do after all sessions, but he maintained throughout the post-interview that he remembered nothing of the past life regression. This is rare, but I wonder if the use of drugs somehow influenced the subject's reactions and memories.

Gerry closed Vitelli's file, set it on top of the other three files, then leaned back in his chair. No mention of manipulating personalities, secret information being carried, or telepathy used to transfer information in a noisy environment. No Morse code or Zener code or missile submarines and data transfers. The only similarity between Alyssa and Wayne's files was the use of hypnosis. Apparently, Ms. Hamilton had withheld files.

He opened his desk drawer and retrieved the file Wayne had given him. He thumbed through the papers until he found the section on Derryl Michael's concerning information that had been summoned forth via a post-hypnotic command or response to a pre-programmed cue, then paused. No mention of Michaels being tested for a particularly high count of PSI. And what about Kinnison? Why so little research on the pedophile? Gerry sighed. How had he known he would have to pay another visit to Alyssa Hamilton?

Chapter Nine

W HEN GERRY DIDN'T see Collin behind the bar at *The Hot Spot*, he
went directly to the tall brunette who was filling a shot glass with
whisky. She glanced at him.

"Is Collin around?" he asked.

"Nope," she replied, and set the drink on the tray to her left.

Gerry glanced at his watch. Nine o'clock. "He's not working tonight?"

The brunette gave him a questioning look.

"Hey, Susan," a guy called from the other end of the bar, "where's my
beer?"

"Coming up."

She produced a cold mug from the small refrigerator behind the bar
and stuck the lip beneath a beer tap and poured. She looked at Gerry and
raised a brow. He stepped back and pointed to the badge clipped to his
belt. She glanced at it, then turned her attention to the almost full mug.
She straightened the glass as the beer foamed, then delivered it to the guy
at the end of the bar.

A moment later, she was standing before Gerry again. "You're that
cop asking about Frankie."

"Right."

She paused, as if assessing him before saying, "Collin didn't show up
for work tonight."

"Is that normal?"

"Nope. He's a straight up guy."

Gerry thought back to the conversation with Collin. "Frankie considered himself some sort of player. Fantasy or not, I don't want any piece of

that action."

"You know his address?"

She nodded, then produced a pen from beneath the bar and grabbed a napkin.

✦

COLLIN'S APARTMENT WAS located on the second floor of a small apartment building in Miami's lower rent district. Gerry tilted the napkin and reread the chicken scratch by streetlight.

"Apartment three-B." He regarded the dingy door in front of him, then knocked.

No answer. He knocked again, still no answer. A closed curtain on the window to the left blocked all view into the dark apartment. To the right, a TV blared through the building's thin walls. Gerry stepped down to that door and knocked.

A short gray-haired man answered. He had a three-day-old beard and sweat stains in the armpits of his T-shirt. The television blasted behind him. Gerry was betting the guy was on helluva *good neighbor*.

The man squinted up at him. "Yeah?"

Gerry pointed at his badge. "Coral Gables PD. I'm trying to locate your neighbor, Collin Norman."

"Aint' seen 'im." The man started to close the door.

Gerry stuck his foot against the door. "Have youseen or heard anything suspicious in the past couple days?"

"Nope." The man shoved harder on the door.

Gerry didn't budge. "You didn't notice if Collin came home last night or was around today?"

"Nope."

"Don't talk much, do yah?" Gerry commented.

"Nope."

"Do you know Collin?"

The man started to open his mouth and Gerry raised a brow.

"I talked to him," the guy conceded.

"Did he have any friends here?"

"The girl next door." The man nodded toward the apartment on the other side of Collin. "I seen 'em talking."

"What's her name?"

"Marissa."

"Thanks." Gerry removed his foot and the door slammed before he had a chance to turn. He stared at the door. "Be sure to give me a call if you ever need the police. I'll hurry right over."

He strode to the other door and knocked. A twenty-something, pretty redhead answered. Gerry smiled. "Good evening, ma'am. I'm Detective Forstner with the Coral Gables PD." He unclipped his badge and held it up. "I just spoke with your neighbor a couple doors down and he tells me you're friends with Collin Norman."

Her eyes widened. "Is Collin okay?"

"He's probably fine. He didn't show up for work tonight, and I'm trying to find out where he might have gone. Have you seen him?"

Marissa shook her head. "He always goes to work. He's saving for culinary school in France."

"When did you last see him?"

"He called Monday, said he had a few things to take care of for his folks and he'd be back in a week."

"Where do they live?"

"Pensacola."

"Do you have access to his apartment?"

She blushed. "He gave me a key last summer."

"Would you mind checking inside, just to be sure everything's okay?"

"Sure." She turned and disappeared around the corner of the short hallway.

A few seconds later, she returned with a key. She brushed past Gerry and hurried to Collin's door. Gerry waited while she unlocked the door, then followed her into the entryway and waited while she continued into the living room and switched on a light.

"There's nothing here," she called. "Everything looks okay." She peeked around the edge of the hallway wall. "Come see for yourself."

That's just what he'd been waiting for.

The short hall led to an eat-in kitchen to the left, and living room furnished with a sofa and two end tables. Opposite the sofa against the far wall sat a seventeen-inch TV, compact stereo, and DVD player on a plank supported by two cement blocks on each end. He crossed to the slider that led to a lanai with two beach chairs and scanned the balcony, but saw nothing that seemed out of order.

In the kitchen, the balled-up dishrag on the counter was dry and the dishwasher had been loaded but not cycled. The garbage pail was nearly full and smelled like two-day-old rot when he flipped open the lid.

Back in the living room, Gerry fingered through the CD's, mostly classical with some fusion jazz. Marissa stood by the sofa watching expectantly.

Gerry pointed to the opening to the back hallway. "Bedroom back there?"

She nodded and he went back. The bathroom on the left was small and neatly kept. Collin's bed, a simple box spring and mattress, was made. His closet door hung wide open and an empty, top dresser-drawer had been left out a few inches. A pair of socks lay on the floor by the dresser. A computer sat on the small desk against the far wall. Gerry let out a breath. A neat freak who wanted to be a chef had left his garbage in the kitchen, his closet and drawers open, and a pair of socks on the floor.

Gerry let out a breath. "What scared you, Collin?"

GERRY DROPPED THE four CD's that contained photos of Jackson's books on his desk at home and sat in his chair. Hargrave settled on the carpet beside him and began dozing. It was only quarter after ten. Late nights were becoming too much for the old boy. Gerry grabbed the first CD tagged *First Half of Book One* and popped it into his computer.

Page one of the book loaded. Gerry zoomed in on the seal superimposed over a single word he assumed was the scribe's name in the last of the four columns. What was it about the lopsided cross that bothered him? He stared at the image. Had he seen it in his studies, travels, or maybe when…

Gerry started, the echo of shadowy images resonating with a flicker of gray light in his mind. He blinked the computer screen into focus. The digital clock read ten twenty-seven. A tremor rippled through his belly. He'd lost seven minutes.

That night in the alley, the precinct had clocked him as being MIA for over twenty minutes. When faced with life and death situations, most cops experienced time slowly. He'd heard long time drunks talk about delirium tremens, but had hoped he hadn't sauced his brain enough to do that much damage, so had attributed that twenty-seven minute difference to a one time anomaly. This seven minute episode implied otherwise. He wasn't sure which was worse: alcohol induced delusions, or just plain delusional. Maybe it didn't matter.

Gerry rose and went to the kitchen. He opened the cabinet door, stared at the bottle of scotch that had sat as reminder the last two years, and reached inside. Hargrave padded into the kitchen, his nail clicking on the linoleum.

"You don't get coffee." Gerry said.

He pulled the coffee can from the cabinet, then closed the door.

GERRY SIPPED HIS coffee, then set the cup on his desk alongside the yellow legal pad, and looked at the computer screen. Four columns filled each book page. The first consisted of dates, the second of one of the four different words in that column, the third a single word, and the fourth with what he assumed was a name followed by the lopsided cross and seal. Familiarity washed over him again, but he forced back the feeling and concentrated on the first column of dates.

The first entry was dated in the year eight hundred and thirty-five. He ejected the CD and inserted disc two, then double-clicked on the last page of Book One. The final date read eighteen hundred and thirty-five. Gerry paused. Exactly one thousand years apart. Had he made a mistake? He scribbled the last date on his pad, then went back to the first disc and rechecked the number.

He leaned back and released a low whistle. No mistake. The book predated the Icelandic Eddas by at least a hundred years. Jackson and his men had good reason to worry. The document was valuable as hell. A pang of regret stabbed at Gerry. The old judge might not get out of this situation.

Gerry fired up his Optical Character Recognition software and set the program extracting text from the photos. While he waited, he printed out the first twenty pages and began with the name beside the seal and the most repeated word in the second column. The word in the column beside the seal was Mótsognir, and the name Freyja was the name most repeated in the third column. Gerry frowned. Freyja was the Norse Goddess, but who, or what, was Mótsognir?

He pulled up Google and searched. The screen filled with hits on Scandinavian mythology, Tolkien, Mótsognir: Norse gods, Asatru and Old Norse. Gerry opened the first link and began reading. After five pages, he cut a single paragraph from the document and pasted it into a Word document entitled Mótsognir.

Mótsognir was one of the older beings of the world and possessed a promethean power of creating. He belonged to the circle of holy powers. The "High Gods", or Aesir, gathered in council to set the universe in order and instructed dwarfs under their leader Mótsognir to make human beings from the flesh of Ymir, the primordial giant and progenitor of the race of frost giants. Ymir was killed by Odin, and the maggots which swarmed in Ymir's flesh gave wits and the shape of men who live under the hills and mountains and are called dwarfs.

Gerry paused. These ancient Asatru considered themselves gods, creators of men, and the Valknut murderer had decided to take up where they'd left off. Gerry rubbed his eyes. Dammit, Reyna been more right than he wanted her to be.

The second link called up a news article on an ancient crypt unearthed by a construction crew. "Hey boy." Hargrave's ears perked. "This must be the tomb Iris was talking about."

He scrolled down to the first of three photos of artifacts found there and caught his breath: a broken sword with the tree of Yggdrasil engraved on the blade. The same sword he held in the hallucination after being stabbed. Up until now, memory of the symbol had been vague, but the mental picture in his mind stood framed crystal clear.

Gerry broke his stare. No way this was the same symbol he'd seen in his hallucination. The symbols were similar—maybe—but couldn't be the same. He scrolled to the next photo and stared at the two daggers he'd seen the creature in his hallucination pull from his belt and cross in front of his chest. Gerry recognized the two symbols carved on the daggers' handles alongside the sun rune as Proto-Sinaitic.

What was a thirty-five hundred year old symbol doing alongside a symbol that didn't make its first appearance for another twelve hundred years? More importantly, how had he seen that dagger in a vision?

He scrolled up and looked at the sword again. How had he seen that sword? Because he had seen it somewhere and just didn't remember, that's how. Those symbols on the daggers weren't foreign to him either. Somewhere, he'd seen those pictures and just didn't remember.

Sherlock Holmes had it right. *When you have eliminated the impossible, whatever remains, however improbable, must be the truth.* There was no other explanation. He had a great memory, but he'd seen those symbols and forgotten.

Gerry closed out Google and began translating the four words in the second column of Jackson's book. Four words repeated on all the pages: birth, death, marriage, and a word that meant coronation or communion. He made a note to ask Janice, then concentrated on the scribes' signatures. These bothered him almost as much as the seal. They were too damned similar. He slumped back in his chair and released a breath. Maybe he should wait until Janice could get Iris to do a complete translation. But he was already reaching for a yellow highlighter from his drawer.

When he finished highlighting the signatures, he found that some entries were punctured with a second or third signature, and close to two thirds of the entries looked as if they were written by the same hand.

Then there was that seal. It matched perfectly, right down to the little indentation on the upper rim. He recalled how the scribes who copied the Masoretic text of the Hebrew bible trained for years in order to learn how to copy the text as good as a Xerox. In the case of the Icelandic registry, not only had they copied the script, but the seal was passed to each successive scribe and the name Mótsognir was then used. The hair on the back of his neck tingled. Catholic priests were considered literal representations of God on earth. Mótsognir was a leader, creator— a god—their god.

Gerry removed the disc from the computer and inserted the first disc of Jackson's second book. A long list branched out across the page.

"Holy shit," Gerry breathed, and grabbed the mouse.

He scrolled down the page. Jackson had called the book a simple registry. Despite the faded ink and sporadically unreadable script, there was no mistaking the complex lineage that filled the screen. Hargrave let out a low sigh. Gerry absently rubbed the dog's ears. Hargrave laid his big snout on Gerry's leg and stared at him with dark eyes.

Gerry glanced at the clock. Twelve-thirty. He grinned at Hargrave. "You looking for a snack?" At the word snack, Hargrave's ears stood at attention and rotated left and right as if he was zeroing in with his radar. Gerry laughed. "Come on, boy. I'm hungry too."

Hargrave jumped up and led the way to the kitchen continually glancing over his shoulder at Gerry.

As Gerry reached into the cabinet for a bag of Hargrave's Old Mother Hubert doggie snacks the phone rang. He picked it up. "Yeah." He grabbed scissors from the drawer.

"The report on Pentz and Norman came back," Lummus said.

"Well, hello to you, too." Gerry cut open the bag.

"It's fucking twelve-thirty and I've been working all day. You're lucky I called at all."

That, Gerry knew, was true. "What have you got?"

"Nothing. No trace of either of them."

Gerry paused in pouring the treats into the bowl. "What?"

"Sam Pentz had a place in Miami Beach, but his current whereabouts are unknown."

"Dammit," Gerry cursed. This was a loose end that would come back to haunt him. "What about Collin, did you get everything back from his place?"

"Swept the place clean. No hint of foul play. There wasn't much to give forensics. We checked the fingerprints, analyzed the kitchen towel, cracked open his computer, and took a light to the entire apartment. Not a thing."

Gerry opened the treats and tossed one to Hargrave. "Bank records?"

"The guy had sixty-two bucks in his account. He's got two credit cards, both maxed, and neither of them used in the past two days. He's dropped out of sight."

Just what they needed, Gerry thought, a possible victim MIA. Hargrave gave a low woof as he begged for more.

"You still spoon feeding that woos of a dog?" Lummus said.

"This woos of a dog will kick your ass with one paw tied behind his back. Find Sam Pentz and Collin Norman." Gerry didn't give Lummus a chance to respond, and hung up.

Chapter Ten

PAIN LANCED THROUGH his ailing body. Judge Jackson grunted, but refused to cry out. *Higher*—no—his arm couldn't go any higher at that angle behind his back without breaking. The blonde appeared in the hallway and stepped inside in the doorway holding his wife Barbara in a choke hold with her free hand clasping Barbara's jaw. His knees weakened further, but his attacker's hold tightened more painfully on his arm. He had prayed some miracle would intervene and somehow keep the blonde from finding Barbara.

"Harold," his wife croaked. The soft light on his desk illuminated her face. Her eyes pleaded in terror.

The grandfather clock ticked off the seconds. Tick. Tick. Tick.

His chest constricted. He wanted to look away, but owed his wife more than cowardice. He met the blonde's blue gaze, and said, "The detective took the books."

The man gripping his arm shoved it higher. Searing pain came hard on the heels of the crack of bones. He cried out this time, but didn't allow his gaze to break from his wife's face.

The blonde twisted her head, farther…farther.

"No!" he cried.

Barbara screamed. The blonde gave her head a final hard twist to the right. A snap echoed, and she went limp. Soundless tears streamed down his face. *Barbara*. Her head lolled forward against the blonde's arm before the blonde stepped back and let his wife's body collapse into a crumpled heap on the carpet.

The blonde shot toward him in a blur. He gasped. The grip on his arm loosened and an arm slid around his back, keeping him upright. A hand grasped his jaw and forced his head to the side. He cursed the weakness the tremble in his old body revealed. Barbara lay dead. He would be next.

Tick. Tick. Tick.

Blond hair fell across his shoulder. Warm breath against his neck brought a shiver. "Go t-to hell," he rasped.

A sharp prick. He stiffened. The needle-like prick went deeper into the flesh of his neck. His heart pumped faster. He arched with the strain. Dear God, what was this?

The mouth withdrew and pain lanced across his neck—a cut, he'd been cut—like the Valknut victims. Warm blood flowed down his chest.

The Lord is my Shepherd; I shall not want. He focused on the psalm he knew so well, his lips noiselessly reciting the verse.

He maketh me to lie down in green pastures:

He leadeth me beside the still waters.

"He restoreth my soul," he said in a hoarse voice.

Blood pumped faster. What was the next line? *Please God, don't let me die until I finish.* Blood soaked his shirt and spread to his waistband.

Yea, though I walk through the valley of the shadow of death... His breath caught with relief.

"I will fear no evil," he blurted in a burst of adrenaline, then added in a whisper, "For thou art with me"

Thy rod and thy staff, they comfort me.

Thou preparest a table before me in the presence of mine enemies.

Thou annointest...

Faster. Pain blasted from his heart. Faster it pumped blood. Heaviness weighted his chest.

Surely goodness and mercy shall follow me...days of my life, and I will dwell in the House of the Lord forever.

The grandfather clock pealed Westminster chimes—

Ding, dong, ding, dong.

Ding, ding, ding, dong.

Ding, dong, ding, dong.

Dong, dong, ding, dong.

—then gonged four more times in the empty room.

PART THREE

A match made in Hell.

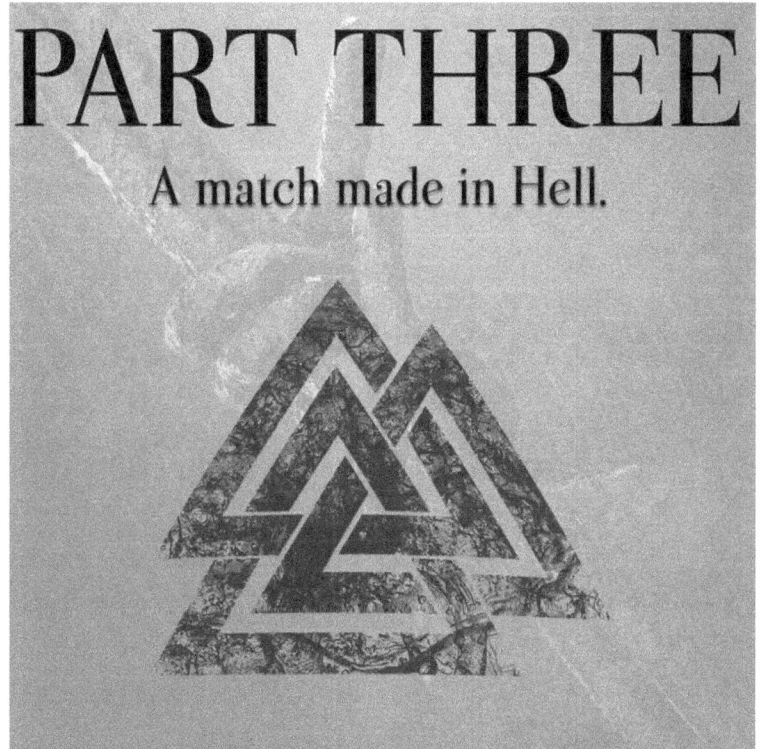

BOUND

Chapter One

FARAWAY OUTSIDE THE dream fog a screen door banged. Gerry started awake. *The back door.* He glanced at the digital clock in the predawn shadows. Five-forty-five. He quietly slid open the nightstand drawer, withdrew his 9mm, then slipped from bed. He paused. Where was Hargrave? Gerry crept from his room down the hall to the kitchen. Hargrave stared at a closed back door.

Gerry brushed past the Shepherd to the door. He grabbed the deadbolt lock and twisted right, but it didn't turn. With a gun in the house, he was a fanatic about locking that deadbolt. How had he forgotten it last night? Gun at ready, he eased open the door and shoved past the screen door onto the back stoop. Gerry stared at the deserted back yard. Anyone who had gone out the back door would have had to vault the six foot high fence. The discs!

He whirled and raced to the study. A desk light shined down on the disks and printouts where he had left them last night. Christ, he'd been dreaming. Despite years of habit, he'd been working so hard on the books and simply forgotten to lock the back door.

Gerry spun the chair and dropped onto the seat. He paused. Strange. He didn't recall ever having to rotate the chair to sit down. Being right handed, the chair always faced right after he had risen. Gerry shot a glance at Hargrave who stood in the doorway. Had he moved the chair? Gerry settled back as if doing so might somehow wipe away the disorder he felt, but his grip on the 9mm tightened.

"You're a creature of habit, Forstner," he croaked in a morning voice. "That's a sign of age." But the reassurance didn't stop him from looking at the mouse and keyboard. They sat where he always left them: keyboard pushed back and mouse at the front edge of the pad.

He reached under the desk to feel the back of the computer where the power supply fan was and his fingers touched warm air vents. A surge of adrenalin kicked his heart rate up a notch. Someone had been there. He stilled. Or were they still around?

He glanced at Hargrave. The dog stared placidly at him. "No one around, boy?"

Hargrave thumped his tail on the carpet. Gerry had relied on the dog's sixth sense for as long as they'd been together, but another slight tremor rolled through his gut. He remembered the affects the blonde had on him at *The Hot Spot* and wondered if dogs could be hypnotized.

Gerry rose and, step by step, checked every room, every closet, even behind the couch with Hargrave trotting alongside without a care in the world. No one was in the house, but someone had been there, and not very long ago.

Gerry returned to his computer and turned on the machine without sitting down. While the computer booted, he inspected the desk, keyboard, and chair. He crouched and ran his hand over the thick sheet of plastic his chair rolled on. He felt a scratch, but it moved. Peering closer, he pinched and pulled up a straight blonde hair.

He held the six-inch stand of hair up for inspection. Brenda, he thought, but the blonde from *The Hot Spot* came to mind. The picture of her face metamorphosed into a scene with her naked in his bed, him over her.

Gerry started. "Jesus," he cursed. "How the hell hard up are you, Forstner?" The thickening in his groin sent a shudder through him. He forced a picture of Dee, brown eyes, darker hair, deeper contours. More stiffening. "Fuck," he growled. He was turning into a freak.

He refocused on the hair. Brenda had entered the house only once— as far as he knew. He looked closer. Straight, light blonde. Could be—he caught sight of his monitor. Where was the logon screen? Embarrassment warmed his cheeks. He had left the computer running. He checked the computer properties and found that the auto shutdown was set for 6 hours. The computer had just shut itself down—just as he had set it up to do.

A strand of Brenda's blonde hair must have hitchhiked on Joey's clothes. As Gerry let the strand fall into the trash the blonde goddess stood within the fringes of his memory, the blue of her eyes stark against a cold, gray world. His breathing hitched. She wore leather like that she'd worn in the hallucination he'd had in the alley. The ringing of a phone intruded. Gerry reached out. The blonde evaporated. Another ring, then a third. He reached for the phone.

"Forstner," he croaked.

"Gerry, it's Dee."

Warmer images of Dee pushed the last threads of the blonde's cold beauty from his mind. He struggled to remember the salient points of the waking dream, but the pleasantness of a much more tangible Dee tangled his mind with thoughts of her beneath him and him inside her.

"Good morning, Dee."

"I'm afraid it isn't," she said. "Judge Jackson and his wife were murdered."

Gerry straightened. "Christ."

The jingle of Hargrave's collar sounded beside the chair. The phone shook in Gerry's hand. Hargrave rested his snout on his knee.

"Valknut?" Gerry demanded.

"None found."

"Forensics?"

"They've already rolled."

"I'm on my way." He slammed the phone down on the receiver.

He stood and Hargrave backed away. Gerry paused. Each successive victim had been at the previous victim's crime scene. Jackson's phone numbers were in Kinnison's phone, but there was no evidence Jackson had been at Kinnison's apartment.

"Fuck me," Gerry muttered.

The Valknut chain was broken.

✦

GERRY BRUSHED PAST Lacy who was photographing Sir Lawrence Alma-Tadema's *A Sculpture Gallery* and squatted beside the judge's body. No Valknut decorated Jackson or his wife's chest and no cut had sliced their necks. *The Valknut chain was broken.* Gerry glanced at the half destroyed desk. The department kept the discovery of the books out of the papers, but the killer had learned of their existence. Had the blonde returned to his house last night?

Gerry looked back at the judge. "Godammit, Judge, why weren't you honest with me?"

Jackson's arm lay twisted behind his back in an unnatural manner. By the pattern of blood and position of the body, he had been held upright as he bled to death, then dropped once his heart finally gave out. Barbara Jackson lay next to the desk. Her neck had been broken. The murders had gotten personal. Finding the books yanked from his grasp less than a day before he'd gotten there had enraged the killer. And he now knew the department—or more accurately, Gerry—had seized the books.

"It's going to eat you alive wondering what I know," Gerry murmured. "And that's how I'll get you."

Gerry pulled the penlight from his front jacket pocket and used it to roll Jackson's head to the right, then shined the light on his neck. Two pin sized dots about an inch apart were located in the same area they had been on Kinnison's neck. A jolt of adrenaline jump-started Gerry's heart. This one hadn't taken forensics to locate. The bite marks were newer.

He straightened and motioned to Kendall. "Get some photos of this."

Lacy strode over. She snapped pictures at several angles before starting on Jackson's library shelves. Gerry's cell phone rang. He pulled it from his pocket and was smart enough this time to check the number. Quin's name flashed on the display.

Gerry flipped open the phone. "Hey, kid."

"Hey," Quin replied. "I got some info about that murder on the Icelandic ship."

"What did you find?"

"Not as much as I wanted. The FBI was called in, and you know how they love to keep their records confidential—even from themselves."

Gerry grunted. The kid had it right. And now that a judge had been murdered, they would be brought in on the Valknut case. He had to get to McMillian, Pentz, and Johnson before the Feds did, if he wanted to get a look at their ancient books.

"I got my hands on the coroner's report," Quin said.

"How'd you manage that?" Gerry asked, before realizing he knew the answer. "Please tell me you didn't go into the Fed's files."

"Okay, I didn't go into the Fed's files."

"Quin."

"Man, this is some weird shit," he said in a serious tone Gerry had never heard him use before. "The guy was drained of all his blood," Quin went on. "The FBI did a thorough check on the body—"

"Let me guess," Gerry cut in. "Two *old* puncture mark scars about two and a half centimeters apart on his neck."

There was a pause on the other end of the line, then, "Do I wanna ask what that means?"

"Depends on how much sleep you want to get tonight."

"Man, you cops got your own brand of weird. How do you live with this shit all day?"

"Don't ask. Anything else?"

"Not a thing. The murder was about as neat as they come. All that blood gone and no way it could have gotten out. No cuts, no holes, like the blood was beamed up to the mother-ship, without the body."

Gerry recalled Bahia Police Chief Decker's words, "Beam me up, Scotty."

"If you want me to dig deeper…" Quin trailed off.

"No," Gerry said emphatically. "That kind of stuff will definitely get the Feds on your ass. You said that was the last thing you wanted."

"Yeah, but I never liked those fuckers."

Gerry laughed, then stopped abruptly and demanded, "You didn't leave them any presents?"

"No," Quin said grudgingly. "Thought about it, but didn't."

"Good," he said. "Cause there aren't any good looking women in prison."

"I know. That's what stopped me. I forwarded a copy of the coroner's report. Let me know how it goes." Quin signed off.

Gerry flipped the phone closed.

"Where's the wife?" Lummus' voice came from the library entrance.

Gerry turned and nodded toward the desk. "There."

Lummus glanced at her body, then stepped into the study. "Anything missing?"

"Mrs. Jackson is still wearing her two-caret ring. The jewelry box on her dresser and the one in her panty drawer both look full. All the paintings are here. The killer was looking for the books. The drawer where he kept them was ripped from the desk."

"Why didn't the security alarm sound?" Lummus asked.

"The alarm wasn't on. It's like he knew the killers, just like Kinnison. The Jacksons were alone. The maid was gone. She took off early last night. Today is her day off."

Lummus nodded. "What about the neighbors?"

"Sheridan and Gonzales are canvassing the neighborhood."

Lummus stepped up beside Gerry and studied the body. "Where's the Valknut?"

"There isn't one."

"Then it's unrelated to the case."

"Not a chance. Take a look at the puncture wounds." Gerry pointed at Jackson's neck. "Plus, the killer knew the books were here."

Gerry thought of Alyssa Hamilton and the Joseph M. Warner Laboratories. Was there a file on Harold P. Jackson? No. Jackson's death wasn't planned, wasn't part of the chain. He—and his wife—got caught in the crossfire.

"Why leave without taking something for their trouble?" Lummus asked.

Gerry gave a single shake of his head. "Who needs trinkets when you're a god who's going to live forever?"

GERRY THREW OPEN his arms as Joey flung himself against him. Hargrave yelped an excited greeting and Gerry hugged Joey tight as he squinted against the soccer field lights, his gaze fixed on Brenda walking away from them alongside a man with Donald Trump hair graying at the temples. Was this her lawyer? From across the field, Gerry could just make out the new bob-cut she'd gotten a few months ago.

She had slimmed down since the divorce, and weighed the one hundred and twenty five pounds she had in college. Perfect for her five foot six inch height. A pang of remorse hit at the memory of how she used to offer herself to him with eager anticipation. Did she press herself against David Weiss' body and coax him to her as she had him?

"Did you see that goal I made, Dad?" Joey said into his chest.

Gerry looked down at his son. Joey knew he had, he'd scanned the crowd for Gerry after kicking the ball thirty feet across the grass and past the goalie into the net. Gerry had been the first one on his feet and they'd managed two seconds of eye contact before a teammate tackled him.

"You bet, pal," he said. "Thirty feet!"

Joey leaned back and beamed up into his face. "No one else made a goal that far."

"No one else," Gerry agreed.

Hargrave wiggled between them and they laughed as Joey released Gerry. They started toward the Impala and Gerry couldn't help glancing back. Brenda had disappeared. She hadn't even bothered to talk to him before or after the game. She simply caught his attention from the bleachers when he'd approached and nodded an acknowledgment that told Gerry she expected him to take Joey for an early dinner after the game as instructed in her voicemail. Her curt nod, then turning her attention back to the game told Gerry she wasn't interested in further chitchat. She had been sitting beside two of the other mothers and the last thing Gerry wanted was a staring match with Brenda's sympathizers.

He shifted his attention back to Joey. The kid had grown what seemed inches since Gerry had moved out. Joey was growing up, and Gerry had to grab every minute he could.

"Ready for the *Pup and Taco?*" he asked.

Hargrave woofed, and they both laughed.

AFTER THE *Pup and Taco*, Gerry dropped Joey at home and met Dee for a late night dinner. Now, on the way home from the restaurant, Gerry wondered how he could get her to stay the night. He had given her a once-over when she sat in the restaurant chair. Not a hint of fat bulged in her jeans, and the thought of those lean legs wrapped around him drove him crazy. All evening, he had purposefully kept his gaze from wandering to her chest—a feat usually accomplished with finesse—but this time, the effort only made him imagine what was beneath her blouse, and that was worse than looking—almost.

"You okay?"

Gerry almost jumped at the sound of her voice. "Yeah. Why?"

"You seem…preoccupied."

That was one way of looking at it.

"A girl could start taking this personally," she said.

"Don't," he blurted, and almost laughed at the irony.

Gerry turned down his street, half glad, half sorry they were almost home. Maybe if they drove around for a while, she would notice his dilemma and offer to help. He passed his place, made a U-turn, then pulled to a stop behind her Alpha Romero. The car really did suit her. He flipped off the headlights, turned off the ignition, then reached for the door handle. A soft hand on his arm stopped him. He faced Dee.

Her face was in shadow, and he prayed his features were as well hidden when his gaze dropped to her breasts. She surprised him with a laugh, jerking his attention back to her face. She slipped an arm around his neck and pulled him to her. Gerry started at the feel of her soft lips against his. Dee paused and tilted her head back to look up at him. From this angle, the streetlight draped across her face and he could see the *you're saying you really don't like this* look. He didn't make a move and a corner of her mouth twitched in what he realized with some resignation was triumph.

"Men are vulnerable," his dad had told him.

How right you are, Dad, he thought as Dee lifted her mouth to his. Gerry didn't need any further prodding. This may have been just a kiss, but it was more than he'd gotten in three years. Before he could decide whether to caress a breast or grab her ass, the arm around his neck tightened and she pulled herself over the armrest and onto his lap. The ass, Gerry decided, and slipped his hands beneath her rear and pulled her close. He tensed as their bodies made contact. Then she kissed him.

Gerry kissed her, tentatively, at first—much to his chagrin. He ran his tongue along her bottom lip and she opened up. Three seconds later, she pulled back. They stared at each other, his heart racing, and him wondering about the slight smile on her face. A few seconds, and his system was already in overdrive. He liked the feeling.

Office romances were a bad deal. No romances were worse. What the hell. He pulled her close and kissed her, this time, sliding a hand up to her breast. She arched just enough to say she liked it and Gerry felt like a horny sixteen year old who wouldn't last more than three minutes.

Football he told himself. Think of football, but all he could see was what Dee's breasts would look like and how her hard nipples would feel between his lips. She gave him another, quick, but hard kiss, then pulled back and hoisted herself back into the passenger seat. Yeah, he wasn't sixteen and neither was she. She opened the car door and he took the hint.

He did a quick rearrangement to the knot in his briefs before getting out, and following her to the Alpha Romero. As she reached for the driver's side door she cast him a sideways glance so sultry his erection ached. She slid into the driver's seat and he closed the door as she started the car.

"I'll call," he said, then cringed mentally at how stupid that sounded.

She gave a low laugh and started the car. Gerry stepped back as she pulled away and watched the lights of her Alpha Romero disappear around the corner when she made the right hand turn. He blew out a long, low whistle, and headed for the house.

Chapter Two

GERRY DIDN'T WAIT for Alyssa Hamilton to ask why he had shown up at Warner Laboratories at 8:30 a.m. without an appointment, and tossed a file folder with the tab heading *Warner Laboratories Valknut victims* on her desk.

She glanced from the files to Gerry. "If you need someone to interpret our research terminology I will—"

"Yes," he cut in, "as a matter of fact, I do need someone to interpret your *research terminology.*" He flipped open the folder to the information Wayne Comerford had found on Darryl Michaels and read, "Case three-three-three-nine. Subject involved in systematic program to create and manipulate personalities for programmed couriers resistant to torture. To date, experiments show the primary personality is not aware of secret information being carried. Experiment number five is successful, as have been the past four experiments. Information has been summoned forth via post-hypnotic command or response to a pre-programmed cue."

She leveled her gaze on him. "What is that?"

"Don't give me that, Ms. Hamilton. This is a copy of the real research file on Darryl Michaels. The files you gave me are worthless."

"I turned over every record we have. I don't know where you got that."

Gerry straightened. "If you recall, you were ordered by Judge Lopez to hand over all files on the four Valknut victims. I want the real files."

She tore a blank sheet of paper from a note pad, grabbed the pen from the executive pen holder in front of her, and began writing. "Talk to our lawyer." She slid the paper across the desk and looked up at him.

"Force me to get another court order and I'll tear the place apart," he warned.

"His number, Detective."

Gerry snatched the paper from her grasp. "Your earlier cooperation was a fine act, Ms.—" His gaze fell on the paper.

Half an hour, the Dairy Queen at Oak and Bleeker.

Storm out of here.

He jerked his gaze to her face. Her right brow lifted slightly, and he blinked. Was she giving him a cue or telling him to go to hell?

"Have it your way." He whirled toward the door.

✦

GERRY SAT IN the Dairy Queen parking lot. Alyssa Hamilton was three minutes late. She pulled up alongside him in a red Lexus and motioned him into her car.

"This should be good," he told Hargrave. Gerry opened his car door. "Watch the car, Buddy." He and got out, and got into her Lexus.

Once she pulled from the parking lot, she asked, "Where did you get those files?"

"That's what I do, find information."

"You're sure they're authentic?"

"My source didn't make them up, if that's what you mean."

"There's no possibility of a mistake?"

Gerry studied her. "You tell me, what other Warner Laboratories conducted psychic experiments on those four Valknut victims? What's this all about?"

"The files I gave you are authentic research projects my department conducted. They're standard tests we use on all our members." She glanced at him. "Come on, Detective, does any of this government action jive with my profile?"

"Your profile?" he repeated.

She returned her attention to the road. "Don't insult my intelligence any more than you want me to insult yours."

"All right," he replied. "No."

She nodded almost imperceptibly. "I wondered how you traced the victims to us."

"You didn't read my mind?"

She gave a disgusted snort. "It doesn't work that way."

"How does *it* work?"

Alyssa glanced sharply at him, and Gerry realized he had revealed more than he intended.

She slowed to a stop at a light and looked him in the eye. "What's happened?"

"You first," he said.

The light changed to green and she eased the car into a steady forty-five miles per hour speed alongside the other traffic. "I do authentic, PSI research. Our goal is to analyze individuals with PSI abilities in order to understand what causes the phenomenon."

"I take it you don't buy into the *it's part of the soul's journey* routine?" Gerry asked.

"That's a philosophical question. We are looking for the physiology. For example, instead of asking why Mozart was a prodigy, the question would be *what about his brain function made him that prodigy.*"

"So where do these other tests come in?" Gerry asked.

"You have other files similar to the one you showed me?"

"Are you saying you don't know anything about this research?" he demanded.

She hesitated. "I've had suspicions."

"About what? You're not some low-level employee, Ms. Hamilton. You're the director. My guess is you answer to some sort of board of directors and no one else. What about the fact you're supposed to have Extra Sensory Perception?"

"Assuming you believe in PSI, Detective, remember, the people I work with have abilities equal to or greater than mine. There is the possibility they can read my thoughts."

"Is that why you wanted this meeting outside the building?" Gerry asked.

Alyssa laughed. "I said there was a *possibility* they could read my mind. Your mind is an open book. No, I wanted out of the building because, if those files are authentic, then my office is bugged."

Gerry burst out laughing. "I'm disappointed."

She frowned. "Why?"

"Can't *you* read my mind?"

"Are you asking me to read your mind, or daring me to?"

"Is there a difference?"

"A big difference. One is an invitation, the other an invasion of privacy."

"Don't tell me you people have a code of ethics."

Alyssa merged into the right lane, then slowed and made a right hand turn into a Wal-Mart parking lot. She pulled into the first available parking spot, slipped the car into park, and looked at him with narrowed eyes. "Do you abuse the power that comes with your badge?"

Gerry felt his face grow warm.

"Maybe there is some universal plan that makes this add up," she went on in a cold voice, "but, if there is, I don't know it. Now, you don't have to buy into what I am, just as I don't have to buy into your version of justice, but to treat me like I'm a piranha ready to devour every fish stupid enough to wander into my pond is insulting." She gave him a piercing look. "Unless, that is, you think the *he's a cop, of course he took the bribe* should be every civilian's mantra?"

Gerry released a slow breath. "Point taken. Let's start over. What do you know about those files?"

The tension in her face eased. "This is the first hard evidence I've seen. My suspicions are all based on snippets of thoughts I've picked up from members."

"I thought you just said—"

"A psychic doesn't have to be looking for impressions to get them. It's like—haven't you unexpectedly become aware of something you weren't looking for? A lie, a possible crime, something you spotted that a less observant person missed?"

Gerry studied her. "These *snippets of thoughts*, were any of them from the Valknut victims?"

"I did not work directly with the victims. However, when I learned that these members were Valknut victims, I studied their cases."

"Are you saying you gleaned psychic information from the files without knowing the men?"

"Think of it this way," she said. "Despite a psychic's specific abilities, our senses are heightened overall. Touch, pictures, spoken and written words, each carry a specific vibration. Psychics can receive information from any or all senses. In other words, the psychic impression can come from anywhere, anytime. Have you ever had, say, a smell trigger a memory?"

"Of course."

"In some ways, the psychic experience is not much different. Energy embodied in the object triggers a contact point that links to the owner's thoughts, actions, feelings, desires, and more."

"Like taped notes," Gerry murmured.

"Right."

"What did you pick up from the Valknut victims?"

Alyssa paused. "The most memorable was John Kinnison."

Gerry felt as if time had stopped. *John Kinnison.* How had he known that would be the case, and why did the idea trigger a wave of chills? Kinnison's face as it had appeared in the papers the day Jackson acquitted him of the child molestation charges flashed before Gerry. The smugness, the confidence that came with knowing he wasn't in any real danger was apparent in his expression. Kinnison believed—knew—that being Charles Thomas' son would save him. Charles Thomas had appealed to Judge Jackson on his son's behalf before he'd appeared in Jackson's court. Jackson couldn't refuse. It was true. Gerry knew it just as sure as if he'd witnessed the meeting…

Jackson shook his head, his gaze locked on Kinnison. "The prosecution knows your guilty, John."

Kinnison straightened. "You can't kid a kidder."

There was something more in Kinnison's face than the smug look Gerry had seen in the newspaper pictures. It was…the absence of fear. Gerry had dealt with worse bad asses than Kinnison, yet, even the worst of the worst got scared. They usually buried fear behind cruelty, but the fear remained. Not so with John Kinnison.

Kinnison flopped down in the same chair Gerry had sat in during his visit to Jackson's home. "I don't give a fuck about this case," Kinnison said. "I've got better things to do." A predatory expression flickered across his face. He leaned forward and Gerry tensed as Kinnison said, "Don't you think it's time—"

Gerry jarred from the vision and blinked Alyssa into focus. She stared intently at him. He glanced at the clock. 9:20. How long had he been out this time? Five, ten minutes?

"Seven minutes."

Gerry jerked his gaze onto her. "I thought—"

"I saw you look at the clock," she interrupted. "You tell me, was it PSI or common sense that told me why you were looking at the clock? You went quiet seven minutes ago and your eyes were unfocused. You were experiencing a psychic vision, Detective." She lifted a brow. "Call it an impression if the word *vision* bothers you."

"What the hell is all this about?" he demanded.

"You want the truth?"

Gerry started to answer yes, then paused.

Alyssa nodded. "Good. Think long and hard, because once you've got knowledge, you can't unknow it."

"Is this going to go away?" he asked.

She shrugged. "Humans have the remarkable ability to make almost anything go away."

"Yeah," he said, and remembered two years of Swiss cheese memory induced by an endless supply of Scotch. Gerry met her gaze. "I want this motherfucker."

"What *motherfucker* would that be?"

"This has something to do with him, doesn't it, the Valknut killer?"

"It's interesting you would come to that conclusion," she said.

He shot her a recriminating look. Her fucking psychology degree was kicking in again. "What did you discover in those files?"

"Darryl Michaels, Brent Douglas and Frank Vitelli had definite PSI abilities," she said. "Though not extraordinary, as far as PSI abilities go."

Gerry frowned. "I have no idea what that means."

"It's relative. Most people have extra sensory abilities of some sort, but they chalk the incidents up to experience, intuition, lucky guesses, that sort of thing. By our research standards, if a person can guess four of ten Zener cards, that's fairly average PSI. Six or seven out of ten is high."

Wayne Comerford had also described Zener cards as being used to measure PSI. "So these guys fell into the average range?" Gerry asked.

"Essentially. I've known psychics who couldn't hit the correct Zener cards a third of the time, but were highly skilled empaths or clairaudients."

"Clairaudients?" Gerry repeated.

She nodded. "Clairaudients hear voices or sounds that give them information."

"I thought we called that schizophrenia."

"There is a definite difference. Though few medical doctors can make the distinction. In any case, your first three victims were definitely psychic, and by nonpsychic standards, they would be considered special. By psychic standards, while we value all abilities, they weren't particularly powerful."

"But John Kinnison was?"

"I've known more skilled psychics," she replied, "but he was well above average."

"How far above average?"

"John would hit eight out of ten Zener cards."

Gerry whistled. "That sounds damned good."

Alyssa nodded. "It is. Which made me wonder why he didn't make a point of cloaking his thoughts. When I picked up no information from the other files, I wondered if those members weren't involved in the extra testing."

"You didn't get anything from the others? You said Kinnison was the most memorable. I thought that meant you'd gotten information from all the files."

"Of your four victims, he's the only one from whom I gleaned information concerning the extra testing, and that was sketchy. Once I finished studying these four files, I delved into other members' files."

"No invasion of privacy, Ms. Hamilton?"

"This testing may be taking place at Warner P. Laboratories, but who do you think is funding it?"

"You tell me," Gerry said.

"I'm not a government employee, Detective. I don't reel in prospective guinea pigs and I don't do PSI research with drugs."

Oddly, Gerry believed her. "Why do you think you picked up information from Kinnison's files and not the others?" He winced mentally at the realization that he was discussing psychic phenomena as if it were a given.

She shrugged. "My guess is that John Kinnison *did* interest the government, which made him feel...special."

"Sounds as if it would be hard not to feel special," Gerry said.

"It's a double edged sword," Alyssa replied. "Knowing things about other people is a rush, but when the things you learn are horrifying, it's not long before you wish you didn't know."

"But Kinnison liked it?"

"Yes. He had visions of grandeur."

"What kinds of tests were they doing?"

"My impression was they were attempting to enhance his abilities."

"Which were?"

"John was a strong telepath. He also exhibited remote viewing abilities. We hadn't conducted in-depth tests to prove that, but I suspect he would have excelled there, as well."

"What information did you pick up in the other files?"

She paused. "Look, Detective, I don't like what is going on here, but I don't know—"

"I'm investigating a multiple homicide, Ms. Hamilton, and right now you're the only connection between the victims."

She lifted a brow. "Am I a suspect?"

Her unruffled attitude tempted him to haul her to the station for a taste of what it is was like to be a suspect, but he knew that wouldn't bother her either. "You run Joseph M. Warner Laboratories," he said. "If the government is involved, the D. A. will assume you're involved."

"You suspect a government conspiracy?"

Gerry paused. A federal connection would explain the tight-lipped attitude of the FBI. "It's a possibility."

"The government isn't your killer," she replied without hesitation. He gave a short laugh, and she added, "Do you think I'm involved with murder?"

He wasn't going to admit it, but every instinct screamed no. "The D. A. doesn't build cases based on what I believe."

Alyssa snorted. "Of course they do. I'll tell you what, produce evidence that you obtained those extra test files legally, then arrest me for murder."

Gerry didn't plan on doing that—didn't believe she was guilty—but her lack of concern irked him and he wished that for just five minutes he could make her think she was a suspect.

"You're looking for a single individual," she said.

Her statement yanked him from his thoughts.

"Every one of your victims knew him—intimately."

Gerry's brain raced, trying to remember if enough information had filtered to the media to give her this idea. "Someone involved in this other testing?" he demanded.

"I doubt it. He's unlike any other creature you've ever encountered."

A chill zipped up his spine. "*Creature*. What the hell does that mean?"

"Just what it sounds like."

"It *sounds* like he's from another world."

Her eyes clouded. "By our perceptions, he is."

Gerry grabbed her arm. "I don't like games."

Her expression cleared. "I don't make the rules."

"If you know something—"

"I can give you pieces of the puzzle, not the answer."

He released her. "This who-do-voodoo bullshit is a waste of time."

"Is it?" she asked. "Just what were you seeing a few minutes ago?"

"I don't know—that is, I don't know what it's supposed to mean."

She laughed. "Welcome to my world."

Gerry studied her. "What are you *picking up*?"

"I sense darkness."

"That's not hard to come up with. The guy is evil incarnate, ruthless."

Alyssa nodded. "Yes. But he has a plan, something he's trying to accomplish. There's a sense of timelessness about him."

Gerry thought of the ancient priests and how the Valknut killer was trying to resurrect the past.

"He is filled with rage," she went on. "But these victims didn't have what he wanted. He's searching for something—someone—else." Alyssa reached out and touched Gerry's face before he could dodge.

He froze as her gaze locked with his, then became unfocused.

A moment of uneasy silence passed before she said, "He wants—needs—you to retrieve the other." Her eyes snapped back into focus. "You have something he wants very badly. He won't stop until he gets it."

"All he's going to get is an eight by ten with bars," Gerry replied curtly.

"Then you will have to kill him." Gerry wanted to snap back that justice wasn't dispensed that way, this wasn't the Wild West, but she added. "You don't know what he's after."

Gerry laughed. "Are you always right, Miss Hamilton?"

She lifted a brow.

Damn her. Even that remark hadn't pissed her off.

"No one is always right, Detective. But I'm right this time."

"No. You're not. I know exactly what he wants. I've got it, he doesn't, and that's how I'll get him." Gerry felt an unreasonable frustration well up inside. "Do you have anything concrete?"

"What do you consider concrete?"

He grasped the door handle and opened the door. "The only connection between the victims is you. That's too big to be coincidence." God, how he hated fucking coincidences. "I won't ignore it, and neither will the D. A." He thought about mentioning the Feds, but felt like he was playing a game of my dick is bigger than yours. He leaned toward her. "I need the truth, Alyssa. If I have to, I'll become Joseph M. Warner's worst nightmare."

"No need to walk," she said as he stepped from the car. "I can drop you back at your car."

He gave a short laugh. She was a cool cookie. "The walk will do me good."

Gerry glanced at the dashboard clock. Ten-thirty a.m. He shut the door and headed east on Bleeker. Damn. He should have let her drive him back to the car. A mile walk would waste twenty minutes.

Gerry halted. Alyssa had said *he.* "Every one of your victims knew *him*—intimately." Did that mean the blonde wasn't the killer? Maybe, but just how intimately did she know him?

Chapter Three

GERRY GLANCED AT the dashboard clock as he turned into the modest Ft. Lauderdale development. Three-thirty. He had to be at Joey's soccer game by 6:30. He considered skipping the match, then remembered the excited note in Joey's voice when he'd left the voicemail—memory of Kinnison's eight year old victim followed.

"Fuck it," Gerry muttered, and Hargrave moaned agreement. He'd get to McMillian and Pentz as soon as he could.

He tried going directly from Warner to Johnson's place, but Herrero had called and said he wanted a preliminary report on Jackson's murder before lunch to hand over to the FBI. Dammit, once the Feds got their hands on the ancient books they would disappear into the federal twilight zone.

Gerry slowed for the next two street signs, then turned down Locust Street where William Johnson's son, lived. Sam Pentz had taken his father's place in the inner circle. Gerry still hadn't located Sam and was anxious as hell to get a handle on what the second generation had going. William Johnson, Jr. was going to fill him in.

William had driven from Ft. Lauderdale to Miami to meet with his father's old army buddies. Was he interested in the immortality the Nazi's had been searching for? Maybe this second generation realized the value of the Asatru books and simply intended to sell them. Selling stolen artifacts was a paltry crime within the Valknut family. Gerry gave a morbid laugh. This case had it all.

Fifth house down Locust was William's.

"Keep an eye on things," Gerry told Hargrave as he slipped the car into park and cut the engine.

Slamming the car door shut, he adjusted the shoulder holster beneath his sports jacket as he headed up the curved walkway to the porch. He took the two steps onto the slab concrete front stoop in one step and reached into his breast pocket for his ID as he rang the bell.

A man a little under six feet tall and in his early fifties opened the door. Gerry bit back a laugh at sight of the bushy mustache that curled at the ends near each ear. A cartoon Snidely Whiplash came to mind and he showed his badge in an effort to get the guy's eyes off his face long enough to force his mouth into submission.

"I'm Detective Forstner," Gerry said. "I'm looking for William Johnson."

"I'm William Johnson."

"Your father was the William M. Johnson who served in the Army with Harold Jackson?"

William's expression saddened. "You're here about Skip's murder."

"Yes," Gerry replied. "I'm hoping you could answer a few questions."

Johnson stepped back. "Sure. He and my father were friends."

He showed Gerry through an archway on the left. A five-piece sectional sofa sat to the right and a wing chair was placed on the opposite wall. Dead center on the wall between them a modest fireplace burned a gas log. William nodded to the sofa.

Gerry sat down, and said as Johnson lowered himself into the chair, "Your father passed away about five years ago?"

"Yes."

"What do you know about your father's Army stint in May of nineteen forty-eight?"

Gerry thought he caught a flicker of surprise in Johnson's eyes, then wasn't sure when he answered in a calm voice, "You're talking post-war. He finished his tour in the Houston Army base. Nothing eventful, as far as I recall."

"I'm talking about Iceland." Gerry asked.

"Iceland—that's right, he had a short tour there. I think it lasted two, maybe three months. I'd forgotten about that."

Gerry pulled out his pocket notebook and found the page with dates. "More like six months, March 8th to July 20th. That's where he met Judge Jackson. Seems hard to forget."

Johnson shrugged. "Dad and Skip served together. I never thought about it. Dad didn't talk much about his post-war duty. It was what he did for our country that mattered."

"You never heard him and his cronies discuss Iceland when you met with them at the VFW?"

Johnson stiffened. "The VFW—Hey! What is this?"

"I know about the stolen artifacts. Judge Jackson turned his books over to me the night before he was murdered."

Johnson's eyes widened. "I had nothing to do with that. It was my father."

"What did your father say happened in Iceland?"

Johnson hesitated. "An ancient temple and Nazi encampment. The temple was used as an underground base for Nazi U-boats and a laboratory for human experiments, women, primarily. The Nazis believed the Asatru priests had the secret to immense physical prowess and immortality, but the secret was with the women."

"The ancient goddess," Gerry murmured. "Do you have your father's book?"

"No. Glen inherited it. The last surviving member gets the whole collection." Johnson shivered. "It's crazy, but Dad believed in immortality. He was devastated when he realized he was going to die."

"Why do you and Glen's son meet with the others at the VFW?" Gerry shot back.

Johnson's eyes widened.

"Where did you stash your copy?" Gerry demanded.

Johnson's mouth clamped shut for a second. "I didn't—"

Jr. was way too nervous for someone who didn't know anything. "Come on, William, you weren't the least bit worried the others would cut you out? The books were quite old. They're worth a fortune. That makes their theft a felony. You have a copy in case there's something to this immortality theory."

"What the hell—"

"When did the judge tell you where his books are hidden?"

Johnson pushed to his feet.

"My guess is last Monday night at the VFW," Gerry added.

"Sam was the one asking about the books," Johnson said in a rush.

"Jackson was murdered for something he no longer had in his possession." Gerry rose as he reached inside his pullover sweater to his shirt pocket and pulled out a photo of Jackson's body. He shoved it into Johnson's hand. "The killer won't stop with him."

"I don't have my father's book," Johnson insisted without looking at the photo.

"The killer might know Glen Pentz has your father's original, but this guy isn't the kind to leave any stone unturned. You were at the VFW Monday night when the original team met. You're part of the inner circle, and he'll wonder why." Gerry nodded toward the picture. "Take a look at what happens when someone crosses him."

Johnson flicked a glance at the picture. The color drained from his face. "I have a copy in a safe deposit box."

"Did your father ever mention anyone interested in the books?"

Johnson handed the photo back in with a shaky motion. "No. What am I going to do? I've got a wife and two teenage kids."

Gerry slid the picture back into his pocket. "I need a formal statement. I can have a unit make some extra rounds, but I'd suggest getting out of town for a few days. Inform the officer who takes the statement where you'll be. The main thing is getting me that book. We'll make it public knowledge we've got the only copy and hope the killer buys it."

Johnson went a lighter shade of pale. "It's the truth."

"That's the problem," Gerry said. "Once you start playing the game, no one thinks you want out. I'll have a team outside your door within half an hour and someone will be here within an hour to take your statement. Get packed."

"How long until you will have the killer in custody?"

"I don't know. If you can remember anything, call. I need those copies ASAP."

"The bank doesn't open until Monday morning."

Gerry opened his notebook. "Give me your cell number and bank name and address."

Johnson rattled off the information.

"Keep your phone close," Gerry said as he flipped the notebook closed, then slipped a business card from within the notebook pages and handed it to him. "If you need anything, give me a call."

Johnson led the way to the front door. Gerry turned to him. "One more thing, how come you arrived at the Almeria Avenue VFW before Jackson last Monday night?"

"I was already there with Sam. He wanted to talk about the books."

"You two boys vets?"

"I did three tours in Nam. Sam never served. I signed him in as a guest."

"What did Sam want?"

"To talk about how we second generation members could get our hands on the books. Sam was interested in money. I was shocked when Skip and Jack showed up. That's when I found out about the break-in at Skip's place."

Gerry nodded. Linnette Howsten: The dead end. His screw up was working to his advantage. "So, you boys didn't have a chance to make any plans?" he asked.

Johnson's mouth thinned. "Look, I'll admit I thought about the money, raising kids is expensive, and I didn't see it was hurting anyone, but Dad died so unhappy..." He shook his head. "I watched him waste away, and the whole time he went on about the secret to eternal life. I loved my father, but I didn't want to end up like him."

"Why bother showing up at the VFW the other night, then?" Gerry asked.

"Like I said, the money's tempting, and somehow, deep down, I still wonder..." He shrugged.

"Curiosity is going to get you in a lot of trouble."

Johnson shook his head. "Yes, and recently, Sam has turned into a true believer."

"How does Sam know so much?"

"He doesn't. But that's Sam, he likes to talk."

Gerry nodded. "We'll see how much Sam likes to talk when I get a hold of him."

✦

GERRY ROSE EARLY Saturday morning, showered, and pulled up to 2457 Sparrow Lane at eight-thirty. He wanted to get there before McMillian had a chance to leave. He opened the car door and Hargrave started to slip past him.

"Stay," Gerry commanded. Hargrave gave a protesting yip, but backed away from the door. "No lip," Gerry warned, and closed the door behind him.

He hurried up McMillian's walkway, then rang the doorbell.

McMillian, still in a bathrobe, answered a moment later. "The FBI was here yesterday," he said tight lipped. "I gave them my books. You can go bother someone else now."

Damn. He'd had a feeling that had been the case when he drove by last night after Joey's soccer game and found McMillian gone. "You don't sound too upset," Gerry said.

"Why should I be? The intrigue was ridiculous and the back-biting grew tedious."

"All that talk of wealth and immortality didn't tempt you just a little?"

"We were young, of course I was tempted. But the whole thing turned into a nightmare. You know what we found in that hellhole in Iceland? Women—those monsters were experimenting on women. Shelf after shelf of jars filled with body parts in formaldehyde, especially heads, breasts, and genitals. Cadavers chained to walls, others in steel cages. It looked like they had been left there to rot when the Nazis cleared out." He grimaced. "Three years after the war ended, and the stench was still sickening."

"Killed for the Nazi cause," Gerry said.

"Those were the lucky ones," McMillian said. "The unlucky ones had the tops of their skulls sawed off. Others died clawing at their bars. I still have nightmares."

"Why'd you keep the book?" Gerry asked, forcing back the image of the poor souls who went mad trying to get out of those cages.

"I threw it in the bottom of a chest with the rest of the war memorabilia and didn't think about it until Glen told us he'd translated a small portion of his book."

"When was that?"

"About 15 years ago. Glen said the priests who wrote the books claimed to know the secret of immortality, super senses, physical strength, that sort of thing. We knew the Nazi's were trying to breed a super race..." He shook his head.

"You believe that?"

"The experiments, yes. The possibility of a super race?" McMillian gave him a contemptuous look. "I'm no Nazi, Detective."

"Your book contained no secrets?"

"It was a simple prayer book like Marshall's. What secrets could it possibly hold?"

"What about the other books?" Gerry asked.

"Charlie had some kind of registry like Harold's. Glen had an alchemy book. He was very secretive about it. William's book was filled with incantations and rituals. Theirs were supposed to be the important books. Harold and Charles' book supposedly proved that those women lived unusually long lives." The last was added with disbelief.

"You don't believe that?" Gerry asked.

"I don't really care anymore. Ten years ago, I wanted to live forever. Now...I'm just glad to be rid of that book. It's been nothing but bad luck."

Judge Jackson would agree, Gerry thought with a pang. He'd been right, the judge hadn't gotten out of this one.

"What was with the back-biting?" Gerry asked.

"Marshal's and my books were deemed worthless. That made our participation unnecessary and, after a while, unwanted. I think the only reason we remained in the loop was to keep us quiet."

"With all that dissention why stay with the group?"

"They are good men—good men who grew old and afraid." McMillian said.

"What books passed to you when other members died?"

"I got Marshal's book."

"What happened to the books of other members who died?" Gerry asked.

"Charles died ten years ago. His book went to Harold. I assume you have those two books. William's book went to Glen."

"When you men met last Monday, did the judge say where he kept his books?"

"Yes." McMillian paused. "I wish the killer had found them. Maybe..."

Yeah, Gerry agreed mentally, maybe. "Pentz's son was at your last meeting,"

"Sam attends all the meetings. He drove Glen for years."

"You told the FBI all this?"

"No. They were only interested in my alibi and the books."

"Did you make a photocopy of your books?" Gerry asked.

"No, and I'm glad I didn't."

Gerry turned to leave. "Thanks for your cooperation."

"Detective."

Gerry paused.

"Do you think the killer will come for me?"

Gerry hesitated. "He's a nasty son-of-a-bitch."

McMillian's mouth tightened.

"We'll make sure the evening edition of the newspaper reports your books are in custody," Gerry said. "I'll talk to the South Beach PD about an extra patrol."

McMillian nodded a wordless thanks and closed the door.

Back in his car, Gerry tried Johnson's number. No answer. Gerry looked at Hargrave. "We scared the piss out of the guy. Think we overplayed our hand?"

Hargrave sneezed.

Gerry started the car. "My thoughts exactly. I say we take a closer look at this genealogy before the Feds put a serious crimp in our style."

Chapter Four

GERRY JERKED AWAKE. He glanced around, the shapes surrounding him vague in the nearby shadows. Slats of graying dawn light filtered through half-closed blinds. A low woof from the side of the bed snapped his mind awake as if a door had been yanked open. He'd been dreaming, but of what? The Asatru priest, *Mótsognir*, in the dungeon. The blonde had been there, too. A dream, but it felt real, more real than life, more alive.

As if looking through the eyes of the Asatru priest, he had watched his assistants remove her robe. Trembling, she stood before him, young, beautiful—and naked. Flowing hair, skin smooth and creamy, breasts full and ripe from weaning her son. Gerry startled at the memory of making love to her. His body tensed, but not with desire. Love, what he'd done to her hadn't been motivated by love. He had he savored her terror. Why?

When he reached out to grasp her tender arm, his gaze had snagged on the hideous ring on his own middle finger. Then the shriek had woken him up. Gerry gave himself a mental shake. He'd immersed himself in this case, the history, the books, and the whole thing had come crashing down on him in a fucking dream. It was a dream. Not him.

He swept his gaze past Hargrave to the familiar sight of his dresser, the corner chair, and finally the clock beside his bed. The glowing red numbers read five forty-two. Like every other red blooded average American, he was home in bed on a Sunday morning.

Despite the assurance, his stomach turned at the role he'd played in the dream. Why dream about being the Asatru priest? He couldn't commit such atrocities even in a dream. In the dream, he hadn't given a single thought to the blonde's feelings, or her son. His only thought had been to make her his goddess—his for all time. How could he be so...depraved?

His mind stretched as if reaching into the cosmos in search of an answer, but he couldn't fathom why or how he might accomplish such a feat. He'd been studying the books last night. What had he read that promoted this dream? Then it hit—memory of finding the name Thomas in the lineage—and Uma Yohanson—washed over him with a chill that radiated from the bone out. The Asatru lineage—the lineage ended with—Fuck, no wonder he'd had that dream.

Gerry yanked his gaze back to the clock. Five forty-five. He needed to call Mom. She was an early riser, but not this early. He had time for a shower and another look at the genealogy before she got up.

✦

GERRY GLANCED AT the single sheet of paper on his desk to his right, his gaze automatically falling upon the name Uma Yohanson located near the end of the single Asatru genealogy branch he'd painstakingly copied. Guilt stabbed at him. He should inform the FBI of this development. He gave a mirthless laugh at the word *development. Involvement* was closer to the truth. He now knew what Alyssa had been talking about, what the Valknut killer wanted. How the guy had learned the truth, remained a mystery, but he knew—and now Gerry knew.

Dammit, he'd never withheld evidence before, but there was a first time for everything. Gerry shoved aside the feeling that Brenda was right, that cops were nothing but power hungry thugs. She had accused him of waiting for the right moment to cash in on the power his position in law enforcement afforded him. He'd countered with the claim that she'd mistaken him for a lawyer. They were far better at twisting the law into their brand of justice than cops, and Brenda liked the quiet, not to mention, more lucrative way, they went about it. If he had gone into law as planned, she'd be coaching him on how to make his next move, like running for the senate.

He fixed his gaze on the clock at the bottom corner of the computer. Hargrave trotted into the room and plopped his nose on Gerry's leg. Gerry absently scratched his ears as he waited the two minutes for it the click over to seven o'clock, then picked up the phone and dialed his mother's number.

Seconds pounded away as the other end rang and finally connected. "Hello," she said.

"Hi, Ma."

"Gerry," she said, delight in her voice, then, "What's wrong?"

"Nothing's wrong. I just have a question. Didn't Manna talk about an aunt named Uma?" He winced in embarrassment at calling his maternal great grandmother by the nickname he used as a kid.

"Not an aunt," his mother replied. "Her great, great, *great* grandmother was Uma."

"Uma was from Holland," he blurted.

"That's right."

"And she was adopted. Right?"

His mother paused. "Yes, she was. Why?"

"By who?"

"Goodness," his mother laughed, "that goes back…has to be over a hundred years. I would have to look at the records. The only reason I recall her off hand is because she was adopted."

"Do you know how she was orphaned?"

"I only know she was left on the orphanage door step with her name and birth-date pinned to the blanket. Her mother was probably an unwed mother."

"No trace of her parents," he murmured, and looked for the umpteenth time at the name above Uma's: Stephana, and her mother was Liesje, and her mother—

"Gerry, what's wrong?"

There was that old 'mom' authority. He couldn't prevent a smile. She was still a force to be reckoned with. "If what I think is correct, I promise to explain. I need everything you have on Uma and her parents right away."

"The records are in a cedar trunk in the attic. I can be over within the hour."

Her brisk, determined tone made him feel like a kid again. She was something. "Thanks, Ma. I'll see you when you get here."

Gerry ended the call. All right. That took care of number two on his list. Now he was going to find out what the sick fuck looking for these books knew that he didn't.

+

GERRY LEANED CLOSER to the computer monitor and reread the sentence displayed there: *Under the guidance of Gothi Sverkir, a divergent sect of Forn Sior rose to power in Iceland in the mid-tenth century.*

He exhaled a breath. The sentence was the opening line in the document from the Arni Magnusson Institute in Iceland, and was the first document he'd read that had been translated directly from Icelandic, instead of Latin, as had been the others he'd read. Which meant he was now reading a more exact translation, instead of third hand English interpretations.

After calling Mom, he'd called Janice. It had been twelve noon in Iceland, and Janice contacted Iris Hjortur at the National and University Library of Iceland. Iris got to work researching documents on Asatru history and, an hour later, forwarded her findings to him and Janice. Mom came and went, and in the last four hours, the three of them poured over documents via phone and email before Janice found this one buried in one of the un-researched manuscripts catalogued as folklore.

"Goe-th-ee," Gerry repeated, sounding out the word as phonetically respelled.

He flipped back to the dictionary Iris had included, and read: *Gothi priests' magical powers come straight from the Norse gods. All Viking wizards are gothi, but not all gothi have the ability to cast spells. They can all open a vey, however. Since their gift comes straight from the gods, they need little training to use the magic powers, only instruction in the correct rituals, which they get from books.*

"Got it, Gerry murmured.

Johnson said his book was some sort of ritual book. Were the books mentioned in this document the ones the judge and his men had taken from Iceland? More importantly, how possible was it the killer thought they were the same? Gerry went back to reading.

> *The gothi grow in power through practice and achieving the Viking ideal, not study. Since the Viking ideal is struggle and war, gothi tend to be capable warriors as well as spell casters. Gifted gothi spend a lot of time away from mainstream society, casting runes and communing with the gods.*

A bona fide prophet who spoke with the gods. Reyna had been right on. Gerry scanned a couple paragraphs back. "Vey," he repeated, upon finding the word. "That's a new one." He flipped in the dictionary to *Vey*

Opening.

Gothi can only use magic while standing inside a vey. A vey is a mystical connection to Valhalla through which the gods send their power. Veys are a maximum of 10 yards square, and a minimum of half that size. Opening a vey is a ritual during which the gothi circles the area to be opened, chanting Norse deity names. Anyone within the vey as it opens can enter or leave at will, but the gothi who created the vey can deny anyone access. A vey is fixed in place, and ceases to exist if the creator moves outside its boundaries. It also ceases at dawn and dusk—whichever is sooner. A vey takes 10 minutes, plus 1 minute per level to open.

Gerry flipped back to the beginning of the document.

Under the guidance of Gothi Sverkira, a divergent sect of Forn Sior rose to power in mid-ninth century Iceland. Legend tells of how chieftains who opposed these gothi died strange deaths at the hands of the mythical warrior princess Freyja. Herself a Gythia, Freyja was commanded by the gothi and was characterized as a combination of the angel of death and a night stalker. This is not wholly out of character for, as we know, Freyja is sometimes identified as the goddess of battle and death, and receives half of those slain in battle, with the right of first choice as hers.

Our blonde, blue-eyed warrior priestess is immortalized by this sect as follows:

When sunlight fails and darkness reigns, Freyja rises from her sleep.

The gates of hell swing open wide as the Gythia after-goer ascends upward.

She walks the earth in search of mortal men her master has judged wanting.

Her kiss of death is beyond sweet, but the last her victim tastes.

And when the sun creeps over the hills, she sleeps, justice done.

Gerry reread the third line. After-goer? He googled the words. Five minutes later, he stared at the page on his screen.

Aptrgangr, after-goers or walkers after death, also known as Drauger, an animated corpse that comes forth from its grave mound or shows restlessness on the way to the burial place. Whichever name used, the undead of Scandinavia was a physical body, the actual corpse of the deceased. The creature has extreme strength. They possess magical powers, have knowledge of the future, can control the weather, shape-shifting capabilities and can move magically through the earth as though swimming through the stone.

Gerry swiveled in his chair, rose, and hurried to the kitchen where the Asatru genealogical tree lay across the table. The last column, communion, consecration. These women were initiated into the priest-hood and consecrated as high priestesses with some sort of *blood ritual*. Gerry stared.

The mother-fucking angel of death goddess was a vampire.

He practically ran back to the computer and dropped into his chair as he found where he'd left off.

This Gythia is also reported as aiding the faithful in battle. These faithful, of course, were none other than those leaders who the gothi supported.

"Big fucking surprise," Gerry muttered before reading on.

Another such legend goes:
> *Freya appears in the battle's last hour, clad in heavy mail.*
> *She lifts her head to heaven and cries out to her creator Mótsognir.*
> *When her eye falls upon the enemy, that alone can kill.*
> *But those worthy of her aid cannot fail.*

A rushing sound filled Gerry's ears and a current of energy made a hit and run pass through his brain. Shivers raced across his body. Memory of the blonde in the dream when she'd ridden her horse and cast her gaze upon him, leaped up so abruptly in his mind's eye, he jerked back as if someone had stepped up to him nose to nose.

"Fuck no," he cursed, and forced the text into focus.

To date, these two poems are the only ones in existence that reference these legendary female warriors.

Only two poems. He wanted—needed more. Who was this blonde

woman? How had she found her way into his dreams? He froze, the weight of what he'd just thought hit. These poems portrayed a legend far beyond anything humanly possible. The poems were characteristic of legends, which described superhuman beings and events. Legends grew out of proportion all the time, confusing fiction with fact. Legends surrounding the Amazon women were a perfect example. Yet he felt— was acting—as if the legend of Freyja was based upon fact.

Gerry leaned back and took a deep breath. Somewhere along the way, he had read something, seen something that clued him into the possibility of this legend, and had then rolled it into a single individual, a woman with blonde hair, who appeared in the last hour to aid those in need. His mind had conjured up an avenging angel who'd come to his rescue. Only, where was the fucking wound? He took another breath and continued reading.

The high priest of the Forn Sior wielded immense power. They advised, chastised, encouraged, and prophesied doom for those Icelandic leaders who ignored their advice.

In the late tenth century, under the command of Olaf Trygvesson, Gothi Hrafn openly embraced Christianity while privately denouncing the new religion as treason. Hrafn died twenty years later and was succeeded by Gothi Ulfr. Ulfr openly condemned Christianity and branded Olaf a traitor. Fortunately for Ulfr, Olaf had his own political problems and couldn't bother with a minor disturbance in the outlying country of Iceland.

Ulfr approached Rögnvaldr, a powerful chieftain, and made a proposition: Heed my advice and I'll add to your lands within fifty miles of your borders. Rögnvaldr was young and ambitious.

Ulfr proved himself a great strategist and guided Rögnvaldr into greater power. However, five years later, Olaf sent a force that crushed Rögnvaldr. Gothi Ulfr went into hiding. Not until eight hundred years later do we hear of a church in Iceland that picks up the legend of another Asatru sect resembling the divergent Forn Sior. A firsthand account of this event dated seventeen eighty-nine, is signed Brother Matthew, and reads:

The devil himself has come in the guise of one of our holy brethren. However, in contrast to our Lord's sacrificed blood given for our sins, this evil one takes his victims' blood as his own.

When word reached us that a devil preyed upon the people, we believed it to be peasant superstition. Despite our efforts, we have never quite stifled their pagan practices. At last, reports of strange deaths induced our Bishop to investigate. My brother and I set out with a small company of the King's soldiers.

We arrived in the heat of the day, for even the soldiers heard of the night evils, and feared them. Swords brandished, we burst into the church. Despite the unearthly silence that met us, the lavish trappings filled the men with greed and many began gathering valuables. My brother and I, along with the captain and four men, began a search.

We discovered a tunnel leading from a room behind the altar. We thought the room below was deserted until reaching a small room where we found four robe-clad women, arms crossed over their breasts as if in final rest, lying in a row on alabaster slabs. I am a dedicated priest, but I cannot deny the beauty of these young maidens. The bloom of youth had yet to fade from their cheeks. Each had hair as yellow as the sun and their bodies had not a single blemish that our torches could illuminate.

Still, my blood ran cold at sight of their ethereal beauty and I began reciting a prayer for protection. A murmur of admiration rippled through the men and I realized the need for quick action if the maidens were to be spared the soldiers' lust. I hurried to the first and laid a hand on her hand. Cold flesh met my warm touch. I jerked back and looked at my brother. He, too, had touched another of the maidens and stared at her in shock. My horror was complete. We were too late. They were dead.

One of the men pushed past me, but when he touched the dead girl, backed from the room, forming the sign of the cross. As my brother and I followed, I caught sight of writing on the end of one of the slabs and paused to lower my torch and read the writing. The name Kelsey was written above another name I have yet to understand: Mótsognir. Hope surged within me. If I had the maidens' names, I could pray for their souls. I raced to the other three slabs, committing their names to memory: Norna, Linnea, and Valda.

By the time my brother and I reached the sanctuary a fire blazed at the altar. My brother screamed and pointed at the Christ hanging over the altar. He raced forward, but I caught him and dragged him from the accursed place.

It was late in the evening before the building burned to the ground and we set out for home. Praise God. We destroyed the false temple and prayed for the souls of those lost.

I write this account now, twenty years after that horrible day, because whisperings have reached us of evils that once again take place in the night.

Gerry carefully opened his desk drawer, pulled Frank Vitelli's file and read until he found what he was looking for.

Flames everywhere! I can't see them, but I can feel them, sense them. I am afraid, not of the fire, but because I can't move. Why? I'm bound— no, it's more like I'm paralyzed, drugged maybe. Yeah, it feels like my mind is muddled, my body lethargic. I must be drugged.

"Darkness—no, wait, a lit room. The room is old somehow, not in this time, and is small. A candle on the wall near the door is the light. I'm lying on a small bed and there's a man. He saved me from the fire. He wants to know what I was doing there—was I a sacrifice? I was lying on some sort of altar. I wasn't alone. Three other woman lay on slabs near me. Everyone thought we were dead and left us there to die when they burned the temple. A temple, we were in a temple.

"Motherfucker," Gerry breathed. Had Frank Vitelli given an account of that temple burning from the perspective of one of the...the what, high-fucking-priestesses?

Chapter Five

SEVEN-THIRTY THE FOLLOWING morning, Gerry dialed Johnson's cell number for the third time. "Come on," he said. "Pick up."

Ring number four trilled in Gerry's ear. Johnson hadn't answered his cell phone all weekend. If he gave his copy of the book to the FBI, Gerry would never know what kinds of incantations were contained there. He started to hang up when Johnson's deep voice came on the line.

"Hello.

"William, this is Detective Forstner."

"Yeah," Johnson said with a swagger in his voice that told Gerry what was coming. "The FBI was here, said I didn't have to worry. They said there'd be nothing in my father's book that could put me in danger."

Gerry silently cursed, then demanded in a cold voice "What did they want?"

Johnson hesitated. "They wanted to know when I last saw Skip, and where I was the night of the murder."

"Are they coming back for the copies, William?"

A pause, then, "No. I was about to destroy them."

"I suggest you be ready to hit that bank when I get there—half an hour." Gerry slammed the phone back onto the receiver. Damn, he was going to miss the department morning meeting. If he recalled, the Feds were supposed to be there.

✦

GERRY DIDN'T BREATHE easy until he and Johnson stood at Gerry's car after leaving the bank, Gerry inspecting the copied book. Old Norse filled the modern, bright white copy paper. This was no genealogy. He would get on the horn with Janice and ask her to get Iris to make this a priority.

He rolled the copies into a baton and pointed at Johnson. "You still sure last week at the VFW was the last time you saw Jackson and the others?"

Johnson blinked. "Hey! What is this?"

"Who was at that meeting?" Gerry demanded.

Johnson's mouth thinned, but, like the good boy he was, he answered, "Skip, Sam, and Jack."

"Who runs the group?"

"Skip. But with him gone, that idiot Sam will be able to do anything he wants."

"What do you mean?"

"Sam is nothing like his father. Glen is a good guy. Smart, knows—well, knew—his stuff. Sam is a wannabe."

"Sounds like this wannabe is going to get everyone killed," Gerry said.

Johnson shook his head. "Skip was always the squad leader, but Sam acted like he was just letting him go through the motions. Sam's always been an ass. He's smart, but that's the problem. He lets everyone know he's smarter than they are and is tolerating the rest of us." He paused, "Any leads on Skip's murder?"

"Nothing concrete."

Johnson shook his head. "Damn books."

Gerry thought of Uma Yohanson' name on the Asatru lineage and had to agree.

"If you think of anything else—" he began.

"I won't. I'm through with this crap," Johnson whirled and strode toward his car.

Gerry stared at his retreating back. Had to love how people lived up to their civic duty.

✦

THROUGH THE OPEN blinds in Chief Herrero's office, Gerry caught sight of two men sitting opposite his desk. The standard issue blue suits and the get-as-close-to-the-ears-without-drawing-blood haircuts screamed federal agents. He glanced back at Hargrave dutifully lying beside his desk, his long snout resting on his paws. Gerry considered bringing the dog into the Chief's office, but knew Herrero wouldn't appreciate the intimidation tactic.

Gerry stepped into the office. "John." He nodded to the chief.

He flicked a glance at the Valknut files sitting on the desk. Hell, he should have brought Hargrave. The lecture afterwards would have been worth seeing the two federal agents jump when Hargrave growled at them.

"Gerry," Herrero said, "these are Agents Morris and Howell."

They didn't bother rising or offering their hands. Gerry stopped in front of the filing cabinets right of the desk and leaned against the nearest cabinet.

Morris reached for the top file. "We've read through your files," he said in a baritone voice that reminded him of the gothi's voice in the dungeon, "and we have a couple problems with your analysis. For example," he opened the file, "what is the connection with Valknut murders and the murder on the," he glanced at the document, then said, "Eimskip."

"Same signature, similar MO. The Valknut is a unique symbol."

Morris looked at him. "You don't think it's possible the murderer read the news report about the Eimskip murder and liked the symbol?"

"Anything's possible."

"This religious Asatru angle wasn't the only connection you made with the victims," Morris said. "With the exception of Jackson, all the victims were members of Joseph M. Warner Laboratories."

"That's right."

"Your report doesn't explain the connection between Warner Laboratories and this Norse symbol?"

"I don't know of one, yet."

"Then what makes you think this symbol has any meaning beyond the killer thinking it makes him look intelligent?"

"If you read my report on the Asatru and Valknut history, you saw that—"

"We read the report," Morris interrupted as he flipped through the pages. "As well as the hypothesis on the killer's motivation, but there's nothing to directly tie the murder aboard a merchant vessel that docked in New Jersey with the murders here in Miami." He looked up at Gerry.

"I don't know what the connection is—yet—but there's no mistaking the Valknut," Gerry replied.

The puncture scars were a side-note in his report. They didn't make sense unless the victims had been members of the cult for years. He wished like hell Reyna's contacts would turn up something on just one of the victims as being Asatru members.

"The MO might be slightly different, but the signature is unmistakable," Gerry said. "The Valknut killer sees himself as some sort of avenging angel, a god who holds the power of life and death. Laurence Sander killed children. Who better to die than a baby killer?" He paused. "How many murderers do you know that can drain a body of all its blood?"

"Apparently," Johnson broke in, "quite a few. The case you worked five years ago had a similar MO."

Gerry shifted his attention to Johnson. Just as his voice implied, his eyes said Gerry hadn't caught the killer the first time. Yeah, Gerry thought, and wondered if they knew anything about the one hundred and fifty murders committed in twelve states over the last seventy-five years where blood had been drained from the body, as had been in the *Keepers of the Secret* murders.

"Similar, yes," he replied. "But, only in that the blood was drained from the victim's body. There may be a connection, but we haven't found one. If you take a look at—"

"I'm not about to take advice from a two bit cop who couldn't catch a killer the first time," Johnson snapped.

Gerry regarded him. "They're waiting, Johnson. Anytime you think you're ready."

Johnson blinked in confusion.

"The *Keepers of the Secret*," Gerry offered in a soft voice. "We heard they lived in the Keys." He paused, his gaze locked with the agent's. "I was there."

Johnson started to push to his feet. "You mother fu—"

"I don't see your translations here," Morris said.

Everyone stopped and looked at him.

"What?" Gerry asked.

Johnson lowered himself back into his chair as Morris lifted a page from the file he held, and Gerry recognized it as a page from Jackson's book. Johnson looked at him. "You didn't include your translation of the books."

"What makes you think I got it translated?"

"You got the news report on the Eimskip translated. It stands to reason you got the book translated."

Gerry didn't flinch from his gaze. "The books are in Old Norse."

"Not that different," Morris said.

Gerry let bit of respect surface. "A friend got the report translated for me."

"Would your friend do the same for us?"

Sure, Gerry thought. The FBI had translators. He only wanted to know who had completed the translation so they can keep a lid on the findings. "I could ask," he said.

"If you'd give me her number I would appreciate it."

"Sure thing. Does that mean you'll need help in translating McMillian's book as well?"

"Yeah," Morris answered. "We'll have to get clearance, but I'm sure that won't be a problem. Tell me about the military information concerning Jackson and his men. Where did you get it?"

"A friend."

Morris didn't miss a beat. "Who?"

"Can't say," Gerry replied. "You can confirm the information with your records. You'll see by my report I've spoken with several of the men. Everything checks out."

"I didn't see a profile or analysis."

"All my notes go to Jennifer Newman. She's the profiling genius."

Morris looked him in the eye. "Did she work up the report you submitted on the Valknut killer?"

Gerry shook his head. "No. That's based strictly on my observations from the crimes scenes and victimology."

Morris gave a tiny nod. "Jot down that number for me and put your cell number down, too. Once we get these books translated we might need to talk."

Herrero shoved a pad and pen in Gerry's direction, and Gerry was forced to admit he half wished Morris had gotten Lummus' spot on his team. He wondered what the two men would do if he suggested it.

✦

"DAMMIT," GERRY MUTTERED as he pulled up to his house that afternoon. Dee's Alpha Romero sat parked behind his mother's Camry hybrid. He glanced at the clock and winced. Dee was early for their date, he was late getting home—and Mom had made a surprise appearance. Fate was a cruel mistress.

He threw the Impala into park behind Dee's car and jumped out. Hargrave leaped to the ground, then sprinted for the house. Gerry followed at a hurried pace, but slowed when he reached the walkway. As soon as he got the front door open, Hargrave raced down the hall to the kitchen.

Female laughter echoed down the hallway as Mom and Dee cooed over the dog. Tension in his shoulders eased. He stopped in the kitchen doorway. The two women sat across from one another at the table, both holding a mug. Hargrave had his snout resting on Dee's leg and she was rubbing behind his ears. Dee and his mother looked up expectantly.

"Sorry I'm late," he said. "I got held up at the department."

"I found a few more papers I thought you might need," his mother said.

"Papers?" *The genealogy.* Had Dee—

"Your mom tells me you're doing genealogical research," Dee said.

Damn. The detective in her had shot right to the surface.

"My mother traced our family tree back to the mid-sixteen hundreds," Dee went on. He groaned inwardly as she added, "Mom did the work years before the internet." Dee grinned. "I got copies of *all* her research."

Gerry glanced at his mother and saw she had a brow raised. He crossed to the table and slid into the chair beside Dee. Hargrave didn't bother to look up. The mutt wasn't stupid.

"Yeah?" Gerry said.

She nodded. "Mom used the National Census, Mormon archives, and libraries. She dug up several relatives."

Her eyes twinkled, and Gerry couldn't resist saying, "Were you grave robbing or were some of your relatives vampires?"

"Gerry." His mother looked shocked.

Dee grinned. "There's one I like. He's in his eighties. The other three, I could do without."

His mother rose. "I think I'll get home."

"Mom…"

"Walk me out to the car," she said.

Dee smiled. "It was wonderful meeting you, Viola."

"You too, Dear."

Too late, he realized. They were on a first name basis. "I'll be a sec," he told Dee.

She nodded, and he shot Hargrave a recriminating glance before walking his mother out. When they reached the car, she said, "Nice girl."

"Yeah." He opened the car door. She got in and he kissed her on the cheek. "Thanks for the papers. I'll call you."

"Is there anything you need?"

"Everything's okay," he assured her. "I'll fill you in once I figure it out."

She nodded. Gerry watched her drive away, then returned to Dee.

He seated himself at the table beside her. Hargrave hadn't budged. Dee smiled. Yep. The detective in her knew.

"Hargrave," Gerry said sternly.

The dog shot him a sideways glance, then reluctantly padded over to his spot near the door and curled up. Gerry looked back at Dee. "It's not—" he began.

"How did it go with the Feds?" she interrupted.

"Okay."

"Did you give them everything?"

"I can't exactly withhold evidence," he replied, and prayed like hell he was a better actor than he'd ever been with Brenda.

"This case has kept you busy."

Gerry blinked at the sudden change of subject.

"Makes me wonder why you would take time to research your family history."

There it was. "Look, Dee—"

"You know how complicated researching family trees can get?" she said.

He had an inkling. "I won't ask you to…step outside procedure to help me."

She said in a calm voice that bellied the intense curiosity in her eyes, "You have an exemplary record. What could possibly induce you to *step outside procedure?*"

The way she said *procedure* made him want to laugh, but he wasn't about to give her that big of an edge. "You have a career to think about."

"Tell you what. You show me the genealogy and we'll see how it goes."

Gerry laughed, but stopped abruptly at the mental picture of a late night session with Dee. His groin twitched. That was all he needed.

Chapter Six

Two HOURS LATER, the Asatru family tree covered the kitchen table: twenty sheets of paper taped edge-to-edge, draping the table by three inches.

"This is fabulous," Dee breathed. "How did you manage this with the Feds snooping around?"

"They're snooping around the witnesses, not me," Gerry said. "Plus, my OCR file and notes didn't come up."

"You mean: they didn't ask," she said without looking up. "It's interesting how only the high priests were allowed to father a first born." She traced a forefinger down the fathers' names on the diagram. "And look at this. The women who bore male children married and went on to bear more children. Women who bore a female as their first offspring were allowed the special communion. Like this one." She pointed to the first name on the lineage. "Asvor was born in eight hundred and thirty-five. In eight hundred and forty-eight she bore a daughter named Ulta. Look, no other offspring are recorded." Dee found Asvor's name on the registry sheet she'd positioned near her elbow. "The following year, she took communion and was renamed Freyja."

Dee looked at him. "It looks like those women were given new names at communion and didn't bear more children. Or, at least, none were recorded. But I'm betting they didn't. It's too coincidental that those who bore male offspring were recorded as having more children, both male and female."

"The consecrated females weren't allowed to procreate again," Gerry said, "and there is no record of them marrying. Like nuns."

"Right. Plus, the women who bore male offspring first were *not* allowed communion. Except this one." Dee pointed to the name Sula. "She had a boy, yet was given communion."

"That one has me stumped," Gerry agreed. "I wondered if the scribe made a mistake."

"That's was my first thought," Dee said. "But someone would have caught the error. This isn't a single document like our birth certificates, but an ongoing record." She picked up printouts of Jackson's book from the chair between them. "It's odd how these entries look like they're written by the same hand." She looked closer at the document. "Sula,—" Dee abruptly looked up. "The sun?" She grinned. "You translated the name?"

He was surprised to feel himself blush "I didn't know they were names at first. Once I figured it out…" He shrugged, feeling like a schoolboy. "I just kept going. I created an Excel spreadsheet."

She glanced at the sheet. "But this is the only one you wrote on the chart."

"Because that one bugged me. Like you said, she's the only one who bore a son, yet was still initiated."

"Her son was Sigrun; Secret victory." Dee blew out a breath. "I wonder what they expected of this kid. People back then chose names that were meaningful. Could be a family member's name, though, which still says a lot about the clan."

She touched the modern paper as if it was the ancient books, and Gerry realized she felt the same reverence he had.

"Imagine what we could learn about these people by studying the names alone." Dee ran a finger down the page.

Satisfaction rippled through him. Her enthusiasm for the project hadn't surprised him. Her knowledge of ancient history, however, had.

"Sigrun got around." Dee pointed to half a dozen places where his name appeared, then paused, slowly comparing the names of Sigrun's children. "There we are." She tapped a name in the communion column. "This must have been a daughter. She was given communion."

Gerry half listened, imagining slipping her t-shirt up and burying his face between her B-cup breasts.

Dee shook her head slowly. "This is a very intimate picture of Asatru practices."

He could taste the salty film on her skin, feel her nipples grow hard against his tongue. He wanted to hear her moan, feel her move against him, feel her fingers in his hair, tightening as he—

"What do you make of the communion?" she asked.

Gerry blinked.

"You okay?" she asked.

"Huh?" The room came into sudden focus, and he realized she was studying him.

"The communion?" he repeated. "A kind of consecration. I haven't narrowed down an exact translation."

Doubt flickered in her eyes and he quickly traced several lines on the genealogy with an index finger. "Some daughter to daughter lines extend ten to fifteen generations." Dee looked at the chart, and Gerry added, "The most prominent priests must have had a high percentage of X chromosomes in their sperm because they fathered a high percentage of females. Those who fathered too many males disappeared from the record until their death."

Her brow furrowed in concentration. "Some of the women who took communion lived a long time. The entire genealogy spans a thousand years." She glanced at the chart and he was relieved to see her refocused on the case.

The phone rang.

"Sorry," he said.

Dee nodded, her gaze on the chart as he stood and grabbed for the phone on the wall near the door.

"Forstner," he said.

"Evening, Detective, this is O'Connor. I've got a Marissa Cunningham on the line. Says she wants to talk to you about some guy named Collin Norman."

"Get a trace on the call," Gerry said, "and put her on."

"Got it," O'Connor replied, and a click followed.

"Marissa?" Gerry said.

"He-hello?"

"Marissa, this is Gerry Forstner. We spoke a couple days ago."

"Detective Forstner?"

"Yes. You called me?" When she didn't reply, he added, "Have you seen Collin?"

She still didn't answer and just when Gerry was sure he'd lost her she murmured a "Yes," followed by a "I-I'm worried about him," in whispered tones that gave him hope Collin was within hearing distance.

"Why?" he asked. "What's wrong?"

"I've never seen him like this."

"Like what? Is he high?"

"*No.* He hates drugs. He said it's stupid to let anything control your life. He hates them."

Gerry had to agree. Collin hadn't struck him as a druggie. "Where are you, Marissa?"

She hesitated. Gerry glanced at the clock. They needed another twenty seconds before locking onto the call. He was betting Collin wasn't at home.

"If he's in a bad way, he'll need help," Gerry said. "I'm not interested in busting him—"

"He isn't stoned," she burst out.

Gerry paused. "Okay. What's happened?"

"He...he looks like maybe he was sick, you know, a bad case of the flu or something, and he took a little too much medication."

"That can happen."

He sensed the hesitation before she said, "You mean it?"

"Yeah. Collin didn't strike me as a guy out for a fix."

"He's not. He's studying to be a chef."

"I remember. I'll be straight with you." Two seconds, he had her. "Collin has some information I need. If I know he has this information, the people I'm after know it too. I'd like to get to him before they do." If it isn't too late, he silently added.

"I'm worried about him," she said.

"I can help."

"He's going to be really mad I called you."

"Maybe, but isn't it better he's around to be angry?"

"Yes," she answered without hesitation. "His parents have a small place in Big Pine Key. We're there."

"The Keys?" Gerry repeated.

"Yes." She rattled off an address.

Right where the *Keepers of the Secret* trail ended five years ago. Gerry shook free of the fear that gripped his heart and grabbed a pencil from the table. He scribbled the address on the edge of the chart.

"Keep him there. I'll be there in an hour and a half." Gerry jammed the receiver button down, released it, then dialed the precinct.

✦

GERRY EASED THE car past the Key pines and tall dune grass that surrounded the packed sand drive leading to the cabin with the Big Pine Key address Marissa had given him. Surf pounded the shore up ahead. Hargrave sat up in the back seat and stared intently over Gerry's shoulder as the cabin came into view to the left.

He drove the last eighty feet and glanced at the Toyota Celica parked in a shell-covered driveway beside the cabin as he slipped the car into park, then looked at Dee. She had offered to come, and Gerry realized he needed someone—needed her. If anything went wrong, if he screwed up, she was the only one who knew that his family tree was part of the Asatru line. He had filled her in on the drive down.

She had listened patiently, sat silent for a long moment when he finished, then said, "If I'd read it in a book, I would never have believed it." And he didn't believe he was back in the Keys, chasing vampire wanna-bes.

He looked at Dee. "You ready?"

"You bet."

She reached for the door and Gerry felt an unexpected stab of regret. In all his explanations, he hadn't mentioned his visions and how the blonde had invaded his dreams. He grabbed Dee's arm. She paused and looked at him.

"Listen," he began, then realized he didn't know what to say. He also realized he didn't want her inside when he spoke with Collin.

She smiled. "You want to talk to Collin alone."

"Actually, I want you to keep watch out here, Collin's afraid of something, and I don't know what." The guilt eased slightly. He wasn't lying.

"That's okay. I've got your back."

He reached over her legs and opened the glove box. He shoved a hand beneath the papers and withdrew the Beretta 90-2. He handed her the gun, butt first. She took it, reached behind her, lifted the bottom of her sweater, then stuffed the gun into the back of her waistband, letting the sweater drop.

"We'll go to the door together," Gerry said. "As long as everything looks okay when Marissa opens the door, I'll go inside. Things are pretty wide open out here. I'll leave Hargrave in the car. Once I get inside, let him out. Stay between the house and the car. If you get so much as a hint of anything funny, yell, and get that Beretta ready. If Hargrave acts strange, pay attention. The dog is uncanny."

"Okay," she said without hesitation, and guilt resurfaced for involving her. He needed her, all right. But she sure as hell didn't need him.

"Hargrave, stay." He nodded at Dee. "Let's go."

They got out of the car and walked across the sand to the cabin. Gerry knocked, and Marissa opened the door an instant later.

"He's in the shower," she said. "He doesn't—" She halted, her gaze frozen on Dee.

"It's all right," Gerry said. "This is Detective Kelly. She's going to wait outside."

Marissa's expression relaxed a fraction.

"Can I come in?" he asked.

"Sure." She stepped away from the door.

Gerry glanced at Dee. "If you need anything…"

She nodded, and he entered the cabin, closing the door behind him. Against the left wall sat an unmade hide-a-bed; a kitchenette ran the length of the wall to the right up to a closed door that muffled the sound of running water. Straight ahead, a sliding door opened to a deck eighty feet from the Gulf.

"Have a seat," Marissa said, pointing to the small table in the kitchen area. "Can I get you something to drink?"

"No thanks." He lowered himself into the chair. "Just sit down and talk to me."

She glanced at the bathroom door.

"He's not going anywhere."

Marissa sat across from him.

"Did he say anything after he woke up?" Gerry asked.

She shook her head. "He woke up about ten minutes ago and got into the shower."

The running water stopped. Marissa's eyes widened.

"It's all right. Collin's not in any trouble."

"He's going to be mad." Her upper lip trembled.

"Maybe," Gerry agreed. "But, if he's smart, he'll get over it."

Her cheeks reddened. "We're not that good of friends."

"Then Collin isn't as smart as I thought."

Marissa's blush deepened. The door opened and Gerry shifted his gaze to meet Collin's. He stood motionless in the doorway, a towel wrapped around his waist.

"What are you doing here?" he demanded, and shot Marissa an accusing look.

"Don't blame her," Gerry said harshly. "You can't expect friends to do nothing when they know something's wrong."

"Nothing's wrong," he snapped.

"All right. Nothing's wrong. I still need to talk to you."

Collin's eyes narrowed. "Why?"

"I need to know what happened the night the blonde showed up at *The Hot Spot.*"

His jaw set. "She saw me call you, then she split."

Gerry frowned. "What—"

"She gave me a look that could kill, then left." Collin shivered.

The memory of that night, Cray's, the assailant, the knife, washed over Gerry with a vengeance. He wanted like hell to touch the spot on his gut where he'd been—thought—he'd been cut. His hand started to shake and he moved it from the table to his lap.

"I saw her at the bar," Gerry calmly replied. "She tried to get past me and I went after her."

"She was gone," Collin said tight lipped. "She showed up two nights later with that guy…the molester, Kinnison, and took your card." Collin started shaking. "He was wearing the same god-awful ring Vitelli wore. Then he ended up dead. First Frankie, then Kinnison, and she saw me call you."

"There were a lot of people—" Gerry began. Collin stubbornly shook his head and Gerry felt this anger mount. "I saw her standing at the end of the bar. She wasn't wearing trendy clothes like you described, but it was her in that black dress."

"She was dressed in blue sequins, shorts and halter."

"Blue sequins—" Gerry remembered Linnette Howsten and her flashy red dress. He gave Collin a hard look. "Put on some clothes and sit down. We—"

Hargrave's frantic barking sounded outside. Gerry jumped to his feet, already reaching for his weapon. "Into the bathroom, both of you, and keep down."

Collin froze, eyes wide.

"Move!" Gerry flipped the 9mm's safety to the off position.

Collin stepped forward, grabbed Marissa's arm, and propelled her into the bathroom, then followed. The bathroom door slammed shut as Gerry plastered himself against the wall beside the front door. He threw open the door. No gunfire followed. He swung into the doorway, gun at ready, and was blinded by twin headlights.

He dropped to a squat and squinted at Hargrave. The Shepherd stood to the rear of the Impala facing the Black BMW that Linette Howsten drove. Dee crouched behind the Impala, weapon drawn over the trunk. The Beamer idled and the driver's side door was wide open, the edge shoved into the dune grass. The glare of headlight prevented any view of the occupants. Hargrave glanced back at Gerry, then quieted, alerting on the vehicle twenty feet away.

Gerry sprinted to the cover of his Impala beside Dee. "What happened?"

"The car stopped when Hargrave started barking. The driver's door opened, but no one exited the vehicle."

"Call for back-up."

"I did." She nodded at her open cell phone by her feet, still connected with 911.

Good girl. They'd be taping everything that came across the line.

"That's our blonde's car." One of them, at least, he thought, then froze. The blonde in the black dress wasn't the suspect. *She* was the coincidence. "Cover the car," he ordered. "I'm going to scout to the right and approach from the flank."

Dee nodded, not taking her eyes off the Beamer.

"Hargrave, come."

The Shepherd back peddled. The blonde had to still be in the car or the dog wouldn't be alerting to it. If so, they had her. But he had to check the trees, then approach the car from the rear so he could see inside the open door. Knowing she had to be in the car didn't comfort him. He prayed Hargrave remembered his training.

Glass crashed from the right side of the beach house. A woman's scream cut short. Hargrave bolted for the house.

"Watch the Beamer!" Gerry shouted to Dee, and raced after Hargrave.

The dog disappeared around the corner of the bungalow. Gerry skidded around the corner a second later. Hargrave was nowhere in sight. A small sheer curtain whipped from a small window near the edge of the cabin. *The bathroom window.* Gerry looked at the ground below the window. Shattered glass lay on the ground.

"Fuck," he breathed, and scanned the grass and trees to the side thirty feet back from him. The foliage was just thick enough that someone could lie hidden. "Fuck," he cursed again. *Where was the dog?* Gerry hugged the wall in a crouch as he inched toward the window.

One eye still on the grass, Gerry eased his head above the windowsill and glanced inside. Collin and Marissa lie on the tile, their heads crocked at an unnatural angle, the inside bathroom door still closed.

Chapter Seven

AFTER WATCHING DEE drive off, Gerry entered his kitchen at 3 a.m., Hargrave trotting behind. He draped his jacket over the chair and set his weapon on the Asatru chart covering the table as he dropped into a chair. Howsten had vanished, BMW abandoned. Her footprints petered out a hundred yards from the house and Hargrave's paw prints circled. He had returned a half-hour later, long after Big Pine Key PD had arrived. Even the dog had lost her scent. Did Linette Howsten kill Collin because he could identify her, or had Collin known more than he'd told Gerry?

Gerry rubbed the back of his neck and blinked the Asatru tree into focus. The whole fucking thing was his fault. He had led Howsten straight to Collin and Marissa How had she gotten in and out like some goddamn ninja assassin? Only a few seconds had elapsed between the sound of breaking glass and when he reached the window.

His phone ding-donged the arrival of an email. He fished the phone from his jacket pocket and opened the email. Wayne Commerford wrote:

thxs for helping with cindy, but you should have warned me you sent her candy :) btw, I dug up another connection between the victims. seems they all have ancestors that emigrated from the same village in iceland. your connection with the asatru church is in the attachment. <eom>

Gerry stared at the message. The Valknut victims had Icelandic ancestry? How had the kid made this connection? A little voice said he didn't want to know.

✦

GERRY STARED AT the lineage, the first four Valknut victims now penciled in. Like him, all had descended from an Asatru high priest. A call to Iris had verified Wayne's findings. As Gerry suspected, *and feared*, he and Kinnison came from the same Asatru branch. On a nearby limb of the same tree, Douglas, Michaels, and Vitelli had a common ancestor: Sula's only son Sigrun.

He still couldn't quite grasp it, but there it was, staring back at him in black ink. In tracing back a genealogy, each person had two parents, four grandparents, eight great-grandparents, and so forth. Ten generations back, a person had 1024 direct ancestors, and of these, one person would be a common ancestor to two or three men. But the Valknut victims weren't just any men. They had PSI abilities, which had drawn the men to Warner Laboratories. Then, out of the ten thousand Warner members, the killer had found them. Only one thing had kept the killer from finding Gerry: the break in the lineage caused by Uma's abandonment, then adoption by an unrelated family.

If Gerry hadn't been assigned the Valknut case and gotten his hands on the genealogy, the killer might never have known he existed. Two days ago, when Gerry found the connection to Uma, a little voice told him there was more. He'd believed the more was his relation to Kinnison. That had been enough of a stretch. But to find out all the victims were related to the cult… Christ. He rubbed his eyes.

Hargrave laid his head on Gerry's lap. Gerry glanced at the clock. Six thirty. Sunlight streamed through the window and across the sink. He needed some sleep, but knew he wouldn't allow his mind to quiet enough to relive Collin and Marissa's murder.

He fucked up. He'd been chasing a phantom. If not for Joey seeing the blonde outside Jackson's place, he would believe she was a figment of his imagination. Something about her had captured his imagination and he'd fixated on her. That fixation had screwed with his judgment and gotten Collin and Marissa killed. If he had just talked to Collin that night, he and Marissa might still be alive.

Fucking coincidence. The two women's hair were different: Linnette's feathered and straight, the other blonde's, wavy, with a softer look. Otherwise, the similarities were uncanny: the shade of blonde, their height, even the deep blue of their eyes. Only the other blonde—his blonde—made him want to—a realization hit Gerry. The blonde in the video was Linnette Howsten, not the blonde he'd been chasing. That's why he felt nothing when he watched the tape.

He wanted to laugh and cry at the same time. Goosebumps raced across his shoulders and down his arms. Linnette Howsten: ninja assassin. The other blonde: anomaly. Gerry's throat tightened. Marissa had called him, trusted him. And Collin. What had he stumbled into? This was the first time Gerry had known an innocent victim before...

The other night he'd woken from that strange dream and heard the back screen door slam. He had concluded that it was part of the dream. If he was wrong, if Howsten had been in his house that night—Gerry dialed Brenda on the cell phone.

She picked up on the third ring. "What do you want?"

"I need to talk to you about Joey."

"You're picking him up on Friday. Why—"

"It has to be this morning," Gerry interrupted. "Before school."

She paused. "What's wrong?"

"Nothing we can't deal with, but we do have to deal with it."

"I have to go to work," she said.

"I'm on my way."

✦

BRENDA OPENED THE front door and Joey ran to his arms. "Dad."

Gerry hugged his son, his gaze on Brenda. She stood dressed in a pantsuit, makeup and hair done, and had never looked better. He wished like hell he could read her gray-blue eyes, but he'd wished that for a long time now.

Gerry set Joey on the floor. "Have you finished your breakfast?"

Joey shook his head.

"Then you better get to it. When you finish, I'll take you to school."

Joey's eyes lit. "Really?"

"Really."

Joey whirled and raced down the hall, cutting a hard left into the kitchen.

Gerry glanced around the hallway. Familiar throw rugs covered the hardwood floors. Brenda's gloves, unopened mail, and silk flowers sat on the hall table a few feet away. She had added a couple pictures on the walls, but nothing that would dampen sounds from the entry into the kitchen.

"Outside," he murmured, and turned.

Brenda grabbed his upper arm. "You're scaring me."

He faced her. Yeah, he thought. I'm scaring me, too.

"Are you okay?" she demanded. "You look different."

"It's not me." He cast a glance toward the kitchen. By the munching sound, Joey was busy with his cereal. "It's the Valknut case," Gerry whispered.

Brenda's eyes flashed. "I knew one of these days your *work* would bring trouble. If you'd thought about anyone but yourself—"

"Brenda."

"Don't Brenda me. I—"

Gerry seized her shoulders. "Listen, we have to talk."

She quieted, her chest heaving. He released her and motioned toward the door. She pushed past him and he followed, gently clicking the door closed behind him as he stepped outside.

He took a deep breath, then faced her. "Serial killers don't usually go after the cops investigating them." Brenda opened her mouth, but he cut her off. "I'm not saying my work isn't dangerous, and I'm saying my choice was something you bargained for."

Surprise flickered in her eyes, and he was surprised at the faint relief her reaction elicited. "I changed the deal," he said. "But that's not what this is about."

"All right," she said. "What is this about?"

"I found a pattern in the Valknut murders. My grandmother six generations back was a descendent of an ancient cult the murderer is trying to eliminate."

Brenda blinked. "What?"

How was he supposed to explain something so bizarre? All this time, he'd worried about an arrest not sticking and the bad guy making his family a target. Gerry's thorough by-the-book arrests put his conviction record among the best in the county and in the top five statewide. He never imagined his heritage would put his family in the crosshairs.

He took a deep breath. "I might become a target, and Joey, too."

Brenda's expression turned skeptical. "Because…*your* ancestor ties you to victims in a high profile serial murder case." She snorted. "Sounds like a B movie."

"The Valknut killer is after some ancient books—books I have. The lineage is there in black and white."

She rolled her eyes. "You're a cop, not some new age idiot who believes in superstitious nonsense."

Gerry couldn't prevent a laugh. That was the nicest thing she'd said to him in years.

She scowled. "If you have these books, that means the killer doesn't know."

"I can't be sure he doesn't know. Listen, Brenda, this grandmother was adopted, but she is my biological ancestor. Her line leads directly to Mom, then me, then Joey. Are you willing to chance that I'll catch the Valknut killer before he finds me or Joey?"

She didn't flinch. "You're a good cop."

"Christ," he breathed.

"Don't get maudlin on me," she snapped.

He threw up his hands, palms out. "God forbid."

She glared, and he dropped his hands.

"I want Mom to take Joey out of town until I catch these freaks," Gerry said.

Brenda raised a brow. "*Your* mother? How about me? I'm his mother."

"I think you should get away, too, but being with them will only increase the risk to you and Joey."

"No way." Her lips thinned. "Where he goes, I go."

"Brenda, this killer is—"

"How long have you known about this?" she demanded.

"I've suspected for a couple days—"

"A couple days! And you didn't say anything?"

"I've hired a man to keep an eye on you and Joey. He's an ex-cop." It was costing a fortune, but Joey was worth it.

Her lips thinned even more. "I don't care if he's Robocop, I'm not letting Joey out of my sight."

Gerry took a step back. All in all, her response was a helluva lot better than anticipated. He had been prepared to take—kidnap—Joey until the Valknut killer was in custody.

"Okay," he said. "But my guy goes with you."

"Where do you have in mind?"

"Disney World."

✦

THE MORNING WAS nearly gone and Gerry was dragging by the time he and Mrs. Pentz parked in front of Golden Years rest home. He looked at her.

"Ready?"

She gave a succinct nod. "We'll show those boys. Won't we?"

Hargrave woofed from the backseat and Gerry grinned. "You bet we will."

She cast an approving glance at the dog, then said to Gerry, "They didn't want to let me in on any of their secrets."

Gerry saw a spark of the heat she'd displayed when she described the visit the FBI had paid her earlier that morning.

"Treated me like an old fool." She giggled. "Well, maybe I am old fool. But only a young fool lets on that he knows that." She patted Gerry's leg. "I knew you'd be giving me a call after those FBI men showed up."

She had picked up on the first ring and told him to get over to her place. A lousy thirty-five years' age difference had cheated him out of the woman of his dreams. "What will you say if we run into those FBI fellas here?"

"You're my lover and I've come to break it off with Glen."

Gerry groaned. She had been inventing alternate plans to his *my husband asked to see Detective Forstner and no one else* plan all morning.

"What?" she asked indignantly. "You don't think those fools would believe that an old gal like me could snag a young buck like you?"

Gerry smiled. "I don't think those fools would believe you'd go for a fool like me."

Mrs. Pentz grinned. "I could convince them."

He laughed. "I bet you could at that."

She reached for the door handle and Gerry grabbed her arm. "Marilyn, I want you to know—"

"Hush," she interrupted. "You don't have to tell me how much is riding on this. I see it in your eyes."

"A lousy thirty-five years," he murmured.

She brightened. "Not too much if you want to give it a go."

Gerry laughed.

✦

THE ADMINISTRATION HAD Glen Pentz in physical therapy when they arrived. "They keep changing his schedule," Mrs. Pentz complained as, forty-five minutes later, they were escorted to her husband's room.

She had raised a fuss, but the nurse—Miss Ratchet, Mrs. Pentz had called the woman when she left the room—had stood firm. Mr. Pentz needed his workout if he was to live a long and healthy life.

"*Long and healthy life,*" Marilyn had mimicked in disgust.

Gerry understood how she felt when the male nurse who escorted them opened Pentz's door upon a room that resembled a hospital ward. The four pine beds and matching wardrobes emanated all the warmth of a cheap hooker, and were packed together like sardines in a can.

Glen Pentz sat on a small couch by the only window at the far side of the room. His gray hair grew unkempt, still thick and curly, especially on the back of his neck. He wore a gray sweatshirt that hung on broad shoulders that could have belonged to man decades younger. Per Mrs. Pentz's+ request, none of Glen's roommates where present.

The male nurse started toward Pentz, but Gerry stopped him. "Mrs. Pentz will let him know we're here."

The nurse hesitated, then shrugged and left.

Mrs. Pentz sat beside her husband and smiled gently. "Glen." When he didn't respond, she covered his hand with hers. "Glen, there's a detective here to see you."

Pentz glanced at Gerry with a vacant expression. Mrs. Pentz's eyes moistened, reflecting the sadness he'd seen the first time they'd met. She missed her husband. She stood, and Gerry seated himself in her place.

"Mr. Pentz, I'm Detective Forstner, from Coral Gables PD."

"Do I know you?" Pentz asked.

"No," Gerry replied. "May I call you Glen?"

A smile brightened his face. "If I can call you Detective."

Gerry grinned. "Sure. Glen, I'm here because there has been some trouble."

Glen shifted his gaze back to the window. "That doesn't surprise me."

"Do you say that because the FBI was here yesterday?" When Glen didn't answer, Gerry said, "I'm here to ask you about the books you found in Iceland."

Pentz looked back at him. "What books?"

"The books you and Skip Jackson found in Iceland."

"Don't remember any books."

"There's no need to be afraid," Gerry said. "I'm not with the FBI. It's all out in the open now. I know about the books, and even have Judge Jackson and William Johnson's books in my possession. No one is angry. I just need to know about your book."

"My son visited me yesterday."

Gerry shot Mrs. Pentz a questioning look. The front desk had said the only visitors Glen had received in the last month were the FBI. She shook her head.

Gerry looked back at Glen. "Did you give the FBI your book?"

"Sam is such a good boy. He takes care of me." Pentz looked at him. "Such a good boy."

"I'm sure he is," Gerry agreed. "What did you tell him to do with your book?"

Pentz's mouth tightened. "Black magic."

"Black magic? You read—" Gerry halted at sight of Pentz's wide eyes. Gerry gave a lopsided grin. "You caught me off guard, Glen. That's not easy to do, you know."

Pentz blinked uncertainly, then grinned back. "Sorry."

"That's okay. I'll just have to keep my eye on you." Gerry gave him a mock frown and the old man beamed. Gerry shifted in his seat and draped his arm casually over the back of the couch. "What makes you think black magic is in that book? Did you pick up a little Old Norse while in the military?"

Pentz laughed and leaned back against the cushion, clearly imitating Gerry's manner. "No. We weren't there long enough for that. After a while, us boys got curious about those books. We got our hands on a dictionary. We didn't get far, though. I got a headache from trying to decipher that chicken scratch. It's Old Norse, you know."

Gerry nodded. "Yes."

"William had a friend whose son was a chaplain in the Army," Glen went on. "Smart boy. He had a history degree from some Ivy League university…Harvard, I think. William got him to translate some of the book." Pentz leaned closer. "We only had him translate a little—you understand, security and all—but it was enough to see it was a book of incantations." He shivered. "Gave me the willies."

"I don't blame you," Gerry answered honestly. "Did you keep those translations?"

Pentz's eyes went vacant. Gerry's heart fell. The lucid man was gone. An instant later, Pentz's face brightened, and he said, "We shit-canned them. After that, we put the books away. Too scary."

"Where is your book?" Gerry asked.

Glen looked at the open hands in his lap. "Don't know."

"You said your son visited yesterday. Would he know?"

He shook his head. "It could have been yesterday, or last week. Hard to say." He paused. "Sam said he would take care of it." Pentz looked at Gerry. "He did, didn't he?"

"I'm sure he did," Gerry said. "You have nothing to worry about."

Pentz gripped Gerry's wrist with surprising force. "I don't want to die. I thought...did Sam discover something?"

"I'll know when I talk to him."

Pentz released Gerry's arm, and Gerry rubbed the place where Pentz had cut off his circulation. If not for his brain, the old man would have a few years left in him.

Pentz sighed. "I didn't think so."

"I'll tell him you asked."

Pentz nodded, and turned a vacant stare out the window. Gerry rose and met Mrs. Pentz' gaze. Her eyes were wet. He stepped outside the room and left her alone with her husband.

✦

GERRY CLOSED THE car door for Mrs. Pentz, then circled the car and got into the driver's seat. Hargrave licked his ear.

Gerry scratched the Shepherd's neck, then looked at her. "When was the last time you spoke with Sam?"

"About a week ago when he called to ask when I was going to see Glen next."

"He didn't say where he was calling from, did he?"

"No," Marilyn answered. "You haven't been able to contact him?"

"No."

She sighed. "I told the FBI to leave Glen alone. Do they have the right to question him like they did? Is—" her voice broke. "Is he in trouble?"

Gerry turned the key in the ignition. "No." Not if he could help it.

"What about Sam?" she asked as he backed out of the parking spot. "He didn't steal anything, but he has that book."

Gerry glanced at her. "You came to that conclusion pretty quickly."

She gave him a recriminating look. "It doesn't take a degree in criminal justice to put two and two together."

He grunted amusement. "No, it doesn't. I doubt Sam is in any trouble." At least not with the FBI, he thought. There was something about Sam Pentz that rubbed him the wrong way. "They want the book." He maneuvered through the parking lot. "I'd like to get to him before the FBI does. Once they have the book, I won't get a look."

Mrs. Pentz snorted. "You don't have to worry. Glen didn't tell them about Sam."

Gerry stepped on the brake at the parking lot exit and looked at her. "You seem certain of that."

She flashed a smug smile. "I asked him. He isn't as feeble minded as people think."

"You mean he's faking?"

"Not exactly. He does have Alzheimer's. If he didn't, I'd have him home. But he has lucid moments, which he delights in keeping to himself."

"Are you saying he was messing with me?"

"No, he liked you. He didn't like those FBI men, though." She gave a triumphant nod. "He didn't tell them Sam had the book."

Gerry studied her. "He told you all this after I left?"

She lifted her brows. "Don't look so surprised, Gerald."

He winced. Mom was the only person who called him by his given name, and then, only when she was peeved. Even Brenda hadn't done that.

"We've been married fifty-five years. A woman gets to know a man."

Yeah, Gerry thought. But how well did a man get to know a woman?

Chapter Eight

GERRY'S CELL PHONE rang just as he pulled into his parking space at the department. He glanced at the dash clock. 11:15. Had to be Brenda telling him she and Joey had arrived to the hotel. He grabbed the phone from the cup holder and looked at the screen. Her mobile number flashed back at him. He pressed the receive button.

"Hello."

"Gerry, it's Brenda. Joey and I have arrived."

Something in the way she said 'arrived' stopped him. "What's wrong?"

She gave a small laugh. "I never could keep anything from you."

"What is it?" he snapped.

"Don't get into a huff. Nothing's wrong. I said we're all right, and we are. It's just that we're all right in a different place than you planned."

"What the hell—"

"Don't start with me," she replied in a cool voice that reminded him all too much of the Brenda he'd divorced. Was this how she kept Joey in line? "Just keep quiet and listen," she said. "I didn't want to go to Disney World. That was a bad idea."

"Bad idea—"

"That's right, bad idea. It's too far away, too many people. What if something happened I couldn't handle?"

He had sent Hammet with her for anything she couldn't handle, but said instead, "I thought you could handle anything."

"Don't be an ass. Just because I have no intention of ending up a widow like your mother doesn't mean I think you're a complete fool."

"Shit," he breathed, the air taken out of him. "Goddamit, Brenda, you never said—"

"Oh, stop," she interrupted. "Just listen. I'm on Plantation Key with David."

"The boyfriend you didn't tell me about?" Gerry said before realizing she'd said The Keys. His gut clenched.

"That's right. It wasn't any of your business."

"Anyone who's around my son is my business," he nearly shouted.

"Cool your jets, Gerry, or I won't tell you where I am."

He gave a mocking laugh. "I'm good at my job, remember? I can find you within the hour."

"All right, find me. Then what are you going to do, take Joey?"

"Myles can't protect Joey. Where's Hammet?"

"Right here. I compromised and brought him."

Gerry suddenly realized Hammet hadn't called to apprise him of the change. As if reading his mind, she said, "He didn't call you because I told him if he did, I'd call the cops and say he was stalking me."

"Mother fucker," Gerry muttered.

"Joey is my son," she said in a voice that said *fuck you right back,* "and I have no intention of taking any chances. David was willing to help. He has a place that's secure."

"What does that mean?"

"State of the art security system at his cabin."

"Cabin?"

She gave a condescending laugh. "If you can call it that. It's more like a chalet."

"You got your lawyer," he shot back.

"And you got your dog. I've already emailed you our address. You can call Hammet from now on to check in."

The phone went dead and Gerry let out a slew of curses that moved him to the front of the long line outside Hell.

GERRY LEANED BACK against his chair as the waitress at the Sand Box collected his and Dee's plates from the table. Shouts sounded from kids in a Mustang convertible peeling out of a side street into traffic, yanking him from another image of Joey with David Myles at every Superbowl for the next ten years. Joey was the best part of Gerry's life, and he wasn't going to let the boy forget it.

Pale yellow light from the sodium streetlamps fell across Dee's soft brown hair. Gerry slid his gaze along the long sleeved cotton sweater that clung to her arms and breasts as if to invite exploration of the curves beneath. God, he needed her. He lifted his gaze and saw her eyes darken. Had she read his mind? If so, would she mind? If the other night was any indication, she wouldn't.

A tingle spread up his spine, dispelling the pleasant picture of Dee not minding. He resisted the urge to glance around. He'd had enough of the PSI weirdness and didn't need Dee asking if they should head for the psych ward instead of home.

She reached for her purse on the chair beside her. "I'm going to the ladies room." A corner of her mouth quirked. "Think you'll be all right while I'm gone?"

Truth was, he wasn't sure, but he couldn't help a chuckle. "I'll keep my hands above the table."

Her mouth twitched into a half smile and she stood. Gerry watched her weave her way between tables and into the restaurant. Movement to his right jerked his attention in that direction. A blur of navy blue in front of him focused into a cashmere suit, but his attention fastened on the slim hand grasping the chair beside him and pulling it out. He lifted his gaze and took in the long blonde hair of the blonde he'd seen outside Jackson's. His eyes met hers, and his pulse leaped into overdrive as she sat down. He hoped like hell she couldn't hear the pounding of his heart.

He'd been looking for her for what seemed like a lifetime, and he had to do a mental check to keep from slapping the cuffs on her. Her only crime had been to run when he told her to stop at *The Hot Spot*. What bothered him now was how she had invaded his dreams.

Gerry opened his mouth to say she needed to answer some questions, when she said, "I need your help."

The plea was bellied by a softly accented voice that washed over him like cool water on dry lips. Iris had that same accent. His groin twitched and he felt himself hardening. *Jesus fucking Christ.* His help? He's the one who needed help.

"You're playing with fire, lady," he growled.

"I'll leave before your friend returns," she said.

"You want my help, I want some answers." The only thing he had on her was obstruction. If she had stopped when ordered, he wouldn't have been looking for the wrong blonde the past week. The thought bubbled up in unreasonable anger.

She leaned forward only a fraction, but Gerry felt as though she came within an inch of his face. He glanced toward the restaurant door, hoping Dee would appear, praying she wouldn't. He looked back at the blonde.

"Please help me," she said.

The childlike way she made the statement grabbed his attention. Some women wanted—needed—a man. Maybe this was his ticket.

"All right," he said. "You help me, I'll help you." He stopped short. What the hell was she supposed to say, *'Why are you in my dreams?'* Instead, he blurted, "Who's Linnette Howsten?"

"Linnette Howsten?"

"What were you doing outside Judge Jackson's place the other night?" Gerry fired back.

Fear filled her expression. "He is one of the men killed by the Aptr-gangr."

"What the—"

"I must find them," she said, her voice insistent.

"You're looking for the books," he snarled. Dammit. He'd been wrong straight down the line.

"Books?"

Gerry straightened. "Who are you?"

"Sula."

"Sula?" he blurted.

Gerry felt as if the wind had been knocked out of him. Was she the one trying to make herself into a modern day gothi? Brother Matthew's account of the four blonde maidens discovered in the Asatru temple leaped to mind.

Blonde, beautiful, ethereal. Four maidens.

Did she somehow know of Brother Matthew's account?

He thought of Vitelli's past life regression. Christ, Vitelli as one of the maidens who'd died and reincarnated as a wise guy was more believable than the woman sitting across from him.

Gerry sliced through the mental haze and grabbed her arm, the same slim arm he'd seen in the dream. "Cut the crap. Assuming the name of an ancient priestess won't bring back the past, and killing people won't—"

His surroundings vanished and he found himself in a dark room. He was staring over his shoulder at a woman dressed in a robe, holding a blonde haired baby. The child cooed, and despair filled Gerry. He faced forward and began walking between two hooded individuals. Fear sliced through him an instant at sight of the labyrinth of tunnels up ahead. He turned a bend a door awaited up ahead.

He wanted to run, but kept walking as if his feet weren't his own. He looked down to see slim, feminine arms at his side. A long white robe hung from his body and small, sandaled feet carried him. His insides began to shake, but his body remained steady.

His gaze fixed on the door ahead. "No!" his mind screamed. What lay beyond that door was a dream, but the thought of stepping through it filled him with terror. "No!" he screamed again.

The door vanished and a rumbling sound grabbed his attention. He stood on uneven ground. Despite the darkness, he recognized the click of a train racing down tracks. A small neon sign glowed in the distance. Squinting, Gerry made out the words *Bear's Taxidermy*. The sun unexpectedly blazed in an evening sky, and he saw a large building behind the shop with the Miami skyline in the background.

A car horn blared and Gerry bolted to his feet. He recognized the street, the restaurant...the empty chair were Sula had been sitting.

"Gerry?"

He jerked left to see Dee staring at him.

"What's wrong?" she demanded.

He glanced around, saw no sign of Sula, then pulled out his wallet and, with shaky hands, grabbed two twenties. He tossed them on the table and looked at Dee.

"Let's get out of here."

"You got it."

In the car, Dee remained quiet. Gerry could have kissed her. When they arrived at his house, he got out of the car and headed for her Alpha Romero. She headed for the house.

He caught up with her at the porch. "What's up?"

"Invite me in," she replied.

"Dee—"

She shoved him against the door and kissed him. Blood pounded in his ears. Gerry turned and pinned her against the door, pressing his erection against her. Dee gasped, then kissed him harder. She wrapped a leg around one hip, pulling him closer. His insides gelled as she arched into him and ground her hip against his hard on. He fumbled the key from his pocket and somehow located the lock even as he cupped a breast with his free hand.

"Gerry," she whispered against his lips.

The lock clicked open and he shoved at the door, practically falling through while still locked in the kiss. Hargrave joined in, tail wagging, and tried to squeeze between them. Gerry pushed the dog aside with his leg, kicked the door shut, then backed Dee against the wall. Hargrave tugged on his pant leg. Gerry swatted him away while Dee yanked his shirttail free and slid a hand under. Fingernails raked his chest. He groaned. An aroma of lavender at the nape of her neck drew his mouth down to taste. He slathered wet kisses as she worked the buttons on his shirt.

Gerry slipped a hand beneath her sweater. Just as he'd imagined, silky smooth skin met his fingertips. Desire to feel every feminine contour pressed against him flooded his senses. He had forgotten how soft and luscious a woman's body felt and tasted. Inches above her flat belly, firm breasts rested in a lacy bra. He slid a hand under and cupped her breast. Bigger than he imagined.

His hard-on throbbed in agreement as he circled a hardened nipple with his thumb. She shoved open his shirt, leaned forward, and ran her tongue around a nipple. Shivers of pleasure radiated to his core. Dee unbuckled his belt, unzipped his pants, and reached in. Cool fingers gently curved around his erection and pulled him free.

"Keep this up," he rasped, "and this will be over in five minutes." *Five minutes? Hell, three.*

"If you don't keep this up, I'd take it personally," she breathed into his chest. "I'm counting on you to make it up to me if it does." Dee shoved his underwear and pants down. They slid to the floor as she ran her tongue around the other nipple.

Gerry freed the button on her jeans, opened the zipper, and slid panties and jeans over her hips. She wiggled until a soft thump of fabric on carpet sounded. He lifted her, started to bring her down onto his erection, then cursed.

"What is it?" she demanded.

"We need a condom."

"I'm on the pill," she said.

"Jesus," he rasped, and slid her onto him.

Pleasure shot through him. She moaned, wrapping her legs around him. He pressed her back against the wall and thrust deeper. She gasped and her grip on his shoulders tightened. He held her ass with one hand, slipped the other between them, past her soft curls, and stroked her. Dee sucked in a breath.

His ears roared. He wanted like hell to make this last, yet wanted to climax so hard his eyes rolled back into his head. He felt the heat mounting, the near compulsion to drive himself into her harder and faster. If he gave in—Hell, he'd make it up to her as soon as they made it to his bed.

Chapter Nine

FOR THE THIRD time in fifteen minutes, Gerry eased the Impala over the train tracks that separated the industrial area from a dilapidated residential/commercial neighborhood. He'd had a wonderful night with Dee, then morning, then lunch. He had needed a break from the case almost as much as he needed her. He wanted a little down time after she left, but the memory of Collin and Marissa drove him.

Finding *Bear's Taxidermy* had been the easiest piece of detective work in the case. He had followed hunches before, but discovering the place actually existed still had him shaken. He had cruised the area three times in an effort to locate a landmark that jarred loose some memory that explained the images he'd seen at the Sand Box. Nothing.

A couple hundred feet from Bear's, he parked the Impala between an abandoned bike shop and a beer distributor. As he killed the ignition, Hargrave sat up in the passenger seat.

"Yeah, we're going in." Gerry grabbed the leash and coiled it in his hand. "Remember your training, or you'll stay home next time."

Hargrave flattened his ears submissively and turned away. Gerry glanced at the seagulls soaring over the bay behind the beer distributor as he got out of the car. The birds' cawing rose above the background city noises, reminding him of *The Birds*. He circled the car and opened the passenger door for Hargrave. The Shepherd jumped to the ground, and they walked the half-block to Bear's.

Gerry halted to inspect the three-story shop. Four stories, he corrected, counting the attic. Just like his dream, a large building—a warehouse—towered behind the shop. A neon sign with fractured glass tubes forming the words *Bear's Taxidermy* hung in the second story window. In the vision, the sign had hung in midair above the house and flashed. At first, darkness had surrounded the place, then he'd seen the sun setting just as it did now.

Dirt and grime covered the shop's plate-glass window, obscuring view of the interior. Gerry stepped onto the cement front stoop and tried the door. The handle turned, but the door didn't budge. He tested the door with a shoulder, but the solid feel confirmed his suspicion that the door had been nailed shut on the inside.

He headed to the rear of the house with Hargrave trotting alongside. Around back, an open field separated the taxidermy from the railway tracks and warehouses beyond. He looked back at the taxidermy. What had he expected to find? He recalled the descriptions of psychic visions he'd read in the Warner files and grimaced. The word 'visions' conjured up pictures of men like Nostradamus and Charles Manson. Of course, Manson had admitted the talking dog had been bullshit. Nostradamus, however, still had a strong cult following. Desperation, Gerry reminded himself, was the only reason he was there.

"Let's get this over with," he told Hargrave, and strode to the back door.

Gerry grabbed the handle and turned, stumbling forward a step when the door unexpectedly opened into a mudroom. Hargrave pushed past and sniffed the crack of the interior door. Four windowpanes filled the upper half of the door. Gerry peered inside. It looked like an old storeroom. He tried the door. Locked.

"We gotta go in," he murmured, stuffed the leash in his back pocket, and unholstered his gun.

He broke the lower left pane with the butt, reached through, and found a deadbolt. He turned it and opened the door. Hargrave shot past. Gun at ready, Gerry eased passed empty shelves, keeping the Shepherd in sight. Hargrave pawed at a door at the far end of the room. Gerry glanced around, his gaze fixing on a second door located ten feet left of the one Hargrave sniffed. Probably the showroom. He grasped the doorknob with his free hand.

"Hargrave," he whispered, and the dog's head swung around. "Come here, boy."

The dog woofed, but didn't budge.

"Hargrave," he repeated in a sterner tone.

Hargrave sneezed. Gerry silently cursed. The Shepherd had never before disobeyed an order. Gerry tightened his grip on the gun and inched open the door. Beyond was a long room with empty display cases lining the walls.

He closed the door and crossed to the dog. "This door?" Hargrave woofed. The dog's confidence should have comforted him, but didn't. "Sit," Gerry commanded. Hargrave sat. "I don't want you running ahead of me this time." Gerry opened the door. Stairs descended into murky gloom. Hargrave snaked past.

Gerry froze. What waited in the basement that the dog wanted so badly? Hargrave had never led him into danger, but Gerry couldn't bring himself to reholster his weapon. He started down the stairs. The fourth step creaked and his pulse spiked. He was acting like a kid watching Chilly Billy.

He longed for those carefree days when vampires and werewolves came on a thirteen-inch screen, blood was black, and fangs white. He slowed, holding the handrail, aiming the Beretta into the gloom. Where was that mutt? At the bottom of the stairs, he stepped onto a concrete floor. The walls were cinder block. The open room he stood in had doorways in left and right walls leading into smaller rooms.

"Hargrave," he called in a low voice.

Nothing. Directly ahead, late afternoon sunlight streamed through cobwebs enveloping a barred, ground level window. Through the right-hand doorway, sunlight illuminated the adjoining room. *Must be another casement window.* The left-hand room was dark.

"Hargrave?" he called louder.

Still no sound. This was not the place to die. How would he protect Joey if he didn't make it out? Gerry's pulse thrummed in his head as he edged right, until he could peer around the edge of the open doorway. Empty. He braced against the concrete and aimed straight ahead at the other, dark room. Unless there was some hidden doorway, Hargrave was in that room.

"Anybody here?" Gerry called.

An answering rustle was followed by a low whimper from the remaining room.

Gerry straightened. "Hargrave, come!" He started forward, then stopped when the dog appeared in the doorway, tail wagging. "Where have you—" The words died on his lips at sight of the blonde—Sula—stepping out of the darkness behind Hargrave. Her blue eyes were even more startling in the dim light.

He leveled his Beretta. "Freeze," he ordered, then called, "Hargrave," but the dog didn't move. "Come," Gerry commanded. Hargrave barked. "What have you done to him?"

"How did you find me?" she countered.

The question caught him off guard. Hadn't he gotten the images from her? Alyssa said that psychic impressions could come anytime unbidden. The hand gripping the gun trembled. He'd pictured Kinnison in Jackson's office, then the taxidermy. *Visions*, Alyssa had called the experience.

"I'm asking the questions," he snapped.

She stepped up alongside Hargrave and Gerry tightened his grip on the 9mm. Her expression conveyed no more concern than if he held a squirt gun. He wanted to jam his eyes shut, then open them to discover this was some crazy dream.

"How did you find me?" she asked again.

"I'm psychic," he blurted sarcastically.

"Second sight," she murmured.

A chill crept across his skin. *Not this, not now.*

"Who are you?" she demanded.

"Jesus, fucking, Christ, lady. That's my line."

"I don't mean your name and occupation," she said.

He couldn't believe it. She sounded indignant. She as the one who found him at the Sand Box, asked him for help. She was the one with connections to the Asatru vampire cult. Had she really came to him in the alley after he was stabbed? She had done something to him that night, then invaded his dreams, drew him to this place. She had Hargrave under her spell. How far down the rabbit hole had he fallen? Chills rolled from his skull clear to his calves.

"You're human." She tilted her head as if studying a monkey in a cage.

In thirty-seven years, that was the oddest thing he'd heard anyone say.

"You know me," her tone turned incredulous.

Memory of the dream with him as the gothi when she stood naked before him, flipped to the vision he'd experienced at the *Sand Box*, when he was her and the gothi had grabbed his arm. The gothi wore the ring with the lopsided cross, the same symbol in Jackson's book. More chills. His skull felt like it was curling up and drying into leather.

She started forward.

"Not another step." His voice trembled and his mouth was dry as dust.

Sula stopped, glanced at the gun, then looked back at him, her expression incredulous. She extended both arms. "I have no weapon."

Gerry ran his gaze down the knit sweater and skin tight jeans that left little room to pack even a blowgun. He almost wished she did carry a gun. That was a weapon he knew how to deal with.

"Turn around," he ordered.

She lifted a brow. By God, she was mocking him.

"Turn around."

Hargrave barked. Gerry glanced at him. The shepherd's lips twitched and he bared his teeth in a ferocious growl. The dog was about to charge.

Sula's head jerked toward the stairs. A shape blocked the light filtering down the basement stairs. She cried out and, in the next instant, a figure leaped from the head of the stairs and landed on the concrete floor between Gerry and her.

The blond man Gerry had seen in the alley stood before him.

Sula bared teeth with long incisors and growled in unison with Hargrave.

Gerry's ears rang so loudly, he barely heard his shout of "Police! Hands up!"

The man turned. Gerry fell back a pace at sight of his glowing eyes. Where had he seen eyes like that?

Linnette Howsten.

Gerry leveled his weapon on the guy. *"Drop."*

The man's mouth lifted in a sneer. Sula shouted something in a language Gerry didn't understand. The guy yanked his attention back to her and replied in the same language.

She hates him, Gerry realized. "Hey!" he shouted, and they both looked at him. "Down on the fucking floor, both of you, before I put you in your graves."

The man's eyes narrowed in contempt. His gaze bore into Gerry. Gerry flushed warm. Sula shouted. Hargrave began barking. In a blur, she leaped on the guy. He spun, and shoved her. She crashed into the wall. Cinderblocks cracked with the impact. Hargrave lunged.

"Hargrave!" Gerry shouted, and fired.

The bullet ploughed through the man's arm as the roar of the gun ricocheted. Blood gushed from the wound, but he didn't flinch. Hargrave latched onto his arm and shook it. Sula rose, shouting in... *Old Norse.* The man shook Hargrave off as if he were a rag doll, and whirled on Gerry.

In the blink of an eye, Sula leaped between them as Hargrave sank his teeth into the man's leg. Gerry fell back a pace. She rammed her elbow into the guy's face. His head snapped back with a sickening crack.

Sweat dribbled down the side of Gerry's face. He swung the gun onto the guy, but couldn't get a clear shot.

"Halt, mother fucker, before I blow your fucking brains out!"

The man whirled. Sula clamped her hands together and slammed them down on his neck. His eyes bulged. She sunk her knee into his kidney. He caught her leg on impact. Gerry circled to get a clear shot. She twisted free. The man lunged, caught her throat in one hand, and deflected her blows with the other. He ground out a statement that Gerry could have sworn was a plea to stop fighting. He had deflected her blows, thrown her off of him, but had yet to strike her.

Gerry pulled the trigger. The bullet entered the man's back at heart level. For a sickening instant, Gerry thought the bullet might hit Sula on exit. But the guy crumbled to the floor and she stood over him, chest heaving, breath coming in hard rasps. A chill—this one of fear—raced through Gerry at sight of her eyes. They glowed like blue hot embers.

"What the fuck?" he whispered, and she looked up.

Hargrave stood beside her, tail wagging. Gerry stumbled back two paces. His heel struck the bottommost step and he collapsed onto the third stair.

"Come." She started toward him.

He leveled his gun on her. His hand shook, but he kept the weapon aimed at her heart.

She halted. "We must leave." She glanced at the dead guy, then back at Gerry. *"Now."*

Gerry croaked a laugh, then abruptly sobered. The fear in her eyes bordered on hysterical. "The man's dead."

"You don't understand," she said. *"He is not dead."*

"I shot him through the heart. The motherfucker is dead."

She shook her head. "He can't die this way."

"Everybody dies when they get shot through the heart."

"Not the Aptrgangr."

The word stole his breath. "I've had enough of this shit." Gerry grabbed the banister and pulled himself to his feet. "We aren't living in the stone age. We don't believe in the boogieman anymore." Even as the words left his mouth, he remembered Alyssa Hamilton's warning, *Never underestimate the boogieman, Detective, and don't doubt your ability to know him when you see him.*

Sula stepped toward him. "Death was at your door. I stood with you when he knocked, and I pulled you back."

The center of Gerry's belly hummed as if plugged into an electrical outlet.

"We shared," she went on. "I saw you as a boy on the pony, the arguments between your parents, the dance with that girl. Your marriage, your son's birth."

"Who the hell are you?" Gerry narrowed his eyes on her. "Where did you get this information?"

"I shared memories with you. It is the way of things. My son." Her voice cracked. "Centuries, and still I have not forgotten."

"Stop," Gerry rasped.

"We must go," she said urgently. "I am strong, but he defeated me once." She looked at the body. "I am stronger now. He will not catch me unawares again." Her voice quieted, "His kind came first. They are older, timeless, the original clan cast from paradise. Stronger...male."

Gerry wanted to race up the stairs and run down the street flipping a finger across his lips like the nut case he had become. A blur flashed across his vision. His gun was knocked from his hand before he could think and Sula gripped him in her arms as if dipping him in a tango. Adrenaline exploded through him. He grabbed her shoulders and shoved. She crushed him to her. He gripped her so hard, she should have crumpled to the cement, but she didn't falter as she lowered her head toward his neck.

You're human, she had said.

He could see his obituary in the Miami Herald: *Head of Miami Task Force Murdered by Alien.* They would analyze his body for the next five hundred years.

Her hair fell across his face like spun silk. Blood rushed through his ears. He pushed harder against her iron grip, but her embrace was like being crushed between two ten-thousand-pound monster trucks. Her cheek brushed his as if in caress and moist lips touched his neck.

"Forgive me," she whispered.

His heart raced. *Is this how women feel when being raped?*

Anger turned to fear, then helplessness when the lips opened in a wet kiss. Tears welled in the corner of his eyes as two sharp pins pierced his neck. Adrenaline rammed through his system in a frenzy of self-preservation. His chest tightened like a massive fist preparing to strike. The tickle of a deep kiss drawing blood to the surface of his skin broke into the stream of energy like cool water across flushed skin. The tickle deepened, then turned hard as if drilling through skin and vessel into the pulsing river of blood.

Gerry startled at finding himself riding alongside the same stream he'd seen in that night in the alley, the moon high overhead. Sheer cliffs rose on both sides of the valley as he horse picked its way along the rocky terrain. Night crickets sang in harmony with faint whale songs from the North Atlantic a league to the east. Suddenly, a cloaked man appeared on the path before him. Fear surged through Gerry. Alarr, the most skilled assassin of his kind. A legend come to life, one part of Gerry thought, while another part recognized the man as the one he had just killed. Gerry's upper lip lifted in a sneer.

"Shh, sweet," Alarr whispered.

Gerry drew the sword strapped to his side and leaped from the horse. Alarr drew daggers and crossed them in front of his chest. Gerry lunged. Alarr flowed aside. They parried, Alarr speaking softly, Gerry snarling in response, until Alarr dropped his daggers and caught Gerry's blade between his palms, snapping it in half. Alarr grabbed him in a hold even tighter than Sula's.

Gerry snarled as Alarr lowered his head and whispered, "Shh." He touched his lips to Gerry's skin.

Something pricked his neck. Desire rippled through him. *No!* His stomach turned in revulsion. His body sagged, then jerked, and he found a new vision flowed from Alarr, something older, more ancient than the dungeon, or of the gothi violating a teenage Sula. He raced alongside a high cliff, a tall, muscled man running beside him. Gerry squinted in the pre-dusk light to discern the man's features.

"They have us walled in," the man hissed, and motioned at the path ahead.

Gerry tore his gaze from the man. A sheer cliff lay fifty feet ahead. He faltered, and the man seized his arm and steadied him without breaking stride. Gerry's gaze riveted onto the fingers gripping his arm, then his own masculine arm as the man released him.

"We must scale the cliff," the man said.

Gerry looked at him. *Jonis.*

Jonis shot forward in a blur.

Fear pumped through Gerry. How could he run that fast—how could he possibly climb that sheer cliff? As if in answer, his feet moved with a speed that left him breathless. He reached the cliff and began climbing. His stomach lurched at the quickness of his movements. He looked up and saw Jonis a few feet above. Wind whipped hair across Gerry's eyes, stinging like tiny whip lashes. He shook back thick, straw-blonde hair— hair like that of the man he'd just shot.

Angry shouts sounded overhead. Jonis stopped and Gerry nearly collided with him. Dozens of mail-clad men stood on the cliff's edge.

"By the gods," Jonis cursed. "They will take us as they did Byrn."

Sorrow filled Gerry. Byrn had been taken captive midsummer, when perpetual day drove their kind underground. A green-eyed woman's face filled Gerry's mental vision. Kristen, human—and Byrn's mate. His captors had used her to force him into battle as their captain.

"They have hunted us too long." Jonis choked the words.

They had been hunted since the beginning of time, Gerry understood. Since man had worshipped something greater that himself. Since the great war that had ripped the universe apart.

"Enough," Jonis hissed.

The bloodlust in Jonis' blazing eyes heated his own blood even as fear rocketed through him, and he poised for one giant leap onto the cliff.

The shouts vanished and Gerry found himself back in the walled community of women. He faltered, the feel of his slighter, feminine body moving lithely down the familiar labyrinth. Memory of his son's cry as they parted still echoed against the corridor's stone walls. The oak door lay ahead.

He struggled to break free of the vision as they approached, but the door opened and they entered the room. Cold hands pulled off his clothes. His gaze caught on a gold band on the man's middle finger. The ring of the Gothi High Priest, Mótsognir. *The same seal in Jackson's book.* Fear overrode sorrow. Gerry wanted to run.

"Come, my prized priestess," Mótsognir said.

A woman stepped from the shadows. She grabbed Gerry's shoulders, then yanked him to her and bit his neck. Darkness enveloped him.

Cold pain shot through his veins like fire. He convulsed, then choked on the damp earth in his mouth. A heavy rumble shook the ground. He cringed. Another rumble—closer—louder. The earth unexpectedly rolled away. Sunlight penetrated his closed lids.

He leaped from the hole, his first steps unsteady. Trees lay a hundred feet away. He started forward, then fell back at sight of a bulldozer a few feet away. The monster belched smoke as the bucket lowered toward the hole. Gerry screamed. The bucket halted and a man leaned from the cab.

"What—" the man began, but Gerry raced for the trees.

An instant later, the forest enveloped him. He had dug into the ground and covered himself when the cool earth began to sooth his stinging skin and he heard voices.

"Where is she?" one man asked.

"Did you see how fast she ran?" another said. "I've never seen anything like it. Where did she come from?"

"That hole you dug."

Gerry suddenly crouched in a dark village street watching a man accost a woman. Gerry shoved the man off the woman and sank his teeth into his fleshy neck. Waves of ecstasy mingled with the memory of the night he'd been wounded by the burglar.

That night turned into another, then another and another, until merging with the despair of learning he had awakened in the twenty-first century. Gerry fought the memories, but hopelessness overwhelmed him. The temple, *her temple*, had been destroyed long ago. Tears streamed down his face. His clan, all that he knew, slaughtered. And his god— Gerry's heart lurched.

She had been betrayed.

The pounding of his heart receded, replaced by weightlessness. Horror, fear, despair, all faded. An unhurried ebb and flow of blood moved in his veins. Peace and serenity enveloped. Pleasure seeped through every pore in an even rhythm like the soft caress of an angel's body. Lips brushed tingling skin between ear and shoulder. Soft as corn silk, Sula's hair shifted against his neck, sending shivers of pleasure to his groin. He reached for the nape of her neck and buried fingers deep in the silken trusses. The heavenly presence receded. Reluctance and shock filled the void.

Gerry shoved to a standing position, trapping her against the railing, and covered a breast with his free hand. Lust shot through him when she pressed into his palm. Pleasure surged, and he realized he was seeing through her eyes, feeling her desire, the need for his touch, his stroke. His breath came in shallow spurts. He was hard as a rock. An image of driving into her burst across his mental vision in vivid color. But the image hadn't originated with him. She had thought it. *She wanted it.* She—

Gerry tore free of her and collapsed onto the concrete. He stared up at her, breathing hard. "What the fuck are you?"

PART FOUR

The fangs of God are waiting.

SPLICED

Chapter One

THE BASEMENT LAY in shadows. Gerry reached up and touched his neck. Two pinpoints of slickness no bigger than shaving nicks lay an inch apart on the side of his neck. Hargrave stepped up and licked his face.

Sula shifted. "We must go. He's waking."

Gerry shoved Hargrave aside. "The dead guy?"

"He isn't dead."

Hargrave gave a low growl.

"He is waking," she said, her voice insistent.

Hargrave backed up a step, his collar tags jingling in the silence.

Dead guys, vampire blondes, and mind melds in basements and dungeons. A chill rippled down Gerry's arms. *Dammit.* He leaped to his feet, turned toward the stairs, then whirled.

"My gun. *Shit.*"

He scanned the floor. If the damned thing had fallen very far, he might not find it. From the corner of his eye he thought he saw the dead guy move. Chills slammed down his back.

"Behind you," Sula said.

Gerry jumped at the sound of her voice, then looked where she pointed and saw the gun lying beside the last stair. He scooped it up and started up the stairs two at a time.

"Hargrave," he called.

The dog shot up the stairs, Sula hard on his heels.

By the time they hit the street, Gerry's heart was running ahead of him. He didn't slow, didn't—couldn't—think. They reached the car. He jumped in and shoved the key into the ignition as Sula opened the passenger door. Hargrave leaped in and over the seat and she jumped into the passenger seat. The engine turned over and the car roared to life as Gerry revved the engine and slammed the gear into drive. He squealed a U-turn and sped away from the taxidermy toward the railroad tracks. Hargrave stepped onto the armrest between the front seats, whined, then plopped his forepaws and head onto Sula's lap.

Gerry glanced at him, then at her. "I'm telling you right now, if not for the dog, your ass would be back there in that basement with that freak." He gave an almost hysterical laugh. "What the hell am I talking about? You're the freak. Shit. *I'm* the freak."

He sent her a sideways glance. "What did you do to me, and...and why did—what was—" *Aw hell, why dance around it?* "Why did I like it?"

Like it? He was still shaking from...he was still shaking because he wanted more. A dead guy coming back to life and him running away like some kid scared of the boogieman did nothing to lessen the mother of all erections still lodged in his pants.

They approached the tracks. Gerry slammed the automatic transmission into second. He needed to strip some gears, and badly. He half drove, half flew across the tracks. Hargrave yelped.

"Fucking live with it," Gerry muttered, and shifted back into drive. "Well?" he demanded of her.

"I am sorry," she said, which pissed him off. "I don't know how to explain. Beings like me are not supposed to exist."

He made a hard left onto a deserted access road. "Did you slip me some kind of hallucinogen?"

Her brow furrowed on confusion.

"I didn't think so." He thought again about Alyssa Hamilton. *"I'll catch the boogieman next week,"* he had told her. *"Right now, I'm interested in finding out who the next victim is, and catching his would-be murderer."*

"How do you know they aren't one and the same?" she had asked.

"Are you speaking of the murderer or the next victim?" he countered.

He still hadn't forgotten looking into her eyes and feeling like he'd fallen into a house of mirrors when she said, *"Why not the murderer and the boogieman?"*

Gerry glanced at the blonde as they passed beneath a streetlight. Her blue eyes seemed to envelope him. He returned his attention to the road.

"What do you know about these murders?"

"I know you are trying to find the killer."

"Try again," Gerry ordered.

Up ahead, a streetlight turned red.

"I know an Aptrgangr has chosen them," she said.

He slowed for a red light, his mind racing back to the Google search that had turned up Aptrgangr. Icelandic Saga—*Drauger*. "An animated corpse that rises from the grave," he said, and made a hard right against the red light onto Arapaho Road. Hargrave slid into him and a car swerved to miss them. A horn blared. "Aptrgangr—after-goer or one who walks after death," Gerry said between clenched teeth as he jerked the wheel right, sending the car flying into a strip mall parking lot.

Hargrave yelped. Gerry brought the car to a jerky halt beneath a streetlamp at the far corner of the lot next to a dumpster, and Hargrave slid forward. Gerry jammed the car into park and faced the woman.

"You're telling me some sort of undead Icelandic vampire is running around killing people?"

"No. Aptrgangr are not dead. Legend made us that. We never died."

Hargrave tried to stand, but Gerry pushed him back onto his belly and repeated, "We?"

"I am Aptrgangr."

"You look pretty fucking alive to me."

"I am alive. Legends of the undead are stories created to cause fear."

Hargrave looked up at Gerry and thumped his tail. Gerry ignored the overture and snorted. "I've heard some doozies, but this one takes the cake." But even as he said the words, he remembered the dreams involving her. The night in the alley, her as the woman the gothi had raped, and only a few minutes ago when she had attacked him and…at least his hard-on had dulled to a low hum. Why hadn't he thought to bring a cross or some garlic?

"How do you know this killer is Aptrgangr?"

"He uses the knot of the slain."

"The Valknut." Gerry stared. "The murder on board the Icelandic ship." Her eyes flickered. He seized her wrist. "What do you know about that murder?"

"He was an evil man," she answered in an angry voice. "He murdered children."

Gerry gave her wrist a hard shake. "That's not what I asked."

"His kind do not deserve to live." Her eyes flickered with a glow.

"*The angel of death and a night stalker,*" Gerry quoted. "*Goddess of battle and death, who receives half of those slain in battle. The right of first choice is hers."*

Her eyes dilated.

He released her. "You killed Baby Killer Sanders."

"I am sworn to kill the unjust."

"Commanded by the powerful gothi," Gerry cited the passage, and she nodded. *Jesus fucking Christ. Move over Jim Jones, you got nothing on these nuts.* "Where is this gothi?" he demanded.

"I am searching for him."

"Searching—but you said he commanded you to kill the guy on the ship."

"No. I said, I am sworn to kill the unjust. My gothi was not there. I haven't seen him not in four hundred years. I know you are searching for him, too."

Hysterical laughter threatened to gurgle up from Gerry's belly. "You don't look a day over twenty."

"I was eighteen when I became Gythia."

And there it was. "And what have you been up to the last four hundred years?" he asked even as the bulldozer reappeared in his mind's eye, her leap from the hole, the men chasing her, her burying herself. Queasiness bumped against his insides.

She leaned toward Gerry, startling him. Her eyes glittered. "*He* tried to kill me."

Gerry didn't have to ask who *he* was. Hargrave laid his head on her lap—*just like Dee.* The dog wasn't acting like he was in the presence of a serial killer—he wasn't acting like he was in the presence of any kind of killer. There was something about murderers. Not people who slew someone in a crime of passion or a barroom brawl, but the kind that plotted and planned, a person who reveled in fear, pain—death. Gerry couldn't remember a single instance when Hargrave had misjudged character.

He grabbed the police radio from the back seat. It didn't matter if Hargrave thought she was the greatest thing since doggie biscuits. He needed answers.

He turned on the radio, depressed the send button, and said, "Dispatch, Detective Forstner here."

"Dispatch. Go ahead, Detective."

Gerry recognized Noel Henderson's voice. "Get forensics and a coroner over to Bear's Taxidermy on 1295 Hillindale. I just shot a male suspect." The instant the words were out of his mouth, when he remembered Uma Yohanson—and Joey.

"What is the description of the victim?" dispatch came back.

Gerry hesitated. The Valknut cult was the most dangerous he'd come across, and by some astronomically large improbability his ancestor had been a part of it. He couldn't confess that tidbit.

"Six foot, blonde, about two hundred pounds."

"1295 Hillindale. Units en route,"

"Out." Gerry let the hand gripping the radio fall to his thigh. "Goddammit."

He started the car, backed out of the space, and accelerated from the lot, headed east on Apollo. An electric generating plant had set up operation in his stomach. He had to get some answers—and fast. How had Sula transferred mental images of the dead guy into his mind—and why had the guy been dressed in gothic clothes. Were the clothes ceremonial? Maybe the cult got off dressing like ghouls.

The words from one of the ancient poems in the old manuscripts Iris had found came to mind:

And when the sun creeps over the hills, she sleeps, justice done.

Gerry glanced at her. "There are many Asatru symbols. Why the Valknut?"

"Hrungnir's heart. The connection between all that is above and below."

"The Valknut can be drawn in one stroke," he said.

"Yes," she replied in an excited voice. "The line without end."

Gerry turned his gaze to the road, radio still in hand. "Ever since that night in the alley, I've been having…visions." He let the words hang, his heart pounding.

Sula tilted her head and looked at him. "The alchemy of our blood is powerful."

"The alchemy of our blood," he repeated, then added, "When you have eliminated the impossible, whatever remains, however improbable, must be the truth."

Sula frowned.

"Something a fictional detective once said," Gerry said.

She stared for a long moment, then returned her attention to the scenery flashing past the window.

When they pulled up to his place ten minutes later, the lust had dissipated. The glowing eyes in the dusky light of the taxidermist's basement, the dead man who had moved, and vampire bites, all felt like snippets of a distant dream.

Gerry shoved open the door. "Let's go."

Inside the house, he strode to the kitchen. The click of Hargrave's nails on the linoleum floor as he trailed Gerry broke the silence. Gerry flipped on the light switch. Sula gasped. He swung, hand on his holstered gun.

She stared at the genealogy tree spread across his table. Slowly, deliberately, she approached the table and sank into the chair facing the chart. She began at the top, pointing at each name, and read aloud in flawless Old Norse. Gerry let his hand fall to his side when Hargrave trotted to her and lay at her feet. Her words dropped to a whisper. Tension thick enough to smother a 9mm round filled the room.

Sula placed a hand on the chart as reverently as Gerry had Jackson's books. She abruptly stilled, one slender forefinger on her branch of the lineage, the other on his. Fear jammed through him. She traced his branch past Uma Yohanson name and the notes he'd made that extended the chart to him and Joey.

The anger he'd kept at bay since Brenda had called resurfaced. Joey was in the hands of David Myles, and they were in some fucking cabin in the fucking Keys. Gerry had run a background check on Myles. The guy wasn't a criminal, at least not one that had been caught—yet. Gerry wanted to believe Brenda purposely went to the Keys to hurt him, but he'd never confessed that he had somehow mentally connected with the *Keepers of the Secret* killer when he had searched the Keys for members of the secret society. He'd never told anyone.

"You are of my people."

He startled at the sound of Sula's voice. "*Your* people?" He crossed to the table. "The books containing these charts only recently surfaced. They'd been buried for two hundred and fifty years." He tapped 'Sula' on the chart. "How did you learn about this, Sula?"

She shook her head. "I am Sula. I watched them enter my name in the eternal list that is chronicled in the Hidden Books of Thoth."

"The Book of Thoth that's buried with Prince Neferkaptah in the City of the Dead?" Gerry recalled stories of how the reader of the book gained the ability to understand the language of animals, cast spells, and enchant the sky and earth. As punishment, the loved ones of those who read the book would die until the reader returned the book. Jesus, the gothi god had gone all the way back to Egypt for his religion.

"The Hidden Books of Thoth were written for those destined to serve for eternity," Sula said.

"Eternity? Christ, a lifetime isn't enough. Your god wants your eternal soul."

"You do not understand," she said. "The legends are true. An eon of careful selection led to our two lines." She pointed at her son's name. "I now see my son was the first. That explains the connection between us."

"Like a perfect match?"

"Mates crafted by the gods. Your line from the gothi, mine from the sisterhood. My kind are called by the gods. Their special gifts flow through us to the world. We are raised in the temple then, through the blot, infused with the life blood so that we can ensure the survival of the weak. I became *Freyja*, high priestess." She laid a finger on the name 'Sula' in the column beside his finger. "I carry out the gods' judgment."

Gerry recalled a passage from the papers Iris sent. *Gothi died strange deaths at the hands of a mythical warrior princess. This warrior princess was none other than the goddess Freyja,* A biblical story in the book of Exodus told of how the Angel of Death swept through Egypt killing the firstborn of all who didn't paint the sign of the Hebrew god over their door.

Angel of Death: God's assassin. Freyja, warrior princess, angel of death and night stalker: Asatru assassin. How were they different?

Gerry shifted his gaze to her face. She had called the experience of biting 'shared memories.' Had he somehow tapped into a past time and place when vampires lived? He stared into her blue eyes. Fuck philosophical questions. Whatever she was, she'd admitted to killing the sailor, and had proven she was strong enough to kill the Valknut victims when she'd fought Alarr. Hell, if his so-called visions were real, she killed others in that Icelandic village. But how did the assassin in her explain the plea for forgiveness when she'd bitten him? Had she begged the victims' forgiveness when she'd bled them to death?

"Did you kill Kinnison?" he demanded.

"No."

"What was your connection with Judge Jackson?"

Her brow furrowed. "Who is he?"

"You were there. I saw you."

Her eyes flashed recognition. "Yes, you were with a boy."

Fear crept up his spine. Just now, she'd acted surprised at seeing Joey's name on the lineage. Yet, outside Jackson's house she'd stared at Joey like she knew him.

If he put her in jail, he couldn't keep her from contacting the gothi and passing on the genealogical information about Joey. The Feds would have a different idea. They would view this as an opportunity to flush out her partner, a killer they believed was just one more human gone bad. Joey would be their bait.

"What were you searching for?" he demanded. "What are you doing here in Miami?"

"I came to find my clan."

"How did you know about Jackson?"

"I awoke six months ago with nowhere to go. My temple was destroyed, my clan gone. Iceland is a difficult place to live without identification or status. While researching my clan, I befriended a clerk at the National Archives. She told me about a man who had inquired about the same names from the same years. Your Judge Jackson."

One helluva coincidence, but Gerry knew she was telling the truth. Jackson knew about the lineage, but hadn't said a word. He had connected the books with the Valknut killings and held out to the very end.

"So you figured Jackson was a member of your long-lost cult. Why didn't you contact him directly?"

"I am alone in a time that is not mine. I came to Miami. Discovered he had no connection, but knew a great deal about names and dates. I needed to contact him but didn't know how to explain."

"How to explain you've been dead for four-hundred years?"

Her gaze sharpened. "We can die by only one means, but we do die. I thought I had died."

Her expression clouded and he knew she was remembering a hole in Iceland, and a backhoe removing the dirt that had covered her. He forced back an impulse to take her in his arms. How was he supposed to deal with the desire she incited in him, the questions she forced him to ask: What was she? What was he?

Maybe he could take Joey and disappear. He had a little money. Mom would help. Sula grasped his arm. Fear and...desire flooded him.

"What are you doing to me?" he rasped.

She stood. Hargrave jumped to his feet. Gerry tried to step back, but her grip on his arm tightened. "No," he commanded, and grabbed her wrist, but couldn't disengage her. *"Hargrave."*

The dog wagged his tail. She leaned close. "Forgive me. I must show you what I cannot explain." Her cool lips touched his neck and he trembled, but wasn't sure if it was fear or anticipation. She nuzzled his neck. Her teeth grazed skin and he tensed in anticipation. The prick followed and he fell headfirst into—Hargrave woofed.

"Gerry?"

Sula spun. Gerry staggered back. His vision cleared. Dee stepped into the kitchen. He lurched to the side, grabbing for the sink.

"What's going on?" she demanded.

He gulped air, trying to force his brain to function.

"My God, you're the blonde wanted for—Gerry, what the hell is going on? Don't move," she ordered Sula.

"It's not what you think," he was saying, knowing it sounded stupid.

Dee's eyes blazed. "It *looked* like you were about to kiss a murder suspect."

It looked that way, but he couldn't say what was actually about to happen.

"I hope the sex is worth your career, Gerry." Dee turned her glare onto Sula. "Twitch so much as a muscle, Blondie, and I'll break your legs." She reached for the phone hanging on the wall beside her.

"Dee," he stepped toward her.

Gerry caught movement in the corner of his eye. Sula brushed him aside like fabric. She caught Dee's wrist and propelled her toward him. He caught Dee as Sula crouched, spun with a leg out stretched, and hooked his ankle. He and Dee went down. Arms and legs tangled.

Hargrave leaped to their side and woofed, tail wagging. Gerry shoved the dog aside and pushed to his feet. His eyes met Sula's in the instant before she grabbed the genealogy. The room swam, and he lurched forward onto the bare table. The table pitched like a ship's deck in high seas, then righted itself. He pushed off, shaking. Sula was gone.

Hargrave shot past him. Gerry stumbled after the dog and through the open front door. By the time Gerry gained the walkway, the dog had reached the end of the block.

"Hargrave!" he shouted.

The dog looped toward him. Gerry bent, grabbed his knees, and gasped for air.

"What the hell was that all about?" Dee asked.

He looked left. She stood beside him, eyes hard, mouth set.

"Our best chance to find the killer," he answered, "and you blew it."

Chapter Two

GERRY GLANCED IN the Impala's rear view mirror as he slowed over the tracks and approached Bear's Taxidermy. Dee's headlights reflected in the mirror. She had followed inches from his bumper all the way from home. The shock on her face when he'd told her about the shooting was etched into his brain. He returned his attention to the road and the police vehicles whose flashing blue and red lights lit the cloudless night. Hargrave sat up in the back seat. Gerry's gut tightened as he parked behind the nearest black and white.

"Stay," he commanded the Shepherd, and got out.

Dee pulled up behind, and hurried from her car to follow.

High-powered battery lights illuminated the showroom, spilling light out the door and windows. Where was the yellow crime scene tape? Gerry pulled his badge from his back pocket and flashed it to the uniformed officer standing on the sidewalk in front of the taxidermy. The guy nodded, and Dee fell into step beside Gerry as he headed toward the taxidermy's front door. Inside the showroom, he stopped at sight of Lummus squatting beneath a window on the east side of the room.

Lummus rose as Gerry started for the basement stairs. "What'd you do with the body?" Lummus called.

Gerry halted. "What?"

Lummus smirked. "The body. You called in the shoot, but there's no body."

Gerry hit the basement stairs two at a time with Dee on his heels, and halted at the bottom. Portable arc lights flooded the basement. No body. No blood. A few feet to his right, a chalk circle surrounded each of the two casings from the rounds he'd fired. A small measure of relief filtered through him. At least he hadn't imagined the shooting.

Lacy appeared in the doorway to his right. "You all right?"

"Where's the body?" he demanded.

"That's supposed to be my line."

His gaze jerked left as Federal Agent Howell appeared in the opposite doorway. Morris stepped up behind Howell. How had they known?

Lummus.

"The guy went down there." Gerry pointed to the casings.

"Who was he?" Morris asked.

How the hell could he answer that one? He couldn't say the man was a vampire. "Don't know. I'd seen him once before, a couple days ago. It's in my report." Gerry thanked God the computers had been online that morning.

"You sure you hit him?"

"Yeah." Gerry started to add 'right between the shoulder blades' and stopped.

"Your team hasn't found any traces of blood," Morris paused. "Could he have been wearing a vest?"

Gerry had seen blood gush from Alarr's arm. A flash went off, and Lacy rose from a squat, lowering her camera.

"Why didn't you call it in from here?" Morris asked.

Damn GPS in his cell phone. They'd tagged him when he called from the parking lot. "The blonde we've been looking for was here. She took off. I went after her."

Gerry avoided Dee's gaze. He deserved everything she threw at him, but he prayed to God she was a better woman than he was a man. Howell leaned against the doorjamb. The man reminded him too much of Lummus. He'd had an attitude before Gerry met him at Herrero's office.

"No blood, nothing," Morris said. "He had to be wearing."

A logical assumption, Gerry thought—for a person who hadn't been there. "Yeah," he replied.

"Where's the blonde?"

Gerry could feel Dee's gaze boring through his shoulder blades. "She got away."

Another flash went off as Lacy snapped another photo.

Morris started to open his mouth. Gerry cut him off. "You can read the full report in the morning." He spun and headed up the stairs. He went out the door with Dee close behind.

She remained silent until they reached his car. "What the hell is going on?" Before he could reply, she added, "I'm not usually that bad a judge of character. I might have misread what happened between us—"

"You didn't."

She paused, clearly uncertain, then said, "I didn't expect you to marry me, but I didn't figured you would be hard up for another woman the next day."

Guilt stabbed at him. He started to respond, then saw Lummus emerge from the taxidermy. He sauntered down the sidewalk. At his car, Lummus gave him a casual salute, then opened the door and got in.

Gerry leaned against the Impala and looked at Dee. "I wasn't looking for another woman. I came here because…because I got a tip, of sorts."

"What the hell does that mean?"

"It means…" he took a deep breath. "You saw how fast she moved."

Dee hesitated. "Yeah."

"Have you ever seen anything like that?"

"No."

"The guy I shot moved even faster. That first night after we went to the *Sand Box* I chased him into an alley where he disappeared."

Dee scrutinized him. "Able to leap tall buildings and outrun bullets. That makes him Superman."

Gerry didn't miss the sarcasm, but only nodded. "And she's Super Woman. But we know Superman and Super Woman aren't real."

Dee glanced at his neck, and a chill rolled across his arms. *Send in the Clowns* blared from his waist. He snatched the cell phone from his belt. A Ft. Lauderdale number showed on the screen, but it wasn't Johnson's.

He took the call. "Forstner."

"Detective Gerald Forstner?"

The voice was a cop's, but not one he recognized. "Yeah."

"I'm Detective Jones of the Fort Lauderdale PD. William Johnson's been murdered. I understand you paid him a visit two days ago."

Gerry's heart lurched. Johnson had two kids and a wife. "What about his family?"

"They're fine. The killer waited outside his house, broke his neck when he took out the trash."

Just like Collin and Marissa.

Linette Howsten.

"Your boys were supposed to keep him safe," Gerry snapped.

Silence met his outburst, then, "I haven't been briefed on the case. I'm the investigating detective."

"Was there a symbol on his body?" Gerry asked.

"Symbol?"

"The Valknut symbol."

"No," Jones answered slowly.

There hadn't been with Collin and Marissa either. "When did it happen?"

"Last night. I need to talk to you. I'm coming down there."

Dammit, just like with Collin and Marissa, the killers were covering their tracks. McMillian and Pentz were next. "I'll get back to you," Gerry said.

"Where can—"

Gerry hit the end button.

"What is it?" Dee asked. "You're white as a ghost."

"William Johnson's been murdered." He hit three on speed dial for Lummus.

Lummus picked up. "Yeah."

"I just got a call from the Ft. Lauderdale PD. William Johnson is dead. Get some protection on McMillian and Pentz."

"You're not in any position—"

"Shut the fuck up. One more word out of your mouth other than 'yes, sir,' and I'll have your ass in a sling before Herrero can phone IA."

A heartbeat of tense silence passed, then Lummus shot back, "Yes, sir."

"Widen the APB net on Sam Pentz. We need to talk to him. I've got a couple things to check out. I'll be in touch." Gerry ended the call, pulled out his notepad, flipped through the pages, and dialed Marilyn Pentz's number.

On the fourth ring, the connection clicked open. "Hello?" Marilyn said.

"Marilyn, it's Gerry Forstner. I need to see you right away."

"Anything."

"I'll be there within the hour."

Dee stared expectantly. "Where are we going?"

He shook his head. "We're not going anywhere. This is a bad—"

His cell phone played another stanza of *Send in the Clowns*. Gerry glanced at the display. Herrero. He'd be suspended while IA investigated the shooting, but without a body, the only thing they could prove was discharging his weapon in the taxidermy. The result would be a long vacation. The phone rang again. With Lummus wanting his ass and Howell gunning for him, he wouldn't catch a break. He considered not answering, but knew they'd already located him. Damn GPS.

He met Dee's gaze. "The shit's about to hit the fan. I'm not taking you down with me." He flipped open the phone. "Forstner."

"Get down to my office, *now.*"

"Am I on suspension?"

"Breaking and entering, discharging your firearm, leaving the scene, a missing body. The mayor's already heard. Yeah, I'd say I don't have much choice. But I want to hear your side before Internal Affairs gets a hold of you."

"I'll be there as soon as possible," Gerry said.

Herrero didn't answer right away and Gerry wondered if the Chief was going to call Howell and Morris and tell them to pick him up before he left the taxidermy. "I could just have the Feds bring you in," Herrero said.

"You could," Gerry agreed, "But IA won't catch up with me until tomorrow. I'll come to see you first.

"I want to see you tonight."

"I'll do my best." Gerry hung up.

He regarded Dee. "I'm sorry. I didn't intend for any of this to happen. You're already in hot water if anyone figures out you knew something and didn't say anything. I won't pull you in any deeper."

He got in the car, started it up, and rolled down the window. "Give me a day. If I come up missing or empty handed, tell them everything: the genealogy, the blonde—" He started to tell her to watch out for Joey, but saw in her eyes she already knew. He shifted into drive, maneuvered around the black and white, then headed down the road.

Five minutes later, on Interstate 95, he spotted Dee's headlights behind him.

Chapter Three

G ERRY WHIPPED THE car onto the shoulder and stopped. Dee pulled up behind and stopped. He left the Impala and stormed to the Alpha Romero. She stared through the closed window. He rapped on the glass and she lowered the window an inch.

"We're on a freeway, you know," she said. "This is dangerous."

"What the hell are you doing?" he demanded.

"Driving."

Three cars whizzed by in quick succession, kicking up exhaust filled wind. He grimaced. *Too many cars to haul her from the Alpha Romero and shake some sense into her.*

"This isn't a game," he shouted over the traffic.

She lifted both brows.

He wasn't sure if her expression said she was waiting for a chance to castrate him or she hoped a car would clip his ass. He stomped back to his Impala and got inside. He studied her in the rear view mirror. He didn't have time to lose her, which was unlikely given the performance disparity between their cars.

"Women," he muttered, and Hargrave sneezed.

HALF AN HOUR later, Gerry pulled up to Intelligent Corporate Services.

Dee fell into step beside him when he reached the walkway. He whirled. "Go home, Dee. Revenge isn't worth your job."

She stared for a second, then burst out laughing. "What an ego."

"I'm not worth it."

She laughed harder. "You think I'm here because I have feelings for you?"

His face heated. "Suit yourself." He started for the building.

Dee kept pace with him. "What—" She forced back a hiccup of laughter and he shot her a recriminating glance. "What are we doing here?" she asked.

"*We* aren't doing anything. You're going to keep quiet. Blow this and I'll lock you up somewhere until this is over."

"Will you strip me naked and have your way with me first?"

He jerked his gaze onto her. He couldn't tell if she was serious or not.

She grabbed his arm, stopping him. "I saw how fast that blonde moved, and I saw the blood on your neck. If I'd seen only the blood, I would have figured you'd gone psycho. But seeing her move like that... What's going on?"

"I'm not sure, and what I think I know, I don't know if I can explain. Look, Sula took the genealogy and—"

"Sula?"

"Yeah."

"God," Dee whispered.

"I've got to get them, and fast. If I can't, I'll have to drop out of sight with my son, and that's no life for him."

"When we leave here, I want to hear it all, no matter how weird."

Gerry wasn't certain he could explain, but nodded.

Raul wasn't on duty at the main entrance. The guy behind the desk, Marcus, was even bigger.

Gerry didn't waste time. He flashed his badge. "Anybody still up at Intelligent Corporate Services?"

"The owner, Kevin Matheson, hasn't come down yet," Marcus said.

Gerry had figured that would be the case. Those geeks were taking over the world one kilobyte at a time. "We're going up to see him." Gerry glanced at the phone half hidden by the upper level of the desk. "Don't call him."

The guy lifted his hands, palms out, and leaned back in his chair.

Gerry headed for the elevator with Dee. A minute later, the elevator doors opened on a deserted office. They strode down the hallway to Kevin's office. The door was closed. Gerry didn't bother knocking.

Kevin's head snapped up from eye level with the monitor in front of him. "What the—" He glanced from Gerry to Dee, then again at Gerry, and leaned back in his chair. "Working late?"

Gerry took four steps to his desk, Dee matching stride, and said, "I want the rest of Linnette Howsten and Harold Balder's file."

Kevin looked surprised. "Rest? The cops from Long Key have already been here. I told them the same thing I told you."

Long Key, Gerry thought. Linette had murdered Collin and Marissa in the wrong county. Long Key cops were bulldogs. "Let's call it an...update," Gerry said. "That way, I won't have to get nasty."

The muscle in Kevin's jaw worked, but he pulled the keyboard off the desk onto his lap and typed. A second later, pages rolled out of the printer at his elbow.

Gerry scanned the printout. Not a Goddamn thing different than the other one. He looked at Kevin. "I want access to their account."

Kevin hit a button on the keyboard. Then scanned the monitor. "Nothing the last two weeks."

"Listen, mother—"

"Let me see that," Dee cut in.

She edged Gerry aside and turned one of the flat screen monitors to face her. She extended a hand to Kevin. His surprised expression melted into uncertainty, then a disdainful curve of his mouth. He handed her the keyboard. She pulled one of the chairs closer, grabbed the cordless mouse to Kevin's left, then began reading the computer screen. With a few keystrokes, the screen filled with a list of incoming calls and faxes for the last month.

Christ, she was one of *them*. Gerry ignored the roil of his stomach and scanned the list. Kevin hadn't lied; there'd been no new activity the last two weeks. Gerry started to demand the real report, but Dee abruptly snatched the document from his hand. She ran a finger down the list. Her brow furrowed, she set the document on her lap, then minimized the list on the screen and pulled up Internet Explorer. She typed TYR in the Google search engine in the upper right hand of the browser screen.

"I already—" Gerry started, but stopped when she typed 'Old Norse' instead of 'Industries,' as he'd done.

The screen filled with a list of hits containing fragments of the words Tyr and Old Norse. Before Gerry had a chance to understand what she was doing, she hit the second link. A list of Old Norse names filled the screen. Dee scrolled down to Tyr: Norse mythical name of a son of Odin, meaning, god.

"Jesus," Gerry breathed. "How'd you—" but she was off again, scrolling up the screen.

She stopped at the name Harold, and Gerry read, *leader of the army, derived from Old English, here "army", and "leader, ruler." The name of five kings of Norway and two kings of England, including Harold II who lost the Battle of Hastings (and was killed in it), which led to the Norman Conquest. After the conquest the name was rarely used, but was eventually revived in the 19th century.*

Dee looked up at Gerry, but he couldn't tear his eyes off the screen. "Try Balder."

She did.

Balder means "prince" from Old Norse. In Norse mythology Balder was the son of Odin and Frigg. Because of the disturbing dreams he had as a youth, his mother extracted an oath from everything in the world that it would not harm him. However, the evil fire god, Loki, learned that she had overlooked mistletoe. Being jealous, he tricked the blind god Hoder into throwing a branch of mistletoe at Balder, which killed him.

"Print the whole thing," Gerry said.

GERRY AND DEE hit ICS's parking lot fifteen minutes later. A serial killer, even if a paying client, was more than Kevin had bargained for. It had taken him less than five minutes to hack into TYR Industries' account and pull every transaction conducted in their five years at Intelligent Corporate Services.

"Where to now?" Dee asked as they approached the Impala.

"You're going home."

"You promised to explain. Besides, you can't study those printouts while you're driving."

Gerry stopped with one hand on his car door. Hargrave sat in the driver's seat with paws on the steering wheel as if to say he would drive while Gerry read the printouts.

Gerry handed the sheaf of papers to Dee. "Get in." He shooed Hargrave into the back seat and climbed in. His phone rang and he snatched it off his belt. It was Lummus.

"Forstner."

"I'm at McMillan's. There's been no trouble here."

"Put some uniforms on his house."

"The Feds are taking him and his wife into protective custody."

Great. Maybe they would shove them into some gray room and conduct PSI experiments. If they took Lummus with them, Gerry would be willing to turn over everything he knew to the G-men and call it a day.

"Have you heard from Sheridan?"

"He tried calling you."

Damn. Leave it to a geek like Kevin Matheson to shield his office against cell signals. Gerry wondered what Kevin knew about the phone company that he didn't. "I was out of range."

"More like 'out of it,'" Lummus said.

Gerry fought rising anger. "Cut the shit."

"Sheridan reported Pentz is fine. He left a couple uniforms on guard until the Feds can talk to the wife."

That meant Gerry needed to get to her first. "Good," he said. "What about Sam Pentz?"

"No sign of him."

"Get on the horn and find out if TYR Industries owns any property in the greater Miami area. Keep me posted." Gerry ended the call and dropped the phone into his cup-holder.

With Glenn Pentz and Jack Macmillan accounted for, Sam Pentz remained the only unaccounted for link to the books.

Hargrave shifted in the back seat and Gerry's mind tuned into the police radio chatter coming from under his seat. Damn dog had pushed the radio off the seat again.

Gerry started the car and pulled from the parking lot. He glanced at Dee, who was reading the printouts, then eased on the brake for the yellow light up ahead.

"How did you know about the acronym?"

She looked up. "TYR had to be an acronym. That reminded me of an old movie I saw as a kid where the killer got a thrill from using word clues the cops missed."

She'd been right. And, like the cops in the movie, he'd missed the clue.

✦

TEN MINUTES LATER, Gerry halted in front of Marilyn Pentz's house.

"Wait here with Hargrave and keep an eye on the house."

"Gerry—"

"I'll be right back. Study those printouts."

He hurried to the front door and rang the bell. Marilyn opened the door. Her gaze shifted from Gerry to Dee sitting in the car. A gentle smile lit her eyes and Gerry recognized approval.

"That's Detective Kelly."

Her smile vanished. "Gerald, what's wrong?"

"May I come in?"

"Of course." She stepped aside and he brushed past.

She closed the door and followed him into the living room. "I can make coffee."

"No thanks," he replied.

She sat on the couch.

Gerry sat beside her. "Marilyn, I need to find Sam right away."

Her lips pursed. "Is he in danger?"

He hesitated. Would this be too much for her? She was a tough lady, but she was seventy-two. "I'm afraid he is."

She shook her head. "I've been worried all day. He called earlier and—" Her voice broke.

Gerry covered her hands with his. "What happened?"

She smiled gratefully. "It's not so much what happened, but more that he seemed somehow different."

"How?"

"He's always been high strung. Geniuses are like that. He is one, you know. Most parents say that because they want to believe their children are special, but Sam is a bona fide genius, MENSA initiate and all." She sighed. "It's really more of a curse than anything. There is such a thing as being too smart."

Marilyn looked Gerry in the eye. "He said his father told him you and I had been to see him. I've tried telling him Glen won't be with us forever. So, naturally, I was delighted he visited his father. But then he began asking questions about you, what you'd said to me, if I knew anything about the investigation. It wasn't long before the questions felt more like an interrogation. When he didn't mention the FBI visiting Glen, I couldn't get past the idea it was you he was interested in. He was angry that I'd brought you to see Glen." Her eyes moistened. "He has Glen's book. What does that mean? I laughed off those books as if…" She gave her head a jerky shake.

Gerry gently squeezed her hand. "As if they were Playboy magazines."

She nodded. "But I was wrong. Wasn't I?"

"You couldn't know."

"Maybe," she said, but the sadness in her eyes didn't dissipate. "Is Sam going to jail for having that book? It doesn't belong to him or Glen."

Gerry wished like hell that was all Sam—or Glen's—only risk. If there was any truth to Sula's claim that the books were part of the Book of Thoth that made them near priceless, and Gerry was betting Sam Pentz was willing to chance his own father's murder for that kind of money.

Gerry released Marilyn's hand. "The man who wants Glen's book isn't so nice."

"He's the man you're looking for."

Gerry would have given anything to be able to say no, but he wasn't going to lie to this woman. "Yes."

"We have to save Sam," she said. "He has no idea the danger he's in."

"Where can I find him?"

She raised a shaky hand to her mouth. "He wouldn't tell me."

"Do you have any idea where I can begin looking?"

She shook her head slowly. "I wish I did."

"If you hear from him, call me right away."

Gerry promised to keep her informed of on any news regarding her son, then headed back to the car. Dee watched him get in, then start the engine.

"Find anything?" he asked as he pulled from the curb.

"Some repeated phone numbers, and a lot of calls to and from country code 354. Do you know what that is?"

Gerry's jaw tightened. "Iceland."

"Isn't it time you told me what *that*," she jabbed a finger at his neck, "was all about?"

He felt his body flush. "I swear to God, Dee, I don't know how."

"Start from the beginning," she urged, and he did.

Chapter Four

A N HOUR LATER, Gerry finished with, "That's what the blonde was
doing at my house."

He had driven back to the station on autopilot, and now sat two
blocks away. He had explained about the *Keepers of the Secret*, the Valknut
chain, how the MO had been broken with Jackson's murder, Joseph P.
Warner Laboratories, and his belief that Linnette Howsten had been a
dead end. He'd been so wrong about that one.

"Howsten isn't the blonde I saw at your house?" Dee asked.

"No."

"There are two blondes?"

"Three."

"The man you shot is one?"

"Yes."

She snorted. "Thank God. I don't think I could have survived the
competition."

"It's not like that."

"No?" she said sharply, then seemed to catch herself. "There's something...hey, wait a minute. The Valknut—Knot Of The Slain. My God."
She went white.

"What? What is it?"

Dee looked at him. "Knot of the slain: K O T S, Keepers of the Secret." She paused, then repeated with emphasis, "K O T S."

Gerry waited for the shock. Instead, he realized he'd known all along
there had to be a connection.

The dispatcher's voice rose above the low background chatter. "1030
at 4049 Ponce De Leon Blvd, Suite 580. EMT and homicide units

respond."

Dee's eyes widened and they said in unison, "Kevin Matheson," then she added, "Someone's on our trail."

My trail, Gerry mentally corrected, then remembered Dee's car in ICS's parking lot.

"Damn," he muttered as she grabbed his arm and said, "My car,"

"Find the radio," he ordered.

Dee unbuckled her seat belt, twisted, and half dove into the back. Light spilled across her buttocks and Gerry wished he'd never laid eyes on Sula. He wished he could drive to the closest seaside hotel. He would make love to Dee until dawn, then, later that morning find a secluded spot where they could skinny dip. Dee was a good woman. She deserved better.

She bobbed up, radio in hand.

"Dispatch, this is Lummus," the radio barked, "ETA, fifteen minutes."

"Roger," dispatch came back. "Be advised, agents Howell and Morris en route."

"Roger," Lummus replied, and the radio silenced as Gerry grabbed his phone from the cup holder and thumbed Brenda's number.

She picked up on the fist ring, and said, "Decided to call me anyway."

"Cut the crap, Brenda. He's my son, too."

She remained quiet for three heartbeats, then said, "Everything is fine. Joey's right here sleeping. How's the case?"

"It'll be a couple more days at least."

"That's no problem. Joey loves going out on the boat."

Gerry's heart twisted, *Myles has a boat.*

He managed in an even voice, "Stay out of sight."

"Sure. Bye."

Gerry turned to Dee. "I'm leaving you here." He pocketed the phone.

"I'm not on duty for another hour."

"I'm not going back home. You're the only one who knows what's going on. I need you safe if things go wrong."

Her gaze cut through him with razor sharp precision. "This is your male ego talking."

"Do you have someone you can stay with after your shift?" he asked.

"You're over the top on this one, Gerry."

"Am I? The guy we talked to an hour ago is dead. Collin and Marissa are dead—now Johnson. Joey's in deep trouble if this madman gets to the genealogy—or gets to me first. This isn't about advancing your career or my male ego or you being able to take care of yourself. Herrero will suspend you. Maybe even kick you off the force for not reporting our conversations. You'll never get a job in law enforcement again. For your sake *and* Joey's, you need to stay clear of trouble—and stay alive. It doesn't matter what I do. I'm finished. They'll never buy the truth." He wondered why he was suddenly able to accept it.

"They have to."

"Vampire assassins roaming Miami looking for me and my son, a dead guy who got up and walked away?" Gerry shook his head. "Not to mention a four hundred year old woman."

Dee snorted. Gerry held her gaze without replying.

She stared. "You're seriously buying into her story?"

"I shot the guy in the arm, then the heart. Even if he wore a vest, I saw the blood gush from his arm. Did you see any blood on that basement floor?"

"Maybe someone moved the body."

"You said you'd never seen anybody move like that."

"So, what's the secret to their long lives?" Gerry didn't reply, and Dee added, slowly, "She was about to show you."

He wanted to melt into the car seat. The way she'd said it sounded dirty. She was right.

"Do you have somebody to stay with?" he asked.

She gave him a deprecating look. "Anyone I'd be staying with would be because I was protecting them."

"I'm not letting you go home alone," he said.

"Then you'll have to be here when I get off duty."

"And if I get tied up?"

"Then you miss staying at my place this time."

✦

THE DASHBOARD CLOCK clicked over to nine forty-five when Gerry turned off his red penlight and set the last page of the printout on the neat pile on the passenger seat. Sitting half a block from Marilyn Pentz's house, he scanned the street for the hundredth time. Since parking the car an hour ago, he hadn't felt so much as a twinge from his weird sense. Hargrave's even breathing in the back seat further validated the feeling

Marilyn wasn't in any immediate danger.

Gerry jammed his eyes shut and rubbed them. The printout had begun to blur fifteen minutes ago, but he'd kept reading. The invoices, bills, contact lists, and phone records spanned the last five years, the time since he'd lost the trail of the *Keepers of the Secret,* almost to the month. Half the incoming caller ID numbers were listed as 'No number available,' and neither Michaels, Franklin, Vitelli, nor Kinnison's phone numbers appeared in the records. Gerry had expected nothing less.

The remote logins and email records contained information about the source whose Internet Protocol address identified a computer on a network. Gerry didn't need Quin to tell him that the address was not necessarily unique. However, a trace of the route might show who owned the computers. Quin would get the list first thing tomorrow.

Gerry's cell phone rang. He blew out a long breath. Herrero had called half a dozen times. Gerry let it ring three times before snatching it from the cup holder. Iris Hjortur's name flashed on the screen. It was one a.m. in Iceland. Adrenaline pumped into his veins. Iris had to be pouring over the parts of Johnson's book he'd sent. He hoped she'd found a clue that would solve the case and the mystery of his insanity.

He hit the answer button. "Hello, Iris."

"Hello, Gerry," her soft Icelandic lilt should have salved his nerves, but reminded him of Sula and of what she had said, *Mates crafted by the gods.*

"Forgive me if I'm calling too late," Iris said, "but you did say to call the moment I had anything substantial. I don't think I could have waited for your morning to speak with you."

"I'm glad you didn't wait."

"Gerry, I must tell you, this small piece of the manuscript—it is a small section, you did say that, correct?"

"Yes."

"And you did promise that if I was interested, when the time was right, you would share the remainder of the manuscript?"

Gerry had shared a small portion of Johnson's book, hoping the promise of receiving the whole thing would assure her silence. When he gave her the pages, he hadn't told her anything other than the book had been written in Old Norse. He wanted to see if she verified the men's accounts of the book's content.

"*Manuscripts,* Iris," he emphasized.

"Oh," she breathed. "Will you also tell me where they were discovered?"

"I'll tell you everything I know."

"I have never seen anything like this," she said. "This manuscript delves deep into secret Asatru rituals I've never heard of. As you said, the language is Old Norse. However, it is interesting to note that there are a few Latin words intermingled."

"What does that mean?"

"The Latin used is technically modern, that is, modern as Shakespeare's English is Modern English. Without further study, I can't be sure what the combination of the two languages mean. Perhaps the priests preserved the archaic Norse much as the Catholics use Latin and the Jews used Hebrew in the temple during Jesus' time when Aramaic was the spoken language. There is no mistaking the Old Norse, however, which means these traditions were passed down from the time of the Eddas."

Earlier, Gerry thought, if the dates in the lineage are correct.

"We see three things," Iris went on. "The initiation of priestesses into the temple, the joining of the high priest and each new initiate—"

"Initiate?" Gerry cut in.

"Yes. It was, and still is, common for those entering any priesthood to go through a ritual that inducts them into the sect. However, while such rituals are common, these particular customs are not. Then—and this is by far the most exciting—we see the ascension of the new priest." Her voice exuded the excitement of a scientist on the brink of a discovery that was about to change mankind. Gerry had found that such discoveries came with downsides that were seldom considered, much less understood.

"Their priest isn't typical," she said. "This man is a god."

"That's not so strange," Gerry said. "Catholics believe the pope is God on earth."

"God represented on earth," she corrected, "not God."

"What's the difference?"

"A very big difference. These Asatru believe their god chooses a body to inhabit."

"That sounds like Christianity's version of Jesus," Gerry said. "God on earth, born as man, inhabiting a human body."

"No," she said. "This god isn't born, but exists as spirit. He carefully selects a human host, then a ritual is performed where he takes possession of the body. Mótsognir—"

"Mótsognir?" Gerry murmured. Memory of the poem he'd read surfaced.

Freya appears in the battle's last hour, clad in heavy mail.
She lifts her head to heaven and cries out to her creator Mótsognir.
When her eye falls upon the enemy that alone can kill.

"But those worthy of her aid cannot fail," he said out loud.

"What?" Iris said.

Memory of cold hands pulling off his clothes intruded into his thoughts. The gold band on the man's middle finger—the ring of the Gothi High Priest, Mótsognir—gleamed in his mind's eye. "Come, my prized priestess," Gerry murmured in unison with the gothi priest.

"Hello?" Iris said.

The steering wheel snapped into focus. "What about *Mótsognir?*" Gerry asked.

She hesitated, then said, "Mótsognir is a parasitic god, one who moves into a host body, then absorbs the host's experiences and knowledge."

"Sounds like he could take over the world."

"There is a sense that he has limitations. He might, for example, gain the knowledge of how to read music, but his fingers would not be able to translate that into actual practice. If he invaded Einstein's body, he would gain the scientist's knowledge, but Einstein's ability to extrapolate beyond his predecessors' work would remain outside Mótsognir's ability. In a very real way, the god bleeds his hosts dry, channeling their consciousness into his own, and therefore draining the host of his soul."

"A psychic vampire," Gerry said. "Even Stoker understood that." As did vampire cults today, he added silently. "How long does this process take?" he asked.

"No time was specified. But the new host was left in the room with the dying host and the high priestess, then emerged later with Mótsognir inhabiting the new body."

"The high priestess and god," Gerry said. "Only one person was privy to the actual ascension. Conclave has nothing on these guys."

"Interesting you should mention conclave," Iris said, her voice excited. "As early as the fourth century, popes were chosen by general consensus or acclamation—voice vote, if you will. However, this lack of organization in election procedures gave rise to rival Popes. In 1059 Nicholas II decreed that the cardinals elect a candidate who would take office after receiving the consent of the clergy and laity. The Cardinal Bishops were to meet first and discuss the candidates before meeting with the Cardinal Priests and Cardinal Deacons for the actual vote. If these books predate the Eddas as I suspect, there might be a connection between Nicholas' decree and the Asatru tradition. The secrecy that shrouded conclave after Nicholas' decree is similar to the Asatru tradition we see in these books."

Gerry couldn't repress a shudder. *Only the new pope didn't steal a person's soul in the process as the Asatru god did.*

"Any idea how a host was chosen?" he asked.

"Not directly. The new host is referred to as young, strong, and of sound mind. It seems safe to assume physical prowess was a major concern. That wasn't the end of the process though. Once Mótsognir emerged from behind closed doors, he had to pass the high priestess' test."

"Sounds as if the high priestess ran the show," Gerry said.

"Matriarchal societies predate patriarchal structures," she replied.

"What's the test?"

"A blood ritual."

Gerry could almost feel Sula's lips against his neck, the silky softness of her hair against his skin. He shivered.

"She must verify that the new host possesses the old host's memories," Iris said.

"Shared memories," he murmured.

"Exactly. These memories merge through the bite of the Aptrgangr."

"The what?"

"The Aptrgangr. The exact translation is the ones—"

"Ones who walk after death," he cut in. "Do you realize you're saying this is a priesthood of vampires?"

"Vampire mythology is complex," she replied. "This cult, however, is not the blood sucking ghouls portrayed in old movies."

Gerry recalled Chilly Billy and wished to God he'd gone to bed like Mom ordered.

"Here we have a completely new twist," Iris went on. "One that takes us into a highly regulated system. By drinking his blood, the high priestess experienced the memories stored in his consciousness. If the memories that existed in the old host were present—she was familiar with those memories because they performed other blood rituals throughout the year—that meant Mótsognir now inhabited the new body."

"You're telling me this high priestess is the head vampire?"

"Essentially, yes."

"What do you make of all this?" he asked.

"I have very little to go on. If I had more…"

"You will, I promise."

She sighed. "I can only hypothesize."

"Hypothesize."

"This is an elaborate and highly ritualistic system. Fear of the supernatural was their main weapon. The god's transference from one body to another implies he cannot die, and his ability to commandeer a body is a supernatural ability attributed to vampire-like creatures. He would, in essence, be the ultimate vampire, draining his victim—the host—of his very consciousness, leaving him a walking zombie after Mótsognir moves on."

That's if the body was allowed it live, Gerry mentally added. If this Mótsognir didn't want to leave a trail of ex-hosts…ex-hosts like Darryl Michaels, Brent Douglas, Vitelli, Kinnison…

"But mythologically, vampires have that same power," Gerry said evenly.

"Not these vampires," Iris said. "They don't make zombies of their victims, only Mótsognir does. Another interesting point is the fact that this sect brought the goddess Freyja to life as nothing less than Mótsognir's personal assassin. She's part of an elite female sect who are descendants of priests and priestesses. She is sworn to defend the priests, which usually meant assassinations reminiscent of ninja warriors who used skill and stealth under cover of night to slip in, kill, then leave unseen."

Gerry's memory spiraled back to Sula's words, *I am sworn to kill the unjust*. His mouth thinned. The unjust as defined by her god. Howsten had killed innocents. Something in the rights and laws of the sect had changed over the years.

"The right of first choice is hers," he quoted the old poem.

"Correct," Iris said. "Also, a cryptic reference to another group is made. I have only their name and the context to theorize upon, but they appear to be of a warrior class, perhaps some sort of protective force or defender."

"They protected the priestesses?"

"On the contrary, the implication is that they are the single barrier between the priestesses and the world."

"The single barrier, like some sort of cop?"

"Or, the final judgment."

"Final, as in death?"

"Yes. There is a connection between them and Mótsognir. There is a passage that reads, *I was born into darkness, but I learned the magic that gave me power to possess another man's body and absorb his soul. No longer do I live as sómaherji. I am free.*"

"*Sómaherji?*" Gerry repeated.

"Yes. Honorable warriors. Their name, Alarr, is derived from a leading class of warriors. They—"

"Alarr?" Gerry blurted, mind racing.

Alarr, the male Aptrgangr. The guy he had envisioned wearing a cape and floating down in front of him onto the rocky ground of some God forsaken path. The guy he had been in Sula's vision with Jonis. *The guy I shot and who should be in a body bag in the morgue.* Gerry jarred back to the present. Iris had become silent.

"Iris, I'm sorry. This information…"

"Yes?" she prompted.

He heard the hopeful note in her voice. "I'll have to explain later. Can you send me your translations?"

"My notes will be finished this morning."

"Thanks," he said. "I'll have copies of these books sent to you ASAP."

"Will I ever know the story behind this?"

"I'll make sure you get the unabridged version, the one the newspapers will never know."

"Oh," she said, a little breathless. "I can't thank you enough. I look forward to seeing the remainder of this manuscript."

"It's yours. Talk to you soon."

She said goodbye, and he ended the call.

Alarr, the assassin's assassin. Gerry's stomach turned. The vision he'd seen of Alarr and Sula had been an assassination attempt. Only Alarr hadn't killed her. He'd buried her in the whole the bulldozer uncovered.

Sula, Alarr, Linnette, and Balder. Gerry hadn't met Balder—or had he?

Chapter Five

H ARGRAVE'S ROUGH TONGUE on Gerry's ear jarred him and he tuned into the low chatter of the police radio in the back seat. Gerry took a cleansing breath and patted the Shepherd. He now could account for three of the four maidens Brother Matthew had found in the temple.

Vitelli, Linette, and Sula—but that wasn't right. Sula had been attacked and buried by Alarr. She hadn't woken up until that bulldozer uncovered her grave. She wasn't one of the four maidens. Who were the other two? Christ, was the modern world ready for two more like them? Was he?

The dispatcher's voice broke into his concentration and he realized Dee's voice had yet to come over the radio's secure channel.

"If you took off to do some detective work on your own…" he said under his breath.

Gerry grabbed his phone and hit speed-dial number two for the department. Lummus had probably already circulated the news about the missing body at the taxidermy and Kevin Matheson's murder. What sort of reception would he get from whoever picked up the phone?

"Officer Wilson."

"Wilson, Forstner here."

A beat of silence passed before Wilson said, "Yeah?"

There it was. "I need to talk to Detective Kelly," Gerry said.

"She's not with you?"

"I dropped her off an hour and a half ago."

"Yeah," Wilson said, "she was here. Now she's gone."

"What do you mean *gone?*" Gerry demanded.

"She was here, then she wasn't."

"Did she say anything?"

"Not to me. Herrero got here half an hour ago and was looking for her. When they didn't find her, he figured she left with you."

"She took off to work the case," Gerry said more to himself than Wilson.

"She'll have a tough time getting around without that little sports car," Wilson said. "It was impounded. She didn't bother getting anyone to fill in for her, either."

"If she turns up, give me a call."

"I'll let the Chief know," Wilson replied.

Gerry just bet he would. Wilson was probably typing a request to have Gerry's GPS location traced, but they'd get no readings. He turned the feature off two hours ago. He ended the call and dialed Dee's cell. Her end rang. Hargrave stuck his snout between the seats. Two rings, then three, and his heart rate kicked into high gear.

"Come on, pick up." After five rings, her voicemail picked up.

"You know what to do," her recorded voice said, then a beep followed.

"Dee, where are you? Call me." He ended the call and dialed Herrero.

The Chief picked up on the second ring. "Forstner, where are you?"

"Dee's missing."

"I know. We're working on it. Get your ass in here."

Gerry stared at Marilyn's house. The old gal never had the books and knew nothing concrete about them. He wasn't taking a chance.

"I'm outside Marilyn Pentz's place. I want someone over here."

Herrero was silent for a minute, then said, "That's how I'm going to get you in here?"

"Yep."

"Fuck this up and I'll throw your ass in jail."

"The second I see the squad car, I'm on my way to you," Gerry replied.

"You have half an hour," the chief said, and hung up.

GERRY RUBBED HIS eyes. Two hours into the three-hour grilling, Herrero had gotten his second wind. If Gerry didn't know better, he'd think the Chief was working him like a real perp. Gerry had been on the interrogator's side of questioning a thousand times, yet hadn't learned how to stick to a fabric of lies when asked to re-explain a hundred different ways at three in the morning.

Herrero flipped through the notes he'd written on a yellow legal pad. "Let's go back to Jackson's house when you saw the BMW."

"Christ, Chief. We need to find Dee."

"If what you're saying is correct—"

"If what I'm saying is correct." Gerry stared. "You think I'm lying?"

"I'm saying, if your hypothesis is correct, she's out working the case."

"She doesn't have the experience."

"You don't give her enough credit."

Gerry rose. "Hargrave's in the car and I need to get him home."

"He's a police dog. He can go a day without pissing and a week without sleep."

"Well, I can't."

"Let's go over this once more."

"You said that an hour ago. I've got to get some shuteye." He headed for the door.

"Don't you walk out, Forstner. It may be your last time."

"I'll be in touch." Gerry opened the door and strode out.

HARGRAVE WAS SOUND asleep in the back seat when Gerry got to the car. The Shepherd sat up when Gerry got in and began slathering Gerry's ear with his tongue. Gerry thumbed Dee's cell. The line picked up. Her name died on his lips when a bold, resonant male voice said, "Detective Forstner."

Realization dawned a second later. "Hello, Harold," he replied.

Balder gave a knowing laugh. "You have something I want."

"Yeah?"

"You and the books in exchange for Detective Kelly."

Him and the books? He knew about the genealogy.

"All right, Harold. Where and when?"

"One more thing. I want a Huey at Opa-locka Executive Airport."

"A helicopter?"

"A Bell UH-1, fueled and ready."

"You're fucking nuts."

"I don't think so," Balder replied unruffled.

This wasn't a move Gerry had expected. "I need a few hours."

"Meet me at Tall Palms Estates at 5:00 a.m. sharp."

Gerry glanced at his watch—only two hours to set up the deal. "You're not giving me much leeway here, Harold."

"Be there or she dies."

"Tall Palms is a big place, must be fifty new houses going up there."

"Look for my black Lexus."

The line went dead.

Gerry headed back to Herrero's office.

GERRY PAUSED BETWEEN two partially constructed houses at Tall Palms Estates and peered around them at the Lexus parked in front of a Tyvek wrapped house three lots down on Elm. The SWAT team's head sharpshooter, Matt Alfonso, had spotted the Lexus. His night scope showed the engine still warm and two heat signatures inside the house.

Gerry ducked around the rear of the house, then flattened against the wall beside a bare-frame doorway. The bullet proof vest he wore would stop a bullet. He wished like hell that a cross or garlic around his neck would stop a vampire. Taking a deep breath, he stepped into the house.

He eased between studded partitions that cut through the future kitchen. Moonlight streamed through windowless openings, casting angled rectangles across his jeans and the plywood sub-floor.

He scanned the window with roughed in sink plumbing underneath and called, "Balder, I'm here. If you want the books—"

A figure stepped out of deep shadows far left of the sink. He stood six-one, two hundred pounds and, even in the shadows, an athletic build registered.

"Hello, Harold."

Balder approached. "Where are the books?" His voice had an edge that hadn't been there over the phone.

"Hold it right there, Harold. I spook easy. Where's Detective Kelly?"

Balder stopped. "I don't see the books."

"Show me yours and I'll show you mine," Gerry replied.

"The books," Balder snarled.

"Careful," Gerry warned. "I can bury the books so deep no incantation or *vey opening* you create will be worthless. Show me Dee, then we talk."

An unexpected sensation tickled his mind. He recognized the psychic *knock knock* in his mind and concentrated on the weird sense. A presence emanated from the shadowy depths beyond Balder. He snapped his mind closed so fast it took a second for the realization to catch up with the fierce pounding of his heart.

Balder raised a hand. Gerry flinched, barely catching himself before taking a step backward. Balder motioned with two fingers in a *come out* gesture to someone behind him. A shuffle sounded and Linnette Howsten, tall, breathtaking goddess, stepped into the moonlight with Dee slung over her shoulder. Alfonso's second heat source. He couldn't have distinguished between Howsten and Dee through the walls of the house. Or maybe Linette didn't radiate a heat source?

Linnette lowered Dee to her feet and spun her around. Gerry's heart lurched. Dee appeared spaced out or drugged. Iris had said the gothi made zombies out of their victims, but the vampires didn't. He recalled Dee's lightning fast reaction when she brought the punk down in the precinct. She wasn't an easy target. What had they done to her to induce this comatose state? His balance abruptly wavered with the same mental force as it had outside the stationery store.

"Get the fuck out of my head," he snarled at Linnette.

Her gaze flicked to Balder and the woozy sensation evaporated.

"Where are the books?" Balder demanded.

Gerry eased a shaky hand inside his sweatshirt and withdrew a CD from his shirt pocket. "Full scans. You know the Feds have the originals."

"Not good enough," Linnette said.

The sensual, husky note in her voice startled Gerry. She didn't have Sula's accent.

"She's right," Balder said through tight lips.

"It'll have to do," Gerry said. "These are full electronic copies. That's the best deal you'll get."

"And the helicopter?"

"I hope you can fly the thing, because I can't."

Balder laughed. "You scared, cop?"

"Scared shitless."

"Three tours in 'Nam," Balder said with the cockiness of a fighter pilot.

If Gerry had worn the wire Herrero insisted he wear, by now, the

Feds would be searching DoD records for Vietnam helicopter pilots living in Florida. But Gerry hadn't been willing to chance Balder discovering he was bugged. Gerry wanted to round up as many of these freaks as possible in one shot. One shot might be all he got.

"Three tours?" Gerry repeated, then asked on impulse, "Was that before the *Keepers of the Secret*?"

Balder laughed. "You almost tracked me down in the Keys."

"We need to go," Linnette cut in.

Gerry's gaze snapped onto her and he felt the spooky tingle again. "So, it's true, you vamps have to be in bed by sunup."

She turned her gaze on him and a wave of a crippling vertigo hit. He seized a stud, his stomach pitching starboard as his balance listed port.

"Don't...like being...called a common vampire?" he wheezed, then added with a sneer, "*Linnea.*"

She gasped. Satisfaction shot through him before he realized the gravity of her reaction, and his stomach roiled. A cool hand clasped his upper arm. He blinked stupidly at Sula standing beside him—then reached for his gun. She shot forward and had Balder's neck in one extended hand before Gerry cleared the weapon from its holster. Linnette gripped Dee in a headlock. The team outside would have seen Sula enter. They would be here any second.

"Freeze!" he shouted. "What about the trade?"

"Leave," Sula ordered. "He wants you and your son."

"How—"

"Leave!"

Gerry motioned toward Dee. "Not without her."

"Release him, or I'll rip off her head," Linnette growled.

Balder made gurgling noises and pounded Sula's head with fists to no effect.

"Let her go," Gerry ordered Linnette. "Then you vampires can finish your spat."

Her eyes flashed. Sula shot across the room in a blur. She knocked Dee aside and kicked Linnette across the room. Balder collapsed like a rag doll. Gerry rushed between studs to Dee. He squatted to haul her over his shoulder. A blur flew past and he fell across Dee, shielding her body with his. Something crashed into the wall beyond Balder. Gerry looked up. Linnette lay near the outside wall. The jagged end of a two-by-four protruded from her chest at heart level. He stared. Another crash sounded behind him. He twisted, pistol leveled on two grappling figures: Sula and *Alarr*.

Alarr shoved Sula. She stumbled back and he leaped on her, pinning her to the floor.

Gerry leaped to his feet and leveled his 9mm on him. "Hold it, motherfucker!"

Alarr bared his teeth, his grip on Sula never wavering.

Gerry jerked the barrel upward twice. "Hands up, or I'll shoot and, this time, I'll put a stake through your fucking heart before you get up."

Alarr laughed. A chill raked Gerry's back at the cold timber of the male vampire's voice, and Sula's words came to mind, *We can die by only one means.* She never said what that one way was.

"Leave." Sula groaned under Alarr's hold.

Their gazes met. In the filmy gray of hinted-at morning, Gerry caught the blue of her eyes.

"Gerry," she whispered, her soft accent discernable in the one word. "Please."

Something in her voice startled him...remorse, longing—

"No!" Alarr cried, and Gerry realized the Aptrgangr read the plea in her voice.

A scrape sounded behind him. Gerry whirled. Linnette inch-wormed toward him, grasping ineffectually at the end of the board protruding from her back. She slammed her chest on the floor, driving the board out a fraction. She gasped for air, then lifted her body again and slammed harder. Gerry forced back nausea. A stake through the heart didn't kill these creatures. He stuffed his gun into its holster, grabbed Dee under the arms, and dragged her toward the kitchen. Where was the goddamn SWAT team?

Linnette rose and reached behind her for the board. He needed that SWAT team—now. Gerry stood, aimed for Linnette's heart, and fired. Sula heaved Alarr sideways as Linnette, thrown back by the force of Gerry's bullet, struck the wall. Alarr stumbled backward. Sula jumped to her feet and Gerry caught sight of something in her hand.

He dropped across Dee as Sula threw. Fingers closed over the hand gripping his gun as the object whizzed across the room. He jerked his gaze onto Dee as she swung his arm up and fired the 9mm. The round hit Linette's shoulder as the object Sula had thrown also hit and she exploded in flames.

Linnette wailed a banshee scream. Flames spread and covered her body in an instant. She raced toward the front door, fanning the fire into a greater inferno. Heat singed his face as she passed. At the door, she took one step outside and crumbled into ash.

A faint scent of honeysuckle filled the air.

"Fire," Dee rasped.

The sweet smell choked him. He grasped the hand still holding the poised gun and looked at Dee. "Yeah," he said. "Fire." He gently lay her arm across her stomach and slipped the gun back into his holster.

Footfalls pounded behind him. "Everyone down!" a man yelled.

Gerry hugged Dee close as men with automatic rifles and flashlights swept the rooms. He glanced toward Sula. She and Alarr were gone.

"House secure," the SWAT team leader shouted.

Two team members squatted over Balder and squeezed the mic on his lapel. "Better send for the coroner."

Gerry turned his attention to Dee.

She lifted a shaky hand and gave his cheek a tap. "Don't wait so long next time," she croaked. Her hand dropped to her chest. "I feel like shit."

Gerry buried his face in her neck.

Chapter Six

THE TENSION IN Gerry's shoulders eased when the doctors at Palmetto General diagnosed Dee with nothing more than a severe case of exhaustion. He held the door for her as she climbed into the passenger seat of his Impala. She hadn't said a word, but he knew the prognosis was due to loss of blood. Red highlights shimmered in her hair against the bright February sun and Gerry wanted to pull back the locks and look at her neck. He closed her door, crossed to the driver's side, climbed in.

"How do you feel?" he asked as he slipped the key into the ignition.

"Like I've got the mother of all hangovers."

Their gazes met. He paused, then hooked a finger in her hair. As he drew it back, he glimpsed two puncture marks before she pulled away.

Gerry let his hand fall to her shoulder. "We have a matching pair. Almost."

She cast a glance at his neck, and he had the distinct feeling she was comparing Sula's bite to Linnette's and thinking he got the better deal. Remembering the mother of all hard-ons, he wasn't so sure. He started the engine and nosed the Impala toward the hospital exit.

Once on the street, he asked, "Do you believe in vampires?"

A moment of silence passed before she said, "What happened at Tall Palms?"

Gerry jerked his gaze onto her. "You shot my gun."

Dee nodded. "I wanted to kill her."

His insides twisted, but he kept his voice level as he gave her a run-down of everything up to Sula throwing the firebomb. "*Poof.* Like magic, Linnette was gone."

"That I remember," Dee whispered. "I'll never forget."

Neither would Gerry. "Herrero put a rush on forensics. He called half an hour ago. Apparently, the firebomb was homemade, sodium and chlorine in a glass vile surrounded by a rudimentary form of Napalm. The vial broke and ignited the accelerant. Only problem is—"

"No sign of human or animal remains where Howsten went up in flames," Dee finished without taking her eyes off the passenger side window.

Gerry accelerated into the highway's fast lane to pass a slow Caddy driver. "Only ashes from the 2x4 in her back," Gerry said. "No one saw anyone enter or leave. The team detected three heat signatures. As far as Herrero is concerned, you and I were alone with Balder in that house." He shuddered. If that wasn't proof vampires were living death, nothing was.

Two heartbeats of silence passed, and Dee said, "You think they're gone?"

No cold chills rolled over him. "No. The team is going through Balder's house. Maybe they'll find out where Alarr had gone."

"Alarr?"

Gerry silently cursed. "The guy I shot in the taxidermy basement...the guy fighting with Sula tonight." He glanced at Dee. Her mouth was set tight.

Dee met his gaze. "She's still out there, too."

"She's not part of this. Alarr is."

Dee's gaze sharpened. "And you know this because you two shared memories?"

"Sula was searching for her gothi. Now that Balder's gone, she'll have to look elsewhere—and stay one step ahead of Alarr."

"Are you going to tell Brenda she and Joey can come home?"

He returned his attention to the highway "I called her about an hour ago. No answer. They're probably out fishing."

Dee's exit passed on the right.

"Where're we going?"

"You have two choices. My house or my house."

"I've been kidnapped, had my blood sucked—" he jerked his gaze onto her, "—been dragged around like Hargrave's favorite chew toy, and prodded by doctors. I'm not sure I'm in any condition for a romp in the sack."

A laugh burst out. "I'm putting you to bed, then getting some shuteye. We'll talk about your fitness to perform in ten hours."

She gave him a come-clean look.

"Okay," he said. "I'm nervous. We both need sleep. Herrero ordered me to be at his office at one p.m. to meet with Internal Affairs. I'll feel better knowing Hargrave's standing guard while I'm gone."

"IA. That doesn't sound good."

Gerry caught the melancholy in her voice and wanted to kill Linnette Howsten for putting it here.

✦

AT ONE P.M. sharp, Gerry knocked on Herrero's office door.

"Come."

He took a deep breath and swung the door open. Lummus and Sheridan stood beside Herrero's paper strewn desk.

"You look like death warmed over," Herrero said.

"Feel worse," Gerry said.

"Wait outside," Herrero instructed Lummus and Sheridan, and they filed out. After the door closed, Herrero blew out a breath. "I'm putting you on administrative leave until IA finishes their investigation. Turn in your badge and weapon."

Gerry had expected the suspension, but it pissed him off nonetheless. He pulled his badge from his pocket, tossed it onto Herrero's desk, then unholstered his gun and dropped it beside the badge.

Herrero met his gaze squarely. "We have a dead body. You and Detective Kelly were the only people in that house. Add the shooting with no body, two dead in Long Key, and Lauderdale PD on your ass about William Johnson's murder. The fact you nailed the Valknut killer is the only thing keeping you on the force." Herrero's phone rang and he picked up.

Gerry sat in the chair opposite the desk. Herrero would think twice about keeping him on the force if he knew Gerry believed two vampire were the murders. Alarr didn't fit into the murders. A careless sense of danger emanated from the male vampire that Gerry hadn't detected in the crime scenes. Gerry had tried placing him over a victim who had been forced to kneel before his greatness, and couldn't. Alarr was too lofty to give a damn about power. Alarr *was* power.

No. The male vampire wasn't at Two Palms to resurrect past glory.

The fury in his cry when Sula pleaded with Gerry to go had revealed the vampire's feelings. Alarr might not be human, but he was male, and Gerry recognized the male reaction. Alarr loved Sula. He hadn't killed her the first time those hundreds of years ago, and he had no intention of killing her now. He wanted her.

Gerry shifted in his chair. But they weren't his problems anymore. Balder and Linette were dead. Neither Sula nor Alarr cared about murdering people or making themselves gods. Even if Gerry wanted to find them, no APB would be issued for two vampires. The Valknut murders were over.

His suspension gave him a couple months off to spend with Joey, not to mention getting to know Dee better. When he'd left the house, she'd been asleep in one of his T-shirts with Hargrave lying in the bed beside her. The Shepherd had lifted his head as Gerry mouthed, "You're not allowed on the bed," then the mutt settled his head back down and nuzzled her arm. Gerry had wanted to crawl beneath the covers and nuzzle every part of her with his day old beard.

The question he'd kept at bay pushed forward: Why had Sula saved Dee? Alarr's name had been on that single firebomb, but Sula had used it on Linnette in order to save Dee—the woman she believed Gerry loved. The look in Sula's eyes when she'd pleaded with him to leave had been love—*a match a thousand years in the making.*

Herrero hung up the phone. "That was IA. They're waiting in 103."

Gerry nodded. One-oh-three was an interrogation room. There would be two or three IA officers grilling him for a week or two, until they were reassigned, or until they got him booted off the force, whichever came first.

GERRY'S HEAD WAS ready to explode by the time IA filed out for dinner. He stretched in the metal-folding chair, pulled out his cell phone, and turned it on. Four missed calls, all from Brenda.

"About time," he muttered, then realized she would never call him four times just to check in.

He punched the code to access voice mail. An automated feminine voice noted the call and time, then Brenda's trembling voice came on the line. "Gerry, Joey's missing. We went into his bedroom this morning—"

She burst into tears and the call ended.

Missing? Gerry's heart felt like it couldn't pump the blood out fast enough. How? Balder was dead. Fear twisted Gerry's insides. *Alarr.* But why—how had he found them?

Sula.

If Alarr shared her memories, could he have learned of their family connection? Just how deep had that mind meld with Sula been? His heart pounded even harder. This was worse than the house of mirrors. How was he supposed to fight a vampire? Any fucking way he could.

Gerry leaped to his feet headed for the door. Alarr caught Sula, discovered he couldn't make her love him, and was now seeking revenge. Why hadn't the possibility occurred to him? Because it hadn't occurred to him Alarr would catch her.

As Gerry pushed through the door he hit the speed dial for Brenda. She picked up before the first ring ended. "Gerry, were have you been?" Her voice trembled with panic.

"Internal Affairs investigation. I had my phone off. Why the hell didn't you call the station—Never mind. What happened?"

"We can't find Joey." Her voice hitched. "When I went up to his bedroom and found him gone, I thought—" She began to cry.

"You called 911?"

"Yes. They're searching the island."

"Where are you?"

"The police station on Plantation Key."

Gerry's breath caught. Plantation Key. The Keys. *Fuck the Keys.* They had his son. He would torch every last fucking vampire down there.

"I'm on my way. Stay there. Keep the phone close." He jabbed the end button.

As he passed the break room, Elaine from IA called, "Hey, Forstner"

"Gotta go. If I'm not back in fifteen minutes, start without me."

"Forstner…"

Gerry slammed the crash bar on the fire exit and hit the parking lot running as the fire alarm blared.

Chapter Seven

"INTERCOM SECURITY," GERRY murmured as he strolled up to Alyssa Hamilton's luxury high rise.

He spotted the elevator straight ahead through the glass door. The numbers above the doors were descending. *Five...four.* He slowed. Three. He reached inside his pants pocket and gripped his keys. *Two.* Gerry stepped onto the sidewalk. *One.* He slowed as the elevator opened and a young couple got off. Five feet from the door, he pulled out his keys as the couple reached for the glass door. The woman exited and Gerry stepped aside as the guy held the door open for him.

"Thanks." He passed the man and headed for the elevators.

Two minutes later, he stood in front of unit four thirty-five. He had called Joseph P. Warner Laboratories. Alyssa Hamilton had left for the day. He hoped they'd told the truth and she wasn't simply 'out of the office' to all callers. Joseph P. Warner Laboratories had better security than her apartment building.

No peephole. Maybe she didn't need one. He knocked, then waited less than thirty seconds when the deadbolt started to disengage, then stopped. Christ. She knew it was him.

Gerry leaned close. "Open the door, Ms. Hamilton."

He held his breath. The deadbolt clicked over and she opened the door. Their gazes met. Even in sweats, she looked formidable.

"We need to talk," he said.

She regarded him for a moment, then stepped aside. Gerry brushed past and strode down the short hallway to the living room. She continued past him to the couch and sat down.

He met her gaze. "You dropped out of sight after the Branson case.

Why?"

"It hurt too much to watch children die."

"They found that little girl a quarter of a mile from the epicenter you told them to search. Ten miles from where they were searching."

"Dead," Alyssa said.

Gerry sat down beside her. "You see them die?"

Her gaze shifted away, but he knew she wasn't looking away, but instead was simply…somewhere else.

"I feel their fear, their pain…desperation." Her mouth thinned. "They call to their parents."

"Would you be able to feel my son?"

Alyssa looked at him. She stared for a moment, then gave a tiny nod. She wasn't saying, *Yes, I'll help you find him*, but instead, *I'm not surprised your son is missing.*

"When?" she asked.

"Sometime this morning, maybe during the night."

"You believe his disappearance is related to the Valknut case. Why?"

Gerry hesitated. He hadn't planned on lying, but how the hell did he tell her a vampire was pissed off because his lady vampire liked Gerry better?

"The abridged version," Gerry said. "This kidnapper is a vampire."

Alyssa's gaze remained glued to his as she said, "What kind of vampire are we talking about?"

"Not the run-of-the-mill Goth worshipper who walks the street," Gerry replied. "But the genuine four hundred year old variety…the boogieman you spoke of."

Her gaze dropped, and she murmured, "He operates in a different reality than we do."

Hope surged through Gerry. "I've seen him three times. The first time, he followed me. I chased him into an alley, but he disappeared down a dead end street and there was no way out, unless he can fly." Something Gerry wasn't sure he couldn't do.

"And the second time?"

"Two days ago, when I shot him."

She blinked. "Shot him?"

"Point blank. By the time forensics arrived, he was gone."

"Is this blonde vampire the Valknut killer?"

Gerry startled. "How did you know he was blonde?"

Alyssa frowned. "Didn't you say so?"

"No."

She shrugged, and Gerry blurted, "Is Joey still alive?"

"I need something of his."

This is it, Gerry thought, and realized he had one more thing to do first. "Give me a sec," he said, and slipped his phone from his shirt pocket. He dialed Herrero's office.

"Herrero."

"Chief, it's Gerry."

"Where the hell are you?" Herrero demanded. "We've got every cop in Dade County looking for you, not to mention the Feds. As far as they're concerned, you fouled this case *and* the *Keepers of the Secret.*"

"Johnson was gunning for me from the start. Why?" Jerry demanded.

"He was working the *Keepers of the Secret* case before the Governor called you in."

"His name wasn't on any of the reports."

"That's because the report was filed with the Bureau," Herrero said. "You know how stingy they are with information. He says he was a day way from cracking the case before you got involved. I don't buy it, but that doesn't change the fact that you need to get back here."

"He's got Joey," Gerry said.

"What?"

"The Valknut killer."

"What are you talking about? We got Balder at the morgue."

"There's someone else. Joey was kidnapped out of his own bed."

A heartbeat of silence passed, then Herrero said, "Get in here. We'll put together a team—"

"Like we did at Tall Palms?"

"Gerry—"

"Don't let the department screw my son out of what he's due," Gerry cut in.

"You're on suspension," Herrero put in hurriedly. "I'll send someone."

"Who, Lummus?" Gerry laughed. "The second you put out the call, the Feds will bumble in and I'll lose Joey forever."

"I can—"

"I had to tell you, Mark. I owe you that much. Remember what I said about Joey." Gerry snapped the phone closed and Alyssa started to rise. He grabbed her arm. "There's more."

She relaxed back onto the couch and Gerry released her. "My son is the last in the line of an ancient Norse priesthood the Valknut killer is trying to resurrect."

"What?"

Gerry heard genuine surprise in her voice and wondered how often anyone caught Alyssa Hamilton off guard. "I know it sounds crazy," he said, "but it's true. We came into possession of three ancient Asatru religious books confiscated from Iceland after World War Two. One of those books is a genealogy that lists the sect's priests and priestesses. An adopted great ancestor of mine was the daughter of a priestess."

"You are a descendant of these vampires?"

Gerry stilled. "I never said the vampires were part of the lineage."

Alyssa gave a short laugh. "You've discovered you're a descendant of an ancient priesthood and have recently come in contact with a vampire. Two and two still equal four."

"You don't know the half of it," Gerry replied, surprised at the relief he felt. Thank God good old logic still had a place. "Speaking of coincidences, what's the connection between the killer and Warner Laboratories?"

"Your killer wasn't inside the lab," she said. "How do you know the victims weren't related to the priests, too?"

Gerry gave a small nod of admiration. He hadn't given her so much as a hint. "How did he manage to leave blood from each successive victim at each of the first three crime scenes?" he asked.

She frowned. "What do you mean?"

"The Valknut was drawn on each victim's chest with blood from each successive victim: Darryl Michaels' blood was found on Brent Douglas' chest. Vitelli's blood on Michael's chest. Kinnison's blood on Vitelli's chest."

"Whose blood was found on Kinnison's chest?"

Gerry shook his head. "We don't know. Forensics hasn't turned up a match, and another victim hasn't shown up with the Valknut on his chest."

Her eyes grew wide. "I see a man filled with darkness."

"A man?"

"He is the possessor," she said as if not having heard him.

A chill passed through Gerry. He'd been wrong again. The cult god had to be Alarr.

✦

GERRY LEFT THE front door open and flicked on lights as he hurried to Joey's room, Alyssa at his heels. "Pick something, anything. If you can't find what you need, we'll break into Brenda's place."

Alyssa went to work, calm and sure, touching items on his dresser.

"What's up, Gerry?"

He whirled at the sound of Dee's voice. She stood in the doorway drowning in his blue terry bathrobe, Hargrave beside her. She split a glance between him and Alyssa.

"This is the Dr. Hamilton from Warner Laboratories I told you about." Gerry turned to Alyssa. "This is Detective Kelly, and Hargrave."

"Detective," Alyssa said to Dee, then dropped her gaze to Hargrave. Her eyes brightened when she met the Shepherd's eyes, then she turned back to the dresser.

"What's wrong?" Dee asked.

"They have Joey."

She gasped. "What—how—I'll get dressed."

"No, you're staying here."

She glared at him. "How the hell can I rest—" she choked. "It's my fault."

"What?"

She touched the scars on her neck, and his heart wrenched. "Dee—"

"I found what I need." Alyssa said.

Gerry turned. Alyssa held Joey's soccer ball. Her eyes glazed. "I don't sense immediate danger. We have time to be careful."

"I'll get dressed," Dee said. "Gerry, I'll need a pair of boxers and a t-shirt."

Ten minutes later, Gerry opened the passenger door for Alyssa while Dee and Hargrave climbed into the back. His cell phone beeped a waiting message chime and he reached for the phone as he started around the front of the car. He pressed the message button as he slid behind the steering wheel.

"Gerry," Chief Herrero's voice came over the line, "I don't think anything I say will make one bit of difference, but maybe this'll knock some sense into you. Sam Pentz's body was discovered. The Valknut appears on his chest and he's missing blood." Herrero paused. "He was found down in the Keys, Gerry. Plantation Key."

Gerry jerked his gaze onto Alyssa. She was staring at him.

Chapter Eight

GERRY KEPT SILENT about Sam Pentz's murder in Plantation Key, yet wasn't surprised when Alyssa ordered him to drive south. As they entered the Overseas Highway, he stepped on the gas. Waterfront condos, hotels and cottages dotted the nighttime landscape on both the Atlantic and Gulf sides of the narrow highway. He was right back where the horror had started.

Gerry glanced at Dee in the rearview mirror. She met his eyes as if aware he was looking, then returned her gaze to the darkened landscape. He flicked a glance at Alyssa before concentrating on the road. Her hand still lay on the soccer ball in her lap.

Hold on, Buddy, he begged his son. *I'm coming.*

By Largo Sound, the car had taken on an eerie silence. Rock Harbor came and went. Sunset Point and Tavernier followed. They crossed Snake Creek in Plantation Key, and rage and fear welled up in a frenzy of energy that made Gerry think he'd lose his mind.

"Here," Alyssa said, startling him.

In a panicked reaction, he hit the brakes, but released them when the car jerked. "Where?" He braked more slowly, scanning the Coontie, Oleander, and Sea Oats lit by the car's headlights.

"There." Alyssa pointed at two luxury condo buildings a block ahead on the Atlantic side.

Gerry eased past the first building, then pulled onto the deserted street between the buildings and cut the engine. Hargrave sat up and leaned forward as Gerry surveyed the seven-story adobe. Ground level floodlights lit the base of the wall. Light bled through curtains on a few apartments on upper floors, but even at 1 a.m., he expected someone to be awake. He looked at Alyssa. Faint moonlight fell across the car, but her features remained in shadow.

"He's nearby," she said.

"One of the condos?"

She placed both hands on the soccer ball. "The surf is loud. An ocean-front home."

Gerry shoved open his door. "Let's go."

Salty air washed over him. With a long remembered response, he shrugged the bulletproof vest into a more comfortable fit as he grabbed the pen flashlight and handcuffs from the door pocket. He was pulling Hargrave's leash from the same pocket when the dog vaulted over the seat-back and onto the asphalt. Hargrave took two bounds toward the ocean and froze, staring in the direction of the water. Gerry jerked his gaze onto Alyssa as she circled the front of the car, soccer ball tucked under her left arm.

Dee stepped up alongside Gerry. A gust of wind whipped back her leather jacket and he caught sight of her holstered Walther. He remembered that her scores qualified her as a sharpshooter.

"Does he sense something?" she asked Alyssa.

Alyssa stopped beside Hargrave. "Joey." She looked at Gerry. "How do we proceed?"

He shoved the handcuffs and flashlight into his jacket pocket. "Let's see what's on the other side of these buildings." He leashed Hargrave and started down the deserted street toward the ocean.

At end of the condo, Gerry halted and peered around the corner. South, the beach disappeared around a sharp right curve. North, palm trees and tall grass dotted the open area between the condo and the nearest sand dune. Beyond the dune, trees covered an acre of beachfront with an open area in their center. Near the shore, the trees thinned to Palms where a stone pier jutted into the ocean.

"Look at this." Gerry waved Alyssa and Dee closer. They flanked him. "There has to be a house in the middle of those trees," he said. "Probably accessed by a private drive."

Hargrave whined. "Hargrave," Gerry called. "Sit." The dog's rear dropped to the asphalt. Gerry turned to Alyssa. "Is that the place?"

"A void," she said "As if space is occupied by…nothing."

He startled. *Alarr.*

"Chaos."

"Alyssa."

She blinked.

"Did you connect with *him*?" Gerry demanded.

She stared at the trees. "Not connected, just sensed a…presence. I veiled myself from him."

"With the white bubble?"

She had instructed them to surround themselves with protective white light where only higher, positive spirits could enter their psychic space. They'd brought holy water, a cross and, as what seemed as an afterthought from Alyssa, a pentagram. He wasn't sure if they were going to cast out demons or cast a spell. A tremor rippled through him. He had stepped into the twilight zone. Gerry reminded himself for the hundredth time that Alyssa Hamilton had proven she *wasn't* a kook. To hell with it. When he got back the real world, Joey would be with him.

She turned to him, clearly reading his anxiety. "Energy exists. Not long ago, people would have branded electricity as a tool of witchcraft. Today, we understand the universe is governed by such physics. Einstein's theory of relativity says that energy and matter are the same. Gurus, shaman, and magi have known this for centuries." She looked toward the trees. "I've never encountered anything like what I'm sensing from him."

Gerry reached inside his jacket and unlatched his Glock's holster strap. He wasn't used to the Glock, but his Beretta was on Herrero's desk. Added insurance came in the form of the Derringer strapped to his leg. At Bear's, Gerry had taken Alarr by surprise, and a 9mm to the heart hadn't done much. The male vampire was faster and stronger than Sula, and could probably dodge a bullet. Two guns or ten might not stop him.

"Radio check." He looked at Alyssa.

She pulled back her hair. Moonlight spilled across her neck, revealing the wire running from ear to collar. On the way out of Miami, they had swung by a place that sold stolen police issue equipment. In all his years as a cop, Gerry hadn't so much as inched outside the law. His father had been a by-the-book cop, and those same values went bone deep for Gerry. For an instant, Gerry thought he caught a whiff of Camacho cigars. They weren't cheap, but his dad smoked one every Sunday afternoon until the day he died.

As a kid, Gerry worried his father would die like his grandfather: strolling down the street one Sunday morning, suddenly crashing to his knees, dead of a massive heart attack before anyone realized he lay there. It hadn't occurred to Gerry his father would be shot by a petty criminal. For the first time in his life, Gerry was glad his father wasn't around. This time, he'd be disappointed in Gerry.

"*Sorry, Dad,*" he silently murmured, but the apology evaporated with the phantom cigar smoke. "I'm turning on the radios," he said out loud. "From here on, use them. They're hypersensitive, so don't speak above a whisper." He switched on his radio and turned away. "Can you hear me?"

"Loud and clear," Alyssa whispered.

"Roger," Dee replied.

Gerry turned to see Hargrave leaning against Alyssa's leg. He abruptly realized the dog had taken to her as quickly as he had to Dee—and Sula. A lump formed in this throat at the mental picture of the warrior goddess, head high as she rode her horse, determination burning in her blue eyes. The gothi god had used her, but in her heart, she was righting the injustice that had slipped past the heavenly gods. Just as she had righted the wrong her god had committed against them when she stepped in the line of fire for him and Dee. Her efforts would be wasted if they didn't get to Joey in time.

"Alyssa," Gerry whispered into the mic.

Her gaze broke from the trees and she looked at him.

"Anything you sense, tell me immediately." She nodded, and he faced the dune. "Let's get a look at what's on the other side of that dune. Hargrave, heel."

The dog fell into place between them as Gerry broke into a run. Ten seconds later, they reached the dune. Gerry dropped to his knees. He grabbed Hargrave's collar and led the way up at a crawl. A partial slanted roof came into view beyond the trees. On the roof, a TV antenna jutted three feet into the air beyond a satellite dish.

"A split level," Gerry whispered.

"That's the place," Alyssa said.

Gerry resisted the urge to charge down the dune to the house. "You and Hargrave wait here," he said. "Dee and I are going in. We'll keep in radio contact. If—"

"I'm going with you," Alyssa said.

He shook his head. "No way."

"You need—"

"We need you alive. We don't know what's in there. If we can't get out, you have to protect Joey at all costs—and Hargrave stays with you."

"But—"

"Forget the movies you've seen where dogs perform like human beings," he interrupted. "Hargrave is amazing, but he isn't trained for clandestine situations." Gerry gave a harsh laugh. "Hell, I'm not trained for it. The danger he'll sense might override training. If I need him, I'll give the order. Only then, release him."

"All right," Alyssa replied.

"Hargrave." The Shepherd's gaze followed as he handed the leash to Alyssa. "Stay." Hargrave hugged close to her, alert and guarding.

Gerry faced Dee. They stared at each other, "Dee, if you—"

"That *thing* violated me. She invaded the part of me that belongs to me alone. I know she's gone, but this isn't over."

Even in the dim moonlight he could see the set of her jaw and, had to admit he agreed. "Okay."

They scrambled down the dune and hurried across the twenty feet of open beach to the trees. Gerry rushed forty feet through the trees, then slowed when the front of a three thousand square foot, split level house came into view. Dim base lights like those at the condo building were located every ten feet around the house. He and Dee hurried to the edge of the trees where a dirt driveway cut across their path. The driveway curved left in a semi-circle in front of the house, then disappeared into the trees toward the highway.

"We're at the front of the house," Gerry whispered into the mic. "The place looks deserted. We're going to check out back."

They stayed within the cover of trees until the rear of the house came into full view. A deck spanned the seventy feet of the house. A glass table sat between two wicker lounge chairs, Gerry's gaze caught on a slider to the right of the furniture.

"The slider," he whispered into the mic.

Dee nodded and they sprinted from the trees across hard packed sand. Gerry kept his eye on the deck's sliding door for signs of movement. At the deck walkway, he stopped. Where was Alarr? The male vampire wouldn't leave Joey there alone. Sula said he wanted him and Joey. Anger bubbled up. Gerry had thought the comment referred to Balder. He hadn't gotten a single thing right about this case. But he knew this had to be a trap. He should have called headquarters to find out who owned the house. Quin would have gotten him the info without alerting the Chief. He should have thought of that earlier. Damn.

He pulled the Glock from its holster, motioned Dee to follow, and cautiously crept onto the wood deck left of the slider. She melted against the wall beside him, Walther gripped in both hands. Definitely beautiful secret agent in disguise. He should have known that from the beginning, too. Gerry pushed the handle. The door slid open a fraction.

Dee grabbed his arm and he jerked his gaze onto hers.

"This is breaking and entering," she said matter-of-factly. "We can't make an arrest stick if we don't do this by the book."

"Arrest?" he repeated. "What jail would hold a six foot vampire?"

"Nothing," she replied without hesitation.

"Nothing," he agreed, and eased open the door.

"We're going in," he whispered to Alyssa, and grabbed his flashlight as he slipped inside, Dee close behind.

Gerry turned on the flashlight and swept the small beam across an island that doubled as a stove, and ran the light to the right, along counters, dishwasher, refrigerator and, finally, in front of them, stairs that had three steps straight up, then made an immediate left. Alarr had to be lurking in the dark, waiting to pounce. Was he waiting for them to penetrate deeper into the house, farther from windows and doors?

"We're in the kitchen," he whispered.

"Upstairs," Alyssa replied.

Gerry crossed to the stairs. Nobody hid in an open-plan dining and living room that extended off to the left. Six high-back chairs stood like silent sentries around an oak dining table. His flashlight beam reflected off cupboard glass doors. Living room furniture occupied the gloom beyond. He should sweep the first floor before going up, but time pressed inexplicably. He paused at the bottom step and slowly shined the light upward, counting stairs.

"Twenty steps," he whispered. "Stay below and cover my back." He clicked off the flashlight and started up.

With each step, his heart beat faster. The seventh step creaked, and Gerry's stomach leaped into this throat. He stopped, listening for any sounds of movement. Dee breathed at the bottom of the stairs. The refrigerator hummed. More distant, a muffled crash of waves. Dead silence came from the second floor. He started up again.

At the top, Gerry stopped. No sliver of light shined through door cracks or windows.

"Clear," he whispered into the mic.

Dee started up. He counted her soft footfalls. No creak came from the seventh step. Good girl. A minute later, they stood in total darkness. Could vampires see in the dark?

"Left or right?" he whispered into the mic.

A heartbeat of silence passed and he feared Alyssa hadn't heard. A high pitched screeching in the ear bud abruptly drilled his eardrum. He yanked the bud from his ear, barely stifling an oath. Dee's elbow jostled his arm as he gave his head a hard shake in an effort to clear the ringing from his ears.

She seized his arm, dragging his ear to her mouth, and whispered, "Radio interference."

Gerry nodded and cautiously tested the bud in the other ear. Light static crackled in a low hum. His connection with Alyssa and Hargrave had been severed.

Stay where you are, Alyssa, he mentally ordered, while praying he could get by without her.

He covered the face of the penlight and turned it on. Gerry splayed his fingers a fraction to allow a little light through and scanned: one closed door on the left, two on the right.

Static still hummed through the radio, but he whispered, "Which door?" into the mic. Nothing. He pulled Dee close and pointed to the first door on the right. "I'm going in. Cover me."

She nodded. He turned off the flashlight. They crept to the door in total blackout, then hugged opposite sides of the frame. With a deep breath, Gerry grasped the doorknob and turned. The bolt clicked free of the door strike, and he froze, heart racing. No gunfire or shouts followed and no glowing eyes appeared.

He eased the door open an inch, and paused. Nothing. He opened the door enough to peer around the edge and turned on the flashlight. The beam cut across the room. He froze at sight of a twin bed against the far wall with a small figure huddled beneath a thin blanket. The edge of a Nike tennis shoe lay exposed at the bottom edge of the blanket. *Joey.*

Gerry raced into the room. He dropped to his knees at the bed and the figure curled into a tight ball. Gerry heard a low whimper as he gently grasped Joey. The boy stiffened. Gerry turned him. Joey lashed out with a punch to his jaw. Gerry fumbled the flashlight. It thudded to the carpet as Joey leaped from the bed. Gerry grabbed for Joey's shirttail, and missed.

"Joey!" he hissed in a whisper, but the boy was halfway across the room, sneakers pounding on the carpeted floor.

Gerry scrambled to his feet, swiped at Joey's shoulder and missed. Dee appeared in the doorway. Joey collided with her and sprang back. Gerry circled his waist and clamped a hand over his son's mouth. A muffled a scream escaped and Gerry yanked him against his chest.

"It's me, Dad," he said into Joey's ear.

Joey twisted in an effort to look up at him. Then went lax in Gerry's grasp. Gerry loosened his hold and Joey spun, throwing his arms around him. Despite the boy's earlier bravado, he trembled. Gerry hugged his son close. In the angled splash of flashlight beam across the floor, moisture burned the corners of his eyes.

"It's all right, pal. I'm here. It's all right." He let Joey cling to him for a moment longer, then pulled back. "You okay?'

Joey gave a shaky nod. Gerry scooped up the flashlight and shined the beam on his neck. No scars.

Gerry blew out a breath. "That was some punch."

"I was scared," Joey said in a bare whisper.

"Me too," Gerry replied. "Now let's get outa here."

Joey stiffened and Gerry looked right to see Dee standing behind him. "Detective Kelly is here to help us," he said. "Let's go." He grasped Joey's hand and started toward the door.

Dee fell in behind Joey. An unexpected tingle traveled down Gerry's spine as they neared the hall. He stopped an instant before the door cattycorner across the hallway opened. Gerry shoved Joey back against Dee. A man stood framed within the doorway.

"Gerry."

Gerry's heart nearly stopped. "Hammet?"

"Yeah."

Without glancing back at Dee, Gerry swung his hand, palm back in a 'Stay here' gesture blocked from Hammet's view by the half open door. He hurried from the room, pulling the door closed on the way out. Two steps from Hammet, he said, "Brenda didn't tell me you were missing."

"How did you find us?" Hammet asked in a hoarse whisper.

Gerry stopped beside Hammet and laid a hand on his shoulder. Hammet had done a short stint with the Dallas Cowboys and still had the linebacker shoulders that had gotten him on the team.

"You okay? Did they drug you?" Gerry asked.

"Yeah. What are you doing here?" Hammet demanded.

"Later. We're getting Joey out." Gerry paused and squinted past Hammet at what looked like a desk sitting against the room's left wall. A large square object sat left of the desk he realized was a filing cabinet.

"I'm glad you're here," Hammet said.

The first hint of light Gerry had seen since they'd ascended the stairs seeped in around the edges of thick curtains behind the desk. He brushed past Hammet and hurried around the desk to the far wall. He grasped the curtain edge and drew it back an inch. Moonlight filtered through thick clouds and illuminated another beach house eighty feet down the beach.

Gerry released the curtain and faced Hammet. "What is this room, an office? What are you doing here? Where's the blond guy, Alarr?"

"Not here."

Gerry's heart beat faster. "He's gone?"

Hammet didn't answer.

"Dammit, Hammet, get your ass in gear."

"I hadn't expected you," Hammet said. "But I'm glad you came, Gerald."

"What—" He froze. No one called him Gerald.

The last, most important piece of the puzzle slammed into place. The lopsided cross. "*...their god chooses a body to inhabit and possesses it,*" Iris had said. "*It seems safe to assume physical prowess was a major concern.*"

Each of the first four Valknut victims had been at the crime scene of each previous victim because *each had murdered the victim before them* when Mótsognir left their body and entered the new host—the murderer. The real murderer was "Mótsognir," Gerry said the name in a whisper. Then remembered—*Balder hadn't been wearing a ring.* Gerry jabbed the flashlight's ON button, jerking the beam onto Hammet's right hand.

A garish gold band encircled his middle finger.

Their gazes locked.

Hammet lunged as Gerry yanked his Glock free of its holster. Hammet rammed a shoulder into his gut. Gerry's body armor jarred his whole torso. He dropped the flashlight and slammed the butt of his weapon between Hammet's shoulder blades. The ex-linebacker thudded to the carpet. Gerry dropped with all his weight and drove a knee into the small of Hammet's back. Air burst from his lungs.

Gerry shook off a wave of dizziness, raised the Glock, then hesitated.

This was his friend. His mind spun with too many possibilities. Iris had accurately described the god. This man—creature—was some sort of spirit-hopping god. A spirit-hopping god who had found a descendant of the vampires he'd fed off of throughout the centuries and planned on making that descendant his next host.

Gerry pictured Joey's eyes widening with fear, then going blank as the parasitic god drained the part from Joey's mind that made him Joey. Gerry's stomach turned. He slammed the Glock down on the back of Hammet's head. He went limp and Gerry felt his friend's neck. A strong pulse thumped against his fingers. He holstered the weapon, then pulled the handcuffs from his coat pocket and snapped them on Hammet's wrists.

Static buzzed an abrupt crescendo in the ear bud. "Ge—y," Alyssa's voice came intermittently over the line. "Up-airs, d-d y- find -ey?"

"Alyssa, what's happening?"

"—ference. To- -uch psy-ic en-rgy. Upstairs. –ey there. Is –ere a hal—ay?"

"Yes," he replied. "We're upstairs. We found him."

"Th-rd –oor."

"Third door?" he repeated. "What about the third door?"

"—careful—" More static. "The door at the—"

"—end of the hallway," they said in unison.

Gerry scooped up the flashlight as he shoved to his feet. He hurried from the room and across the hallway into the doorway of Joey's bedroom.

"Dee," he whispered.

She rose from beside the dresser.

"Watch Joey," he ordered, and ran down the hallway.

At the third door, he turned on the flashlight as he swung the last door open. Total darkness didn't mask the bone deep thrum that pulsed inside the room. He swept the darkness with the flashlight beam. Against the right wall, a figure lay chained to a twin bed. *Sula.* He realized that somewhere deep inside he'd known he'd find her here.

What had they done to her? But he knew. Only Alarr's touch could have kept her on that bed despite the chains that coiled her legs, crisscrossed her torso, securing her arms at her sides, and wound three layers thick across her neck. His heart ached at sight of her slumped head lying against the thick chain nearest her neck.

Gerry made a sweep of the room with the beam, saw only a dresser on the opposite wall and an open empty closet, then crossed to the bed and knelt. He felt for a pulse. Sula's neck, cold under his probing fingertips, felt as lifeless as the maidens Brother Thomas had described. Did vampires have a pulse?

She took a sudden, shallow breath. Gerry heard Dee gasp behind him. He glanced over his shoulder and saw her standing with Joey. Gerry pushed to his feet. A heavy rattle of Sula's chains caused him to stop and he looked back as her eyelashes fluttered open. In the dim light of the flashlight, he saw her eyes focus, then her dry lips part in surprise. Her gaze shifted past him and her face relaxed.

"Your son." Hoarseness marred her soft lilt. She looked at him. "Leave."

"I have to get you out of these chains." Gerry stuck the flashlight between his teeth and reached for the links.

She gave a slight shake of her head. "I'm too weak."

He paused, fingers barely touching the chain crossing her breasts, and shook his head stubbornly.

"Go," she whispered.

"Gerry," Dee urged. "She's right."

He twisted and looked at her as he grabbed the flashlight from between his teeth. "She saved our—your—life back at Tall Palms. I didn't abandon you. I won't abandon her." He hesitated. Mótsognir, in Hammet's body, was handcuffed in the other room. That still left Alarr. "We're getting Joey out first." Gerry pulled his Glock from the holster as he hurried to his son. He grasped Joey's hand, then strode down the hallway to the stairs.

Silence. He started down.

They reached the sliding glass door in seconds.

Gerry squatted eye level to Joey and grasped his son's shoulders. "I'm going back, pal." Joey swallowed, and Gerry's heart constricted. "We don't leave friends behind. Do we?"

Joey shook his head. "No way."

The determination in his son's voice startled then strengthened him. No matter what happened to him, Joey would be all right. "Go with Detective Kelly. We have another friend who's waiting with Hargrave. You do what Detective Kelly says. It's important that I know I can count on you."

"I will, Dad."

Pride welled inside Gerry. He would make sure they both made it. He hugged his son close before standing and facing to Dee, "You know the drill." He handed her his Glock.

"I've got my Walther."

"I know. But a weapon in each hand is better. Keep both guns ready. Get to Alyssa, then have her and Joey get as far away as they can." He pushed them out the door and watched them race down the walkway toward the beach. He retrieved the Derringer strapped to his leg as Dee and Joey made the trees, then he turned, flipped on the flashlight and raced back up the stairs.

Sula lay perfectly still. Gerry sat on the bed beside her. Was he too late? He stuffed the Derringer into his waistband and grasped her shoulders. Her eyes shot open. Recognition flooded her expression.

"What are you doing here?" she rasped.

"Why didn't Alarr bury you like he did the first time?" Gerry demanded.

She frowned. "The Alarr?"

"Why not just bury you like he did the first time—or take you away? Why did he bring you back to Mótsognir?"

"I don't understand."

But Gerry did. Anger rammed through him. She didn't know Mótsognir had contracted a hit, or that Alarr had saved her life by burying her. The swords buried with her had been hers *and* Alarr's. Alarr had meant to return for her. But she hadn't stayed around the mock grave long enough to discover the truth. But why had Alarr delivered her to Mótsognir now? What hold did the gothi god have over him? Eternal life as he'd promised the murder victims?

"To hell with it," Gerry muttered. "We're getting you out of these chains."

"I'm too weak to break them," she whispered.

He leaned in close. "Not if you have blood."

"You can't—"

But he was already drawing her close. Chain shifted with a low clank as he nestled her face against his neck. His heart pounded and his insides trembling like a bowl of jelly. You've done this before, he told himself, *and liked it.* Her hair fell across his arm, soft, just as he remembered.

"Drink," he whispered.

Sula remained still.

"Come on," he coaxed. "Who knows how much time we have?"

She didn't respond.

"Sula."

"I need too much," she murmured.

"No," he said. "Not too much. Remember? We're a perfect match."

Understanding hit like lightening. He'd always been intuitive, uncanny at sorting out clues in a puzzle with too many missing pieces. But something had changed after that night in the alley...after Sula had bitten him. He hadn't become like her, not fully, nor like Alarr. But he had changed, had become...more.

"You saved my life in the alley," he whispered. "I can't let you die." When she didn't stir, he added, "He's out there, Sula, your Gothi, the god who took your life, your child *and his children*. The first four victims here in Miami were your son's descendants."

The narcissistic bastard had used women for centuries in a way that was much worse than rape. He had taken body, mind and soul, and changed them into something nonhuman, something tailored to feed his lusts. Now, he no longer discriminated according to gender. The Valknut victims' bloodlines were all he cared about.

Gerry bent his head until his lips brushed Sula's ear. "He can still come for me, for my son. We don't know how to kill him."

A moment of silence passed and he wanted to shout, shake her until she got as angry as she had in the taxidermy basement when she'd laid Alarr on his ass. She shifted, her lips grazing his neck.

Gerry tensed. *I need too much*, she had said. Would he die, or worse, this time become like Alarr? If he did, would the holy articles in his pocket send him to hell, or maybe set him on fire?

Despite anticipation, the tiny prick to his neck startled him. Shivers rolled down his spine. His balance wavered. The thrumming in his ears mingled with the rush of blood through his veins as Sula drew deeply. Black and white Chilly Billy rose in his memory, then faded into the familiar sight of battle lines of men arrayed before him on a moonlit field.

He became aware of the rhythm of the horse he sat upon, and scanned the open expanse to the far hill until his gaze caught on Sula astride her mount. She drew him, and he gave into the rush of wind that surged, then lifted him. He startled at the unexpected lightweight feel of his body, but couldn't tear his gaze from the crystal blue eyes that pierced his soul. His body ached. He longed for her, to hold her, for her to hold him.

When he reached her, he opened his arms and she stepped into his embrace. Her coolness seeped through his chainmail, searing his warm body as he pressed her to him.

"Take what you need," he whispered.

She nestled closer, melting into him, inch by inch, her chill seeping into his very soul. His warmth pooled in his center, bleeding into her essence, drawing from the farthest reaches of his outermost cells. Cold surrounded him in a thin steam of hot ice. His body grew heavy. He wanted to fall into himself...into her. Wrap around her, bind each cell to hers. Become one. Mind, body, spirit. Cold. He shivered. He wanted—needed—sleep. Sleep beside her, forever.

Gerry spiraled into a gray murk. Cold wind whipped through him. The wind cooled, then warmed. A glow permeated the shadows ahead. Thunder erupted. Heat seared his skin, then poured into his blood and shot through him. Wind roared, tossing him, jarring his bones. Time flowed in quicksilver. Quiet. Alone.

His freefall stopped with a hard thump. His eyes shot open and he found himself lying on the sand outside the house. He looked about wildly. Where was Sula? His gaze snagged on two petite footprints angled toward the side of the house. Had Sula carried him—a thud sounded on the sand behind him. Gerry leaped to his feet, yanking the Derringer from his waistband. His head spun. He shook his head against the lightheadedness and focused on a man standing twenty feet away.

Hammet. He'd torn free of the handcuffs. But how—*Alarr had released him.*

Hammet laughed softly as if reading his thoughts. Gerry squinted to focus his vision on Hammet and forced the images and sensations of Sula from his cloudy brain.

"I need your body," Mótsognir said with Hammet's deep voice. "I will be your son's father until he comes of age."

"Over my dead body," Gerry ground out in a whisper.

He gave his head a shake to clear the cobwebs and leveled the gun on Mótsognir. His aim wavered and he clasped the weapon with both hands, then hesitated. What would happen if he shot a god?

Mótsognir gave a small nod. "I need your body. Once I take possession of you, the missing books will be mine."

"How did you find out the books still existed?" Gerry forced thoughts of Joey from his mind. He couldn't give the god a chance to pick up on his thoughts. He had to keep him talking.

"I was looking for a suitable host when I was guided to John Kinnison," Mótsognir replied.

Gerry could only stare. *Guided?* The psycho believed in divine providence. "You wanted their psychic abilities. But it didn't work, did it? Their bloodline didn't do you one bit of good." Gerry remembered Vitelli's past life regression. "How'd you like reliving the destruction of the temple through Frank Vitelli's memories?"

Mótsognir's smile faded.

Gerry recognized the advantage and pressed on. "Finding out one of those girls had lived must have turned you inside out. Saved by a lowly soldier. One helluva coincidence." Hell, maybe coincidence wasn't so bad after all. Gerry started laughing. "*That's* providence"

Mótsognir's face contorted in rage.

"White lig-Ger-!" Alyssa voice abruptly shouted into his earpiece. "Vis-lize -ite li- shooting fr -our feet and up ov- -r head t- encase you."

Gerry froze. Alyssa shouldn't still be within radio range. He had ordered her to take Joey and get out.

"Do -t!" she shouted.

Gerry kept his gaze on Hammet—Mótsognir—and pictured *white light.* A bubbling ball of transparent white light burst in front of his mental vision. He startled. Chills rolled down his body in contrast to a warm glow that pressed in on him. Pressure against his head dropped him to his knees. He saw Hammet's lips moving, yet heard nothing but a rushing wind in his ears.

His eyes bulged. He jammed his eyes shut. Blood jammed through his veins and pounded in his ears. He jerked his gun up, gripping it with both hands, and blindly fired. The pressure on his head seeped into his skull. A dog barked. Someone shouted. Gerry opened his eyes, but blaring light filled his vision. Was this the white light? What had gone wrong? The light rammed into his mental vision, blinding him. He jammed his eyes shut harder, but the light saturated his body, mind...soul.

He cried out in pain. The gun slipped from his grasp. The barking grew louder, a distant echo down a long, narrow pipe. His skull felt ready to splinter. He became oddly aware of the soft tissue in his brain. It shifted as if compressed. A woman's shout broke through the chaos and the barking filled his ears.

The pressure evaporated and Gerry's mind did a mental-recoil that felt as if his head had snapped back onto his neck like on a rubber band. Hargrave stood two feet away, barking wildly at Hammet. But Hammet was staring at the house. Gerry whipped around. Alarr stepped from the far side of the house. Sula suddenly appeared in front of Gerry. Hargrave whirled and stared at her.

"Freyja." Mótsognir took two paces toward her.

Alarr started forward. She snarled something indistinguishable. Alarr halted. She jerked her attention onto Mótsognir and threw out a harsh sounding string of sentences. He ground out a phrase and her eyes began to glow.

Her palpable anger startled Gerry. His mind raced with the sudden realization that Sula wasn't the first high priestess the gothi god had ordered murdered by Alarr. *A legend come to life* her memory had told him, *an assassin's assassin.* Sula had searched for her gothi not to reunite with him, but to demand answers.

"She knows the truth," Gerry said.

Mótsognir's gaze jerked onto him.

"She knows you ordered her death."

"Stay out of this," the gothi snapped. He looked at Sula. "We must perform the blot. Three hundred years have passed and I have not sustained a host. I have chosen this one." He pointed at Gerry.

Blood rushed through Gerry's ears. Something Iris had said hovered at the edge of understanding. The Alarr were the legend. Who else— sómaherji. *I learned the magic that gave me power to possess another man's body*—Gerry stared at Mótsognir. Christ, it couldn't be possible.

"Hey, Alarr!" Gerry shouted.

The male vampire's gaze riveted onto him.

Gerry forced a picture of white light surrounding him as he recited, "I was born into darkness, but—" the rushing air around him metamorphosed into energy, "—I learned the ma-gic that gave me power to possess another man's body and ab-sorb his s-soul. No longer do I live as s-som-*sómaherji*. I am free." He gasped for air. The gothi son-of-a-bitch was invading his mind. His throat constricted. "That-that's from the Hidden Book of Thoth."

Alarr's attention swung onto Mótsognir.

The pressure in Gerry's head eased. "Who were the honorable warriors, these *sómaherji*?"

"The *sómaherji*," Alarr repeated without taking his eyes off Mótsognir.

Even through the rush of air around him, Gerry heard the deep timbre of the vampire's voice, its authoritative resonance and…courage.

"*Our* brothers," Alarr said.

Gerry swung his gaze onto Mótsognir. *No longer do I live as sómaherji.* The gothi god used to be one of them. The pressure inside his skull amped up. He cringed. Hargrave snarled and began barking.

"Freyja," Mótsognir said in a harsh voice, "we must perform the blot. *Now.*"

Hargrave's ears went flat and he bared his teeth.

"Freyja," Mótsognir's voice grew urgent. "I need you. I must have rest."

The warmth around Gerry began to recede, replaced by a bone deep cold that seeped through his skin. This was nothing like the peaceful cold he'd shared with Sula. This was the fate that had awaited Joey if Gerry hadn't found him.

Alyssa, Gerry mentally pleaded, *get my son to safety.*

"Wh- light!" she shouted through the radio. "Holy wa-r. Thr- it on – im!"

"Get the—" the order to get Joey away died on Gerry's lips when Dee stepped from the side of the house, her Beretta gripped with both hands pointed at Mótsognir.

"Freeze, you son-of-a-bitch!" she shouted.

"Dee," Gerry rasped.

"Freyja," Mótsognir insisted.

Sula shifted her gaze to Gerry. The rushing air around him subsided and the roll of the surf filled his ears.

"What's this?" Mótsognir looked from Sula to Gerry. "Yes," he said in a soothing voice, "you want him." He approached her. "We can have him, Freyja. Once he is mine, he will be yours as well."

Dee stepped to the side and Sula glanced at her.

Mótsognir edged closer. "We can be together again."

Hargrave growled.

Sula looked at Mótsognir. "You betrayed us." Her voice was soft, sad.

"Never," he insisted.

She shook her head slowly.

Gerry reached into his jacket pocket and pulled out the small vial of holy water and the cross.

"Freyja," the gothi god pleaded.

Gerry flicked the lid off the vial and lunged, flinging the water onto Hammet as he thrust the cross toward him.

The gothi fell back a pace but the water spewed across his shirt. Fear rocketed through Gerry when droplets splashed on Sula.

"Sula." He took a step toward her, then stopped when the gothi's eyes cut to him and a laugh rumbled from Hammet's massive chest.

"Look, Sula." His voice dripped with condescension. "This human, how ignorant he is. He believes *His* symbols can harm us."

Confusion washed over Gerry.

"Why don't you fall down on your knees and pray to your god, human?" Mótsognir taunted.

Gerry wondered if he shouldn't do just that. What was he supposed to do? Had Alyssa gotten Joey away? Time, he needed to ensure their escape. He shoved his free hand into his pocket and yanked out the pentagram.

"Have you another *holy* article to banish us with?" The amusement died on the gothi's face, and his features contorted in fury and pain. He hunched into himself and backed up. "Where did you get that?" he snarled.

Sula retreated a step.

Movement flitted in the corner of Gerry's eye, then Dee cried out and Gerry glimpsed her crumple to the sand in the instant before Alarr appeared beside Sula. Sula pivoted and slammed her elbow into the male vampire's jaw. His head snapped back, but he held his ground. Hargrave latched onto Mótsognir's pant leg. He kicked Hargrave back ten feet. Sula leaped in a snap-kick to Alarr's jaw. He slid sideways, deflected her leg in midair, and toppled her backward.

Hargrave spun and lunged at Mótsognir again. Mótsognir grabbed Hargrave's chest and tossed him against the house. The Shepherd yelped and fell limp to the sand. Gerry crawled to Hargrave's side. The dog's breathing was quick and shallow.

Sula leaped to her feet as Alarr snapped out a sentence in Icelandic. She hesitated. Alarr seized her arm. She pivoted, twirling under his arm and twisting his arm like a jump rope. Gerry winced, expecting a crack of shattered bone.

"Stop, Alarr!" Mótsognir shouted. "She's Hrungnir's heart."

Hrungnir's heart—understanding flooded Gerry. Knot of the Slain. The Valknut drawn in one stroke. Earth, Hell and Heaven. Protection against evil spirits. Chooser of the slain…the beginning and end. The high priestess was the key, the nexus. Something in her—her blood—connected earth, hell, and heaven—and this psychopathic god controlled her. Used to control her, Gerry corrected as Mótsognir rushed into the fray.

Something metallic reflected in his hand. Gerry recalled the firebomb Sula had thrown at Linette and aimed his Berretta before realizing Mótsognir gripped a Taser.

"Sula!" Gerry shouted as electricity crackled and arc-light flickered.

Mótsognir thrust the Taser at Alarr and the male vampire spun.

"You swore to free her—" Alarr began.

Sula seized his shoulder, yanking him back. The arc leaped from Mótsognir's hand and connected with her fingers. Flames erupted. Alarr whirled. The flames raced up her arm as if on a lightning fast trail of gunpowder. Alarr grabbed her free wrist and started to yank her into an oxygen-quenching hug. Sula's eyes abruptly glowed deep blue, her gaze fixed on his face.

"No!" he shouted.

Sula pivoted so fast she blurred as she ripped free of Alarr an instant before she evaporated in a flash of blue fire with a loud pop that seemed to pierce Gerry's eardrums.

Nothing remained but scorched sand.

Gerry dragged in a ragged breath, tears so near the surface, he could taste them. Alarr had tried to save her, but she hadn't allowed the sacrifice.

A hideous cry from Alarr broke the spell. He seized Mótsognir.

"You can't!" Mótsognir cried. "Our law forbids murder of our own kind."

"*Our own kind,*" the vampire sneered, and yanked Hammet's neck to his mouth.

Mótsognir screamed as Alarr tore into his flesh. Blood spurted onto the vampire's face and pumped down Hammet's neck. He gurgled another scream. Mótsognir beat wildly at Alarr's back with a thick fist, his resistance slowly ebbing, until his arm fell to his side. Gerry looked wildly about the sand for his Derringer. Mótsognir gurgled. The vampire was killing him, killing Hammett. Gerry spotted the gun and dove for it.

His fingers closed around the cold steel and he came up on his knees, the weapon pointed at the two men.

Hammett's body lay limp in the vampire's arms. For an instant Gerry confused the pose for the intimate embrace he had shared with Sula and confusion washed over him. Then he glimpsed Alarr's face and the fire in his eyes, and the confusion vanished.

Gerry's hand trembled, the gun shaking, and he feared hitting Hammett, but it didn't matter. Hammett was dead. Alarr drew on Mótsognir another long moment before throwing him to the sand. He stared at the body, chest heaving, blood covering his full mouth and running down his jaw.

Gerry wondered if he was waiting for the god to emerge from the lifeless husk. He grasped the gun with both hands in readiness, then forced back a bubble of hysterical laughter. If this powerful vampire couldn't stop a spirit, what chance did he have? At last, Alarr faced him. Hands still shaking, Gerry kept his gun pointed at him. Indecision flickered in his expression, then the vampire was gone, leaving a cloud of airborne sand that settled into deep footprints heading toward the highway.

Gerry waited, the gun shaking so badly he couldn't have hit a rhinoceros at point blank range. Wind whistled to his left and he swung the gun around, but saw only night. On the other side of Hargrave, he heard Dee's nearly soundless crying.

At last, his arms ached so badly they finally dropped to his lap with the Derringer. He lowered his head to the ground and closed his eyes. Gerrry jarred when something wet rasped across his check, then relaxed under Hargrave's attention. He sank his fingers into the Shepherd's thick fur and felt warmth.

Shadows of dawn hinted at early morning light and Gerry discerned a dark line in the sand ten feet away from where he had crashed to his knees. He ran his gaze along the line in a full rectangle back to its beginning, then flicked a glance at the gothi god's last victim and shivered. Mótsognir had been creating a vey opening. Gerry pulled himself onto his knees and crawled to the center of the vey opening where Sula had died.

Epilogue

Giants walked the earth in those days. Men of celebrated heroism, honorable warriors who were sons of the gods and earth's daughters.

G ERRY'S ATTENTION SNAGGED on the words *honorable warriors* and his fingers tightened on the open folder on his lap. He forced his grip to loosen and tuned out the activity in the bullpen outside his office as he continued reading Iris' email.

The Old Norse word used in this passage of the *Hidden Book of Thoth* for honorable warrior is *sómaherji*, the same word found in the pages you first shared with me two months ago. Of itself, this has little meaning, but this passage is too much like the biblical verses Genesis 6:1-4 to be easily dismissed.

> *And it came to pass, when men began to multiply on the face of the ground and daughters were born unto them, that the sons of God saw the daughters of men that they were fair and took them wives of all that they chose.*
>
> *And Jehovah said, My Spirit shall not strive with man forever, for that he also is flesh: yet shall his days be a hundred and twenty years. There were giants in the earth in those days; and also after that, when the sons of God came in unto the daughters of men, and they bare children to them, the same became mighty men which were of old, men of renown.*

The next passage in the Hidden Book of Thoth reads: *When Nidhogg, brother of Odin the most high and captain of the sómaherji angels, offered mankind truth from Yggdrasil, Odin grew incensed and made war with*

Nidhogg and his children and cast them to Midgard where they await the final battle.

When you understand that Nidhogg is the dragon who lives at one of the three roots of Yggdrasil, the cosmic tree that connects the nine worlds, and Midgard is the world of men, the similarity to man's temptation in Eden and the war in heaven between Jehovah and Satan is too obvious to miss.

Gerry paused, Sula's words returned. *"His kind came first. They are older, the original clan cast from paradise."*

He startled with the memory of running alongside Jonis. *"They have hunted us too long."* Gerry heard the words as if Jonis was speaking them, and remembered the meaning in the vampire's words: *They had been hunted since the Great War that had ripped the universe apart.*

Suddenly Gerry understood what he hadn't allowed himself to grasp at the time. They, the Aptrgangr, were those angels who had been cast from heaven after warring with God. They were *the sons of God who came in unto the daughters of men… the same who became mighty men which were of old, men of renown.*

And they were vampires.

What kind of god created holy beings as vampires?

Unexpected anger tore through him. Sula was—had been—human. She had been made what she was by a fallen angel who would be God. Gerry's chest constricted. Had she found peace? Where did her *kind* go after death? Not long ago, he wouldn't have considered such a question. Now…now he had no more answers than he had before this began.

He refocused on Iris' email.

Also, Nidhogg is referred to as captain of the *sómaherji* angels and as brother of the most high. Captain of the *sómaherji* angels is a direct correlation to Michael the archangel, and Nidhogg as the brother of the most high mirrors the legend of Loki Laufeyjarson, a son of the giants Fárbauti and Laufey, and foster-brother of Odin.

To solidify Nidhogg and Loki's identities as one and the same, the final battle referred to could easily be what, in Norse mythology, is called the *fate of the gods*, the end of the world battle, waged between the gods, led by Odin, representing order, and their aggressors, Loki, and his children, representing chaos. Because prophecy reveals the battle's outcome, the gods know that Heimdall, the White God, guardian of the gods, will fight Loki, and neither will survive. However, not only do Loki, gods, giants, and monsters perish in this apocalyptic fight, but almost everything in the universe will be destroyed. *Armageddon.*

Though not mentioned in these passages, it is interesting to note that Loki is known as a master shape shifter, which further reflects Satan's role in the Garden of Eden when he changed shape and appeared to Eve as a snake.

Loki and Nidhogg as the single entity that embody Satan, Michael the Archangel, and God's brother all in one, has far reaching implications, the most interesting of which is found in his role as *sómaherji*, the Alarr, which is the clan of Aptrgangr: Ones who walk after death—creatures we today call vampires. After all, if the brother of the most high is a vampire, than the most high, too, is vampire.

Satan God's brother. This wasn't the first time Gerry had heard that theory. But God, a vampire?

"He believes His symbols can hurt us." Mótsognir's had said of the holy water and cross. He hadn't feared the Christian symbols, but he had feared the pentagram. Why fear Satan and not God? Why fear one brother and not the other?

A tremor traveled through Gerry's midsection. He'd studied religion, but put no faith in it beyond its historical value. He hadn't truly believed in God or Satan.

Alarr: honorable warrior. Sula: Asatru assassin. Mótsognir: sómaherji god. Vampires as gods…gods as vampires?

From the corner of his eye, Gerry saw Dee approach across the bullpen. The familiar psychic *knock knock* sounded inside his mind. He mentally locked the door as the knock sounded again, and tossed the folder containing Alyssa's latest missing child case onto his desk drawer. He closed his email. His cell phone played *Send in the Clowns* and he glanced at the caller ID as he and rose to meet Dee. Brenda's number flashed on the screen. He really needed to program a special ring for her number.

From the authors

We hope you enjoyed *Knot of the Slain*, the first book in the Blood Angels series. Next, follows *Land of the Giants* where our protagonists will chase down more of the Blood Angles on Easter Island. Please enjoy a preview of *Chain Reaction*, the first book in our Phenom League series.

Evan and Shawn
T. C. Archer

CHAIN REACTION

The Phenom League

For love of country and a woman, Jordan Pierce must sacrifice his humanity.

Former Chicago Detective Jordan Pierce put his life on hold in order to protect America's secret weapon against the Nazis; The Manhattan Project. But he can't protect himself against the disease eating away at his humanity. Jordan discovers how much of his soul this infection has devoured when he falls in love with the woman who could destroy America. Choosing her, means choosing the monster he's becoming, making him the most powerful man he's ever known.

Chapter One

October, 1942

TENSION FERMENTED IN the air like a sour mash whiskey. By chance, skill, stealth, and deceit I had kept my secret. But tonight I strode down the halls of Chicago University's Eckhart Hall with a feeling my time had run out.

Every evening I reported for duty as The Manhattan Project's head of nightshift security not knowing what I missed during those midday hours when I lay dead to the world. Along with the bizarre sleep that immobilized me, the strange infection raging through my body made me dislike food and drink, stopped my smoking habit cold turkey, and switched me into permanent high gear. The worst part was the dread I barely kept at bay, knowing the people I worked for would turn me into a lab rat if they discovered the truth.

My gut coiled tighter as I entered Security Chief Lopez's office at six o'clock sharp. Lopez stood in front of his desk, hat in hand, while rifling through a stack of files. He looked over his shoulder and our eyes met.

I halted. His bloodshot eyes told me something was wrong even without the uncharacteristic loose tie and rumpled black suit. He straightened and raked strands of greased hair over the bald spot in the back of his head.

"Pierce," he said, "there's been a security breach."

Relief washed over me. This had to be a repeat of the one and only *security breach* we'd had a couple of weeks ago. In a fit of depression, Miss Therese Hance, a mathematics major here at Chicago University, had written a poem. I still recalled the verse verbatim:

> *Dear little neutronian who lives on a nucleus in an atom of my knee, if you do not stop jumping around, you are going to cause an atomic blast and blow up the universe.*

With the top-secret race to beat the Germans to the first nuclear chain reaction going on at Chicago University, the poem hit too close to home. When Miss Hance's professor, Dr Albert, found the poem on her desk here in Eckhart Hall—Dr Albert had some vague awareness of the research going on—he passed the poem along to Oppenheimer, and Oppenheimer panicked. Lopez and I barely prevented the scientists from having a collective nervous breakdown.

I gave Lopez a *not this again* look. "Which student wrote another poem? Miss Hance didn't know a thing. It'll be the same this time." Then I added before he could reply, "Don't tell me you bought into the story about how her studies in group theory gave her a subconscious knowledge of the scientific research being conducted here."

Lopez shifted and I caught sight of the bright red, *Eyes Only*, top-secret folder beside the pile of folders he had been thumbing through. I started. An *Eyes Only* report could only have originated with General Groves, head of The Manhattan Project. This was no student poem.

"We intercepted a radio message north of the Ontario border last night." Lopez grabbed the folder and extended it toward me. "The code-breakers say the message contains the correct amount of Uranium 235 needed to sustain a chain reaction."

"The true U-235 amounts?" I blurted, mechanically reaching for the folder.

Our big edge over the Nazis was the knowledge of how little Uranium 235 was needed to start a chain reaction. Of the two isotopes of uranium, U-238 and the rare U-235, the Nazi's head scientist, Werner Heisenberg, believed they needed a uranium concentration of ninety percent U-235 to build an atom bomb. According to our head scientist, Enrico Fermi, only a twenty percent concentration of the rare isotope would reach critical mass. The disparity was enough to keep the Germans busy doing nothing but enriching uranium until we drove them back to Berlin. But we had to attain the first nuclear chain reaction to ensure victory.

I dropped my stare to the folder and forced my fingers to close around it as Lopez's hand fell away. A bona fide breach here at Chicago Pile One? No one in the outside world knew what was really going on in Eckhart Hall's *Metallurgical Lab*. The real liability lay a block away at Stagg Field. The scientists were building an atomic pile in an abandoned squash court beneath the field's west grandstands. Damn it, I'd warned

Lopez someone would get suspicious at seeing scientists constantly running between Eckhart Hall and Stagg Field, briefcases clutched so tightly their knuckles turned white. Suddenly Miss Therese Hance's poem didn't seem so farfetched. Who else had noticed strange activity at Eckhart Hall?

"Who else besides the CP-1 scientists have this information?" I asked.

Lopez's mouth thinned. "You, me, and General Groves."

Groves and Lopez were above suspicion. The transmission had to have come from one of the fifty-two scientists working on the project. They all understood the ramifications of an atomic weapon in the hands of a madman like Hitler. I couldn't believe any of them capable of selling out their country, much less the rest of the world.

I swung my gaze up to Lopez's face. "If the Nazis find out Heisenberg's equations are wrong…"

"And the Nazis get their hands on the correct equations…"

We both let the unsaid words hang: *The US could lose the war.*

"Any leads?" I asked.

"Nothing. I rang your apartment an hour ago when the report hit my desk, but you must have been out."

I nodded. Here was the reason for the dread I'd experienced tonight. A crisis like this could draw attention to the fact I was always *out* during the height of daylight hours. My service during the Great War combined with my position as a detective on the Chicago Police Force had gotten me through the security check for this job. Keeping a low profile had kept my secret safe—until now.

"What are our instructions?" I asked.

"Sit tight and observe until the spooks finish their investigation." He nodded at the folder. "It's all there. I've already requested a list of the scientists who have access to the U-235 information, as well as a few other topics so the librarians can't guess who or what we're after."

"When will the report be available?" I asked in a tone I hoped didn't show my disbelief. Waiting for our counter intelligence experts to mull over mounds of information wasn't General Groves's style. Groves was the kick-ass type who single-handedly spearheaded the construction of the Pentagon, the world's largest office building.

"When they're ready," Lopez said. "We've got to catch this guy, but can't chance alerting the scientists to the possibility we have a spy. Any panic, and the university might discover this isn't the harmless metallurgical laboratory our government claims. Those bleeding heart academics will strip us naked and toss us ass first to the media wolves. In the meantime, we go on alert. Our inside network is working to pinpoint where the information originated."

Suddenly, the folder felt like it weighed a ton. I'd never expected to be holding one of these super secret reports. My thirty-nine years of age made me ineligible to fight this war, so I'd consoled myself with the knowledge Chicago cops were needed to keep the streets safe here at home. When I'd been attacked in the alley eight months ago, I'd put my life on hold while I hunted for the fiend who attacked me. Now, I'd set aside my search in order to aid the war effort because I was even more afraid of Hitler's Nazis and Mussolini's fascists gaining control than I was of what I had become. The longer I put off finding out who infected my body with this sickness, the less likely the chances I'd be able to reverse the disease. I hadn't allowed myself to think about what I might become if the disease ate me alive.

"We can't let those bastards win the war," I said.

Lopez's mouth thinned. "I have to fly to Washington. You're in charge while I'm gone."

"Me?" I forced back shock. "What about Banks? He's your dayshift second in command."

"You're head of nightshift. Groves says you're in charge when I'm not here."

My mouth went dry. Lack of seniority enabled me to do this job. I wanted to ask when he would return, grill him on every tiny detail in the red file I gripped, anything, to keep him talking and here at CP-1.

His gaze bored into me. "You got this handled?"

"Yeah," I replied.

Without another word, he donned his hat and disappeared out the door.

I stared at the open doorway and muttered to the empty room, "As long as I can find the leak before sunrise."

Chapter Two

I HAD READ only eight of the eleven pages of the *Eyes Only* report when I got the call. Two minutes later, I stood outside the closed office door of Dr Leonard Heinrick, stopped by the smell of cold blood seeping from the room. A lot of blood. What stopped me wasn't the heightened sense of smell that aroused boyhood memories of the way my father smelled when he returned from the slaughterhouse where he worked, but the stomach-churning odor of decaying blood.

I fought back a rising panic. Why the hell hadn't Lopez caught a plane an hour later? As head of security, he should be standing here instead of me. At the very least, he should have locked down the lab and given me authority to run my own investigation. Instead, he'd tied my hands and left me waiting for information from the eggheads.

Movement on the other side of the door's frosted glass startled me from the dread and I recognized the blurred form of Officer Of the Day, or OOD, Colonel McHenry. I opened the door. He stood near the desk in the cramped office and turned, revealing the mutilated body of Leonard Heinrick. He lay on his back, arms at his side as if at attention. Blood had pooled in his right eye socket. Crimson stained the front and sides of his starched white shirt where his throat had been cut, and over a quart of blood had puddled on the floor under his head.

A chill snaked up my back. The precision throat slice reminded me of the way Lawrence 'Lucky Larry' Fiato liked to kill—when he had the time to enjoy his work.

"You didn't touch anything?" I asked in reflex as I forced my legs to carry me forward. The stench of dead blood made me want to vomit. Week-old hamburger would smell better.

McHenry marched to the door, quietly shut it, then faced me, hands clasped behind his back. "I secured the crime scene, then called you from the office next door."

I didn't know what *secured the crime scene* meant—the Army wasn't known for doing things like the Chicago PD. I swallowed back rising revulsion as I unbuttoned my suit jacket and squatted beside the body. The disease flowing through my veins made me crave warm, living blood. *Dead* human blood made my gut roil as if I'd taken a nosedive in a Douglas A-24 Banshee.

I made as close an inspection of the body as possible without disturbing anything. Nothing obvious was missing. Heinrick's wallet bulged in his front pants pocket and the Prexa Swiss-made Chronograph Manual watch he wore was still strapped to his left wrist. No other wounds were visible, but forensics would have to tell me what his backside looked like. The rotting odor I knew Colonel McHenry couldn't smell forced me to choke back a gag. I'd seen my share of blood and death. At fifteen years of age, my six-foot height and sprouting beard got me into the Army during the Great War, where I saw enough death and dismemberment near Maginot Line in France to last a lifetime. Now I couldn't get past the violent aversion to cold, *dead* blood.

But I'd have to deal with my loathing in order to find the killer. The stabbing to Heinrick's eyes indicated torture and the slice to his neck was professional. A trained killer had infiltrated the sterilized ranks of Chicago Pile One. I had to work fast. Espionage, torture, and murder mounted a greater problem than being out of communication during the midday hours when I lay unconscious.

We couldn't afford to draw attention to the lab with the kind of security found on military instillations, so we kept security light. I'd strapped on the Colt .45 General Groves had insisted Lopez and I keep in our desks in case of emergency, but neither McHenry, nor any of his civilian-dressed officers—we had to make the daily business look like a typical university operation—carried weapons. A policy that had to grate against McHenry's military mind. Yet strangers didn't enter Eckhart Hall without notice. So how had someone waltzed into Heinrick's office noticed?

I stood and walked a circle around the corpse. More important than the how was the why? Scientists had reasons to be jealous of one another: status, projects, publications, and occasionally romance created friction among them. But these motives seldom led to murder. Was Heinrick's murder related to the security breach or another matter altogether? The easy answer was that Heinrick had passed on the priceless U-235 information, then outlived his usefulness. But I had a feeling there'd be no easy answers.

I steeled myself against the nausea, squatted again, and drew the stench deep into my nostrils. In two seconds, I knew Heinrick had been dead approximately four hours. "You were killed around quarter after six, Heinrick," I murmured.

"How can you tell?" McHenry asked.

I looked up, having forgotten him. "Hypostasis." I drew an imaginary circle around Heinrick's eye with my forefinger. "See how pink his skin is here? That's an indication the blood is settling in the lowest parts of his body. The pinker the skin, the earlier the time of death." I glanced at McHenry, not adding that hypostasis commenced approximately six to eight hours *after* death and isn't fully pronounced for eight to twelve hours. Truth was, I couldn't explain how I knew the age of dead blood, and I'd grown tired of trying to understand the strange ability.

I dropped my gaze back to the bloody neck. "Just a guess. The coroner will have the final say."

"Security is on full alert," McHenry said. "We're on lockdown. If the killer is still here, we'll find him."

I nodded, not saying, *If he isn't one of the staff or military personnel.* Inside jobs were the hardest for military police to accept. Traitors in the midst of patriotic zeal hit hard.

I rose. "I assume none of the evening staff are missing?"

"No."

"You have someone checking on the day crew?" If the murder turned out to be an inside job, he could be in Canada by the time the day shift showed up and we discovered him missing.

"Banks is on it," McHenry replied.

"How about the office?" I asked. "Anything missing?"

"Don't know. Security still has to inventory the contents of the safe."

I glanced at the combination safe by the desk where Heinrick stored his classified documents. What McHenry called a safe was a fortified steel file cabinet with a combination dial about the size of my fist with a sturdy lever type handle. Every scientist had a similar safe. Some had two drawers like Heinrick's, others four. If the thief had accessed the safe, he wanted us to think otherwise: the drawers were closed and the cabinet looked unmolested.

I took two steps to the safe and pulled my handkerchief from my back pocket. Using the handkerchief to cover my fingers, I jiggled the handle and yanked. Locked.

"I'll have the contents inventoried and dusted for prints," McHenry said.

Spies preferred photographing documents instead of stealing them. Missing documents were always assumed to be in foreign hands, and steps taken to discredit, invalidate, or obfuscate the secrets within. The killer had made no efforts to hide the fact he was a professional, so why hide the fact he'd stolen documents? Now everything in the safe would be considered compromised. My gut said because he hadn't been interested in the safe's contents.

"Who found the body?" I asked as I scanned the sides of the safe.

"Dr Nichols."

Dr Gladys Anne Nichols, thirty years old—seven years younger than me—had four degrees from Vassar, Wellesley and Cornell. I had reviewed her personnel file a week ago when she arrived, but hadn't met her. I thought she worked dayshift.

"Where's she now?"

"Roma's office."

"I'll have a chat with her. Let me know when the Chicago PD arrives."

"General's orders are he talks to you first."

I jerked my gaze onto McHenry. "Chicago PD hasn't been notified?"

"You have to talk to General Groves first."

The implacable set of McHenry's jaw said he wasn't saying more, but I wasn't in the habit of leaving dead bodies lying around.

"You haven't reported the murder yet?"

"The Army doesn't report to local police."

"This isn't a military installation," I said.

"You were going to talk to Dr Nichols." He turned to the side, indicating I should precede him out of the room.

I stared for a long moment, but knew he wasn't going to budge until I left the crime scene. I strode from the room, McHenry closing the door behind us and taking up guard in front of the door as I kept going. "Damn Army by-the-book-board-up-their-asses attitude," I muttered as I turned the corner in the hallway. I used to like that about the Army when I served. I guess I was young and dependent back then.

A moment later, I halted in front of the closed door where Dr Nichols waited. The name painted on the glass read: Dr Enrico Roma, the alias of the great scientist and Nobel Prize laureate Enrico Fermi. The alias didn't fool anybody but the ignorant. Light shone through the milky glass window. I blew out a breath. The last thing I wanted to do was interrogate a hysterical woman.

I opened the door and stopped dead at the sight of a shapely blonde leaning against Fermi's mahogany desk. I stared as realization sunk in that the Veronica Lake look-alike standing there was the same egghead pictured in her personnel file. The glasses she'd worn were absent and, despite the red-rimmed eyes and drawn expression, the single overhead light warmed the creamy complexion that had looked bland and colorless in the photo.

Thick blond hair slid across her face in a broad wave and flowed down slim shoulders. Suddenly, I understood the reasoning behind the functional bun in the picture. Despite the legs that mesmerized a man all the way down to the high heel straps, the tweed skirt and blazer she wore emphatically stated the bombshell figure was off limits. But the moment a man laid eyes on her luxurious hair all bets were off. My breath caught with bloodlust as I drew in her scent from across the room.

Gray-blue eyes stared from behind the drape of blond hair. Her gaze flicked to my waistband and I realized she'd glimpsed the colt holstered beneath my suit jacket.

"You wear your gun like a gangster," she said.

I startled. Her voice, low and sultry, held a shaky note, but I knew the remark was payment for my staring.

"This incident requires I carry a weapon." My drill sergeant used to berate any reference to the word gun. *"Your gun is between your legs, son. Your pistol or rifle is called a weapon."*

She continued to stare and guilt stabbed at me. She'd discovered a colleague who'd been brutally murdered, and I stood in the doorway gawking at her. I swallowed, feeling like a school.

"Dr Nichols, I'm Agent Pierce, head of nightshift security." Her fingers tightened around a lace handkerchief gripped in her right palm. I didn't want to step closer, but had to. Her pheromones were making my blood, or what was left of it, crave an infusion from her veins. "What happened?"

Her gaze dropped to the hankie and she began working the fabric with both hands. "I was working late and needed Leon to come to the lab.

I couldn't get the Geiger counter to calibrate. I knocked. When no one answered, I opened the door and…" Her eyes swung up to meet mine. "So much blood." Her gaze remained locked with my eyes as if demanding a response.

"I'm sorry," I offered. "I thought you were assigned to dayshift."

She swiped at the corners of her eyes with the handkerchief. "I switched shifts yesterday so Leon and I could calibrate the new equipment."

I nodded. The scientists worked a twelve hours on, twelve off schedule seven days a week. We were in a race against Nazi scientists while men died in Europe, North Africa, and the Pacific. "Did you notice anything unusual tonight?" I asked.

"Nothing."

"Hear anything strange on the way to Dr Heinrick's office, pass anyone in the hall?"

She shook her head. "Maybe he's still here."

Something in the way she stared at—through—me, searching for answers and fearing what she might find, threatened to tip me off balance. "The murderer is gone," I replied in a level voice.

"How do you know?"

"A hunch," I said, and meant it.

"Why kill Heinrick?" she said. "Why not Compton or Fermi? But Heinrick…" Her voice trailed off.

"Are you saying Heinrick didn't know anything worth killing for?"

"I suppose we all know *something* worth killing for. Each scientist on this project is top in his or her field. But the project will go on without Heinrick. If we lost Oppenheimer, or Fermi, the project would be delayed, if not brought to a standstill."

"Did you enter Heinrick's office?"

"No, I took one look and ran."

The response, given without hesitation, or guile, made me wonder if this woman ran from anything.

"This was the first office I came to," she said.

Her story made sense, and my instincts said she was telling the truth. I had learned to trust my sixth sense, especially the last eight months. This ability was another one of those things I couldn't explain, like being conscious of the way her pheromones where working on me double-time.

"Are you staying in the dorm?" I asked.

She nodded.

"I'll have someone escort you there."

Desire to go with her shot to the surface with the heat of a volcano. I pictured white skin, full breasts, and blond hair between perfect thighs. I forced my breathing to remain even, and the swelling in my shorts abated. I'd never experienced such sudden, intense lust. If I escorted her back to her room I would drink her blood—and God only knew what I would do to her afterward. My pulse jumped with the thought of her warm blood flowing past my tongue down my throat... and her tight walls closing around me as I entered her.

"I have to complete my measurements before the day shift," she said. I jarred from the erotic thought. "There's not enough equipment to go around," she added.

I nodded. "Of course."

Clipped footsteps sounded almost noiselessly on the linoleum floor of the hallway and I recognized McHenry's walk two seconds before Dr Nichols's eyes shifted over my shoulder.

"Pierce."

I glanced back to see him standing in the open doorway.

"The general wants to talk to you."

A measure of sanity reasserted itself. I had to get away from her, *now*. "Could you escort Dr Nichols back to the lab?"

His expression lightened. "No problem." He stepped aside and motioned toward the door with an open hand. "Dr Nichols."

She cast me a farewell glance and headed toward the door. I tried tearing my eyes from the gentle sway of hips as she walked past, but couldn't, and felt the heat swell to the surface again. I had to find one of the small rodents whose blood I drank to keep my thirst for human blood at bay, or go back to Heinrick and hope the congealed blood in his decaying body would make me forget the craving. Rising desire twisted my insides and I feared even Heinrick's dead blood wouldn't work against the warm, pulsing blood of Dr Nichols.

I waited until their footsteps receded down the hall, then started forward. My gaze caught on Fermi's portable chalkboard on wheels, and I stopped. Equations filled the board that would have looked like Greek to me in my former life. Now, they sparked a story in my mind. Differentials, integrals, and algebra flowed in an almost perfect melody. The first time I saw calculus after becoming infected with this disease, I stared, fascinated. After flipping through a text on advanced mathematics I found in the small but well stocked CP-1 library, I could visualize the differential as rates of change, the integrals as sums, and functions as shapes and movement.

I stared at the puzzle of Fermi's equations, one side of my brain working the numbers, the other side stuck on the murder. Heinrick's eye had been stabbed in a careful, deliberate manner to inflict maximum pain *without* killing. Yet no one had reported the screams, which must have penetrated his office walls. Why? Like the equations on the board, the evidence didn't fit. Except, equations could be fixed. Heinrick would be dead forever.

I stepped up to the chalkboard, picked up a stick of chalk, and tapped down the chalkboard alongside the offending column of calculations. Halfway down, I fixed an exponent and turned a minus sign to a plus, then fixed the equation below, which didn't equal zero as Fermi had written. I circled the answer and connected the derivation on the right hand side of the board to the bottom equation on the left, which now equaled each other. I stood back. Harmony now flowed between the equations. I didn't know what they represented, but they were now correct.

The first time I stood in front of this chalkboard and recognized a mistake, I had walked away. If anyone discovered my abilities, I would be consigned to hell in some biological laboratory I dared not contemplate beyond the knowledge of its existence. Later that night, I found a communiqué on my desk from General Groves reporting ninety-eight men had died, including Rear Admiral Daniel Judson Callaghan and Captain Cassin, when the USS San Francisco sank during the battle of Guadalcanal. Groves had handwritten a single sentence on the Teletype page: *This is why we're doing this.* I had rushed back to write my solution, but found Fermi had erased everything. Since then, I didn't chance leaving Fermi's mistakes uncorrected.

I set the chalk back in the tray and brushed my hands on my trousers. As for my personal problem, even if I found a cure for the need to drink blood, I would still never be the same after this war, no one would. Yet, whatever I was, I would still be alive. Many men wouldn't be.

About us

T. C. ARCHER is comprised of award winning authors Evan Trevane and Shawn M. Casey. They live in the Northeast. Evan has a Ph.D. in electrical engineering, and Shawn is a small business owner. Their collaboration began on a lark with the post WWII film noir story *The Pickle My Little Friend*, and has evolved into nearly a dozen works, which includes their new series *The Phenom League*, and Daphne Du Maurier winner the romantic thriller *For His Eyes Only*.

Other Titles from
T. C. Archer

Full Throttle

For His Eyes Only

Chain Reaction Book One in the Phenom League

Trouble at the Hotel Baba Ghanoush

Fontana's Trouble

The Pickle My Little Friend

Kirsoval Series

Winter in Paradise

Yeoman's Curse

Sin Series

Sin Incarnate

Coming Soon

In the Company of Kate

Behind Enemy Lines: The Phenom League

Sin Series

Sin Revisited

Sin Reborn

Blood Angels Series

Land of the Giants

www.ingramcontent.com/pod-product-compliance
Lightning Source LLC
Chambersburg PA
CBHW071250170626
46809CB00001B/155